REBEL

Heather Graham

REBEL

A TOPAZ BOOK

TOPAZ
Published by the Penguin Group
Penguin Books USA Inc., 375 Hudson Street,
New York, New York 10014, U.S.A.
Penguin Books Ltd, 27 Wrights Lane,
London W8 5TZ, England
Penguin Books Australia Ltd, Ringwood,
Victoria, Australia
Penguin Books Canada Ltd, 10 Alcorn Avenue,
Toronto, Ontario, Canada M4V 3B2
Penguin Books (N.Z.) Ltd, 182–190 Wairau Road,
Auckland 10, New Zealand

Penguin Books Ltd, Registered Offices:
Harmondsworth, Middlesex, England

First published by Topaz, an imprint of Dutton Signet,
a division of Penguin Books USA Inc.

REGISTERED TRADEMARK—MARCA REGISTRADA

Printed in the United States of America

Dedicated
in loving memory to
"Papa,"
my father-in-law,
Alphonse Pozzessere,
who will live in our
hearts forever

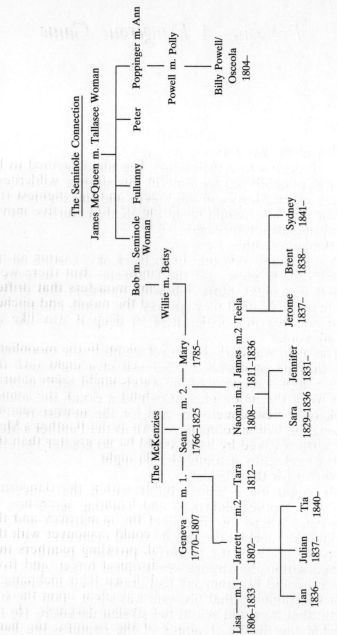

Prologue: A Dangerous Game

May 1862

The night was eerie.

Indeed, more than eerie. The night seemed to be an exceptionally savage time in this strange wilderness, where every whisper in the breeze and the slightest ripple of the water could mean the stealthy, furtive movement of a deadly predator.

Human, or other.

A full moon rode the silken black sky, casting an iridescent, ivory glow over the landscape. But there were clouds that night, puffy, billowing monsters that drifted along invisibly until they covered the moon, and pitched land and sea into a darkness so deep it was like an ebony void.

The night was dark, but never silent. In the moonlight, the chirping of insects, the screech of a night owl, the subtle ripple and wave of the water, might seem natural. But when the moon pitched behind a cloud, the sounds took on a new dimension, and for the newest recruits among the Union company known as the Panther's Men, the terror evoked by battle could be no greater than the terror evoked by a south Florida night.

Not so for their leader.

He could move imperceptibly within the dangerous forest of reptiles, darkness, and haunting screeches. In this place where the pines met the mangroves and the hammocks touched the sea, he could maneuver with the ease and grace of the powerful, prowling panthers that lurked within the strange semitropical forest, and from which he and his company had drawn their nickname.

It was rumored that his walk was silent upon the soft earth; that he could see in the stygian darkness. He respected the deadly creatures of the swamps, the hammocks, and the sea, but he didn't fear them. He led his men through trails most men could never see, and followed those trails to places no sane man would usually dare to tread. He could move across this savage landscape and become one with it. Silent, mercurial, subtle, he had been known to startle his own men with uncanny appearances and disappearances. Like a panther, he moved with ever-quiet care, always watching.

Stalking.

Tonight, they had left their horses a quarter of a mile back on a high hammock and he had led them on foot to this inlet far from civilization—indeed, far from all that seemed human in any way. They were south, even, of the old Seminole war outpost Fort Dallas, though he had assured his men they were still in the area designated as Dade County, so named in memory of the late commander killed in the Second Seminole War.

He knew this land well.

Word was that though he wasn't Indian himself, he had kin among the Seminoles and had learned the swampland and the sea around it just like a red man. Rumor also had it that he had kin among the panthers and gators, and so he could run in the semitropical jungle like a cat and make his way through the brackish waters like a great streamlined lizard. At first glance, the major might have indeed been bred among the Indians, for his collar-length hair was as ebony as pitch and his long lean body was as hard-muscled and bronzed as any wild Indian's. His eyes added to the illusion, for though they were blue, it was a blue as dark as cobalt, and upon occasion, they seemed as black as a pit in hell, and as dangerous.

It was good that he was a dangerous man.

For he led his troops into dangerous places.

And now, in the darkness, the troops of Major Ian McKenzie waited. Waited and watched—or listened, at the very least, when the clouds so covered the moon that watching became impossible. They had waited now for hours in the damp, insect-laden inlet along the extreme southeastern coast of the Florida mainland because there was a chance they might catch the Moccasin, one of the most notorious Rebel spies to work the Florida coastline.

A coastline that invited subterfuge.

A coastline most Union troops despised.

An assignment to Florida was like an assignment to hell to most men before they ever marched forward into battle and drew a weapon. The peninsula itself was a no-man's-land, impossible for the Rebs to hold, impossible for the Union to take. Endless miles of coastline made the Union blockade laughable. Likewise, endless miles of coastline made the state vulnerable to Union attack at any time. Jacksonville had already changed hands several times. St. Augustine had been taken by Northern forces, and was still held by the Federals. Down in this arena of war, the naval base at Key West had remained firmly in Union hands, but as to the rest of the state, hostile forces were always at work. Florida had been the third state to secede from the Union. Her Confederates were staunchly loyal to what they considered their great Southern Cause, yet there were very strong pro-Union forces in Florida as well. Though Reb troops raised in Florida were most frequently pulled out of the state to engage in the heavy fighting taking place in Virginia, Tennessee, and other areas of the South, the Florida peninsula was incredibly important to the war effort. Florida provided a large portion of the beef and salt that sustained the Southern troops.

Thus it was important to the Union that this hellhole and those helping to see that supplies ran endlessly into and out of it were controlled.

Therefore, the Moccasin had to be caught. Since the hanging of the Rebs suspected of espionage in the north of the state a few weeks back, the major had determined that he and his men must be the ones to capture this particular pain in their backsides.

The Moccasin had been a scourge to the Union for some time now. Too many times, when Union ships had tried to stop blockade runners, the Reb captains had known about the Federal ships ahead of time—and backup had been waiting, lurking just within the next inlet, behind the next dune. Ships carrying firearms were breaking through the blockade and reaching Rebel troops through the Florida inlets; gold was making its way into enemy hands. Union men straying beyond the St. Johns River out of St. Augustine had fallen far too often into the hands of desperate Florida troops, and those Rebel troops were causing great havoc harassing Federals along the waterway.

Major McKenzie had been given free rein to do what harm he could within the peninsula, with the order to destroy the actions of all spies, blackguards, traitors to the Union, and blockade runners in whatever manner he saw fit. He hadn't been given a customary assignment, and he wasn't compelled to bow to customary authority.

This was not a customary place, nor could he and his men possibly fight the war in a customary way. Nor had the major been his customary self since that hanging. The major never had cottoned to the military acting as the law. Men died in battle. That was a sad fact. But to him, if the Federals started taking the law into their own hands too many times they became nothing more than predators, and the whole point of the war would be lost, because they'd no longer be fighting for the unity of the country, for home, glory, and honor; they'd be nothing more than murderers themselves.

"A ship! Major, by God, you were right!" old Sam Jones whispered in the night.

Though they had seen their commander's uncanny ability to fathom exactly when and where things were going to happen before they did, some of his men had silently doubted that a ship would actually have the audacity to risk this section of the bay.

"Steady, boys, we can't take a ship right now, and we don't want anyone getting wind of us and carrying off the cargo we can take," the major warned back. His voice seemed to come out of nowhere. "We want the landing party, gentlemen." He was silent just a moment, then his deep, soft voice seemed to ring with passion. "We're here to seize the Moccasin."

The spy stared at the fast-approaching coastline. *Almost home!* the Moccasin thought, and was glad, for the war was a wearying effort, more trying than ever recently, and frequently the spy was sorry he had ever, in a surge of loyalty, become the Moccasin and slipped into playing such a dangerous game.

It was just that the spy had believed, passionately, in the Southern Cause. In States' Rights. The Confederacy now was like the fledgling band of the colonies before

the Revolutionary War, fighting for the right to independence, for the pursuit of life, liberty, and happiness—in
their own way. If only others understood, there would
be no war.

Still, the pain plagued the spy. And still, too often
now, the fear.

The Moccasin had been thinking a very long while
now that it might just be time to curl up like a ball
python—and quit. So far, all that had been done was
good. Rebel lives had been saved. The spy's information
had all been good, and the spy's movements had been
well planned.

But times were changing. Perhaps it would be possible
to slither into the water now, and disappear into legend
and history.

And have a life again. Bitter now, perhaps, but one
touched by hope. If only . . .

In the small inlet, just before they might have run
aground, the ship was brought to a slow, smooth halt.

"Cast dinghy!" the captain ordered. He was a good,
gruff old man who had sailed the seas as a scavenger
before the war and the Cause had inspired every able
man with so much as a rowboat to try to best the Union
forces and break the blockade. The Moccasin had sailed
with this captain before. They were close; good friends.
Neither had ever sought riches from the war. Although
the spy's main contraband was usually quinine, ether,
chloroform, or laudanum, and the main objective was to
save lives, the spy had caused serious mischief, and was
well aware of it—and of the union broadsides pasted up
in every possible Yankee port advising that the Moccasin
was far more deadly than any regular snake, and was to
be taken, dead or alive, shot or hanged without mercy
at the discretion of the captor.

The Moccasin didn't dare think about such threats—
or the fact that they would be carried out. Fear made it
impossible to function.

Tonight, the spy wore a face-concealing dark slouch
hat and a large, encompassing greatcoat with frocked
shoulders and numerous pockets. The pockets were
filled with correspondence, gold, and hard Yankee cur-
rency, and laudanum. The weight of the coat was such
that it would be easy for the spy to drown if cast over-

board, but it would be equally as easy for the spy to cast off the coat if necessary and, if possible, retrieve the coat at a later time.

But things should go smoothly this evening.

This was a no-man's-land, by the spy's home. And staring toward the land with sharp eyes, the Moccasin could see nothing amiss. The moon kept creeping behind clouds, but when the clouds parted, a strange yellow glow illuminated the earth. The water, with or without the moonlight, seemed black. Trees were encased in silent shadow. In a sudden burst of yellow moonlight, the Moccasin scanned the shore. Nothing. Nothing . . . except . . .

"Wait!" the Moccasin said, and the captain, about to order a man to row the spy in, paused.

"You see something?" the captain demanded, frowning and trying hard to peer into the night.

Yes, something. Something had moved in the shadows. The Moccasin was suddenly filled with dread. Twin red lights suddenly seemed to peer from the trees. The Moccasin felt a tightening grip of panic begin, but then breathed more easily again, nearly laughing aloud with relief.

"What?" the captain asked anxiously.

"A little deer," the spy said.

"Ah . . . A deer. You're certain?"

"Yes."

"Jenkins, bring the Moccasin in," the captain ordered one of his young seamen.

"Yessir!" Jenkins said, saluting. The captain turned to the Moccasin. "Be careful. Please."

"I will, sir."

"Remember, your life is far more valuable than your cargo, no matter how precious it may be. *You* cannot be replaced. You must remember that."

"I will, and I must go now, sir."

The captain nodded. He appeared unhappy, as if he struggled for the words to say more, but could not find them.

As if he, too, had suddenly been filled with the same sense of dread.

For a moment, the Moccasin was made uneasy by his

manner, and felt a strange chill, one as foreboding as the haunting night with its eerie yellow moon-glow.

"Be careful," the captain said again, gruffly.

The Moccasin nodded, hiding a smile, eyes averted downward. "I know my business, sir."

"We should move now, sir," Jenkins said uneasily. Jenkins believed in his duty, and he'd die in this war if the good Lord called for it, but he hailed from Jacksonville, and he hated swampland, and he hated this southern region of the state where a deceptively beautiful coastline was but a slender thread of land that bordered the dense watery jungle of the Everglades.

The Moccasin nimbly scrambled over the starboard side of the ship, following Jenkins down the small drop ladder to the dinghy waiting below. Jenkins quickly slipped the oars into the water, and the dinghy shot across the night-black sea. The coastline loomed ever closer.

"Stop!" the Moccasin whispered suddenly, overwhelmed by a feeling that all was not well. No more flashes of eyes made red by the moon's sudden reflection peered out, yet the spy was certain they were being watched. That something awaited them. The heavy breathing of some great horrible creature seemed to echo in the darkness. The trees were too still. Nothing stirred; no insects chirped.

Jenkins ceased to row. The dinghy, caught by the impetus of his previous strength, continued to streak through the water despite Jenkins's efforts to position the oars to stop its progress.

Then the trees came to life. The moon was gone, darkness had settled, but the Moccasin heard the sounds as men slipped from the trees, rifles aimed at the dinghy.

"Surrender, come in peacefully, and your lives will be spared, you've my guarantee!"

The moon slipped free from the clouds. Eight men in hated Union blue had come from the trees. They were in formation at the water's edge; four on their knees, four standing, all aiming their rifles directly at the occupants of the dinghy.

"Lord A'mighty!" Jenkins swore. He didn't even glance at the Moccasin; to him, escape was impossible.

He'd rather face a Union bullet a hundred times over before daring to put even his big toe into the water here.

The Moccasin would not surrender.

Could not surrender.

The Moccasin stared at Jenkins with both panic and contempt.

"We surrender—" Jenkins began.

But before he could finish, the Moccasin had already dived deep into the water.

"Damn the wretch!" Ian swore, shedding his cavalry jacket and swiftly unbuckling his scabbard while kicking off his boots. "Men, keep your guns trained, get the Reb in the rowboat, and watch the surface for our friend emerging from the shallows. Gilbey Clark—" He hesitated just briefly. Gilbey was his new man. But a good man. "Gilbey, take the trail up a hundred yards; Sam, follow him at fifty. Sharp eyes on the water!"

He turned, running out into the shallows, then leaping into a dive that took him into the depths near the dinghy. Fool spy; they all carried their contraband in their clothing. This idiot would go down like a leaden ball.

But though he dived and surfaced in the area of the dinghy again and again, he could find no trace of the spy.

Nor did a body float to the surface.

It was night; and though he did have excellent vision in the darkness, even he was nearly blinded. Yet he instinctively believed that the spy was not dead; the spy had dived into the water because the spy was someone who knew how to swim, how to navigate the water and the shore—even in the darkness.

He made one last dive and came up triumphant: the spy's heavy-laden coat. Dragging it along with him, he swam toward shore, then came to his feet to wade the rest of the way in. His sodden cotton shirt was plastered to his chest; his wool uniform pants felt even worse.

"There! There!" came a sudden shout.

Ian forgot his discomfort and ran to the shore. Up ahead, he could see a shadow rising from the water; Gilbey Clark had seen the apparition as well.

"Halt, or I'll shoot!" Gilbey called out, raising his rifle.

But Gilbey didn't shoot. Ian came behind him, bursting out of the blackness of the night. He laid his hand upon Gilbey's rifle, lowering it. "No shooting; I'll take the spy," he said. Then he added softly, "Alive."

He raced past Gilbey, heedless of the ground against his callused bare feet. He heard a cry which should have been a final warning to him that all that he had feared secretly within his heart, but hadn't wanted to believe, was true. It didn't quite register, he was so intent on the pursuit. In a little spit of sand between tree roots and shore, Ian caught up with the Moccasin at last. He threw himself upon the spy with a fierce burst of speed, grappling the spy, intending to bring the enemy down, winded, before he could be knifed or throttled in turn.

The catapulted weight of his body forced the spy down to the ground easily enough.

They were soaked with sea and sand. Ian caught his balance, easing from the figure beneath him and rolling his enemy face-upward at the same time. Without missing a beat he straddled the spy.

The Moccasin was pinned to the sand.

The moon's light was abundant.

Even with soaked hair tangled in seaweed and lashed about her face, the Moccasin was exotically beautiful. Neither night nor water could completely dim the shimmering gold of her hair, and the glowing moonlight only helped illuminate the unique color of her eyes, a hazel so fused that the color was not green at all, not brown, but nearly as gold as her hair. Her lashes and brows darkened to a honey. Her face was delicately, artistically formed with a small straight nose, elegantly high cheekbones, a stubbornly square chin, and a beautifully shaped, generous mouth. Her cheeks were flushed to give a warmth to her coloring; her lips were naturally tinged a cherry except that now they were held in a thin, grim line and they were a mixture of white from tension and blue from the cold.

Ian drew back. *In his mind, he had suspected this. In his heart, he had refused to believe it.*

He didn't know what she saw in his own features then, but it was apparently enough to draw the last of the color from her features. Yet in her own dismay, it seemed she sensed his momentary weakness in his discovery of her, and took full advantage of it, suddenly jerking back an arm to strike him with a serious punch to the jaw.

She was really quite amazing.

She could move about a ballroom as if she floated on air; she could smile and disarm the most hardened soldier, make it seem as if the sun were suddenly warming his face. She was petite, and could appear as delicate as the most fragile rose. Yet it wasn't as if he had been unaware of the power of will and strength within her slender frame; he had simply forgotten it in his anger and dismay.

Her punch was as hard and well aimed as that of a trained boxer, hard enough to shift his balance, and after she had hit him, she thrashed and struggled like a wounded gator, trying to free herself from his weight, his hold.

He couldn't let her go. Would never do so.

She thought that freedom from him would be her only salvation. He knew better. Remaining his prisoner now was her only hope for life. He had learned the bitter lesson that he could not always save Rebel spies and soldiers from being hanged. Indeed, until the day he died, he would not forget the pain of seeing his own kin dangled at the end of a rope. The anguish now lived with him, marched to battle with him. It was a nightmare within him, waking, sleeping, one from which he could never shake free.

The tempest of his emotions seized him in an excruciating grip. He caught her wrists and slammed her back to the sand, glad that his force was such that she cried out as the breath was knocked out of her. She stared up at him, frozen, apparently believing that he would kill her himself, here and now.

It was the best thing she could possibly believe.

"So you are the Moccasin," he said, and his anger was so deep that his words and body shook with his effort to remain still. To control the sweeping range of emotions that tore at his heart and soul. Remembrance, fear, rage, pain.

And desire. Suddenly and wildly awakened. *For she remained Alaina. Curved, warm, vital, and alive, beneath him. Alaina, with her catlike eyes, her smile, her laugh, her temper. Her recklessness. Her dedication, her passion . . .*

To her wretched cause.

His words tumbled out of him again in a rage.

"So you are the bloody, damned Mocassin! How dare you?"

She was shaking as well, staring back at him. She spoke through her blue-tinged lips. "And you're the Panther. The bloody, goddamned Panther. Stalker. Traitor! Dear God, this is Florida!" she cried. "You are the traitor here. How dare you?"

As her voice faded, Ian became aware of the soft footfalls of his men as they surrounded the pair.

Sam Jones, Ian's right-hand man at all times, stopped the others with a swift motion of his hand. The eight men who had ridden with him tonight, all specially chosen by Ian himself, stood as silent and still as sentinels. Waiting. They would follow his lead. Whatever it was.

They were Federal men, loyal to the Union. But their first loyalty was to Ian. They had ridden with him many times. He had taught them to survive; he had kept them alive.

Tonight, he was exceptionally grateful for their loyalty.

Except that he hoped they didn't realize how the deadly Panther *was shaking right now, that he was afraid in a way he'd never known fear before. Afraid . . .*

For the Moccasin.

Because he knew what could happen to spies. He'd seen what could happen, firsthand.

"Major," Sam said softly. "We lost the Reb from the ship. He panicked and drowned. We went in; there was nothing we could do."

Ian winced inwardly. It was war. Death came daily. Still, wasted life never ceased to appall him.

"All right, Sam," he said, and he was surprised at the quiet in his own voice. "Brian, Reggie, see to the body. We'll head back to base camp." He looked down at the woman.

The Moccasin.

"Don't try to escape me again."

Her tawny eyes were upon his. "Will you shoot me?"

she asked him, and he was glad it seemed she really needed an answer to that question.

"My men get nervous in the swamp. God knows, sometimes we shoot at anything."

It was a lie. His men were superb. They never panicked, and they were some of the finest marksmen in the South.

He came to his feet, then drew her up. He stared in silence while the men bustled around them.

He set her up on his horse, Pye, an Arabian mix bred on his family plantation. Pye wasn't afraid of snakes or swamps. Pye had ridden the peninsula with him for a very long time. Since the war had begun, Pye had lived in the swamp.

Ian mounted his horse behind the Moccasin.

He tried to still his own shaking, still the fear and fury that ripped through him.

Alaina was the Moccasin!

God in His heaven, what did he do now?

No more than thirty minutes of riding in a tense silence brought them to a small grouping of cabins, built up on stilts, deep within a hammock. The cabins were all but hidden by a massive wall of pines that broke just before the small clearing.

Having reached that clearing, Alaina began to shiver. The night air was very cool. She was dressed in men's breeches, a cotton shirt, and high boots. Even her boots remained uncomfortably sodden with seawater.

She was so close to home. The home where she had grown up. She was close to help. Salvation. Yet if she were to be saved, then Ian McKenzie would die, because he would readily give his life before allowing his captive to be seized from him.

She would be hanged.

No!

Something in her heart cried out that it couldn't happen. But, oh, God, what a naive fool she had been! It now seemed inevitable that this day should come.

She wished fervently that he had ordered his men to drag her through the swamp on foot. That would have been better than riding with him. *Feeling* his rage, his horror that she was the Moccasin. It seemed to burn from him, from the arms that held Pye's reins around her, from the hard-muscled wall of his chest. He was fire tonight, and she would be consumed in it. Cast into Rebel hell.

He seemed to be a mass of heat and muscled tension, and yet the very feel of him when he touched her was somehow colder than a northern ice floe. *As if he could not bear to touch her. . . .*

Perhaps that was well. Ian seemed to be a broad-shouldered, yet slender man. His appearance was deceptive, for it was his height, over six feet, that made him seem more lithe and lean when he was actually quite powerfully built. If he were to touch her, he might readily snap her neck, break her right in two.

Yet when they reached the clearing, he jumped swiftly from Pye. Briefly, his cobalt eyes lit upon hers. Blue fire. He turned to his men. "See to the prisoner!" he ordered brusquely, then quickly strode to one of the cabins. He couldn't bear to be near her, she thought. He was afraid that he'd strangle her, tear her limb from limb with his bare hands.

What would that matter, she wondered, feeling a sudden rise of hysteria, if she was to be hanged anyway? A quick death at his hands might be preferable.

Ah, but he was the famed Major Ian McKenzie. He'd never lower himself to the cold-blooded murder of a prisoner. Justice—Union justice—would have its way.

When Ian was gone, she realized that his men had been left as surprised as she. But one of the men quickly sprang to action. "My name's Sam. Don't try to escape, now, ma'am. Pye will just throw you, you know."

Pye would throw her. The horse was as irritatingly loyal to his master as were Ian's men.

Sam reached up to help her down. She didn't know just how badly she had been shaken by the night's events until she realized she could barely stand. Another soldier rushed to her side, supporting her. He looked at her with dazzled, dark brown eyes. Too bad this boy wasn't her jailer, she thought. She'd be free in no time.

"Thank you," she told him very softly.

Ah, but that was why they had called her the Moccasin. She'd eluded those sent to trap her time and time again.

Tonight, though, she would not escape. For in Ian's eyes, she was condemned.

Again she wished she could cry out; she wanted to explain. In a way she wanted to shriek with pain, for all she had seen in his eyes. And in a way, she wanted to rail and beat against him for being all that he was. The Panther.

"Come along, ma'am," Sam said. "I imagine the far cabin's yours for the night. Gilbey, see to fresh water for the lady. Brian, post a guard."

Sam escorted her to the cabin, keeping a hand loosely on her elbow as he helped her up a ladder to the platform flooring. Sam was polite, but firm. He lit a kerosene lantern, illuminating the cabin. "You should be comfortable enough," Sam said. "Bed and blankets—clean sheets to wear while your clothing dries. Not much else here, I'm afraid. Ah, there's a sliver of soap and there's your pitcher and bowl. Gilbey will bring fresh water for washing and drinking. I'm afraid the bunk, the desk, and the chair are all the furnishings we have."

"Well, Sam, I am quite impressed," she murmured, attempting to do so with spirit.

There was a light rapping on the door. The young soldier with the deep dark eyes, obviously fairly new in the command, appeared with a big pitcher of fresh water, pouring some directly into the wash bowl for her.

"Sam," he whispered, "it is a she, all right—is *she* really the Moccasin?"

"She's the Moccasin," Sam said wearily. "So it seems. Now get on down, Gilbey. Ma'am," he said to Alaina, "we'll leave you now."

Sam came down the steps. Brian was sitting guard. Sam decided that he'd best take up that position as well. He sat, leaned against one of the thick pine support beams that kept the cabin sitting high off the ground. He pulled out his whittling knife and a piece of old oak he'd been working on a long time. "Go tell the major she's in the cabin, set for the night," he told Gilbey.

"But Sam—" Gilbey protested.

"Go," Sam said.

Gilbey obeyed.

The temptation to wash the salt from her face became

more than Alaina could bear. The fresh water felt delicious. She forgot her peril for a moment, drank deeply,
then swore softly and impatiently and shimmied her way
out of boots, breeches, and shirt. She doused herself in
the fresh water, even pouring it through her hair. Then
she stood shivering again; there was no fire in the cabin,
and though the late spring night was probably no less
than seventy degrees, chills could set in. She found the
clean sheet on the bed and wrapped herself in it. She
sat cross-legged on the bed. They had left her water and
a lamp. Probably far more than the Moccasin deserved.
At least she would not die in sea-salted misery.

But that thought brought a sudden sob to her lips. He
had been so terrifyingly furious. Ah, but no matter what
his fury, he had dismissed her so cleanly! She might
never see him again. She might die without ever having
a chance to say . . .

To say what? They had chosen different paths, and
nothing could change that. She had hated him often
enough. She had to hate him now. She did hate him. . . .

She didn't hate him.

She hugged the sheet around her. She seemed to be
ablaze on the inside, riddled with fear, with fury. She
could demand mercy, surely . . .

Oh, God, not from him. Nor could she cajol, plea,
bargain. She'd always told herself that she would die
with dignity if she was caught. She'd never beg or
plead. . . .

But she'd do so tonight, just to touch him. Except
that, oh, God . . .

She leaped to her feet in a whirl of frustration. She
had to set her mind to finding a way to escape. She
couldn't plead or cajol, because he wouldn't believe a
word she said. She couldn't bargain, because there was
no longer anything she had that he might want. Again,
a soft sob of rising panic escaped her.

Then she heard footsteps on the ladder, and she
swung around quickly. The door to the cabin opened.

And he was there.

He had changed to dry clothing. His skin seemed very
bronze in the lantern light; his eyes did not appear blue
at all, but rather a deep and penetrating black. He stared
at her so long that she thought she would scream and

beg him to shoot her and get it over with. Just when she thought that she would simply save everyone trouble and die on the spot, he spoke at last.

"The Moccasin," he said softly. Then, "Goddamn you."

"No!" she heard herself cry in return. "Goddamn *you,* Major McKenzie. You betrayed your state, not I!"

A lock of jet-black hair fallen over his forehead obscured what emotion she might have read in his eyes. Perhaps it was to her benefit; perhaps she didn't want to know all that lay within their cobalt depths.

"Indeed. My state betrayed my country, madam. But that doesn't matter now; politics don't matter now. And whether God Himself is on my side or yours doesn't matter, either. What matters, my dear Moccasin, is that you have been captured by the enemy, while I have not."

Involuntarily, she sucked in a quick, fearful breath.

"Yes, I've been caught. So . . . Major McKenzie, just what do you intend to do with me?" she demanded with a false bravado.

He raised an arched, ebony brow. "What do I intend, madam? How does one deal with a deadly snake? Perhaps I should use against you every atrocity blamed upon the Yankees by such delicate hothouse belles as yourself. Plunder, rapine, slaughter!"

"Ian, surely . . ." she breathed.

But cobalt fires of fury remained in his eyes, in the wired tension of his lithe, powerfully muscled body.

And he had already started toward her.

A shriek seemed to tear apart the satin-rich darkness of the night.

One scream. Cut off.

Gilbey, having relayed his message and returned to the cabin in the major's wake, leaped up from his position on the ground by the support pole.

"Did you hear that?" he demanded of Sam.

Sam kept whittling. He shrugged.

Gilbey persisted. "I know she's supposed to be the Moccasin and all—"

"She is the Moccasin." Sam remained calm. He had

completely ignored the high-pitched, terrified shriek. Gilbey didn't know how he could do such a thing.

"Sam, this is bad. I've never seen the captain so mad, and that's a fact," Gilbey said, shaking his head worriedly. "I mean, sure, she's the enemy and all, but . . . the major always said before that we weren't hanging anybody. He's always said he wasn't judge and jury, and he wasn't going to head any lynch mobs. But I've *never* seen him so mad. Do we leave such a young—a young . . ."

"Lovely?" Sam suggested without looking up.

"Lovely, sweet—why, she's just a stunning young girl, and that's that! Do we leave her to the major when he's in such a temper? He could really hurt her. He looks as if he's ready to kill her."

"He's not going to kill her," Sam assured Gilbey, his words soft and assured as he sat whittling his wood.

Gilbey walked over to stand in front of him, hands on his hips. "How can you be so damned sure, Sam? How can you be so all-fired certain?"

Sam looked up at him. "Haven't you guessed yet, Gilbey? He ain't gonna kill her, Gilbey, 'cause she's Alaina."

"Alaina?"

"Alaina *McKenzie*. Dammit, Gilbey, she's his wife."

Gilbey's jaw dropped, then worked hard before he could manage to speak again. "Wife? The Panther—married to the Moccasin?"

"Well, now, they do say that all things are fair in love and war," Sam murmured. "Perhaps passion ought to be added into that saying as well," he added dryly. He looked up at the moon, then glanced toward the cabin above him.

It was the war. The war had done terrible things to them all. Especially to the McKenzies, all of them, even with their special brand of honor, loyalty, dedication, and love. Brothers who had stuck together through thick and thin, and plenty of bloodshed in the shaping of the state, were suddenly torn assunder in their beliefs. Brother against brother, father against son.

Man against wife.

He felt a great wave of empathy for both Ian and his Southern wife. Alaina McKenzie couldn't know yet just

what had been driving Ian so hard of late. Or why he'd
be so ruthless now. And as to Ian, well . . .

Sam thought that the two of them might well be wondering just how and when they had started on this road
so stained with bitterness and fraught with anger.

Had lover become enemy, or enemy become lover?

It had all begun quite some time ago. . . .

Chapter 1

May 1860
Cimarron

"**B**y God, what the *hell* . . ."
Ian first saw the strange party assembled on his lawn when he led Pye off the river barge and looked southward toward his home, Cimarron. A group of young men, several in uniform, faced a young woman. The woman held a sword, as did one of the uniformed men.

What rude and dangerous folly was taking place upon his father's lawn?

He leapt upon Pye and raced wildly toward the fray, ready to rescue the victim.

Except that there was no victim. He heard her laughter just as he reached the perimeter of the group, and reined in quickly, and thus got his first good look at his unknown guest—and saw her in action.

"Parry, you say?"

"Aye, dear mistress, and still, it's the strength of the thrust that gives man the greater advantage!"

Laughter rose from the male audience at the play on words.

"The strength, you say—of the thrust? Parry, thrust, parry, thrust, so?" Her voice was soft, sweetly feminine—with just the slightest edge to it. She was deceptively delicate, elegant and angelic-looking. She didn't bat an eye at the innuendo. She played them right along.

Indeed, Ian thought, there was something about her voice and manner that should have warned the young swains that she knew what she was about. She held a borrowed cavalry sword in good form in her right hand.

The sword seemed quite incongruous, for she appeared to be the epitome of the most perfect, charming Southern belle. Her day dress was a white and teal brocade, suitably chaste for afternoon wear, yet stylishly underscored by corset and petticoats in a manner that evocatively pinched her waist, flared her hips, and enhanced her breasts.

Her hair was a soft tawny gold; her eyes, at this distance, were a color to match its splendor. Gold, as well, cat's eyes, and right now . . . they carried the slightest sparkle of the predator.

She knew she could take her man.

She suddenly moved forward; there was a quick clash of steel as she met her opponent and dueled with lightning-swift speed, grace, and cunning ruthlessness.

Her opponent's sword flew in an arc across the lawn and into the bushes.

Having reached his home just in time to see the strange confrontation, Ian McKenzie found himself quite curious about the petite and tantalizing beauty who had just managed to make a fool of the cocky young man.

The bested fellow wore the uniform of a cavalry lieutenant. His name was Jay Pierpont; Ian had met him briefly at the Tampa base. To his credit, he handled his defeat with grace and a rueful sense of humor.

"Brava!" he cried.

Laughter welled within the crowd.

"Jay! You've been taken by a woman!" someone teased.

The woman in question turned to Pierpont's tormentor. "Well, my good sir, naturally, for I've had ever so talented a teacher in Jay." The lithe beauty applauded in delight. "We've proven that a man's great strength is not his best weapon, but rather the quality of thought within his head."

"Gentlemen!" Jay cried. "The damsel is an amazingly apt student."

"Certainly. I learned everything I know from this soldier in the last ten minutes!" she agreed.

Laughter rose again, and the sting of Pierpont's defeat was soothed. Pierpont bowed to her; she curtsied deeply.

The dozen or so young men who had been on the lawn

then moved in more closely, all vying for her attention, fluttering like a swarm of moths about a flame.

Her laughter was like wind chimes on the air. Her smile, Ian decided, was absolutely lethal. Indeed, he couldn't remember ever seeing such a vivacious beauty, so graceful—and so arrogantly confident in her wiles—in all his days. She had flirtation down to graceful science, a dazzling art.

The young men about her were fools, he thought. She was playing with all of them. He was, at that moment, ruefully amused to realize just what a tug she might have pulled upon his own heartstrings, were it not for Risa. But since he was contemplating marriage with the very poised and beautiful daughter of Colonel Angus Magee, he could easily take a step back from this little charmer and pity the men who might be caught in her web. Still, she was quite incredible—and he was about to leap down from Pye and insist upon an introduction. But he heard his mother's call from the porch, "Ian!"

The maternal delight in her voice was such that she necessarily became the woman of the moment for him. He edged Pye from the crowd on the lawn and loped up the final yards to the house. Before he reached the porch he swung his leg over Pye's sleek haunches and took a flying leap from the horse that landed him directly at the first step to the porch. He hurried up the steps, plucked up Tara McKenzie, and spun her about the porch. "Ah, Mother! I have missed you! As always, you are radiant."

Tara laughed, landing breathless on her feet again, reaching up to take his cheeks between her two hands and study the depths of his eyes. "Ian!" she said, laughing, "my dear firstborn, my pride and joy—you are quite the consummate flatterer! I know that you're deeply involved with your military career and the affairs of the world, and you probably haven't given your doting mother a single thought. But that's quite all right. I am so glad that you could make it here today!"

"I have three days' leave—and two days travel time back to Washington, Mother." He hesitated, growing serious. "I've some important personal matters to discuss with you, and I don't like the way the nation's going,

I'm afraid. There may be some decisions to be made soon, and I want time to talk with Father."

Tara frowned, and Ian was sorry he had spoken so quickly. His mother was no simpering belle, and most certainly no naive hothouse flower. She remained, as she approached middle age, a beautiful woman. her golden hair hadn't dulled a bit from the time Ian was a child; she was slim and graceful, the perfect mistress for his father's beloved Cimarron. But though she embodied genteel Southern womanhood, the scope of her world was much larger. The precarious position the McKenzies had always taken regarding the Seminole question in Florida had caused Tara to be very aware of politics at all times. Ian knew by looking at her now that she was probably far more aware that the country was holding together by tenuous threads than most of the male guests enjoying Cimarron's hospitality.

"Things are even worse than they seem?" she inquired softly.

"Right before I was stationed down at Key West, I had been in Washington. I was at John Brown's hanging. As much as I see the justice of his sentence, I think that his martyrdom will help shed much more blood than he ever managed alive. I think there is no way this breach can be healed. . . . We're heading toward war," he told her quietly.

Her frown deepened. She shook her head. Like many people, Tara didn't want to believe that the country could split apart, that there could be war. "I know that there is a wild and furious faction in Florida. We are a slave state, after all, and men can be adamant about keeping their property. Still, people are so split here with all the military bases that the state could well go to war against itself. But, Ian, surely saner heads will prevail."

"Not if Lincoln is elected president, I'm afraid. Mother, you know the sentiments of most of our neighbors!"

"I doubt if Lincoln will even be on the Florida ballot," Tara said. "Really, his being elected remains a long shot."

Ian shrugged. Perhaps so. But the military had kept him traveling and he'd seen Abraham Lincoln speak when he'd gone on leave with friends in Illinois, and he was certain that those who had never seen the man were seriously underestimating him.

Ian shook his head. "Well, nothing is happening to-morrow. Nothing will happen until the election, that much is certain. But still . . . I look forward to your party today, though I do assume the Democrats and Whigs are at it already within!"

She shook her head suddenly. "There's been some argument, but quite frankly, the majority of our neighbors are slaveholders who see your father as an eccentric—an important, powerful, wealthy and respectable eccentric, but an eccentric, nonetheless. Then, of course, there are those who claim they don't give a fig about slavery; they are furious about the question of States' Rights. As you say, though, it's in the future—even if it is the near future. Tea is about to be served. Freshen up quickly, dear, and come down. You are the best birthday present imaginable for your father; he is like a child waiting to see you."

"Are Julian and Tia home yet?"

"Julian has been working in St. Augustine, you know. He should arrive by nightfall, and he is stopping by Tia's academy to bring her home as well. Hurry, dear."

"Indeed, I will."

He kissed her on the forehead. "I shall be down directly, Mother."

He hurried through the breezeway and up the stairway to the second floor of Cimarron, down the long hallway, and to his room. He meant to hurry, as he had promised, but every time he came here and looked out on the vista that was his home, he had to pause.

He loved Cimarron. Deeply.

As the oldest male offspring of Tara and Jarrett McKenzie, he was heir to Cimarron. He had always known it, and always taken the responsibility gravely. He wasn't sure if his love for the house and grounds had been taught to him, or if he and his siblings hadn't just been born lucky. His younger brother, Julian, quite naturally loved his home. But to Julian, the pursuit of medicine was everything, and so he had become a doctor. Ian's baby sister, Tia, felt an equally warm pride in Cimarron, but Tia loved the world at large. Like their mother, she was intrigued by people and politics, and she was contin-

ually restless and anxious to travel. It had been quite
difficult for his parents to persuade her that she must
remain in Madame de la Verre's Finishing School for
Young Ladies long enough to emerge with at least the
facade of a proper education.

Cimarron . . .

The house was grace itself. His father and uncle had
designed and built it when this area inland on the river
from Tampa had been nothing more than wilderness.

His room was exceptionally large, as was the entire
house, which seemed a waste now that he made use of
it so infrequently. His bed was a large four-poster, made
of oak carved in England: a masculine creation with lion-
carved feet and winged griffins upon the headboard. It
sat against the far wall, facing the hearth on the inner
wall. Upholstered chairs were angled before the hearth,
and a massive oak two-way desk sat center in the room,
with chairs on either side. A wardrobe and dresser filled
the north wall, while the south was taken by his washstand and a second wardrobe with a full-length mirror.
The colors were dark with the richness of the woods.
The Oriental carpet that lay beneath the bed was in
brilliant blues and crimsons, and the sash curtains a rich
blue tapestry as well.

The second-floor windows were actually French doors
that led out to a balcony. Ian stepped out and gripped
the balcony railing. From there, he looked out over the
slope of the land, to the river to the north; and to the
stream that branched from it, habited by manatees and
river otters, and some of the most glorious birds ever to
touch down upon earth. He turned slightly, looking to
the deep pine forests to the south that surrounded the
little pockets of white civilization which had now
sprouted here. At the far end of one of the forest trails
was a copse, and within that copse, a freshwater pool
created from springs beneath the ground. On the lawn,
the grass, even in winter, was an emerald green. The
river flowed a deep, dark aqua, the pines rose with ma-
jestic beauty toward a powder blue sky.

Ian watched a small eagle soar across the sky. A feeling of peace settled over him, only to be disturbed by a
growing unease within him. He loved this place, this life.
And he felt as if he were somehow tied to a boulder

rolling pell-mell, out of control, that would crash into the very foundation of the house, and cause it to fall.

He gave himself a shake. Saner heads would prevail, his mother had said. But already, among so many of the well-educated and well-read men in the army, talk had grown very serious. It was quite odd, of course—if it did come to war, often the men who had fought together before would be the ones riding out against one another. The nation's finest military schools had always drawn their cadets from across the country; naturally, now, the officers in the United States military all hailed from every region. If it did come to war . . .

Whichever side he chose, Ian would be fighting old roommates, classmates, teachers—and friends.

Possibly his own relatives. He winced, telling himself he had made no decisions yet. No decisions had been called for yet. The country had come to the brink of war before and compromises had been made. Still, what the hell should he do?

Keep praying, he advised himself.

He turned and reentered his room, found fresh water in the ewer on his washstand, and quickly freshened up. Still, he had tarried too long. He arrived in the breeze-way just outside the dining room in time to see the servants clearing away the meal and to hear the company all lifting their lemonade glasses in a toast to congratulate Peter O'Neill on his engagement to Elsie Fitch.

Congratulations were in order. Elsie was pretty, sweet—a bit vacant in Ian's opinion—but for a man like Peter, that was probably best.

She was also very, very rich.

"Ian!"

His father's voice. Behind him.

Ian forgot everything as he was engulfed in his father's hug. Jarrett took a step back from his son then, coal-dark eyes examining him. "You look fine, son. Indeed, a damned fine sight for these aging eyes."

Ian laughed. "Speaking of aging, happy birthday, Father."

"A very happy birthday. My children will all be home. I'm anxious to spend some time with you—hear about the world."

"Father, I'm not quite certain you want to know about the world. You can't begin to imagine the situation—"

"Trust me. I've seen a great deal. I will manage to view in my mind's eye all that you tell me. I fear deeply for our country, and our state. News coming here is, of course, so often very slow, but it doesn't matter; you can feel a surliness building like storm clouds. The failure of the National Convention seems to have set a new breeze stirring. There is a dangerous, ugly mood to the country now."

"The division in beliefs is growing so deep, I fear that it can never be repaired."

"We'll talk later," Jarrett said. "I believe your mother has just sent the gentlemen to the library, and a flock of young ladies will soon be heading toward the stairs to nap for the evening's festivities. Naturally, I suppose you might prefer to be swamped by young ladies, but your uncle will want to see you and the not-so-terribly-young ladies will spend just a few minutes with the gentlemen, so your aunt will get to give you a kiss and hug as well."

"I saw Uncle James and Aunt Teela not so long ago. Did they tell you?"

"Indeed, it seems they see more of you than we do, since you've been spending so much time at the base at Key West. Come, let's head for the library, and get out of the way of the feminine stampede!"

"As you wish, sir," Ian said. With a grimace, he followed his father.

As Jarrett had warned him, they had just slipped into the library before it seemed the breezeway was filled with giggling, fluffy creatures, all in skirts filled with so many starched petticoats that they could probably stand for building supports. A few, daughters of old friends, caught sight of Ian and gave him welcoming hugs and proper kisses.

In the melee, he thought he saw a swirl of teal brocade flowers and delicate ivory lace: the golden blond beauty who had been holding court with her fencing party upon the lawn.

Before he could question his father about the girl, however, his aunt appeared in the hallway. "Ian!" she greeted him with pleasure, and he met her with a hug and a kiss on the cheek, and when he looked up again, the little spitfire siren was gone.

"Wait. Please, wait. You must wait!"

Alaina had almost managed to escape the house. Almost.

She had reached the rear set of doors that opened from the great breezeway to the dense pine forests beyond it. At the sound of her name being called, she hesitated just briefly—but too long. Peter O'Neill had seen her. And now he was hurrying toward her.

"Peter, get away from me!" she ordered firmly.

But Peter kept coming, a pathetic-dog expression on his face. A handsome face—at least, she had thought so before today. His eyes were soft liquid blue, his features purely patrician, and his hair was a rich light brown and handsomely long to the collar, the ends curling naturally. He was elegantly dressed in a gray frock coat, starched white shirt, and brocaded vest. Now, though, perhaps for the first time, she looked him up and down and felt no emotion. His liquid eyes were not beautiful, but weak.

Still, his grip upon her wrist was strong.

"I *have* to talk to you!" he said urgently. He tugged upon her arm with force.

She could have broken his hold. She could have threatened to scream. Peter would have dropped her wrist like a hot potato—he despised scandal of any kind. Against her better judgment, she allowed him to lead her from the doorway.

A mistake. She discovered that she'd been drawn into the butler's pantry. Her only escape was back out the way she had come, which Peter blocked, or the kitchen doorway, which was currently blocked by a dolly containing the meats from the smokehouse for the evening meal.

She stared at Peter, folding her arms over her chest. Her heart was racing.

Ah, well, perhaps love dies hard, she mocked herself. Young love. In truth, she wondered even now if she had been in love with Peter, or in love with being in love.

And then, of course, she wondered if she was battling the hurt he had cast upon her with a staunch effort to convince herself that she didn't care about him and he wasn't just a cad, he was ugly in the first order!

"What is it, Peter?"

"I would have told you that my father was determined I must marry Elsie Fitch had I only had the chance!" he cried out. His words were clearly in earnest. If she hadn't felt quite so completely humiliated when his engagement had been announced at tea, she might have stepped forward, touched his cheek, told him that it was all right.

But it wasn't all right. Peter had been to visit her island several times with his father, seeking help from her father for his orange groves. And he had sworn his undying love and devotion, and that it would be just a matter of time before he dared declare it to all the world.

Well, today he had made his declarations to the world. With the majority of the guests having arrived at Cimarron to enjoy Mrs. Tara McKenzie's afternoon tea, Peter O'Neill had stood up, with Elsie by his side, and announced that they would be married. Until that moment, she had been having a wonderful time. Her father did not often leave their island in the far south, and she very seldom mixed with society. Despite his scientific status and renown, her father was not among the monied classes, and they were friends with the McKenzies of Cimarron only because they were best of friends with the McKenzies of Mirabella. Alaina hadn't been accustomed to the rush of attention she'd received from the young men today, and admittedly she certainly felt exhilarated. Mature. Wanted. It had been amusing to test her talents for flirtation. Ironically, she had even thought that it might be fun to make Peter just a wee bit jealous.

But then had come his announcement, and she had somehow stood there and smiled throughout, wondering if her teeth would chip, break, and fall out of her head, she was bearing down on them with such desperate effort.

Then, of course, there was the matter of Elsie Fitch. Elsie wasn't the world's greatest beauty, but she was attractive enough, with her dark brown hair and huge dark eyes. She had giggled to some of the young ladies and whispered that they had just been in love forever and admitted that if they didn't get married quite soon, they were simply so infatuated with one another that they'd be planning a very hasty wedding indeed!

"Peter, apparently you are going to marry Elsie, and I wish you every happiness. Now let me pass."

"Alaina, you don't understand."

"Marriage. A bonding of two people. You will take Elsie, and no other. I understand the concept perfectly."

"Alaina, don't be so flippant!" Peter cried, and she realized that *he* seemed to be losing *his* temper. She was the injured party here. "Alaina, I nearly died watching you tease and taunt those other men today. I wanted to stop you behaving like such a reckless hussy—"

"Hussy! Peter, I will not be flippant. And I will not listen to you be crude. I will not be anything with you at all! I wish to pass by and be away from you. In truth, I tell you again, I wish you every happiness; now let me by, and do remember, what I do with any other men in the future is not your concern!"

But when she tried to step past him, she felt a fleeting alarm. He took her by both shoulders and backed her to the wall, suddenly speaking very quickly. "Alaina, for the love of God, don't torment me! We've no time here. God, can't you tell how I want you? I'm a desperate man, Alaina, you have made me so. Come away with me, into the woods—"

"Into the woods!" she exclaimed. "Into the woods— with you?" Oh, God, she was going to start laughing, or crying. The woods! That had been exactly where she had been headed, but she had been going alone. Alone! She was desperate to be alone, desperate not to feel his touch, not to feel so betrayed, so *foolish*!

"Alaina, I love you, I have to have you. When I watched you today, I thought I would explode with jealousy. You must be mine. You don't understand, you must listen to me, I adore you! God, I'm so sorry that it can't be marriage, but we can make the best of what we have. I am rich, not just in my father's land, but in my own right. My mother left me a trust fund. I can—"

"Peter, stop! I can't believe you are saying these things to me. I can't believe that you would even begin to imagine that, now that you're pledged elsewhere—"

"Don't be a fool, Alaina! Sweet Jesus, Alaina, see the

truth of it! No respectable young man will ever be allowed to ask for your hand in marriage."

"No respectable man would ask for my hand?" she repeated rigidly.

He didn't seem to comprehend the hardness that edged her tone, the sudden and complete dislike in it. He rushed on determinedly. "Oh, my dear, you must realize this! Your father is all but penniless. You've been raised in the absolute wild with the savages! But that needn't upset you, because I truly adore you, Alaina, I will give you everything, absolutely everything that I can. . . ."

His words trailed away. She stared at him incredulously. His mouth came closer and before she realized his intent, he was kissing her, pressing her harder against the wall, his body plied against hers in a way that clearly defined what he expected of her, his tongue persistently forcing its way into her mouth.

Amazement held her perfectly still for several seconds, then she felt his hand, fumbling at her bodice. Fury seared into her. She slammed upward with a knee, and the second he howled and stepped backward, she slapped his face with a vengeance. "Peter, take your despicable proposals and go to hell!"

"Alaina!" he croaked. He was in agony, but whether it was because she refused his outrageous proposal or because she had kneed him with such force, she couldn't tell. Nor did she care at that moment. She could endure no more of the rich and respectable Mr. Peter O'Neill. She took full advantage of his weakness and pushed him away from her, then fled swiftly out of the pantry and back out the double doors, across the lawn and into a grove of harboring trees.

Chapter 2

Ian heard the softest murmur and felt a whisper of breath against his nape. "The usual place!"

The young ladies had departed upstairs to rest quite some time ago. Now the matrons were leaving the men to their brandy and cigars.

The whisper had come from Lavinia Trehorn, the lovely and wickedly sensual thirty-year-old widow of the late, lamented, much-older-but-filthy-rich Lawrence Trehorn.

And though Ian had definitely determined that this time home he would tell his parents he intended to enter into an engagement with Risa immediately—Risa *was* beautiful, poised, well educated, and well acquainted with the military, and the love and longing she stirred within him would surely be the kinds that lasted forever—marriage might be a long time coming.

A very long time.

And the prospect of love and marriage was a completely different concept from that of Lavinia. Lavinia was at a point in life where simple essential lust had become rather like breathing; she sought no commitments.

"What was that, Ian McKenzie?"

Ian blinked. The sensual scent of Lavinia's musky perfume remained behind to distract him.

"Ian McKenzie! Explain yourself, sir!"

He realized that Alfred Ripply, the gin-blossomed shipbuilder from Tampa, was querying him on his last statement. Something he had said about the state of the Union—and couldn't begin to remember right away.

The whisper in his ear had thrown him.

He cleared his throat, then paused, aware of another female stare upon him. He could feel the burning gaze of the young woman who was refilling brandy glasses in the parlor.

Lilly.

Lilly was his friend. She was an exotic young woman whose physical makeup combined the very best of her Indian, Negro, and white blood. She despised Lavinia and was trying—while being a competent servant all the while—to impart to Ian with the power of her stare alone the fact that he shouldn't follow Lavinia. He arched a brow back to Lilly, reminding her that he was as yet an unmarried man, over twenty-one . . . and certainly able to stay out of the evil clutches of such a woman as Lavinia—except for that "evil" he was growing rather anxious to share.

Lilly let out a barely audible sniff.

Lilly was a free woman; there had never been slaves at Cimarron. Ian's grandfather, who had brought his sons to Florida, had despised the notion of slavery. Cimarron was a plantation, and it worked as such, but they managed to do so, and do so well, with paid labor.

Lilly had come to them at the end of the "Third Seminole War," as the government called it. It had been the last cry of a devastated people, and Ian had understood the brief but bitter hostilities better than most, since his closest kin, outside his immediate family, had Indian blood running in their veins.

Lilly had actually lived among a very small tribe of Creek Indians residing inland from Tampa Bay. Her husband had joined with the warriors who were once again seeking some semblance of justice. The last conflict had ended much as those wars waged before it; the Seminoles who had survived remained spiritually undefeated, and had retreated deeper into the Everglades. The whites had gladly washed their hands of a nasty battle.

Ian had been incredibly grateful not to have been involved. There had been no Indian trouble in Florida when he had made his decision to accept his appointment to West Point. He had graduated as a lieutenant, but he'd have gladly resigned his commission rather than take arms against the Seminoles. Thankfully, at the time hostilities broke out, his command had been in Texas. Then he'd been assigned to the hotbed brewing out in the Kansas/Nebraska arena before being ordered down to Key West to work with the men there attempting to chart the hammocks, rivers, and streams through the Everglades. The traveling he had done throughout the country had left him certain that he could speak with an educated opinion concerning the very grave state of the Union at that moment.

But he was damned sorry he had said whatever it was that he had. He didn't want to argue politics right now. Lavinia's whisper had been far too enticing.

He glanced at Lilly. Lilly shook her head, worried about him. He smiled. Lilly should understand his attraction to Lavinia, and the fact that he could take care of himself without risking his own future plans or injuring any sweet, young, innocent girl. After all, he was going to marry a very proper young woman, but there would be endless plans to make, and God alone knew when his wedding might actually take place. Meeting Lavinia was pure entertainment for both parties, with no one getting hurt in any way. He wasn't in love with Lavinia, and Lavinia knew it. Neither, of course, was Lavinia in love with him. They had become friends in the short times he had been home, and Lavinia was a widow who had now taken on a number of lovers, quite discreetly, of course. Lavinia was, and had said so frankly, quite enormously fond of good sexual entertainment without the silly restrictions of society. As a widow—one who would lose her dear departed husband's bank accounts to his brother should she remarry—she could see little reason in denying herself what pleasures and amusements might remain to her.

"McKenzie! Ian McKenzie! You make no sense, sir!" Alfred Ripply said, banging his cane against the polished hardwood of the library floor. "You sit there and say that John Brown deserved to hang, and in what is nearly the same breath, you say that Lincoln—that hideous long lank of malformation!—seeks no evil against Southerners, only strength in the Union!"

Ian sighed, glancing at his father where he stood across the room, an elbow leaned against the mantel. Jarrett McKenzie remained as tall and supply muscled as ever; his stance hadn't altered a hair in all the years Ian could remember. His father's dark eyes were grave against his handsome, dignified features; his hair, nearly

jet-black, was just becoming touched with silver. Ian and
Jarrett had certainly had their differences over time, but
now, in many ways, they were discovering they were
very much alike. In the last few years Ian had come to
realize that he didn't just love his father; he admired
him very much. Jarrett's opinions had definitely influenced much of his own thinking, but his life experiences
had served to convince him of the rightness of his beliefs, at least in his own soul. And that was where, Jarrett
had always taught him, it mattered most.

"John Brown is, in my opinion, sir, a sad case. He
believed most heartily that God had sanctioned his
deeds in the pursuit of a higher goal. However, I say
that he deserved to hang because murder is a crime punishable by hanging according to our laws. John Brown
willfully and brutally murdered many men, claiming to
do so in retaliation for raids into anti-slavery territory
by pro-slavery men. Brown didn't have the right to be
judge and jury for those men."

Ian rose and bowed to the men in the room. His uncle
James—up with his family for Ian's mother's annual
birthday gathering for his father—was watching him
oddly. Ian offered his uncle a quick, wry grimace, then
turned back to Ripply and the others. "Gentlemen, if
you'll excuse me, I believe I'll see to the wine list for
this evening. Father?"

Jarrett was evidently aware that his son was heartily
sorry he'd ever allowed himself to become embroiled in
such a conversation. Ripply wanted total agreement with
his own beliefs, and nothing less. And he probably had
no conception of just how ugly the argument over slavery could become.

He hadn't seen some of the atrocities committed out
in Kansas, Nebraska and Missouri as each side struggled
to prove that God had commanded their credo to be the
right one.

"Indeed, Ian," his father said. "Please do so."

And he was free.

Naturally, he didn't need to see to a wine list. Such
arrangements had all been taken care of long ago. His
father didn't know about Lavinia; he only knew Ian
needed to escape, and he understood.

He decided, however, that he'd best make his exit in the direction of the kitchen.

And that was why, although he never saw the young lady involved, he clearly heard her kissing O'Neill—and then slapping him.

Ian disliked O'Neill. O'Neill, whose father had just announced his son's engagement to the cotton heiress Elsie Fitch, was rumored to have fathered several children already, scattered about the state. And if rumor held true, he had denounced each unwed young woman when her condition became apparent. O'Neill was probably considered conventionally handsome, and obviously he could be a charmer.

When Ian entered the kitchen and happened upon the kiss and the slap, he was quickly certain that whoever the luckless lass might be, she was in his house and therefore deserved his protection. Assuming she wanted it.

But when he forced back the dolly to enter the pantry, O'Neill was alone, somewhat bent over, nursing his cheek—and more of his anatomy, so it seemed. His face reddened so that the hand imprint on it seemed to deepen when he saw Ian.

"Excuse me, Ian. Difficulties with an *affair de coeur* which must now be *fini*. I'm afraid that one was in love with me," he said ruefully.

"Indeed. It certainly sounded like it," Ian said dryly.

"She was totally inappropriate for marriage," Peter said defensively.

"You do seem to have that problem with the women who attract you."

Peter reddened still further. 'My father would have none of it."

"But at least the concept of marriage did pass through your mind this time," Ian said politely.

Peter gave him an awkward smile and lifted his hands. "You've been around in the world, Ian," he said. "You know how women can be. This one is . . . *wanton*. A little hellion. So ripe she was bursting. She wanted me. I couldn't deny her. Believe me, Ian, I'd have had to have been a rock to resist her. You cannot imagine—"

"Peter, spare me, and spare my father's house your theatrics, and whatever callous cruelty you might bestow on your *inappropriate* women." He started to walk by, then hesitated. "You're not toying with a servant in my father's house, are you?" For a moment, he was afraid that Lilly might have been involved.

Peter drew himself upright at last, watery blue eyes spitting hatred. He knew Ian disliked him, and he was furious that Ian should have come upon such a scene. "Certainly not! And if rumor does truth justice in any way, Ian McKenzie, you've no right to condemn other men for their affairs with women."

Ian arched a brow, yet he managed not to reply. He wasn't about to argue with Peter or try to explain the difference in enjoying the company of a mature and independent woman and seducing a young innocent. But then again, maybe he had no right to condemn Peter after all; he didn't know the woman involved. And he was growing somewhat anxious.

The hell with Peter and his problems.

The usual place. Lavinia could be impatient. She'd only wait so long.

"Take care in my father's house, Peter," he said softly.

"Or what?" Peter demanded, his tone surly.

"Or I will have to make certain that you do," Ian said evenly, then stepped past the man and hurried through the doorway that led back out to the great hall.

As he left the house, he could hear the sounds of angry voices spilling from the library. He forgot Peter, and he wanted to forget the overwhelming sense of doom that seemed to hang over his country.

He felt a burning sense of nostalgia for the way it used to be. For the slow, easy days when there was little to disturb the way the river rippled, when barges moved slowly and lazily by and the day-to-day life at Cimarron was like clockwork. When the pines sheltered the land, and the crystal pools cooled a man's flesh from the heat of the sun. That was his world. Unique from the North; unique, even, from most of the South. Much of his world still remained a wilderness, civilization bordered by primitive blues and greens. His crystal pools were like no others; the sunshine here was brilliant, the sunsets radiant with vibrant colors. His land was like an Eden.

Mmm . . . Eden.

Private, secluded. Seductive. He was going to be very

glad for a few minutes' respite with Lavinia in his own private Eden.

Before his whole damned world careened straight to hell.

Alaina hurried along the path, her footsteps light and quick upon the pine-carpeted forest floor. She hesitated just briefly, looking back. The trail from Cimarron was empty. Peter O'Neill was not following her, ready to insist anew that there could be something between them in private, even if . . .

Her cheeks burned.

But she wasn't being followed. She had left Peter doubled over, and no one had seen her; no one had followed her. She could escape. And after the events of the afternoon, she was desperate for some time alone.

To cool down.

She knew where to go. To the soothing refuge where she'd been headed when Peter had so rudely stopped her.

There was a beautiful freshwater pool just ahead, or so she had been promised. A pool as private as Adam's and Eve's own Eden, locked away in the depths of the forest that began just where the Cimarron lawn ended. Ian McKenzie's cousin, Sydney, had assured her she would find the pool easily enough, and that it was magnificent—gloriously clean and crystal clear, fed by underground springs. Sydney knew, of course, because she was a McKenzie herself, though not one of the McKenzies of Cimarron. Sydney had grown up in the far south of the state, as had Alaina, a part of the state still referred to as savage by those who felt they had completely civilized central Florida.

Such sentiments usually amused Alaina, and also gave her a certain sense of pride—which allowed her to feel at least a little contempt for the numerous young ladies at the Cimarron party this afternoon who were whispering about her—and her father—as they supposedly lay down to nap. She hadn't needed Peter to tell her that she and her father were, in a strange way, not exactly preferred society to a number of the very rich mothers and fathers in the state. From her experience, young ladies never did nap when they supposedly did so at

social events—they gossiped. But it didn't matter to
Alaina; she just didn't give a damn. Young ladies didn't
swear, either, of course, but since her father was far
more intrigued with plant life than human, he'd never
realized in the least that he might have neglected her
"proper" upbringing.

And thank God he didn't have the least idea that she
was uninterested in either resting or hearing what might
be said.

Or that because of his eccentricities, she might not be
considered decent marriage material. God! That Peter
would dare say such a thing to her. And to imagine
that she had thought herself in love with such a crude,
detestable man, that she had considered marrying him!
After all that he had suggested to her . . . Oh, God. She
was mortified.

She stopped short. There it was. The pool. Large, with
small bubbles appearing here and there from the deep
springs beneath. Great oaks dipped their branches down
upon the water. The water was so clear, she could see
all the way to the depths.

She was dying to swim. She had started off for the
pool, intending to plunge in, and she hadn't been worried in the least before what people might think.

But now she felt that she had to remind herself that
no decent woman would run out into the wilds of Cimarron and go swimming.

Well, she had just been informed that she wasn't exactly decent material to begin with!

She spun around, inspecting the clearing. Insects
chirped softly. A blazing sun burned down. Her temper
burned as well, and the water was so inviting. She
wanted so desperately to feel it, to feel as if she could
wash away Peter's touch—and his hateful words. The
men were busy with brandy and port, the women were
gossiping. The pool was a private place, known only by
the McKenzies.

She sat upon a heavy pine log and began industriously
working at the ties on her elegant dress boots. With
some difficulty she next shed her gown, petticoats, and
the corset that was threatening to asphyxiate her. She
paused just a moment, thinking that she remained somewhat decent in her chemise and pantalcttes. But then

again, if her clothing didn't dry quickly in the sun, she'd have to return to the house—and the gossips—quite damp. If she stripped down and kept her clothing in perfect shape, took her swim, dressed, dried her hair in the sun, and returned to the house, no one would be the wiser. And besides, she still felt Peter's horrible, horrible touch. Breathed his scent upon her flesh. . . .

She slipped from the rest of her clothing, carefully arranged it all in a pile a distance from the water, then gasped just slightly as the cool spring water touched the hot fire of her flesh.

Chapter 3

L avinia wasn't there.

She hadn't come to elegantly drape herself upon the log, and she didn't even await him angrily, pacing up and down, ready to argue before impatiently insisting that there was always too little time, they must make up. . . .

Well, he had tarried too long. Maybe she thought that he wasn't coming, that he'd had other plans. He silently cursed the fools who had waylaid him.

First, the warmonger Alfred Ripply.

And then, in the pantry, that damned pompous rooster Peter.

He gazed at the log. It was her place. The heavy old pine log.

She liked to perch upon it, knowing full well just how elegant she could look, sitting very straight, long legs curled beneath her, pale features guarded from the sun by a parasol.

He warned himself that he had best cool the fires within him. Lavinia was apparently irritated that he hadn't run when she had beckoned. He sat down upon the log, wondering if he shouldn't be grateful he had missed his chance with Lavinia. He hadn't particularly intended to be chaste, but it appeared a greater power might be forcing him to act like a man contemplating marriage—to a good woman who understood his inner turmoil.

But right now the tempest within him was maddening. He'd needed, wanted, an escape from his thoughts.

He ran his fingers through his hair.

He was going to be called upon very soon to make some very hard decisions.

Peaceful, rational men and women were still saying that there couldn't be a war.

But Ian had seen firsthand the passions of those who might well bring about bloodshed. None of this had happened overnight. This argument had been in the brewing since the founding fathers had written the constitution—and left out the question of slavery.

Now the explosion was coming.

And if it did come to war, what in God's name was he going to do?

No way out of it; Florida was a slave state, most of the planters here did depend on slave labor. Ian would have to fight against his own friends and neighbors.

Sighing, he stared up at the sky. It was so blue. It was what he loved most about being home. Winter did come, and rains came, and wild, deadly electric storms came to ravage the Florida peninsula, especially in the Tampa Bay area. But winter never stayed long; the sky was so seldom hung with gloom. Most days were radiant like this late spring afternoon, with the sky cast in a magnificent clear blue. And when the days weren't radiant . . .

Well, he loved the storms as well. Loved the wild, angry slash of lightning across the sky, loved the feel of the wind against his face, loved to ride the flatlands in a fury on Pye right before a storm broke.

It would have been so nice to forget it all—for a time, at least—in Lavinia's simple . . . lust.

A slight sound in the water startled him from his thoughts just as he realized that a pile of feminine clothing lay by the log, right before him.

He spun around. What he saw sent a flash of heat ripping through his torso and limbs—and straight to his sex.

The minx. She was here.

He'd found her. She hadn't left him after all. Through the clear water, he could see her swimming. She was full of surprises. He'd always imagined she hated the water, and that she would never dampen her perfectly groomed hair.

But there she was. Moving about in the water with the grace and speed of a dolphin and the lithe, almost magical beauty of a mythical mermaid.

He smiled, instantly forgetting the state of the world.

He began to strip.

Her pile of feminine clothing was neatly folded.

His fell upon it with reckless speed.

Alaina was blithely unaware that she had been joined in the crystal spring.

Today reminded her of swimming at the reefs off the Keys. Of the wonderful occasions when she accompanied her father out, and while he fished, she swam. The reefs were different, of course. The reefs offered a magical array of color, with fish in dozens of different shades, pale and bright, darting through the water. There, she swam with the current, and the salt stung her eyes. The water, except in winter, was balmy warm.

Here, the water was crisply cool. And clear, unbelievably clear. She could see the clusters of rock, the plant life, the pattern of the sun. There was no force like the current in the ocean, it was really completely different, and yet . . .

The feeling of being beneath the water's surface was every bit as magical. It was like entering a different world, a world where silence prevailed. She felt at peace, buffered from pain, embraced by a place eloquent in its very quiet.

She luxuriated in the clean feel of the water against her body in the clear view it afforded her, diving deep, surfacing for a swift breath of air, seeking the depths once again. She was indeed most accustomed to swimming in the salt of Biscayne Bay right off her home islet, and though she had been in the fresh and brackish waters of the nearby rivers often enough, she had never experienced anything so delightfully clean and cool on her eyes as this.

It was wonderful. It was enough to take away the hurt, anger, and humiliation that had seemed so monstrous before. It was a world where she could just feel. Far beneath the water's surface, she couldn't hear a thing except for a slight rush of the water as she moved within it. High overhead, the sun burned, casting its rays down like crystal beacons to guide her on her journey throughout her watery Eden.

Oh, God, she loved it! Loved the tranquillity and beauty of the water.

Then she felt . . .

Hands!

Large, powerful hands. On her, gripping her, touching her. They encompassed her waist, slid like mercury to her breasts, cupped them, palms over her nipples, fingers then stroking downward over her abdomen, then lower still into the triangle of hair between her legs.

Oh, God, that wretched bastard Peter had followed her, determined on making her see that she wasn't a decent young lady at all, and that she must see things his way.

But he didn't seem angry.

And he was too strong to be Peter. . . .

She was so stunned and frightened that she twisted wildly to fight the intruder, but the more she writhed, the more she felt those hands on her naked flesh.

Touching. Intimately touching.

And she couldn't free herself from the power of them.

Dear Lord . . .

It couldn't be happening.

But it was.

Oh, God! It must be Peter! It had to be. Who else might have come after her, who else would come to the spring pool? What an idiot she had been; he must have thought that she had come here just waiting for him, wanting him to persist no matter what she had said. . . .

No!

She couldn't bear that he could hurt and humiliate her so, and then dare to come after her, make indecent assumptions.

Water filled her mouth, her lungs. Idiot! She had breathed it, trying to scream, trying to fight. She was choking, gasping, dying! She twisted anew and tried to kick her legs to propel herself to the surface. She managed to shove herself forward into her attacker's chest, and only then became vaguely aware that his skin was dark.

She realized that she was facing a well-muscled chest, thickly covered with crisp dark hair. Dark hair that narrowed at the waist, then flared richly again to nest the long, thick rod of the man's—

Oh, God!

Why was she praying? God had deserted her.

What had she so carelessly done, in diving into the temptation of the pool?

She kicked harder, frantically. She was losing air. It wasn't possible, but she was becoming a victim of the man—and the water. She was in danger of drowning. Black spots began to obscure her vision. She couldn't even be afraid anymore of being raped and perhaps murdered by a stranger. She couldn't think at all anymore. . . .

Sometime later—just seconds, minutes? Surely no more!—her vision began to return. Her face was out of the water. She was being towed through it. An arm was around her torso, a hand just below her breast. "Oh, God, God!" she gasped out, and began to struggle once again against the hold upon her. She tried to strike, to kick, knee, disable this man however she might.

In the midst of it all she suddenly heard, "Woah, stop! I'm just trying to keep you from drowning! Dammit, those are vicious knees, woman . . . ah, but then, you must be Peter O'Neill's young hellion—my Lord!"

Her eyes met his. Deep, dark cobalt, they reflected the very depths of the water.

"The young fencing mistress playing havoc on the lawn!" he exclaimed.

She was released. She tread water a foot away from him, staring at him in horror.

He was dark, all right. His hair was nearly black; his strong, striking features were well sun-bronzed. His eyes were all but black, assessing her, ripping over the length of her, piercing into her.

Ian McKenzie.

Ian.

She really wanted to expire. Right then and there.

Ian! The great man's oldest son. James McKenzie's nephew. Heir to half the known world, so it seemed. Built like an Atlas to take his part in the world as master of Cimarron. Towering, hard, handsome, independent, remote; the powerful young military man who had already made himself legend throughout the peninsula, to white men and red alike.

It had been years since she had seen him. Since he had stolen her father's attention, and she had been both infuriated by him . . .

And fascinated.

He was no stranger; she knew him. Yet he had changed in those years since she had seen him.

She had been young, but she had come to know him. She knew his deep, probing attention when something intrigued him. She remembered the passion and intensity with which he had asked her father questions, the determination he had shown to learn, and his capacity to absorb what was taught him.

Ian McKenzie.

Oh God! What had she done to deserve this? What ironic cruelty fate had cast upon her!

She hadn't even realized he was home. She hadn't seen him at Tara McKenzie's afternoon tea; but then, she had fled from it rather quickly.

And it seemed he must have somehow witnessed at least a part of the exchange between her and Peter O'Neill.

Could humiliation kill? Dear Lord, what had he heard, what did he know?

What had he seen?

Then? Now?

What had he . . .

Touched?

Oh, God, but she wanted to die. Fall straight back into the cool, encompassing depths and never break surface again.

"Ian!" At last she managed to speak. To gasp out his name.

Then, perhaps, the greatest insult of a sadly humiliating day assailed her.

"Do I know you?" he inquired with polite amusement and a slight edge of wariness.

She stared at him, astonished, then let out a furious oath and turned to swim away.

But a hand fell upon her naked shoulder as he jettisoned past her.

A hand that had touched her before. Slid proprietarily over breast, down her ribs . . . between her thighs. Again she burned, her flesh burned, the water couldn't cool her.

"Wait!" he demanded.

Wait! Never! She tried to shake off his touch, the steel

grip of his fingers. She stared at him furiously, near tears, but determined she wouldn't cry, no matter what. She was naked in the water with him. With Ian McKenzie. Like the wildest hussy in all the world. *Indecent.* It had been easy to tell herself she didn't give a fig about her reputation when she knew in her heart she was innocent of wrongdoing, that she'd done nothing to sully her name, but now . . .

"No, I will not wait! How dare you, how dare you, how dare you?" Her words came in a tumble, fast and furious. "How dare you touch me—"

"The dramatics are completely unnecessary," he said irritably. "Hold still. I don't know who you are, but I thought you were someone else," he informed her. His eyes swept over her in a way that bluntly reminded her of her state of undress. "And apparently you were expecting someone else as well."

She swore, violently, thrashing the water, trying to strike him. He caught her wrist. She was mortified to realize anew just how clear the water was. She could see every inch of his naked body within it.

He could see every inch of hers.

"I was not expecting anyone! I—"

"You weren't waiting for Peter O'Neill?"

She would have to kill him—or implode and die herself. "Damn you, I am not Peter O'Neill's mistress, I—"

"Indeed? Just whose mistress are you?" His voice had grown very grave; the deep, dark blue of his eyes was touched by the sun's reflection on the water in a disturbing way. She realized both his strength and sensuality at the same time, and damned herself more viciously as hysteria grew within her. Her frantic twisting and struggling wasn't doing her the least bit of good. Oh, dear God, her father lived in the clouds, but this kind of scandal involving his precious one and only daughter would surely kill him!

"Let me go, let me go, this instant!" she shrieked, her nails tearing against his wrist as he held her.

But his fingers tightened angrily around her wrist. "Who are you?" he demanded heatedly.

"Let me go!"

"Who are you?"

"You're supposed to be such a great, damned gentleman! Let me go!"

"My pool, my property. You're a trespasser."

"I'm a *guest!*"

"Spare us both; tell me who you are."

He wasn't going to let her go. His grip remained as sure as iron. They would stay here together, naked in the water, treading water forever.

"I'm Alaina, Alaina McMann, and I used to see you rather frequently when you visited your aunt and uncle—*and my father*—down near the remnants of Fort Dallas. *Now let me go!*"

He did release her, not because she had demanded he do so, she was certain, but because he was just so completely surprised. And she would have moved then, except that it seemed that his eyes, so piercing a cobalt against the bronze of his strong features, had pinioned her there, in the water. "Alaina!" he gasped in a voice rich with both fury and contempt. "Alaina? Alaina!" One kick brought him skimming through the water once again. His hands were on her shoulders as he easily tread the water with legs only. He didn't even seem to realize that he had touched her again, he seemed so outraged. His eyes appeared black; his hold upon her was brutal. His voice thundered. "Alaina McMann, swimming naked in a pool, waiting to meet *Peter O'Neill?* Sweet Jesu, young woman, someone should have taken a switch to you years ago. What in God's name would your father say?"

"How dare you! I wasn't here to meet Peter—"

"Peter O'Neill! That absurd dandy?" he lashed out, not hearing her protest.

"He's behaved no worse than you!" she informed him, astounded that she was defending Peter; but in such a shattered state, by then it didn't matter to her.

Yet he continued to stare at her as if she were the most disobedient and evil young child he had ever seen. "You apparently don't begin to see how stupidly you've behaved. Something should be done. You're not a child, but you're acting as recklessly as one. You should indeed be cast over someone's knee and seriously reprimanded!" He again repeated the one question that ripped cruelly into her heart. "What were you thinking? What would your father say?"

He was older than she, but not by that much, only by five years. Yet it still seemed he was thinking of her as the little girl he had seen so many times years before. He hadn't realized that she had grown up, that she was a mature and independent woman now.

Able to fight her own battles.

She would force him to realize it, she determined.

"Me? *I* should be switched? You bastard! You are the one at incredible fault here. You should be beaten senseless. Hanged, no less. What would *your* father say about you? Swimming naked in a pool. Recklessly, irresponsibly. Like a child. A—a—grown child. Diving in here, accosting a young lady, a guest in your home. Damn you, damn you, a thousand times over, accosting *me*—"

"When you wished to be accosted by someone else?" he demanded. His eyes narrowed sharply upon her. "I didn't accost you, Alaina McMann, but perhaps you should be forewarned: A naked nymph swimming bare as a jaybird in a pool certainly appears to be inviting a man's intentions," he said angrily. "Any man's intentions."

"Oh! Oh!" What a fool she had been. It was a private spring pool, yes, private to the McKenzies.

And Ian McKenzie was here.

Again she tried to wrench free from him. He was incredibly strong and determined. She slammed at him with such a vehemence that she heard a grunt from him, but he didn't intend to let her go. Suddenly his arms swept completely around her as he struggled to her keep her still. It was far more wretched a position than any she had been in before; she was flush against his naked body, and thereby forced to stillness at last.

No, she was actually desperate to be dead still then. Because his body was all but meshed with hers. She could feel the crispness of his chest hair against the softness of her breasts, touching her so tightly in the water. It was such an acute sensation she wanted to scream.

There was more to feel. More of him. oh, it was all so much worse! She could feel the hardness and heat of his muscled form, feel his hips, his thighs . . . feel . . .

Her cheeks burned. The very length of her body
burned.

Dear God, oh, God . . .

Her struggle with Peter O'Neill now seemed like such
a petty nuisance. She'd known how to move then, how
to get the upper hand, how to hurt him and free herself.
Her father had taught her how to fight. He'd taught her
a great deal himself, and he'd given in to her every whim
as well, hiring a fencing master when she declared an
interest in swords, teaching her how to ride, how to aim,
how to shoot, how to dislodge an attacker.

But now, when she so desperately needed her lessons
to pay off, she couldn't free herself.

And even the pounding of her heart seemed to bring
her more closely against the force of this man. More
aware of the length of him.

She couldn't meet his eyes.

Had to meet his eyes.

Had to . . .

Find a way to escape his touch.

Swearing beneath her breath and pathetically close to
tears, she tried very hard to stare defiantly up into his
eyes.

Fighting wasn't working.

She could take no more of this. Feeling him. The heat,
the fire, the sheer strength of his hold. How could he do
this? Perhaps it didn't occur to him that this could be
the most humiliatingly uncomfortable moment of her entire life; perhaps he thought that her nudity was a casual
thing to her, since he was convinced she had been intending to entertain Peter O'Neill and had probably entertained him—or other men—before.

She wanted so badly to hurt Ian McKenzie for the
way he was looking at her—slash him through with a
sword!—but she was further infuriated to find herself
absolutely impotent against him.

She couldn't bear it. Not a second longer. Pride be
damned, truth be damned, nothing mattered but that she
escape him and the fiery brand his length seemed to be
imprinting upon her.

"Please . . ." she just barely managed to breathe the
word.

She shook.

The whole of her seemed to burn. She had never known such physical distress in all her life.

She was ready to beg for release and agree with anything the man had to say just to gain her distance from him and put some clothing between them.

Too late.

For even as her whispered plea sounded from her lips, she heard the movement of foliage.

And voices.

People . . .

"Oh!" An appalled hurt feminine sound.

"Oh!" A furious, shocked masculine sound.

"Ohhhh . . ." spoken simultaneously.

She froze. Indeed, there were people behind her. She wanted to sink into the water and disappear. Forever.

There was, certainly, something of the gentleman in Ian McKenzie. For several seconds he was as frozen as she. Then he moved: swiftly, deliberately. Alaina discovered that she was no longer flush against his chest, but propelled protectively behind his back.

Yet over his shoulder she could see that the McKenzies' private Eden was not so very private.

The very, very rich, elegant, and beautiful Mrs. Lavinia Trehorn, her brown hair artfully piled in a riot of curls atop her head, stood at the water's edge near Ian's discarded military-issue blue dress uniform and Alaina's own neatly folded feminine attire.

Peter O'Neill, his cheeks lobster red, his breath rushing in and out of pursed lips, stood at her side, taut and rigid with fury.

"Oh, Lavinia, you were right!" he grated out, shaking. "You do know Ian, and indeed, you knew where he could be found, and Miss McMann is very definitely with him, so it appears! Yes, they are certainly together. And he is—what was it you said, Lavinia? He is 'comforting the poor lamb'—and doing so quite well. In fact they both looked damned comfortable, I'd say!"

"Ian McKenzie!" Lavinia said with stark reproach, her perfectly formed lips trembling ever so slightly with an even more perfectly formulated dramatic touch. "Ian, I thought that, oh . . ."

She appeared angelic, and wounded. She looked as if she would faint.

Still, it was Peter's next single word that seemed to ring in the pine forest long moments after the two of them had spun about and departed back to Cimarron—with the latest, most incredible gossip.

For Peter stared long and hard at Alaina, cheeks red and puffed, eyes burning with offended fury as he lashed out, "Whore!"

Chapter 4

"He is an unmitigated ass, and I'll kill the damned bastard!" Ian murmured in a deadly voice.

Alaina barely heard him.

She had to escape the pool. She had to get back to Cimarron and find her father before others did. She didn't know what she was going to say.

The truth. Her father would believe her.

Yet as she streaked across the water, a sudden cramp knifed into her leg. She gasped, clutching her calf. Ian swam up beside her, eyes almost black now with fury, yet his voice, though very deep and husky, was surprisingly calm. "What is it?"

He was reaching for her.

"No! No! Don't you touch me! Don't you come near me again!"

He arched a brow, then swam past her, believing her words.

But the pain knifed through her again. She allowed herself to fall beneath the water's surface while she tried valiantly to massage her cramped limb and bring functioning life back to it. She ran out of air and tried to surface. She couldn't kick. *Float!* she commanded herself. She surfaced, but the pain was so intense she went down again.

Incredulous, she realized that she—Alaina McMann, who had been swimming all her life, who could hold her breath well over two minutes—was drowning. Again, little black dots were forming before her eyes. They were beginning to fuse together. She had to make the surface one more time. Once again. And no matter how awful and detestable, she was going to have to call out to Ian McKenzie with a word she could scarcely bear to issue to him at this time.

Her face broke the water. She managed a choked out, "Help!"

Then the blackness seemed to encompass her, leaving only the tiniest pinhole of light. . . .

Her vision slowly returned, her mind dragging just behind it. She had been brought to the soft, grassy bank at the pool's edge, near the fallen log. She lay naked on her stomach while a dripping naked man hovered over her, forcing the water from her lungs.

She coughed, sputtered, and swung around in horror, eyes wide as she stared up at Ian. "Oh, God!"

She leaped to her feet; too fast. She staggered. He steadied her. She struggled.

"Look at me!" he commanded fiercely.

She found herself doing so.

His eyes appeared blacker, fiercer than ever. His anger was such that she thought he did mean her harm.

"Were you trying to kill yourself over that fop? You little fool! He isn't worth spit!"

"What? I wasn't trying to kill myself!"

"But you were in love with him?"

"Oh, God!" She shook her head wildly, vehemently. "Please, dear God, will you let me get dressed—"

Still tense, he arched a dark brow. "You apparently didn't mind jumping naked in a pool when you thought it was Peter O'Neill who'd be joining you."

"Let me go!"

He did so. She raced straight for her clothing, fumbling terribly in her haste. She was aware that he dressed smoothly and competently at her side.

Naturally! she thought snidely. *Men!* He was far more accustomed to stripping and dressing than she. He was completely clothed, from uniform jacket to polished boots, scabbard, and sword, while she was still struggling with her corset.

"May I?" he inquired politely at her back, reaching for the strings.

"No, you—"

But he already had his hands upon the ribboned strings that constricted the corset, and he had a knee set gently against her back to wrench them in.

He was accustomed to corsets as well. Obviously. La-

vinia had probably taught him all about corsets. All that
he hadn't learned from previous experience. Oh, God,
were all men such loathsome creatures? Interested in
sex, prestige, and money, and not at all concerned if
those things came in one package or in several!

She was shaking as he helped her into her afternoon
tea gown as well, but when the dress was in place, she
quickly pulled away from him to sit upon the log again,
slip into her dress boots, and lace the ties. She realized
that he was standing there, arms crossed over his chest,
watching her with blue fire in his eyes all the while.
When she was about to rise, one of his Union-issue-
booted feet landed on the log beside her and he leaned
low, more or less imprisoning her there upon the log.

"Where do you think you're going?" he demanded.

She stared at him, incredulous and, despite herself,
more than a little intimidated. Ian McKenzie stood very
tall, and as she was quite aware from newly gained firsthand experience, he was composed of good solid muscle
for all that length. He was an exceptionally striking man,
with his strong features, pitch-black hair, unusual dark
blue eyes, and cleanly defined brows. His five-year se-
niority suddenly seemed like quite a bit as well; his jaw
was set in a fashion that told her he knew what repercus-
sions would befall them both over what had occurred
here. He was angry, quite naturally. She felt a little chill,
thinking that surely he could not mean that he really
intended to kill Peter O'Neill. Of course he did not. Still,
looking at him at that moment, she was glad that she
was not O'Neill.

Not that Ian seemed to regard her with much less
contempt. Those penetrating eyes of his raked over her
in a manner now that quite clearly condemned.

She returned his stare.

No. She would not let him cow her.

"I have to go back and talk to my father, and you
should be quite worried about doing the same. Not that
men aren't given every license in the world to behave
like absolute animals, but since this has all occurred at
your father's house, he just might be rather perturbed
about the whole thing."

"My father will understand what occurred from my

end; he is a concern, naturally, but not my main concern at this time."

"Boys will be boys, right? Your father certainly can't be angry with a man acting like a man!" she muttered heatedly. "Well, this might surprise you, but my father is a rational human being who loves me—"

"Indeed, he loves you. And there, Miss McMann, may lie the real depths of our problem."

"We haven't a problem, Mr. McKenzie. I'm quite sure that the ever-lovely Mrs. Trehorn will quickly forgive you this transgression, and you will find yourself cheerfully sleeping with the widow once again. As to me, I'm rumored to be a witch, so the fact that I apparently indulge in the sins of the flesh now and then will be no greater detriment to my life than anything else I have already faced. Now, if—"

"So that's it!" Ian murmured.

"What is what?" Alaina cried with frustration.

Those blue eyes struck her hard, seemed to impale her. "He promised to marry you. But his family didn't deem you good enough."

She had simply been humiliated enough.

"The next time I hear you described as a gentleman, I believe that I will . . . throw up!" she exclaimed vehemently. "now, if you please—"

"I do not please. You have compromised me."

"What?" she all but shrieked. "I compromised you? Don't be absurd—men are allowed to . . . to dally with . . ." She felt as if she were choking again. "Men are *expected* to seek out the company of . . . fallen women!"

"This is an incredibly delicate situation," he said.

Again she felt the pressure of his gaze, eyes sweeping over her, something very hard, calculating, and still furious within them.

"There is no situation," she assured him. But his cobalt eyes remained dark and compelling as he stared at her.

"Miss McMann, how do I put this delicately . . ."

"Why bother to be delicate about anything at this point?"

"Indeed," he said, eyes flicking in a cool assessment over the length of her once again. Then they fell upon hers and sharply narrowed. He demanded bluntly, "You're not expecting Peter O'Neill's child, are you?"

She couldn't have been more stunned if he'd slapped her across the face. For a moment she couldn't reply.

Her silence seemed to convince him he had guessed correctly. "Ah, poor girl. Dear God, was that why you were trying to . . . kill yourself?"

She felt as if she were strangling again. The temptation to lash out at him was more than she could control. She tried, really tried, to gouge his cheeks with her nails, but he was far too fast for her, catching her wrist with a pressure that brought a cry to her lips. "No, damn you, I am not expecting Peter O'Neill's child, and I did not attempt to kill myself. I would never attempt to kill myself, especially over a despicable man!"

"Are you quite certain?"

"Are you daft? Indeed, if I ever do try to kill myself, I'm quite certain I will know."

Pure annoyance swiftly crossed his features. "I meant about O'Neill's child."

"I have never been more certain about anything in my life!" she cried out furiously. "Not that it's any of your concern!"

He suddenly released her wrist. Arms crossed over his chest, he paced in front of the log.

A feeling of deep unease crept through her. If she tried to rise and run past him, he wouldn't let her leave.

"I really have to go!" Alaina informed him, fighting the nervousness in her voice and attempting a strict-sounding authority. "You know, I will prosecute you if you continue to force me to stay here. Brute strength is not the way to solve anything."

"Indeed. So it seems that cunning and treachery are best, in sword play and in life?" he asked softly.

"Oh, this is absurd," she grated, refusing to argue with him.

Ian stared at her, and again she saw anger in his eyes and in the set tension of his face, but there was more: Something both strangely weary and knowing was there as well. When he spoke, he sounded oddly beaten. "You know that we cannot simply go back."

"Why not?"

"By now Peter has less than subtly let everyone know

that you and I were having a tryst at the pool. Your father is crushed and humiliated; mine is furious that I would so abuse the daughter of a friend, a good and decent man. My uncle, as well, will be absolutely appalled, since my acquaintance with your father came through him. Your father," he added with a certain wry amusement, "might want to call me out as well—he may be a scientist, but when it comes to you, he is still no less the romantic."

"You think that my father will challenge you to a duel? That's so silly; it's absurd, it's—"

"You forget that we do live in the gallant South, be it the far wilds of that most honorable section of our country!" The sound of his voice was bitter; she didn't know if he was mocking his homeland or himself. He continued, "Your father must demand some manner of satisfaction, and I would heartily hate to hurt the poor old fellow."

"Oh, how dare you, you arrogant boor! Assuming that you'd be such a power against my father—"

"Forgive me," he interrupted dryly.

Alaina was still for a moment, infuriated but aware that it was entirely true that Ian could kill her father with the flick of his wrist. Her father was aging, and he knew nothing but his books and science.

She struggled for a sense of dignity and told him, "There is nothing to be done; it is a mess, and that's that." The realization of just what a mess it was suddenly bore down upon her, along with the seriousness of it all. A Southern gentleman such as her father was definitely required to demand satisfaction if his daughter had been compromised. "Oh, my God, my poor father."

"Perhaps you should have thought of him *before* stripping and plunging into a pool like a siren from the depths."

"You are insufferable! I thought myself alone! Any decent man would have—"

"Alone? Or waiting for Peter O'Neill?"

"You are never going to get the chance to kill my poor father in a duel because I am going to kill you within the next few moments, Ian McKenzie."

He lifted a hand. "The motive behind your indiscretion is of no importance at this moment."

"Indiscretion? Indiscretion!"

"Miss McMann, call me rude, call me judgmental, but I am afraid in our society proper young women just don't go around naked!"

She should have learned better by then, but after all, she did have the barrier of her clothing now. She leaped from the log, anxious to impart some kind of physical harm to him.

It was an attack he hadn't been expecting; with his one boot angled upon the log, he fell off balance with her impetus, and they landed down hard upon the soft embankment together. For a moment she was on top of him, staring down into his surprised eyes.

Maybe she had grown up just a bit too rough. Because she was ready to give him a sound blow with her right fist to his jaw. But male pride apparently seized hold of him just in time, and she found herself lifted and slammed beneath him.

He was atop her, hands on either side of her head as he leaned against them to keep his weight from bearing down upon her. His face was just inches from her own.

"Settle down, hellion. My God, but you've acquired a frightful temper!" he told her angrily.

She had a temper? He was a damned madman. "You haven't seen the half of it yet," she assured him, eyes narrowed with warning. She could kill him. Simply kill him.

"You might have been better served to grow up under the influence of a stern matron—"

"Don't you dare insult my father."

"Miss McMann," he said, quite grave then, and pushing himself to a position where he straddled over her— arms irritatingly crossed over his chest. "I would never dare insult so gentle and good a man as your father. And there lies the base of this disaster."

"If you will just let me go—"

"You can't go, and surely you must know it."

"But—"

"Peter O'Neill is a vicious young braggart who will do his very best to create all the havoc he can out of this situation. Lavinia is hurt and believes herself scorned, and under such circumstances she will likely be even more vicious than Peter. By the time this story gets to the second listener, we'll have been fornicating so passionately in the bushes that the birds were blushing and we were never aware of their arrival."

"So what is your suggestion?"

He hesitated, his next words seeming to pain him. And still, no words could have astounded her more.

"Obviously," he said flatly, "we have no choice but to marry."

Alaina felt the blood draining from her face. "No," she said softly.

He shook his head, staring down at her, and she wished again that she might have just disappeared into the cool depths of the pool. He didn't care for her; he had no desire for her. He considered her a poorly reared, careless little wanton who had just gotten them both into a terrible situation—but he would do his duty.

Oddly enough, she felt like laughing. Peter had told her that no respectable man could ask for her hand in marriage. No family held more regard within the state than the McKenzies. It was all so sad, and so damned ludicrous.

"Apparently you didn't hear me," Ian said irritably. "We have no choice."

Did he think that she was one of his military men? That he could command her to his will?

"No, there is always a choice."

"How will your father feel, Miss McMann, when all this is thrown upon him?" he inquired with chill courtesy.

She bit fiercely into her lower lip. How would her father feel? Devastated. No matter if he understood that she had just wanted to swim in the clear pool. It might come out that she had indulged in a foolish crush on Peter O'Neill, and the very fact that his daughter had been caught naked . . .

She didn't want to think about it. She didn't want to imagine what her father would think and feel. He would most certainly feel that he had ruined her life by not raising her properly.

"There will be scandal no matter what," she whispered.

"Maybe. And maybe we can circumvent Lavinia and Peter."

"How? There is no way to do that. No matter what, we must go back. No matter what we say, it will appear that you are marrying me simply because we were caught and because you have to do so, and the scandal—"

"We marry before we go back," he interrupted impatiently.

"That's quite impossible—"

"No, actually, it's not. Reverend Dowd did not come to my father's party today due to a fierce toothache; he is home with his wife and brother-in-law. It's a half hour's brisk walk there and a ten-minute ride back, since we can borrow a horse from him. We return to the party quite distressed that our marital status was discovered before either of us has had a chance to tell our respective parents of our decision to elope."

"But I am not of legal age."

"The ceremony will be legal unless your father chooses to have it annulled."

Alaina just stared at him blankly. He had the answer: the perfect answer. Because he was right. To salvage their standing within the world—not to mention the devastated feelings of their parents—they would have to marry.

And again, he was right: It would be far better to marry, pretend that they had done so quite some time ago, and therefore deflect the efforts of Peter and Lavinia to see that they were totally mortified and humiliated and to create horrible friction—and perhaps even bloodshed—within their families.

But as she looked up at Ian, her heart seemed to falter.

Marry. Ian McKenzie.

He suddenly seemed a great deal older; distant, different. A determined man who knew his own mind and would brook no opposition to going about life as he saw fit. Waging what battles he determined he must win.

She couldn't be his *wife*. She suddenly felt quite ill, well aware that she might never rid her life of the tempest she had inadvertently brought about today. She didn't want to admit she was afraid of the demands that he would make upon a wife, afraid to cast her soul into the hands of a man who was convinced she had caused all this with her own salacious desire to seduce another man—one he seemed to heartily despise.

She didn't know Ian at all; oh, Lord, except what she had learned today.

Not true! She had known him once. She knew that he had spent time in the hammocks and swampland down south with his uncles and cousins, he spoke both the Hitichi of the Mikasuki tribes and the Muskogee of the Seminoles. He'd learned the hard lessons of an Indian youth, and Sydney had told her once with pride that Ian could wrestle a full-grown male gator—and win. The trouble between Ian and Peter might well have begun many years ago, because she remembered now she had heard that when they were boys, Peter and Ian had come to blows because Peter had made a disparaging remark about the Indians. Ian had bloodied Peter's nose and cost him a tooth, but controlled himself before further damage had been done.

Maybe she had known him at one time, but she'd been a little girl then, his baby cousin Sydney's friend, trailing along after him, Jerome, Brent, and Julian as they fished and trapped the river, bay, and woods.

That was long ago. A different time and place. A different world.

Now, it was quite true: They were strangers; she really hadn't seen him in years.

Oh, yes. She had seen him. Seen him from head to toe, in the crystal-clear water.

She couldn't breathe, couldn't answer. She still hadn't answered when he rose, reached down, and pulled her to her feet. He took her hand, threaded his fingers through hers, and started walking.

She followed in silence for a long while. Peter and Lavinia had naturally returned by now. They wouldn't go straight to either Jarrett McKenzie or Theodore McMann. Perhaps Peter would go to Tara McKenzie, pretending to be terribly distressed about her son's actions. Or perhaps Peter and Lavinia would just begin a whispering campaign that would take its time getting through to the poor, side-blinded scientist Teddy McMann, and the pillar of the community, the highly respected Jarrett McKenzie.

She suddenly pulled back, tugging on the hand that held hers.

"Ian, you're not thinking this through. This is . . . marriage," she said breathlessly, seeking out his dark blue eyes with the gravity of it all in her own. "How do we live with this? We can't just—"

"Do you see a way out?" he inquired politely.

"But, my God, this is so serious."

"Indeed."

"Divorce will be a greater scandal."

His eyes lit upon her. "There won't be a divorce. Not now. I have to return to military service. I travel frequently; you'll seldom see me. And our pathetic little problems aren't really going to mean much, I don't think. In a very short while . . ." he shrugged. "There might well be a war on, and what has happened today really won't mean a damned thing."

"War?"

He didn't reply; he was walking again.

"War?" she repeated. "Ian, there won't be a war! If there is trouble, Florida will simply secede from the Union. Other states will do the same; they'll form a new nation. Damn you, Ian—"

He didn't respond to her. He was in a hurry.

Brisk was a poor description for the way that he moved. She was practically running to keep up with him, and more breathless than ever, which made argument incredibly difficult.

The next thing she knew, she was plowing into his back in front of the reverend's pretty, picket-fenced lawn. Ian opened the gate; she followed him through. Within a few steps, they stood before the reverend's door, waiting.

Marriage. It was binding. It would change her life, change her dreams.

"Ian."

He didn't hear her.

"Ian!" She was shaking again; she couldn't seem to stop herself from doing so.

He looked down at her.

She moistened her lips. "I can't. I . . . can't."

"You have to. You rolled the dice when you decided

to skinny-dip. Now we deal with the lot we've been cast."

"Well, you know, it might have helped the roll a hell of a lot if you hadn't been naked and in the water . . . groping! And lusting to *fornicate* with the widow Trehorn!"

The door opened at just that moment. A silver-haired woman, her gentle brown eyes wide with shock, plump pink cheeks red as cherries, stared at Alaina—aghast. The word *fornicate* seemed to hang in the air.

"Mrs. Dowd!" Ian said cheerfully.

Once again Alaina wanted to sink into the crystal pool of water she had left behind. Apparently she had said the word *fornicate* really loudly. It just wouldn't go away.

Mrs. Dowd arched a brow to Alaina, but gave no other response to what she had heard. She addressed Ian with pleasure, her voice barely faltering. "Why, Ian, what a surprise, do come in. We're so sorry to have missed your father's party—"

"I'm quite glad that you did, and I'll explain why to you and the reverend, if I may."

"Of course, of course. Do bring the, er, young lady in."

Alaina winced. Her reputation had surely just taken another plunge.

But she quickly discovered that Mrs. Dowd was a kindly person, and Reverend Dowd was a gentle man as well, as thin as his wife was plump, with bright, mischievous blue eyes that seemed to delight in the concept of this secret elopement. Ian's description of what went on was so earnest and close to the truth that Alaina was amazed herself at the deceptive courtesy he displayed in explaining her part in it. She had simply stumbled upon a beautiful pool and been tempted beyond all human resistance, and, well, Ian admitted, his part in it hadn't been quite so innocent, but now . . .

"Now," Reverend Dowd said quite simply, "the matter must be remedied." His glance at Alaina was quite kind.

"I shall get my brother-in-law down. His eyes are failing, but his hearing is quite good. He'll do quite well as a witness," Mrs. Dowd said determinedly. "Harold, you must marry these two young people at once."

The Reverend Harold Dowd took both Alaina's hands and offered her a crooked half smile. "Marriage, then, young lady. It's one thing if a man presses you to it, quite another if it's the devil's doing!" He winked, indicating Ian at her side.

"I have pressed her into it, Reverend," Ian said.

"One and the same," the reverend muttered with humor. "Let me get my book of prayer, then . . ."

He ambled off. Mrs. Dowd had gone for her brother-in-law. Ian suddenly had Alaina's chin and was lifting it in a rough hold that wasn't gentle in the least.

"I'm sorry that Peter O'Neill hurt you and deceived you. I don't know what went on between you, and I'm doubly sorry if you still find yourself enamored of him. Bear in mind, though, from this day forward, it is over."

"There was—"

"And madam, if you ever think to betray me with any other man, know that I will render your backside skinless before throttling you."

Startled by the sudden vehemence of his attack, Alaina found herself both hurt and furious again. Ian McKenzie and his damned sense of duty! He believed that she had slept with Peter O'Neill—and yet he would marry her anyway because it was the right thing to do.

No respectable man would marry her . . . so Peter had said. But here was Ian McKenzie. In a way, she couldn't wait to see Peter's face.

Except that . . . she couldn't marry him.

"You are a monster, the very devil, Ian, and I can't possibly do this! And what of you? All of these threats that you make against me—"

"Ah, but Alaina, I have always known my duty."

"As I have not? How could you know, how could you know anything about me anymore, how dare you think—"

"We are here because I came upon your stark-naked body in a pool in broad daylight," he reminded her dryly.

Her cheeks reddened vividly.

"You—"

His whisper was suddenly a violent breath against her ear. "You stand forewarned, Alaina!"

"*You* stand forewarned!" she whispered in angry

reply. "You have brought this about; you remember that it is nothing but a charade."

"A charade? We are here, Alaina, because it is all damnably real!"

"We are here because you—" Alaina began, but she quickly fell silent as Reverend Dowd came forward.

"Ian, Alaina, are we ready? There was a few legal papers which must be filled out and signed first," Reverend Dowd said, beckoning them over to his cherrywood desk.

She couldn't do it. She couldn't do it. . . .

Ian was propelling her forward, and she could not resist. She couldn't marry Ian, yet neither could she bear to think of what her father would suffer if she did not.

Marry him, just marry him! she told herself. He wasn't going to give her any other choice. She would have the satisfaction of showing Peter he was a fool, that he had lost her for the most ridiculous of reasons. Ian was going back to the military; she could go on living just as she had, except that she would be Ian McKenzie's wife.

Respectably married.

"Alaina?" his voice sounded harsh.

He had already filled out the reverend's papers with impatient carelessness and speed.

Alaina printed in her name, her father's and mother's names, and her place of birth. She signed her name.

Ian's hand was upon her arm.

She found herself back in the parlor, at Ian's side. Reverend Dowd cheerfully instructed them on just where to stand, taking a position before them, his prayer book in his hands.

Mrs. Dowd's brother-in-law—ninety if he was a day, but tall, spritely, and cheerful—was standing at Mrs. Dowd's side. Grinning, cupping his hand to his ear to make sure he heard all that was said properly.

It was all so unreal. Alaina even felt as if the room were filled with fog, as if she dreamed. For this could not be happening.

But it was happening. Ian spoke his vows in a clear, ringing voice.

Alaina barely managed to whisper her own.

They came to the part about a ring. she discovered that Ian had set a heavy signet ring onto her finger, one

that was naturally quite huge, and would have fallen off
her if she hadn't wound her fingers into her palm. Then
Ian was being instructed to kiss his bride. Again, his
fingers were nearly brutal as he lifted her chin.

Oddly, his lips were fire . . .

Forming over her own, imparting a liquid force and
heat that startled and seared her, and left her trembling
as Ian's mouth lifted from hers and he gave his attention
back to details with Reverend Dowd.

Certainly they could borrow a horse. Their haste was
fully understood. Their secret regarding the exact date
of their marriage would be kept.

Within another five minutes, Alaina found herself
mounted in front of Ian on a very handsome bay. And
they were cantering at a steady gait back along the carriage trial that led from the Episcopal church back to
Cimarron Hall.

Alaina felt his arms, and the fire that seemed to com-
pose his body and limbs, and again she felt a strange,
shimmering chill.

She had begun the day thinking herself in love with a
man she now despised.

Oh, and it was true! What a naive fool she had been!
She had started this all by shedding her clothing . . .

Dear, God, she would never do so again!

Because she was now ending the day . . .

Married to a hard, angry, man. A *compromised* man.
Ian McKenzie. A force. A power.

A man she had actually known most of her life, yet
who was still a virtual stranger.

His arms tightened around her as they rode. The heat
of his fire seemed to encompass her.

She shivered all the more.

She looked up at the sky and saw that the sun was
sinking. It appeared to be a fierce, blazing ball of or-
anges and golds upon the horizon. There was nothing so
beautiful as a Florida sunset, and yet, Alaina thought . . .

It foretold the night.

And she was quite suddenly afraid of the darkness
to come.

Chapter 5

Ian was angry with himself.

Furious.

He was equally furious with her—naturally. Especially now, as she sat before him, skeins of golden hair free and tangling about his chest and face as they rode hard against the wind.

If she and Peter O'Neill had picked another time and place to play their games, none of this would have happened. He wouldn't be married to one woman, when he had been all but engaged to another.

Yet no matter how it infuriated him that Alaina McMann had shed her clothing in his pool, he couldn't deny—to himself, at least—that they both might have been out of the water and decently clad before Peter and Lavinia had come upon them if he hadn't been quite so consumed by the sight of her and so irrationally irritated to discover that so lush a beauty as Alaina had been seduced by so wretched an excuse for humanity as Peter O'Neill.

Had it been a strange form of jealousy? The time during which he had actually touched Alaina intimately had been brief; yet the impressions of all that he had felt were forever embedded in his memory. He thought wryly that God had created woman—and so man had wound up cast from Eden. How ironic, for God had created a perfection in Alaina McMann that was surely the worst temptation of man. Her breasts were firm, rounded globes, her waist was wasp thin, her hips flared. She was slender, but, dear God, was she shaped. Maybe that was why he had not recognized her. The last time he had seen Alaina, she had been reed-thin. A devilish little hoyden, running free on the sand. But he should have recognized her face, though her features, too, had matured to a delicate beauty quite different from the time he had seen her last. Still, those eyes, those golden eyes, cat's eyes . . . sensual eyes, taunting eyes. He had seen that beautiful blend of color only in her eyes. How had he forgotten?

Time.

And his irritation with Peter O'Neill.

Which had now damned them both to this charade, as Alaina had called it.

Well, just what had he intended? He still didn't know, except that he'd been obsessed that they must marry, and determined that he must somehow force her to his will. He'd be damned if he'd let Peter O'Neill have the opportunity to slander him, or any of the McKenzies.

And as to Alaina, well, it was easy enough to twist her arm when her father was threatened. Still, he had rushed forward with little thought of the future; he'd only known that he'd not let Peter O'Neill return to Cimarron and destroy everyone there. Yet now the deed was done. He could mock himself. What now? He'd shackled himself to a woman O'Neill had known; perhaps she was still in love with Peter, despite Peter's treatment of her. If she went near Peter, he thought with sudden fury, he'd slice them both to ribbons.

The thought suddenly astonished him, and he gave himself a furious shake. What in God's name was the matter with him, that he could find himself seized by such overwhelming thoughts of violence?

"What now?" she whispered suddenly, and he realized that he had reined in at the lawn's edge, that he just sat there waiting, feeling the last golden rays of the sun beat down upon them.

"Well, now, my love, we play out the charade," he told her.

She twisted slightly, her face rising to his. Cat's eyes questioning . . . perhaps just a little uncertain, delicate face strangely grave and very beautiful. He thought about the way she had teased and flirted on the lawn— and the cunning power with which she had bested her opponent at swordplay. A burning tension tormented the length of him, and for the first time since he had begun with this obsession, he reminded himself that she had grown into a rare beauty indeed, perhaps one of the most beautiful women in all his acquaintance. Then he mocked himself, wondering if he hadn't realized it all the time, if he hadn't been as obsessed with the feel of her flesh, the curve of her breasts, as he had been with his fury against O'Neill.

Marriage.

A damned stiff payment for obsessive desire.

She looked forward again, long blond hair tousled from the ride and teasing his nose. He gritted his teeth and leaned low against her to whisper against her ear, "We face the barracudas."

He felt a slight trembling within her.

"Afraid?" he mocked.

Her shoulders squared. She twisted again, cat's eyes narrowed as they fell on his.

"Of what?" she demanded.

"Facing them all down."

"No," she assured him flatly.

"Ah, then, are you afraid of me?" he demanded.

"Never," she assured him coolly, yet she looked quickly back to the house and he thought he felt the slightest trembling within her again. . . .

He suddenly nudged his heels hard against his borrowed horse and they bolted across the lawn. One good thing, he thought: Alaina McMann could ride like the wind, swim like a fish, run like a deer. She was nature's own child, her father's daughter all the way.

He reined in at the house, leaped down from the horse, and reached up to help her down. Cat's eyes touched his. He swept her down before him, close against him. She slid against the length of his body to the ground and he whispered to her, "Remember the game, my love."

Rich honey lashes fell over her cheeks; she was still shaking. Whatever game he was playing, this was not so easy for her.

Was she in pain? Because of Peter O'Neill? The thought was enough to give anyone apoplexy.

He caught her hand. He gave her no more chance to protest, but drew her along with him into the house.

Cimarron was aglow. Lights blazed within; the exuberant sound of fiddles filled the night. As they stepped into the breezeway, Ian saw that the doorways to the parlor and the library had been opened to the grand hall to create a massive ballroom of most of the downstairs. Guests danced, milled at a punch table, talked, flirted, teased—and argued.

Ian saw that gossip had preceded them home—but that his parents and Teddy McMann had apparently united against it. His mother and father stood together at the rear of the punch table. His mother was chatting away with Teddy. Teddy, his light blue eyes looking a bit lost, was valiantly trying to keep up with Tara and pretend that nothing in the world could possibly be wrong.

Ian noted that though Peter stood by his newly announced fiancée, he was also close to the musicians. Peter whispered something to the men as Ian and Alaina walked in and the music came to an abrupt and jarring halt.

For a moment, they were frozen in an awkward tableau; fiddles remained poised, dancers remained upon the floor—and all eyes turned toward Ian and Alaina.

Including those of Teddy McMann and Ian's parents.

"Don't you dare stand there looking guilty," Ian warned Alaina.

"I'm not guilty!" she said indignantly.

His hand rested upon her back and he felt the stiffening of her spine. Good. They'd both need stiff spines to get through the night.

"Ian!"

His brother, Julian, younger than him by a bit more than a year and nearly his twin in appearance, suddenly came forward to greet him. They embraced one another warmly. As they drew apart, Ian grimaced, recognizing the light of pure devilment in Julian's eyes.

Whatever was up, his brother surely intended to torment him in private. In public, Julian intended to stand by his side, and damn all those who would come between them.

Ian ignored the continued silence in the room and the stares focused upon him as many of Cimarron's guests waited in both tense and delighted anticipation for what explosion might now erupt regarding the scandalous gossip that had been circulating the last few hours.

Ian spoke, greeting his brother with an enthusiastic

return, ignoring the rest of the room. "Julian, dear boy, but it's good to see you. You do know Alaina—"

"Of course, how could I not know Alaina?" Julian said, his smile charming, his voice husky with admiration as he bowed over her hand to kiss it. "Alaina, you have grown into quite the most bewitching woman in all the state."

Julian's voice wasn't loud, but it carried—as it had been intended to do.

Alaina murmured a thank you. She was very stiff, and Ian became aware that she watched her father, and he saw the pain in her eyes.

Julian stepped closer to his brother. "Give me a lead here, Ian; I'll follow."

"Get the damned musicians to start up again," Ian suggested softly. "And . . . and tell Father that I am sorry for any discomfort I have caused him, and that I must beg his understanding and indulgence in what I am about to do. I'll speak with him as soon as I can suitably reach him."

Julian arched a brow, as if he, like many others in the room, had been so drawn by the spectacle of Ian's appearance with Alaina that he hadn't realized the music had ceased. His lips curled slightly, and Ian was well aware his brother was anxious to know why he must ask their father's indulgence.

But Julian spun around, catching the eye of the lead fiddler and lifting a hand in question. The fiddler hastened to comply with such a query from a son of the household.

The sweet, melodic sounds of a waltz suddenly filled the room once again. Ian bowed to Alaina and swept her into the dance. She moved with him quite easily, as naturally graceful on land as she was in water. Her small chin was tilted; her golden cat's eyes blazed. "They are all staring; what are we accomplishing here? My poor father—"

"Your poor father will be just fine. Laugh, smile, pretend you are enjoying yourself. The gossips will soon have their due."

"Will they? Listen! They talk so loudly, they must not even care that we hear."

As they danced, Ian found himself smiling with grim

but genuine humor. Moving about the room, they indeed caught snatches of feveredly whispered conversation.

"Do you believe they've had the audacity to arrive together here?" demanded an old biddy.

"The very nerve of it!" replied her soldier partner.

'Living in so savage a land, she has naturally been raised as little better than a savage. . . ." That from a young Tampa mother.

"Teddy's poor wife dead . . ." That from her husband.

"She's a hussy . . ." An ugly old crone Ian was quite certain he didn't even know.

"But for Ian to respond so, in his *father's* house!" A dignified old soldier.

"There was talk of a *proper* marriage between Ian and a colonel's daughter. . . ." A younger soldier.

"She bewitches men. . . ." A jealous old maid with a very large nose.

"But her father simply must accost him, do something!" Another elderly man, retired military from Tampa.

"It is quite deliciously awful!" one matron admitted to her balding partner. She caught Ian's eyes on her; she flushed crimson, but met his stare for several seconds before backing down.

"Imagine, the McKenzies of Cimarron involved in so sordid an affair!" She said with a loud sniff as they danced away.

He saw that his brother had reached Jarrett and Tara and given his message. He gave his brother a barely perceptible nod, which Julian easily read. He moved across the room nimbly, ducking amid the dancers, to reach Ian's side once again. "May I?" he inquired politely to Alaina.

Her golden eyes touched Ian's, but she readily slipped into Julian's arms.

Perhaps far too readily, Ian thought irritably. But he moved quickly through the crowd to the place by the punch table where his parents stood with Teddy McMann. He knew that the buzz of gossip about the room grew as he addressed his mother, father, and Teddy, but he kept his voice low. He'd be damned if he'd add fuel to the fire. "Father, Mother, Dr. McMann, I wish to make an announcement tonight, and ask that you will all stand by my side—and that of your daughter, sir," he said to Teddy. "Most assuredly, you have heard what gossip has been intended for your ears by now, and I pray that your belief in both Alaina and me has allowed you to keep faith in us despite it."

Ian was surprised to see that his mother appeared to be far more amused than outraged. "See, Teddy," she assured McMann, slipping an arm through his, "I have told you that there can be nothing to these vicious rumors. Though I am quite curious to see how my son intends to dispel them."

Teddy McMann was slim, of medium height, with a head full of snow-white hair and clear, gentle eyes. He studied Ian, then reached out a hand, grasping Ian's. "She is all that I have, Ian. I have known nothing but honor from McKenzies in the many years I have made this state my home; I will trust in you, as it seems my daughter has chosen to do."

Ian looked over to his father. Jarrett was not amused; he was concerned. Arms crossed over his chest, he leaned closer to his son, making their conversation private. "The lady seduced you at the pool? Or you seduced her? Are the rumors true?" he demanded quietly.

"No one was seduced, Father," Ian replied honestly. "It was an accidental situation."

"Men can survive such accidental situations; Miss McMann is ruined. You do realize that. Teddy McMann stands there, his heart breaking, certain that he has destroyed his daughter's life through his selfishness in living on an island to pursue his vocation."

"If you are reminding me, Father, that there is but one honorable way out of a difficulty caused by vicious gossips, I assure you, I have taken the matter in hand." He hesitated, glad that he'd not had much chance to talk to his father yet, and that he'd never mentioned his intentions to marry the colonel's daughter, Risa Magee. "Father, Alaina and I have already wed."

Jarrett started at that, his brows jutting up, jet-black eyes assessing his son carefully. Whatever his thoughts on the matter, he wasn't going to express them then. "I'll give you a moment to tell Teddy McMann; I'd not like to see his heart fail when such a surprise is revealed to everyone in this room. I shall ask the musicians to take a break, and allow you to make the announcement as you see fit."

Jarrett stepped away from his son. Ian turned to Teddy McMann, who was watching him with the eyes of a man who had been kicked—but was still determined to seek good in his attacker.

"Mr. McMann, you deserved much better from me, sir, but I think now is the best chance I have of letting you know that Alaina and I . . . have married."

Teddy stared at him blankly.

Tara McKenzie, at Teddy's side, gasped.

"I'm sorry, Mother," Ian murmured quickly.

"Married?" Teddy inquired. "But how could this be? When did such a marriage take place? My daughter keeps no secrets from me—"

"It's your right to annul our wedding, sir, if that's your choice," Ian told him.

Teddy shook his head. "I'd never deny Alaina what she wanted; I'm just so . . . stunned."

The musicians had stopped playing again. Jarrett Mc-Kenzie stood on the raised dais at the far end of the breezeway where they had played. "Ladies, gentlemen . . . if I may ask your indulgence for a few moments, it seems we have another announcement this evening, and one quite close to home. I will let my son do the honors."

Ian turned, seeing where Julian stood with Alaina. He walked through the crowd, which parted obligingly for him. Then he took Alaina's hand and returned to the dais with her. "Friends, honored guests," he said, staring across the room, his eyes alighting upon many of those who had most cruelly vilified them. "Circumstances have called upon me to make an announcement I'd intended to share privately with my parents first," he stated, his tone chagrined. "But since I'm afraid my eagerness to be with the woman I love was prematurely discovered, I must share our happiness with all of you, here, tonight, as well. Ladies and gentleman, I present to you my wife, Alaina Mc . . . Kenzie."

The room made a collective gasp. There were whispers of astonishment, and relieved laughter as those friends who wondered at the morals of the heir to Cimarron Hall and the botanist's daughter were assured all was well.

"But, but—when did this wedding occur? You mean to tell me your parents knew nothing?"

Ian glanced across the room, recognizing the sweetly concerned female voice. Lavinia's.

Ian drew Alaina to him. She was staring at him, with those beautifully unique eyes of hers exceptionally wide. Her cheeks were flushed to a startling rose. Her look of horror might have been mistaken for adoration. Her hand fell upon his jacket as his arm circled around her. The silky softness of her hair teased his cheek and lay like pure gold against the dark navy of his uniform. The clean scent of her body seemed to subtly infuse the air he breathed, and holding her thus, he was reminded of every lush, firm curve of her body. A fever was awakened within him, making his story come easily, passionately to his lips. "I'm ashamed to say that my parents knew nothing. Yet I believe they will both forgive me; having seen my bride, they can well understand my feelings." His voice trembled just slightly.

The perfect touch.

He wasn't so much an actor; his apparent emotion was actually simple lust.

She pulled away slightly, looking up at him. A pulse beat furiously against her throat. Her breasts rose fashionably above the bodice of her gown. He knew exactly what lay beneath the fabric. He brought his fingers to her cheek, and lowered his mouth to hers. He heard the softest breath of protest, but ignored it. His lips formed over hers; tongue teased, delved. She was warmth, sweet liquid fire. A sudden, knifing ache of desire was awakened in him in a way that left him shaken. She'd aroused him before, naturally—a young, perfect, naked woman in the pool. . . .

This was worse.

He drew his lips from hers. Her eyes spit fire. Her lips were damp and swollen; she was struggling for breath. And he found himself wondering furiously if she was still in love with Peter O'Neill, and indeed, just how and where O'Neill had touched her.

Congratulations were called out to them. Yet among

all the kind words came one far different cry. "I don't believe it; it can't be, they must be lying!"

Peter O'Neill. Ian saw the man standing then in the center of the room, facing them. He felt Alaina grow tense, and the spiral of emotions inside him tightened dangerously. He manage to ask politely, with just an edge of warning to his voice, 'Why, Mr. O'Neill, are you calling me a liar, sir?"

"Peter!" O'Neill's gruff old father called out the quiet warning.

Peter grated his teeth. He didn't dare call Ian out. Peter was a fair swordsman, but Ian had gained a reputation in the military for being deadly. Peter also risked his own newly announced engaged status if he made too much noise about another man's marriage.

Peter rallied quickly. "Ian McKenzie, not on your life, sir, would I call you a liar. Surely you have legal documentation. I confess, I merely express the amazement of everyone here, and naturally, my concern for Miss McMann."

"I thank you for your concern!" Teddy McMann suddenly called out, his voice strong as he approached the dais. "Quite frankly, I am delighted to discover that there is little I need ever fear for my daughter again, since she is in the care of our Major Ian McKenzie, though I hope she will accept my love all her life."

"Papa!" Alaina whispered softly. Escaping Ian's hold, she fell into her father's arms, hugging him.

"I say congratulations are definitely in order!" Julian cried out. "Champagne, my friends, all around. Here, here! To my brother Ian. And to Alaina, the most elegant, magical creature in the world. Ian, to you and Alaina!"

Bedlam then broke out. Ian didn't see his bride again for quite some time. He found that champagne was pressed into his hand, and that he was moving through his home, passed from friend to friend, and onward. A very warm hug suddenly assailed him, and he discovered that he was being held by a tall, slender young woman with stunningly dark eyes and hair, and an ivory and rose complexion so perfect that she almost seemed unreal. His sister, Tia.

"Ian! You devil. You didn't whisper a word to us. I

hadn't even realized you'd seen Alaina McMann in forever. Of course! You've been down in the south quite a
bit lately, right? But not to tell us, oh, Ian!" She stepped
closer. "Or *is* it a lie? Did that scandalous episode at
the spring occur? Ian—"

"Tia!" he moaned. "Behave."

"Ian!" she returned. "Tell me this at least—are you
really married?"

"Yes. Now, Tia, please, act like the charming young
lady of the house and don't get the guests all staring at
me again, eh?"

She kissed his cheek. "Did Sydney know before
now?"

"No, no one did," he told her. "Tia, you know that
you'll get the whole story eventually—you'll torture it
out of someone soon enough. For the moment—"

She smiled, then hugged him again. "Love you, big
brother," she said softly.

His arms tightened about her, then he released her,
just in time to find himself being engulfed by his cousin
Sydney, his aunt and uncle, and his cousin Jennifer and
her husband, Lawrence Malloy, and then his cousins,
Jerome and Brent, his best friends since childhood, all
of whom were baffled, but discreet.

The night wore on.

He saw that Alaina stayed beside her father, not letting him move away, even though she, too, was being
buffeted from well-wisher to well-wisher. Those who had
most probably reviled her so soundly just moments
before.

But she was married now. Into the McKenzie clan.

His cousin Sydney, friends with Alaina from birth,
seemed especially pleased with events, though puzzled.
He felt her eyes on him continually as time wore on. He
stared back at her, then noted throughout the evening
that Peter was watching her as well, as if he meant to
corner her.

Sydney McKenzie was stunning. Tall and slim, she had
her mother's emerald eyes and her father's raven hair.
James McKenzie was half-breed Seminole, and his Indian blood had come down to Sydney in a way that
made her exotically beautiful. Her eyes were a product
of her white blood; her hair was Seminole, thick, lus-

trous, straight. Her flesh was flawless, golden. If Peter O'Neill went anywhere near his cousin that night, Ian would skewer the man.

He took a deep breath. He was hardly thinking in a civilized, rational manner.

Alaina McMann had done this to him.

Alaina *McKenzie*. He had married her. He suddenly felt exhausted.

"Ian?" He turned to find his mother before him, her gaze upon him betraying nothing of her thoughts. "Because of the distance to their home, Alaina and Teddy would have been staying here for the night even before . . . your announcement. Lilly has seen to it that Alaina's things have been moved out of the guest room, where she would have been staying with a number of the other young ladies, to your room."

He stared at his mother blankly for a moment. "Ah."

She frowned, blue eyes studying him carefully. "Ian, you are married?" she inquired softly.

'Yes, Mother. We're married."

"Well, then, you'll want your wife with you."

His wife . . . with him. A part of his world.

He didn't know if he exactly wanted her with him; but he certainly did want her.

Marriage . . . so high a price for desire!

What of life, what of tomorrow? What of the colonel's daughter, and the life he had imagined he would lead?

He inhaled. "Mother, I'm really sorry—"

"Ian, don't be sorry. You have lived your life in a manner that's made us quite proud; we trust your decisions. Besides," she murmured, "maybe one day I'll tell you how your father and I came to be married. Teddy is a good man; your bride is beautiful. Julian is right. She has surely grown into one of the loveliest young women I have ever seen."

"She's indeed lovely," Ian murmured. He didn't add promiscuous, reckless, and hot-tempered.

His mother kissed him on the cheek and slipped away. He turned and found himself with Teddy McMann again. Teddy was studying him with his soft, trusting blue eyes and Ian was annoyed to discover himself feeling twinges of guilt. "Sir, I do have documentation that we are legally wed," he said.

Teddy nodded gravely. "McKenzie, I'm not quite sure what went on here, and quite frankly I don't want to know. I admit . . ." He hesitated. "I love my daughter; I would gladly die for her. But I'm afraid that my love has made me indulgent and Alaina has always done what she has pleased. She rides, shoots, fences, swims . . . I'm grateful she's found you, McKenzie. For she might well lead a lesser man on a merry chase. God bless you, son!" Teddy said, and moved into the crowd again, perhaps looking for his daughter. Where was she? Ian wondered. Then he saw her. She was with Tara, and she was quite white. She was probably learning that she had been moved into Ian's room at Cimarron Hall.

"Ian!"

He swung about. His brother Julian and his cousins Jerome and Brent were lined up before him. Julian carried a bottle of their father's finest whiskey.

"With careful observation, brother, you'll note that Cimarron's guests are leaving already, and of those who are staying, most have retired upstairs," Julian said.

"Before the night wanes further, we McKenzies need to toast you!" Jerome told him gravely. Like Sydney, James's sons carried their white and Indian blood in a striking manner. Jerome had deep cobalt eyes like Ian's own, strong, bronze features, and a touch of auburn to his dark hair. Brent was green-eyed with rich, heavy Seminole hair, so dark it seemed to shine blue-black. They were all of a near height, every one of them over six feet, and built similarly as well. Jerome had studied engineering and shipbuilding while Brent had attended medical school with Julian.

"The first of our generation of McKenzies to marry, my good lad," Brent said. "Well, other than Jennifer!"

"And marry Alaina; how very curious," Jerome added.

"Come outside, away, to the porch," Julian urged in a whisper. "This is a McKenzie-only toast."

Ian found himself propelled outside. They didn't stay on the porch, but wandered to the lawn, a fair distance from the house, passing the whiskey bottle back and forth as carriages departed from Cimarron.

"So you have married our Alaina—and without a one

of us knowing a thing about it!" Jerome said, eyeing him questioningly.

"In a way, of course,' Brent added, "we're like her next of kin—Jerome, Sydney, and I."

"She grew up by us," Jerome reminded Ian gravely.

"Right. If the rumor had come back about her being at the pool with someone else . . ." Brent said.

"We'd have been called upon to defend her honor, naturally, since she had no brothers of her own," Jerome informed him.

"However, since we're *your* cousins—" Brent said.

"Closest kin," Jerome noted.

"Excuse me, I am his brother," Julian interjected. "That actually places me as closest kin."

"All right, we're second-closest kin. We want to know exactly what really happened," Jerome said.

Ian hesitated. Then he shrugged. "We had both decided to go swimming. We ran into each other. We were . . . seen."

"So you're not married," Jerome said with a frown.

"My dear, closest kin," Ian said, "if this toast is for me, you can hand over the whiskey bottle."

Brent, in possession of said bottle at the moment, handed it over. Ian cast his head back and took such a swallow that he burned inside from throat to gullet. He lowered the bottle, took a deep breath, and discovered the three ringed about him in a semicircle, staring, waiting impatiently for his reply. He drank deeply again.

They still stared, patience waning.

"We are really—and legally—married."

"But how in the devil—" Jerome began.

"Marriage is quite damned easy, and you'll manage well enough once you get to it. You just keep saying 'yes' or 'I do' when you're asked a series of questions."

Jerome slowly arched a brow, looking to Julian and his brother. "I'm not quite sure why I'm concerned here. I believe, actually, that he and Alaina deserve one another."

"She's capable of being every bit as sarcastic," Brent agreed.

"Determined and stubborn," Jerome agreed.

"Pigheaded," Brent elaborated.

"Umm," Julian murmured. "And *he* is a tyrant. Ian

always thought he had the right to be the leader with us—"

"I was oldest," Ian said, taking another long swallow of whiskey. It didn't burn as badly as it had at first, and it seemed to be taking a few of the razor-sharp edges off the night. "I did have the right to lead."

"Well, there you have it!" Jerome said dryly. "My ancient cousin—older than you and I by what, Julian, a little more than a year?—likes to take command. Alaina refuses to do what she's told by anyone. This is just wonderful. They should get along like oil and water. A marriage made right in heaven. The question remains: When did it occur—and why?"

Ian arched a brow. The night was growing very late; the moon was nearly full and directly above them in the dark sky. He might well stay here forever if he didn't answer them, and if he could count on secrecy from anyone in the world, it was these three. The whiskey was warming him; he was tired. He'd spent his journey home worrying about the state of the Union, and he'd ended with this. His head was pounding, and he did have a newly acquired wife with whom to come to some understanding before the night ended. "All right, my dear, closest kin, I've now been married several long hours at the very least. It occurred because the young lady seemed to be escaping an unhappy situation. It seems she believed that Peter O'Neill intended marriage—to her, rather than Elsie Fitch," Ian said.

"I'll throttle him," Jerome said darkly.

"No—should the need arise, I'll take care of the man myself. Nothing happened at the spring pool, but since no one other than my family and Teddy would believe the truth, I thought we'd best marry quickly."

"Ah!" His brother and his cousins stared at him with a collective sigh.

"But it is—really—legal?" Jerome said.

"Reverend Dowd married us."

"It's quite legal," Julian murmured. "But what a strange situation. The last time I saw you, there was a colonel's daughter involved in your life."

"And then there had been rumors about Alaina, of course, and I'd been under the impression that she—" Brent began, but broke off instantly.

"That Alaina was involved elsewhere?" Ian demanded with an edge.

"Sydney had thought that she was expecting to marry elsewhere soon, and that she was in lo—interested in someone. I now assume it was Peter O'Neill. Well, that's over," Brent said quickly. "Look, look back to the house. The lanterns are being doused."

"The past doesn't much matter, does it?" Jerome demanded with a level gravity that reminded Ian very much of his Uncle James. He reached out, gently grasping the whiskey bottle from Ian's hands. "You're wed to one another now. And since you've done the honorable thing, perhaps you should do the courteous thing as well, and return to the house."

Ian took the whiskey bottle back from him. "Indeed, I should."

Ian left his brother and cousins standing on the lawn. When he reentered the house through the breezeway, he found the servants clearing the remnants of the party. The guests had departed or retired. There was no sign of his parents, Teddy McMann—or Alaina.

He strode up the stairway and down the hall to his room. He hesitated. He felt as if his body had become one pounding drumbeat; he realized that the sound of his heart had become that excruciating pulse, and that the burning glow of the whiskey remained electrically about him.

He pushed open the door and paused.

All lamps had been snuffed in the room, but someone had built a fire in his hearth against the dampness, and the room was further illuminated as the doorway to the balcony remained slightly ajar. Moonlight spilled in. Enough moonlight to show him that his bride was curled into a protective ball on the far side of his bed. She was so curled, in fact, and so far on one side, that a breeze would send her falling to the floor.

Irritation seized him, along with the haunting knife of desire she could so easily arouse. He walked over to where she lay, looking down at her in the moonlight. Her eyes were closed; tears dampened her cheeks. She looked young. Angelic. Sympathy rose within him, until he wondered if she was crying for her lost love.

He reached down to touch her. Her eyes flew open;

she hadn't heard him come into the room. Moonlight spilled over her, making her face very fragile, her eyes twin circles of glowing gold. Her lips trembled, and one word issued from them in a broken sob. "Please . . ."

He drew away, afraid of the turmoil that raced within him, certain that he must either wrench her up and inflict some violence or walk away completely. He strode to the balcony windows and stood there, tension creating an ache in him from head to toe. He heard her sigh of relief. Did she think that he was leaving?

He turned back, unbuckling his scabbard to set his cavalry sword on his desk. He took a seat in the large leather wing chair behind his desk, setting the whiskey bottle he had carried in down by his feet. He leaned back, closing his eyes to mere slits, watching the firelight play before him, damning himself anew for his reckless-ness by the pool, and determining his position here now. He had a wife, one he hadn't intended. She hadn't wanted a husband—at least, she hadn't wanted him as a husband. But she was truly a fool if she thought that he intended to go through all the years of his life as a cele-bate husband because she had intended on capturing a different lover.

So . . .

He frowned, sitting very still.

She had risen. Slipped from the bed. Her nightgown was an ivory shade, beautifully laced. Sheer. She covered it with the matching robe that had lain at the foot of the bed. Barefoot, moving with barely a whisper of sound, she came near to where he sat, looking down at him. Apparently, she thought he slept.

She bent, plucked up the bottle. He heard her sniff of disdain. She set the bottle on his desk and moved across the room to the balcony.

He gave her a second, then came silently to his feet. By instinct and long habit, he buckled his scabbard back on.

Then he followed.

She wasn't on the balcony. He looked up and down the length of it.

She was on the lawn, he realized. She had slipped down the rose trellis and was moving across the lawn toward the woods.

"Damn her, what is she up to?" he muttered aloud. He swung his body over the railing and caught the trellis himself, climbing down it. She hadn't the least idea that she was being followed. He kept twenty feet behind her as she scampered along the trail that led to the pool. Ian paused behind an oak as she stood in the center of the pool's clearing, staring at the water.

Then a man suddenly rose from the night shadows that encompassed the log at the water's edge.

Peter O'Neill.

"Alaina!" he called softly.

She spun around, long hair and gown flowing like liquid gold in the moonlight . . .

To meet her lover?

Chapter 6

"Alaina, I knew you'd come!" Peter O'Neill called out softly, coming toward her.

"O'Neill!" The quiet of the night was suddenly shattered with the deep thunder of another voice.

Peter went dead still and deathly white.

Alaina froze as well, not certain if she was more stunned by Peter calling out her name or Ian calling out Peter's.

It didn't matter. What mattered was the horrible tableau created here. She'd been so desperate to escape *his* room, Cimarron Hall, *him*. She was accustomed to wandering where she chose at home; there, it didn't matter, there was no one near them, and their closest neighbors would never harm her. She'd been quite certain that Ian McKenzie had passed out with his whiskey bottle; she'd seen him with his brothers and cousins at the far edge of the lawn and she had prayed for just such a respite. In a thousand years, it had never occurred to her that Peter O'Neill might be here now.

But he was. And she knew exactly what it looked like. Peter, in this copse. Awaiting her.

She could feel herself shaking inside with a strange depth of fear unlike anything she had ever known before. Ian stared at Peter, and Peter returned that stare. Peter wore a dress sword. He pulled it from its scabbard, causing Alaina's heart to skip a beat. But then he threw the sword out on the ground. "McKenzie, we'll not have bloodshed. I'm not armed!" Peter cried out suddenly.

Ian McKenzie deftly unbuckled his scabbard, letting it and his cavalry sword fall to the ground.

"No bloodshed," Ian agreed, but his tone was deadly; his blue eyes appeared obsidian. But even as he spoke, the trail behind them suddenly came to life with the sounds of branches snapping and footsteps falling.

Julian, Jerome, and Brent burst into the copse, pausing just behind Ian.

"Jesus," Julian breathed, surveying the scene.

Alaina felt Jerome and Brent staring at her. Neither spoke. She knew what was in their eyes: fury at her betrayal. They were her friends, Sydney's big brothers, almost her own.

But they were McKenzies. The look in their eyes was merciless. Ian McKenzie had married her. She repaid him thus.

"Well," Peter said, finding a certain courage. "Will you look at this! The great and powerful McKenzies! The white boys and the breeds, towering talents with guns, fists, and blades, and all lined up before me." He lifted his arms. "If you think you can just murder me in the woods and get away with it because you are the great McKenzies, you had best reconsider. My uncle is a state senator. You'll hang, every one of you."

"No one is going to murder you, O'Neill," Ian said, his voice deep and quiet. "Not now. But if I ever catch you near my wife again, I will kill you."

Peter shrugged. Then he started to walk out of the clearing, away from the McKenzies. But he paused by Ian. "McKenzie, you just might find yourself having a rough time keeping your wife away from me," he taunted, and he made the mistake of giving Ian a fierce shove.

"Please—" Alaina started to say.

Too late.

Ian lunged for Peter. The two went down in a split-second flurry. Ian was on top of Peter. There was no contest. Peter didn't get in a decent blow. Ian caught Peter's right jaw. Peter howled.

"Stop it, stop it, please!" Alaina cried out, rushing forward, wondering if she could somehow stop a murder by casting herself between the men. Then again, Ian might just as happily kill her.

She never reached the fighters. Brent caught hold of her, an arm firmly around her waist. "They'll handle it, Laina," he told her softly.

As Ian raised a fist to strike again, Julian and Jerome came behind him, his cousin hanging on his arm, his brother on his back. "Ian, he isn't worth it, he isn't worth it!" Jerome hissed.

The two were able to drag Ian off his enemy. Julian knelt down by Peter. "He's out, but he'll be fine. Luckily, Ian, you didn't break his jaw."

Brent released Alaina and stepped forward, stooping down by O'Neill as well. "Let's get him back to Cimarron," Julian said. He and Brent took the burden of Peter and started back along the trail to the house. Jerome hesitated briefly, a hand on Ian's shoulder, his eyes momentarily touching Alaina where she stood by the pool, barefoot and determined not to betray her shivering.

"Cousin?" Jerome murmured.

Ian, tense as a bow string, eyes hard on Alaina, spoke quietly as well. "I'm fine."

Jerome nodded. "Well, then, good night." He turned to follow his brother and Julian down the trail. Alaina very nearly shrieked out to him that she wasn't fine at all, and that he had to come back and protect her. From her husband, his cousin.

She didn't cry out; she couldn't get her jaw to work. Ian didn't move. He just stood there, dark hair fallen over a dark blue eye, features set in so grim a line he might have been composed of stone.

"Well?" he murmured quietly.

"This wasn't what it appeared—"

"Oh?"

"I had no idea he would be here."

"You just felt the urge to run out to the pool and strip and swim again?" The sarcasm in his voice was as cutting as a blade.

"No, I just felt the urge to escape your house, you, your room—"

"You dislike my house so much?" he inquired politely, arms crossed over his chest as he began to take steps toward her. "I'd rather thought it a handsome place, and I'm quite fond of my own room."

She was on the defensive, turning to face him to keep from being cornered as he circled around her. "I detest your house and your room," she whispered. "I—"

"But you weren't meeting O'Neill?"

"No."

"Ah, well, say that you didn't arrange a meeting with O'Neill. Doesn't it ever sink into that foolish little head of yours that running about naked can be dangerous?" he demanded furiously.

"I'm not naked—"

"Naked this afternoon; half naked now, Mrs. McKenzie!"

The way he said the words make her cringe inwardly, snapping out his own name with such contempt and anger that she had no choice but to fight back.

"No!" she cried. "No, I am not in danger, from you or anyone. I am not a weak and sniveling little thing ready to become a victim, sir. I can defend myself—"

"You can defend yourself?"

"I am excellent with a sword, sir."

"Well, I didn't notice that you brought a sword with you here," he commented wryly, "but that aside, are you really so excellent that you feel you can defend yourself from all would-be attackers?"

"I took lessons for years. I bested a cavalryman quite easily this afternoon," she informed him uneasily. He was circling her again. She had to keep turning to keep him from being at her back.

"Fine, then. Have at it with me," he said. He gaze seemed like onyx. Hard, unyielding. Brutal.

"Have at it?"

"Indeed."

"You want me to . . ."

He reached to the ground and drew his sword from his scabbard, tossing it toward her. It spun in the sandy dirt at her feet and she stared down at it before staring back at him.

"Pick it up," he commanded. "Mine is a good sword. Peter's is a silly dress sword, but I shall take it as my weapon and give you the advantage."

"Don't give me anything," she warned him, wondering at what idiocy was driving her now. He was absolutely furious, she knew. And yet, he seemed as cold as ice. It made him all the more dangerous, his complete control.

"Pick up the sword; fight me."

"For what?" she whispered.

A grim, taunting smile curled into his lip. She felt her breath catch, for his hair fell in dishevelment over his forehead, his gaze was ice-hard, and the taunting curve of his mouth was oddly sensual against the rock hardness of his handsome features.

He had Peter's sword in hand. He swept it through the air and gave her a mocking bow. "You can defend yourself; so you have said, when I warned you of the dangers of your recklessness. Fight for your honor. Best me, and walk away. Run back to your island with your father. Lose, madam, and your honor is mine."

"My honor will never be yours!"

"If you can defend yourself as you claim, no man could take it from you, am I right?"

"I can defend myself!"

"Are we agreed on the terms?"

"The terms?"

"My terms."

"We are not—"

"Yes, we are agreed; it is the very crux of the argument, for if I were any stranger with ill will and the violation of your chastity in mind, I would simply seize what I wanted—were I to win."

"No one can seize anything from me."

"So you say. Then fight me."

"I *will* win!"

"Pick up the sword, girl. Defend yourself. Show me how infallible you can be, and that I need not worry about your half-clad midnight meanderings to bring shame upon our marriage. The sword! Pick it up!" he roared at her.

Convinced that she'd be skewered on the spot if she did not, Alaina bent down quickly for the sword, leaped back, and prepared to face Ian. "You're a fool," she cried out. "I know how to use this and if you—"

His sudden movement sent the steel of his sword clashing against her own. The force behind his blow was staggering, but she kept her grip firmly upon her own weapon. Picking up the skirt of her nightgown in her left hand lest she trip on it, she determined that she must go on the offensive herself, before the force behind

his blows weakened her arm. She could move like lightning, and she went after him aggressively with a series
of swift blows, nearly dancing across the soft earth of
the pool's embankment with the speed and grace of her
movement. He fell back, and she felt a moment's tri-
umph. Then she realized that he was falling back
merely to allow her to expend her energy while he
feinted every blow. She had pressed him backward a
good twenty feet when his sword suddenly started
swinging in a series of arcs that she parried just by the
skin of her teeth.

She was forced back the twenty feet she had gained.

They both paused for breath.

He made a sudden blur beneath the moonlight with
his blade—one that she feared for a split second would
indeed cost her her life as his steel just missed slicing
into her breast.

She wasn't cut. The delicate lace ties of her gown were
neatly severed instead.

She knew better than to grow angry; a cool head was
needed here. But she was infuriated. She began to attack
him again with a swift series of blows. She was so swept
up in her tempest that she made a swinging strike that
would have severed his legs at the calves had he not
been swift enough to leap from her attack and land on
the fallen log just behind him. Not willing to lose the
advantage, she attacked instantly, determined to bring
him to the ground where she could rest her sword point
against his throat and thus end the matter.

The log shattered; he lost his balance, falling flat upon
his back. She leaped over the scattered pieces of wood,
certain of victory, but just as she came for him, he made
a miraculous flying leap back to his feet, striking her
sword with a merciless blow that would have broken
her arm if her fingers had not instinctively let go of the
reverberating hilt.

Her sword flew, arced in the moonlight, came to rest
point down in the earth about ten feet away.

She stared into the deep, damning blue of Ian's eyes.
She started to make a mad leap for her sword. His suddenly struck the ground before her, embedding his blade
in the earth there in a manner that brought her to a
dead halt.

She stood very still as he came around her, drawing his weapon from the ground. He raised the sword to her again, the tip of it resting just below her chin.

"Madam, do you surrender?"

She refused to answer, then inhaled sharply at the sudden flick of his weapon. But his blade didn't touch her flesh. It lifted the fabric from her right shoulder. She felt the softness of the sheer gown and robe falling from her right side. She willed herself not to move. A second flick of the sword lifted the gown from her left shoulder. With the delicate lace ties slit, the length of the silky gown and robe pooled to her feet, and she stood naked in the moonlight, facing him.

He studied the length of her. Assessing her, his gaze amazingly dispassionate. He leaned upon the hilt of his sword. "Well?"

"Well?" she whispered, the breeze swept around her, seeming to touch her with strange fingers, so cool against the growing heat of her flesh.

"You have been beaten."

"Never *beaten*, Ian; you have merely cost me my weapon."

"You are beaten, and the point here is that you must learn that you can be beaten. If you would duel, you must meet the terms. Ah, the terms. I believe you're supposed to seduce me."

The breeze grew very chill; she burned against it. She remembered the feel of his hands, his lips. . . .

"Seduce you! That was not in the terms!"

He grinned at her distress.

She moistened her lips. "I'll die before I ever make any attempt to seduce you, Ian McKenzie," she said without heed to her circumstances. She was standing there in front of him naked, and he was most probably still convinced that she had somehow made arrangements to meet Peter even after she and Ian had married. Perhaps she had best control her own temper and appeal to something in him other than the fury she knew she all too easily aroused. She curbed her tone to be very quiet and softly condemning: "You're not behaving in the least like a gentleman."

"Really, my dear wife?" His dark brows shot up. "Well, bear this in mind; Had you been acting like a lady at any time in all this, we'd not be standing here now. Hmmm, let me think a moment . . . No. No, it's true; I've yet to see you behave like a lady."

"You should be horsewhipped, McKenzie," she snapped. She wanted to lash out at him so badly. She felt so absurdly on display, feeling the breeze all about her naked flesh, trying not to move or tremble, to waylay the heat that burned so fiercely in her. She would not feel intimidated, yet she was shaking . . .

Awaiting . . .

His touch.

"I should be horsewhipped? For . . . ?" he inquired politely.

"For criminal nastiness! Now, it's really very late. We need to return to the house," she told him briskly. She started to reach down for her gown and robe. The point of his sword fell into the fabric, pinning it to the ground. She looked slowly up into the hard blue darkness of his eyes.

"I think not," he said. "You like to be naked by water, and you detest my house and room. So we shall stay right here."

She couldn't talk, couldn't move, and was suddenly both very afraid of what he intended, yet trembling with the fire and anticipation of it. She couldn't bear it. She decided to abandon her gown and simply run, yet the second she leaped to her feet, he caught her arm, and she was spun around and swept cleanly from her feet. She landed flat upon her back on the cool earth, breathless, staring into his eyes.

His thumb moved in soft line across her cheek. "I won; you lost."

"When you fight to defend your honor, sir, you do so until the last."

"But you have surrendered."

"I have not; you have merely seized my weapon."

"Sometimes it is wisest to accept defeat."

"I refuse to be defeated."

"Well, then, think of it this way: Those taken in battle must accept the victor's conditions."

She started to argue further; no words escaped her lips, for his mouth formed over hers with a stark demand that both angered and aroused. The pressure of his body bore her down; she was keenly aware of the rough wool of his uniform against her flesh and the soft sweet musky scent of the water's embankment beneath her. More than anything, she felt the hot fire of his mouth, the savage demand of his tongue, invading and caressing, brutal, sensual, violating, coaxing, stroking again. . . .

Then his hand curved around her breast, thumb against her nipple until she would have screamed with the sensation had she been able. She writhed with the encroaching whiplash of fire that seemed to dart through her, burning from those points where he touched her. His mouth flooded her body with warmth; his touch upon the naked flesh of her breast seared through her center and spiraled somewhere deep within her.

She gasped for breath, digging her fingers into his hair as his mouth left hers to suckle her nipple where his thumb had teased. She tried to form words to protest, but her mind failed to oblige her and she continued to do nothing more than gasp and twist and writhe, tearing at his thick black hair, dismayed to realize even that touch seemed oddly sensual to her fingertips. His hand slid slowly along her side, curving around a hip. Slid between the two of them, and then between her legs. The pressure of his thumb slid intimately down through the triangle of blond hair, parting her, stroking the most sensitive and intimate of female places.

She tensed like a jackknife, a scream forming in her throat. His mouth covered hers again with a frightening ardor and passion. She realized she'd not begun to estimate his strength until that moment when she lay pinned beneath him, realized his every movement was not guided by passion alone.

She pressed her palms against the hardness of his chest, but the force of his weight was such he didn't begin to feel her protest. Nor could she cry out, for his kiss consumed her words. She twisted and writhed anew, on fire, seared by sensation, yet wild to escape the threatening pressure of his body. Her knees were thrust apart by a sudden supple movement of his body and the insistence of his weight. His chest and legs remained clad in wool; his hips were naked. She felt his hand and sex rubbing against her. A massive shudder swept through her. He burst into her with a single hard smooth thrust

so knifing it instantly broke all barriers. She never
screamed, for she could not. Involuntary tears of pain
instantly pooled in her eyes. She clenched them tightly
together, turning her head to her side as his lips broke
from hers at last. She felt him looking down at her, just
as she felt the fierce burning at the juncture of her legs.
She wished fervently that she had the power to buck
him off. She wished a giant bird would swoop down out
of the sky and tear him from atop her—and perhaps tear
him into little pieces in the bargain. She waited for him
to apologize.

He did not. He held still, watching her.

He began to withdraw.

Only to plunge into her again. She bit fiercely into her
lower lip, then felt his hands on her face, drawing it
forward. She opened her eyes and met his. Even as she
managed at long last to croak out "No!" she felt herself
somehow stilled by the cobalt fire in his gaze and rigid
tension in his face. She tried to part her lips to speak
again. But again his mouth formed over hers. Demanding still . . .

Coaxing. Bringing liquid warmth.

Slowly, the warmth of his mouth seemed to ignite the
burning between her thighs. The heat remained; the
agony began to still. She found herself enfolded in his
arms, his hands sliding down the length of her back,
forming over her buttocks, drawing her more flush
against the increasing furious pulse of his thrusts within
her. Her fingers curled into his shoulders, nails digging.
Pain faded to a dull throb. The burning was part agony,
part pleasure. She prayed for it to end, yet something
else had begun within her. Something she needed, something that was a different kind of ache. She hated his
touch, his stroke, and yet . . .

She yearned for it. She had wanted to escape it. Now
she twisted and arched to feel it, to feel the growing
sweetness pervading her.

A rigor seemed to seize him; then a violent thrust
brought him so deeply within her that she shuddered
with the force of it. Then once again . . . and the mercury
of his climax filled her anew with a sense of liquid, burning fire. And almost as instantly, he eased his weight

from her, adjusted his Union-issue trousers, and lay staring up at the sky.

Naturally, as a maturing young woman, she'd had her fantasies regarding men and women and love. And admittedly, they'd had to do with Peter O'Neill. But they'd never gone much further than pretty pictures of Peter on his knees, asking for her hand, rising to capture her lips in a blissful kiss while the sun shone down and the birds chirped melodiously.

Never had this particular picture—herself lying naked in the woods, hair entangled with grass and leaves—entered into the realm of imagination.

Yet she lay perfectly still for an instant, sorely pained, humiliated, and suddenly, with his body warmth gone, quite cold.

Then Ian's deep voice broke the stillness that had settled over the night as he mused contemplatively, "So you hadn't slept with him . . . as yet."

She rolled over and socked him hard in the stomach. She *had* to get away from him. He hadn't had a chance to tense his muscles. He cursed, leaping to his feet, but a second too late, as she sped past him to dive into the pool, desperate to ease the pain in her body and soul.

By the night, the fresh spring water was wickedly cold. She surfaced with her teeth chattering, half afraid that he had dived after her. He hadn't. He stood by the pool's edge, watching her, her gown and robe in his hands.

"What the hell are you doing?" he demanded crossly.

"Swimming . . . bathing!"

"Get out."

"Go away."

"Get out! It's very late now. And if you think I'm leaving you here, Alaina, you're insane. Get out here."

"Not yet. I—"

"All the water in the world will not wash today away. Get out here."

She was freezing, so she determined to comply. Shivering, she emerged a distance from him, only to realize that he had her clothing. She twisted the length of her hair, wringing the water from it as he came impatiently to her.

"I'll help you dress."

"I don't want your help."

"Madam, it's *undressing* with which you don't seem to need assistance."

"McKenzie, I will find a way to best you! I'm telling you, I don't want help."

"But you need it."

She could either accept his assistance or lose her clothing, so it seemed. He helped her. The ties on her sheer ivory robe were slit; naturally the robe fell open. She grasped it together, spinning away from him, trying again to escape him. But again he stopped her with a firm grip upon her arm.

"Alaina, where do you think you're going?"

She stood stubbornly still, staring at him, then allowed her lashes to fall.

"Back to that hated house and my hated room?" he queried softly. He caught hold of her chin and raised it so that their eyes met. His voice grew more harsh. "Alaina, what did you think? We were married today. It wasn't what you wanted; it wasn't what I wanted. It was what was necessary. But it's done now, and if you didn't realize it yourself, I gave you fair warning that I wasn't the type of man to courteously refrain from sleeping with the woman *I had married.*"

"Oh, indeed, you did do me the great favor of marrying me!" she cried. "Other respectable men wouldn't have married the botanist's wild daughter, but you're the great Ian McKenzie, and you do know your duty!"

"I did what was necessary," he said, eyes narrowing. "But have it as you will; this marriage was forced upon us both. I'll be damned if I'll be denied what small pleasures might be wrested from it."

"Small pleasures . . . Oh!" She wanted to strike him again; but he was far too prepared for a wild attack by her right now. She spun around, wanting to run back to the house ahead of him just to have a few minutes' respite.

His hand was on her.

His damned hand. Swinging her back around with a sudden, savage force.

"Ian—"

"We go back together, Mrs. McKenzie."

"No, Ian, I just—"

Despite her protest, he swung her up in his arms and started through the moonlit forest trail. "We go back together, just like any married couple."

She looked up into the set, grim lines of his face. "We *are* just like any normal couple," she seethed. "The husband drinks a bottle of whiskey with his good friends, then ravishes his wife. Isn't that customary?"

She was startled to see a wry smile slip into his features.

"How nice. I hadn't begun to imagine anything so charmingly usual and domestic when we stood at Reverend Dowd's this afternoon."

She let out a soft oath of impatience. His arms tightened around her, and she realized that he had come to a halt at the edge of the lawn, looking back on the house.

"So you hate Cimarron," he breathed. "What a pity, my love, that you must hate your home."

If she weren't quite so bogged down in her own bruised torment, she would have told him that she had lied before to hurt him, that she loved Cimarron. The house was beautiful, the epitome of grace.

But she was hurt.

"It's your home, not mine."

"Oh?" he queried.

"My home is on the bay."

"Your home is now where I choose it to be," he told her curtly, walking again. He paused once more, and she realized they were just below the balcony area that led to his room.

"Perhaps, in the future, it will have to be somewhere without rose trellises," he muttered, and started walking again.

"Where are you going?" she demanded.

"Through the front door. It is my home," he told her.

"But what if—"

"If someone sees us? Why, we're behaving like your customary young newlyweds. I doused myself in whiskey with my friends and ravished you by the pool. And now . . . ," he paused with a shrug.

"Now what?" she asked worriedly.

"I imagine that in my attempts to be a good husband, I'll have to drink more whiskey, alone, I'm afraid—my very good friends all seem to have gone to bed for the night at last. So let me see . . . I douse myself in whiskey, and then . . ." His cobalt eyes had a hard, devilish glitter to them as he gazed down at her. "And then ravish my poor, downtrodden bride—inside the house this time. Whether you despise Cimarron and my room within it or not, Mrs. McKenzie, it seems that my bed is destined to become a place you'll have to learn to love."

"Ian, please . . ."

"What?"

His gaze, sharp as an icicle, fell upon her. She tried to speak. "I need to be alone. I . . . you . . ." she stuttered.

An odd sensation of warmth swept through her; she couldn't go on. He entered the house through the front door, but they met no one in the breezeway, nor as he carried her up the stairs to the second story. Moonlight spilled through the open French doors. Embers still crackled in the hearth against the spring night's chill. The room was illuminated in a mix of the ivory moonlight and the red touch of the fire. It was a very handsome room. But a masculine room. His room.

Dear God, but she wanted to run. To understand what had happened without feeling his arms imprisoning her. Without the sound of his voice invading her. Without his touch. . . .

"McKenzie, put me down. Now."

She spoke desperately, but it sounded more like she was screaming as he obligingly dropped her. She'd been dropped down to the comfort of his bed.

She could see his features clearly; despite the dim light, shadows touched his face. She knew that he stared down at her, that he stood with an angry tension—created, perhaps, by the sound of her voice—knotting his fingers into his palms so that his hands were fists at his sides, and despite herself, she gasped softly, cringing from him.

She swallowed hard, trying to remain perfectly still, thinking that he would reach down with force and wrench her close again.

But he didn't.

He didn't touch her.

He just stared a moment longer. And she was disturbed by something that sounded like a contemptuous sniff.

Then, to her amazement, he turned and walked away. His door opened.

And closed.

And he was gone.

Chapter 7

The intelligent, comfortable thing to do—in lieu of controlling his temper and remaining in his own room—would have been to sleep in his brother's room. He chose not to. Not only would his brother be there, but his cousins as well, and he wasn't up to whatever torture they might devise to taunt him regarding the state of his affairs.

He chose the stables, taking another whiskey bottle from the cabinet in his father's den, then finding a comfortable spot in the hay in Pye's stall. He drank enough whiskey to sleep rather quickly—and awaken with a blazing headache. Then, to his dismay, as his eyes opened at last, he discovered his father's butler, Jeeves—as hard, straight, ancient, and wise as a stick of old ebony—along with Lilly, staring at him where he had slept.

"There he is. The bridegroom," Lilly said.

Jeeves arched a brow. "Happy man."

"I tried to warn him that he dare not play with that white witch! Ah, see the consequences."

"Lilly, the consequences occurred because I *didn't* play with the white witch, as you would call Mrs. Trehorn," Ian said sourly. "Now, if you two don't mind—"

"Now, you know, Major McKenzie, we don't mind a thing—being the servants, of course," Jeeves told him. "But your father is in the dining room and has asked to see you when you awaken. I imagine your father-in-law will want to see you, too, eh?"

Ian groaned softly, leaning his head against the wood of Pye's stall. Pye skittered uneasily, not liking the company of others at all.

Jeeves was almost like having a third parent. He wasn't just black, he was ebony, but he wasn't a slave, and though he had a been a slave at one time, he hadn't been one in a very long time. He had watched out for the McKenzies with a stern eye since they had been young children. He didn't think of himself as a servant at all; he was family, and everyone knew it.

"I'm sure that my father is righteously angry, yet it is Teddy I dread to face," Ian murmured.

"You've faced both men already; I think they are both concerned with your plans for the future. I've taken the liberty of preparing a bath in the kitchen," Jeeves said.

Ian stood. His head spun. "Fine. Thank you."

Lilly sniffed. "I'll get him clean clothing. Had the young master just stayed in that room when he should have done so . . ."

Ian stood carefully, eyeing her sternly. "Indeed? And come to blows at my father's birthday party with that fool Alfred Ripply?" Ian inquired.

Lilly didn't look at him; she hadn't been around quite long enough to earn the place Jeeves had within the family. "Now, I'm no one, of course, but it does seem to me that Alfred Ripply's ideas are the popular ones hereabouts. It might be wise if the major were to learn to keep silent about his opinions."

Ian paused, then shook his head. "I cannot form my political opinions by what is considered popular. Excuse me, Lilly."

Ian brushed past her, irritated by the *tsk*ing sound she made beneath her breath. He hurried to the house, plucking hay from his uniform. He happened to pause, looking up to his balcony.

Alaina was there. Blanching to pale white as she saw him below, drawing twigs of hay from his jacket. He paused, hands on hips, and stared at her. He was certainly scowling fiercely, since his head seemed to be splitting. She returned his stare briefly, before spinning about to retreat back into his room. He went on into the kitchen, where his bath awaited.

Lilly had brought him civilian clothing, black cotton breeches and a white shirt. He bathed and dressed quickly, anxious to be done before his parents, a sibling, or a stray guest might come upon him. He paused at the dining room door, seeing that Teddy McMann was the only occupant within the room at that time.

"Good morning, Teddy," he said quietly. He entered the room. Lilly came in behind him, ready to offer him coffee, which he needed quite badly.

"Good morning, Ian," Teddy returned gravely. Ian held Theodore McMann in very high regard. He'd been perhaps ten years old when he had first met Teddy McMann, when the botanist had bought his little islet in the far southeastern corridor of the state. Teddy had been impressed with Ian's knowledge of the area, and though Ian had been a boy, Teddy had always listened to him seriously. In turn, Ian had learned about the properties of plants from Teddy, and he'd learned to appreciate with a greater fervor the unique environs of semitropical Florida. He'd visited frequently over the years. Except—apparently—not frequently enough as of late. Not frequently enough to see that Teddy's little nymph of a daughter had grown into a siren.

"Teddy . . ." Ian began, then hesitated just briefly. "Forgive me; I meant you no disrespect. I'm sorry, truly sorry. I wish I could explain in some way—"

Teddy, soft blue eyes filled with sadness, raised a hand to him. "Ian McKenzie, were it not for one thing, I'd think you the finest spouse in the country for my daughter."

Startled, Ian arched a brow. "Sir, I assure you that although the circumstances were strained—"

"Ian, it's not the circumstances; it's the future."

"The future?" Ian queried carefully.

"Don't sound so surprised—Major. You're an intelligent man who has had a clear view of all that is happening lately. I know you're acquainted with many of the main players in the drama unfolding before us."

"Teddy—"

"There will be war, Ian."

Ian inhaled deeply, then shrugged. "I'd rather thought myself the only person who believed the present circumstances would lead to war. Most Southerners think that each state that wants to can just choose to secede—and that will be that."

"Ah, yes, and a confederacy of Southern—cotton—states can be made. A quiet, glorious revolution, provided for in the Constitution—as just and heroic as our founding fathers splitting from the old tyrant, England.

That's what they think. Many think it will never go so far," Teddy said wearily. "Compromise has been met before. Great statesmen have worked long and hard on that road, but Ian, you've seen a lot. And you could have said a lot more to that arrogant buffoon Ripply yesterday. It was before your time, but I can remember when South Carolina nearly seceded with the Nullification Crises over the tariffs the state didn't want."

"But Andy Jackson threatened that the United States government would take forceful action if the state attempted such a thing," Ian reminded him.

"But compromise was actually achieved by the statesmen arriving at a solution to the tariff argument," Teddy finished, shaking his head and adding, "Can't happen this time. You've got to remember—whether Old Hickory was a bastard to the Indians or not, as your uncle is fond of reminding me, he was a national hero. Martin Van Buren has already determined not to act like a president—the election is still to come and the man has apparently all but washed his hands of the calamity to come—and I don't think there's a man out there who can come into office now with a chance of stopping certain cotton states from seceding, and I know you feel the same way."

"Our very heroism and progress has all but damned us," Ian murmured.

"What?"

Ian shrugged. "I was invited to a barbecue just outside the Capital my last trip. Colonel Robert Lee was there—he was my math teacher when I started out at West Point—and we spent some time talking. He personally thinks that a lot of the politicians in what they're calling the Deep South are hotheads. But he pointed out that our very growth has made the situation all the more grave. He was in Mexico, you know, fighting with Winfield Scott when we achieved victory there. And when Santa Ana was beaten, all the property that became ours just made the question of slavery all the more combustible. Look at the Missouri Compromise—and by God, I'm telling you, you can't imagine the violence and horror already occurring in Missouri and Kansas! In the dark of night, men murdering other men in front of their families in support of ideals—and I defend no side for such slaughter! Still, many people are praying that it will never come to war."

"And what will prayers do? Whose side will God be on? More importantly, Ian, whose side will you be on?"

"I am one of those men, sir, who pray that there will never be two sides between which I must choose," he said determinedly.

"Whose side, Ian?"

"We don't even know just what Florida will do as yet—"

"Florida is a cotton state. She will follow other cotton states. In fact, Florida leaders have long been outspoken on matters of economy, slavery, and the power of local government."

"Frankly, sir, I don't know exactly what I feel right now, or what I will do if I'm forced to take a stand."

"You're in the military."

Ian smiled. "A great many Southern men are, sir. And many of us are aware that decisions may have to be made in the future. I assure you, it isn't something we take lightly. You are talking about men who studied together, teachers and students, soldiers who have saved one another upon different battlefields. I have good friends among the Northerners. I know Philadelphians who sympathize with the Deep South, and I know Southerners, as well, sir, who call anyone against the Union a traitor. Teddy, think about Richard Keith Call, who served as our governor at one time—"

"And as head of the army efforts against the Seminoles during the war in the thirties," Teddy reminded him dryly.

Ian grinned; Teddy was determinedly going to remind him that Call hadn't always been a friend of the McKenzies.

"The point, Teddy, is that old Richard Keith Call is very much a Southerner—no one could love Florida more—and yet, he is pro-Union. Most men are against the concept of the federal government making decisions on slavery for the slave states—Americans don't like to be told what to do, and perhaps Southerners even more so than most. God knows, perhaps it is the fact that our economy is so based on slave labor that it allows people to believe that God himself must condone commerce in human beings. Men have to convince themselves that the Bible assures us it is moral to keep men in bondage—and to sell their wives and children from the auction block at St. Augustine. Still, many of the men who will shout the loudest that Abraham kept slaves, according to the Bible, will be the first to believe in the American union of states."

"Warmongering abolitionists do believe that slavery is unconscionably wrong."

"Indeed," Ian agreed.

"The McKenzies believe this to be the truth."

"Teddy, you know how I feel; my beliefs on that matter are no secret. I have never failed to be truthful."

"And there's my point," Teddy said.

"What, sir, does that mean?" Ian demanded, growing aggravated.

Teddy shook his head. "I fear, Major McKenzie, that you may eventually lose your precious Cimarron. But the election is still to come. Perhaps there will be a miracle and reason will prevail throughout the land. Somehow I doubt it. And still, whatever the future brings, you have married my daughter. So, what are your plans? What are your orders when you leave here?"

"Actually, I'm to go to Washington. I have maps with me to be recorded in the Capital."

"What do you intend to do with your wife?" Teddy asked bluntly.

"To—er, *do* with her, sir?"

"Where will she live?"

"Well, sir, I—"

"Hadn't thought of that as yet? Because you don't really have a home for her, since you hadn't really planned on marriage."

"I'd always planned to marry, sir—"

"But not my daughter."

Teddy McMann's flat determination on the truth defied pretense. "Sir," Ian said simply, "Cimarron is one of the finest plantations in the whole of the state, and it is my home."

"But you'll not be in it. Nor do you know where you'll be for any length of time."

"To this day, the government is still attempting to make sense of the Florida wilderness. I imagine I'll be coming back and forth from the Everglades for the next several months at least." He hesitated. "Unless things change quickly."

"Ian, under those circumstances, I'd like to take my daughter home with me."

"I do assure you, sir, that the marriage is legal—"

"Which is not the point. You have married; she is your wife, and I don't contest that. I'm not making demands; I'm asking to bring her home with me when your leave has come to an end until you are given a more permanent command."

Ian hesitated, feeling uneasy, and not at all sure why. Teddy's area of the state—near where Ian's aunt and uncle and cousins resided—remained, in truth, a very savage land. He loved the area himself; his father owned numerous untamed acres down in the south, but hadn't chosen to live there, as James had. Still, Ian had loved his extended trips down to his uncle's home all his life. The region hadn't been entirely ignored by men and women of vision, but events had somewhat conspired to keep growth to a minimum over the last twenty years.

During the Second Seminole War, the Indians had retreated deep into the Everglades. Before the arrival of the Seminoles, in the great age of Spanish exploration, missionaries had come to the area to attempt to bring the Church to the earlier Indians, the Calusa, the Tequesta, and others. But the Indians had died out over the centuries and been absorbed by the Seminoles; the Spanish missionaries had died out, been murdered, or recalled as well. Eventually the Everglades became a Seminole refuge.

But the Florida Keys and the southeast coast were also havens for wreckers and salvagers—as they had been since white men had first come with valuables in their ships. Men of less than desirable character often frequented the ruins.

Ian never would have thought to worry about his uncle's family, living as close to the abandoned fort as they did. James had wanted the isolation of the far south. James had fought many a battle; he could take care of himself, and he had taught his sons and daughters to do the same.

And he was a half-breed who had defended his mother's people fervently throughout the conflict. The Indians would never harm him or his family. James McKenzie was safe in the Everglades. Against white trash, and—frequently justified—red fury.

But for others . . .

"What is it, Ian?" Teddy demanded.

Ian shrugged. "Well, I was just a child at the time, but I'm afraid to admit that I was thinking of what happened to Dr. Perrine." Dr. Henry Perrine had been a medical doctor, and something of a diplomat-turned-botanist, just like Teddy. He'd been murdered by Indians on the morning of August 7, 1840. Ian had been a young child then, but he could still remember his parents talking about the affair.

Teddy's lip curled into a half-smile. "Ian, Perrine was killed in the last years of the Second Seminole War. The war is over."

"Violence flared again just two years ago—"

"And my property was fine."

"Teddy, you moved in with my uncle. I remember my father saying so."

"Your uncle's family remain nearby, and I'm not a fool. And I'm a good man who has always been friends with the Seminoles. Most of my workers are Indians or blacks or mixed-breed men and women."

"Teddy, Dr. Henry Perrine was a good man. But—"

"Perrine was living on Indian Key—where that detestable lout Housman had been king of his salvage and wrecking empire, I wager!—when the Indians attacked. Housman had himself a little empire going there with his Tropical Hotel for visitors and his own mansion. Housman had suggested that the United States government pay him two hundred dollars a head for every Seminole he could murder. I imagine the Seminole war party that killed Perrine meant to slay Housman. And that was long ago."

"Ironic justice," Ian said. "Housman and his wife escaped, and though Perrine managed to hide his family, the *good* man was the one who was killed."

"I don't understand your fears, Ian. Alaina has lived all her life on our little islet. I'm no fool, and at any threat of danger, I would turn to your own kin."

Ian bowed his head. "I don't understand my unease,

either, sir, to be quite frank. I just know how difficult communications can be."

"For other people. Not you, Ian. Let her come with me."

"Sir, I must agree. Since I do not have a home prepared for her to be with me, your request sounds reasonable."

Teddy appeared greatly relieved. "I won't say anything to Alaina; I'd like to let that decision come from you, if you don't mind, unless she chooses to do otherwise. And we'll see to the future from there," Teddy told him. He hesitated. "Son, I tell you, my fear is this: My daughter is a great deal like the South. She doesn't like to be told what to do. And everyone wants to be right. Yet when it comes to battles, right and wrong seldom matter; all that counts is greater power."

"I've no intent to hurt your daughter."

"And she will have no intent to hurt you, I imagine," he replied, sounding so sorrowful that Ian was startled by a momentary chill. "Well, with the months ahead of us settled . . . Have I told you about my new lime trees?"

Ian smiled, shaking his head. "No, sir, you have not."

"Sit down, don't let me keep you from breakfast. I'll tell you about my work."

Teddy excitedly began to tell him about his citrus groves and his aloe plants. Ian helped himself to bacon, eggs, fish, and fresh-baked bread, and listened. Teddy had always been exceptionally close to Ian's Aunt Teela, who had assisted an army surgeon at one time and now used many of Teddy's plants for salves and herbal remedies. Ian believed that Teela's and Teddy's interests had influenced his brother and cousin in their pursuit of medical careers. Listening to the man who was now his father-in-law, Ian was startled by how quickly time passed by, and he'd yet to speak with his own father.

He excused himself and went in search of Jarrett. He entered his father's den and thought at first that he had come upon his father, only to realize, when the man turned, that he had found his uncle instead.

"Ian," James said, a trace of amusement in his voice.

"Uncle James, I was looking for my father."

"I was, too. Jeeves has told me that he is out riding with your mother. Strange, isn't it? Your mother has thrown this party for your father every year since she came here. He gave up protesting two decades ago. It has always been one of the finest social events in the state. I was anxious to be here this year. I wanted to remember what it was like."

Watching the uncle with whom he had been almost as close as his own parents since childhood, Ian felt the strangest unease settle over him. "Sir, my mother will continue to hold my father's birthday sacred until the day she dies."

"So I imagine," James said lightly. "Can you fathom this, though, Ian? I feel the oddest sense of dread. And not of the things one might usually fear—I'm not afraid of fighting, I spent so long doing it. I'm merely afraid of what is happening to a world in which we all managed to hold fast to one another, no matter what outside forces tore at us."

"You think it will come to war?"

"I know so. We have been heading toward it many years now." He hesitated, then added quietly, "Do you know, Ian, that I despise the uniform you so customarily wear?"

Ian arched a brow, taken aback by the vehemence in his uncle's words. He knew full well the history of his state, and that his uncle had, at times, fought against the U.S. army during the Second Seminole War. But James had also remained close friends with many men who had been in the army. Ian's father's mother had been a very proper white woman from a Charleston family with impeccable lineage; but James's mother had been Seminole, his first wife had been a half-breed as he was himself, his oldest daughter's bloodlines were at least half Seminole, and even his children by Teela were definitely influenced by their Indian blood. James's ties to the Seminole and Mikasuki Indians in the state were close—and there was no way out of the fact that the Florida Indians had suffered terribly at the hands of the United States army.

"Uncle James, you know that I—"

"I know, Ian, that your father couldn't have raised a more honorable man—and that you'd die yourself before allowing violence against any of your kin. I love you like my own, Ian, but I do despise the uniform, and I am afraid of the future before us."

Ian was quiet for a minute. "There is a chance that the situation will die down. It has happened before. There have been compromises—"

"Oh, indeed. And weren't you the one telling me about the bloodshed in Kansas that came out of those compromises?"

"Yes."

James studied him a moment, then shrugged, a slow smile curling his lips. "Well, I've got you looking incredibly grave when you're a bridegroom. My apologies on such a day. So you've married Teddy's daughter, the little hellion. I wish you happiness—and strength."

"You disapprove?" Ian asked.

James shook his head. "I live in an area scarcely populated. Your wife practically grew up with my children, as you well know. My God, Ian, she followed you all about when she was just a little girl."

"I remember," Ian murmured, adding softly to himself, "I remember now."

"I love Alaina dearly. But I know her well. And actually, come to think of it, I think the two of you deserve one another."

"I've heard that before. Do you compliment us, Uncle, or offend?"

"I leave my statement as it stands." James walked across the room, setting an arm around Ian's shoulders. "I think I'll take a ride around Cimarron myself. Brent has decided to leave tomorrow for South Carolina, and your cousin Sydney, Aunt Teela and I are going to go with him for perhaps a month as well, and leave Jerome to see to the far southern homestead. Brent has been asked to serve at the new hospital near your cousin's old family home, and he's going to take up residence there."

"I didn't know."

"He probably didn't have time to tell you; you've been quite active since your return."

"I think I'll ride with you, if you don't mind," Ian told him.

James arched a brow to him. "You've a bride about—somewhere."

Ian nodded. "But I need to ride around Cimarron. I

think I need to hold on to something here as well, today."

James studied him a moment, then nodded.

And Ian felt a greater sense of dread than ever within himself. It was strange. So many of the people in the South, in his own home state, were jubilant. The thought of separation was an exciting one to them; they saw their way of life going on forever.

Ian felt, at that moment, that maybe he and his uncle and Teddy were the only ones in the country to realize that nothing could ever be the same, that the world was about to be shattered.

No matter how he tried to deny it.

There was no sanity left.

On the lawn sweeping toward the stables, he saw Jerome walking around from the front porch. His cousin met his glance. They both grinned. Old ways died hard. They started to run simultaneously, both moving like the wind, determined to outrace one another.

They reached the stables at the same time, laughing. "Beat you to the far edge of the river," Jerome said.

"You're on."

They sped into the stables, each going to his horse's stall, slipping bridles over their animals' heads, then leaping bareback atop them. They cleared the stable entry together, then Pye took a small lead. They both veered around James, who was just reaching the stables himself, shaking his head. "They turn to men," he muttered. "But men just take a very long time to grow up." He stared after his son and nephew, then suddenly darted into the stables himself. A second later, he was riding bareback, flattened against his horse's neck, and tearing belatedly into the race.

Chapter 8

Alaina wasn't quite sure why she felt so angry and tense—and ready to pummel Ian McKenzie.

She had wanted to be alone—and he'd left her alone.

But he'd emerged from the stables this morning covered in hay, making her wonder just who he might have been with. They weren't involved in a love match; she told herself that she didn't really care in the least. Of course, if he had been with someone, that someone was Lavinia. Naturally, Alaina's pride was taking a beating.

But Cimarron was down to family now, and the McKenzie family surely all realized that Ian had done the proper thing, had saved her reputation, and that was that.

But even by late afternoon, Ian hadn't returned.

During the day, it had been quite fine with Alaina; she'd managed to spend time with her father. Teddy—even he was irritating her!—was strangely at peace with the entire affair, demanding no explanations whatsoever from her. His feeling about the matter seemed to be the same annoying consensus taken by everyone involved: Ian was an exceptional and honorable man who had done the right thing. She was somewhat hurt that her father didn't even seem to realize that just a day before she'd had innocent feelings and beliefs that had been shattered; but then, she and Ian both had done their best to lie, and Teddy probably thought it would be worse on her to demand to know the truth than to accept her lies.

By dinnertime, she was deeply embarrassed.

At the party, Ian had made a tremendous show—claiming before the world that he'd been swept off his feet.

Tonight, it seemed, the pretense was over.

If she'd expected to be coddled by Ian, of course, she'd have truly been a fool. But it still seemed unfathomably painful to have such an awful fight at the pool— one that had led to a clash of steel—and then lose all innocence so bluntly upon the ground. She had wanted privacy to nurse her wounds—now she wanted to skewer him.

At least none of the second generation of McKenzics was in the house; Tia and Brent were returning social calls along with their cousins, so Tara said. Jarrett McKenzie was out on business. Alaina did her best to be cheerful through the meal with her father and Tara. She hoped that her effort didn't fail miserably.

By dusk, her father retired to the library with a brandy, and she sat on the porch with Tara, sipping sherry and watching the sunset. It was an oddly beautiful time, and though her mother-in-law made no attempts to either excuse Ian or explain him, Alaina had to admit that she felt a comfortable warmth from the woman who had surely been stunned to acquire her as a daughter-in-law. "Life is so strange," Tara mused. "Sitting here, as we are now, is one of my favorite things in the world to do. To watch the sunset—it's so glorious. And Florida is the last place I ever thought I'd want to be. Gators and savages—that was my opinion of this place." She smiled, and seemed especially beautiful. The soft night light shadowed any sign of age about Tara, and her features were lovely, peaceful. "Naturally, of course, I'm now quite fond of my in-law 'savages'—though I admit, I do still detest the gators!"

"I grew up with them," Alaina told her, smiling as well. "I've never grown particularly fond of either alligators or crocodiles, but I can't envision any other life. I love the sun, the heat, the water. I can't imagine being taken away from the sun."

"Well, then," Tara murmured softly, "it's a good thing you did marry a Florida planter—you won't have to leave the sun."

For some strange reason, the words, as gently spoken as they were, sent a strange chill through Alaina. She stood then, pretending exhaustion, and bid Tara good night. Tara rose as well with a rustle of petticoats and the soft scent of roses. She hugged Alaina tightly, and Alaina was afraid she'd burst into tears. Tara was so good, so generous, so determined to make her feel at home, to feel wanted.

She definitely wasn't wanted by her husband—the man who had done the "honorable thing" for her.

Alaina managed not to burst into tears and to smile good night to Tara, escaping just in time. Yet when she ran from her mother-in-law, she ran to Ian's room. Once she reached his door, she hesitated.

She longed to be elsewhere. The desire to escape was almost overwhelming. Except, of course, she didn't need to escape a husband who seemed to have no intention of returning home.

Inside his room, she found the pretty mulatto maid, Lilly, waiting for her. Lilly had seen to it that she had a hot bath waiting and a clean nightgown. She liked Lilly very much, with her slightly accented singsong English. Lilly told Alaina that her father had been a half-caste from Louisiana, and her speech had the softness of a French accent to it. Lilly's presence was somehow reassuring— Alaina was remarkably happy to have her there.

The tub was delicious, hot as fire and sweetly scented with lavender. The water eased her troubled heart and soul, and Lilly saw to her every need.

"Lilly?"

"Yes, Mrs. McKenzie?"

"You've been exceptionally kind."

"I work here, missus."

"That doesn't mean that you have to be kind."

Lilly, offering her a huge towel as Alaina stepped from the tub, smiled. "You put a stop to that devil woman, missus."

"Lavinia?"

Lilly nodded gravely.

Alaina turned away. She wasn't so sure she stopped the "devil woman" at all; in fact, she wondered if her husband wasn't keeping company with the demoness at that very moment.

Lilly suddenly smiled, as if reading her mind. "You know the devil woman is gone?" she inquired.

Despite herself, Alaina smiled. "Is she?"

Lilly nodded gravely.

"Well, I suppose that's good. And whatever your reasons for being so kind, I'm grateful," Alaina said.

Lilly nodded, serene in her own thoughts, and helped Alaina into the cotton nightgown.

"It's not a gown for a bride," Lilly commented.

"It's the perfect gown."

"Just because the devil woman is gone?"

"Because Ian McKenzie is not here, the night is cool, and I am going to sleep." Yes, it was the perfect gown for a bride without a bridegroom.

She was suddenly anxious for Lilly to leave so that she could feign sleep as quickly as possible. It was his room, after all. He would surely come back sometime tonight.

"Thank you, Lilly," she told the maid.

"You need me, you call me. Anytime, missus, you understand?"

Alaina smiled. Lilly's voice was so passionate, and she was grateful. She had definitely found a champion within this household.

"I will, I promise."

Yet when Lilly left, Alaina sat at the foot of Ian's huge, masculine bed with the lion's claws for feet and the griffins upon the headboard.

"You are a monster, Ian McKenzie!" she said out loud, clinging to her anger.

But suddenly she burst into tears. It was quite terrifying to realize what she had done with her life. More terrifying still to imagine the days and months—and years!—to come. The deed was done, but what now?

Sometimes he would sleep in the hay, sometimes he would not?

He was in the military; he was only on leave, she knew that much. She knew, as well, that he'd been on various assignments across the country for the last year, but she had no idea where he was assigned now.

Or what he would expect of her.

But he'd *married* her, performed the great sacrifice for the sake of her reputation. And he'd expect her to take a place in society as his wife.

The thought caused her to tremble. Nothing that she had done seemed so terrible as the thought of leaving her father alone. They had very good servants, and her father had excellent workers to help with his groves. Not slave labor, though admittedly she'd never really given much thought to the right or wrong of the institution. Slaves were a very expensive commodity, and whether Teddy had ever purchased slaves or not, she did not know. The McManns, comfortable enough on their islet, still were not among the type of monied class that could really afford slaves.

She needed to be with her father. Tomorrow she'd assure him that she'd stay with him. Could she make that promise? Yes, she thought determinedly. Somehow she had to convince Ian that she must return home with her father while he—while he did whatever it was exactly that he did.

She wouldn't ask; she'd just make a statement of fact, and do what she damned well pleased.

It was what men did, wasn't it?

She leaped off the bed, anxious to find a bottle of brandy, or something that would help her to sleep. She knew there would be something in the room—everything at Cimarron was perfect. Indeed, Cimarron seemed to glide like a well-oiled wheel. The home was grace itself— a fact which suddenly seemed overwhelming to her. She was a part of this now. The beautiful house was yet so very foreign—and she was suddenly married to the heir to it all.

She hurried to Ian's great double-sided desk and began rifling, pulling open the drawers. The top drawers were filled with bills, receipts, and ledgers, but in the lower right-hand drawer she found what she sought—a choice of brandy, whiskey, or rum, along with sturdy shotglasses.

"Hmm . . ." she mused. Then she heard a rapping at her door—a pounding, actually, more like thunder. "Alaina!"

Not Ian. It was a feminine voice.

"Yes?"

Sydney McKenzie came sweeping in like a whirlwind, green eyes alight with curiosity and amusement. "Alaina! My God, how strange!" Sydney skirted around the double desk, taking a seat on the opposite side. "I don't think I really believed in this marriage until this moment, finding you here! You've really done it, you've gone and married my cousin. Oh, my Lord! And he's already driving you to drink! Pour me something, too, please. How delightfully decadent! The men are always in their dens or libraries sipping whiskey, so we might as well do the same."

"Whiskey it is," Alaina said, pouring out two shots and taking a seat at the desk facing the fireplace. She sipped the fiery liquid, staring at the blaze. If she narrowed her eyes slightly, the blaze went hazy and warm.

"Whiskey it is? That's all you can say?" Sydney demanded, taking the desk chair opposite her. "Alaina, that's not at all good enough. You are, of course, going to have to tell me the truth, and there's no great romantic story to it, I know. Ian has been . . . well, it's certainly no great secret he's been sleeping with the well-endowed Mrs. Trehorn for quite some time. And as to marriage! He was very nearly engaged to 'the perfect army wife, a most intelligent beauty'—as he wrote to my father. And naturally, Alaina, being your best friend in the entire world, despite his despicable behavior, I'm well aware that you were madly in love with—with—"

Sydney, never afraid of speaking her mind, and actually never afraid of anything at all, suddenly broke off, staring in ashen horror toward the door. Alaina stared at Sydney, but Sydney suddenly leaped to her feet. Her voice was a squeak. "Ian."

Alaina leaped to her feet as well, swirling around. Indeed, Ian. He'd come to the doorway. His uniform was gone; he was dressed in a white shirt, black breeches, and high riding boots. His eyes appeared almost black as they fastened on Sydney, then on Alaina.

"Ah, little cousin, how nice to see you," he murmured, moving into the room. "And you, too, of course—my love," he addressed Alaina. "Am I interrupting? How rude of me. Ladies, do enjoy your whiskey. I think I'll do the same."

He wasn't drunk, Alaina ascertained, but he'd definitely been imbibing. He pulled out the chair she had just vacated, urging her back to it. "Sit, my darling. And Sydney, perhaps you'd be so good as to keep us company."

"Actually," Sydney said, "it's late. I think that I should go to bed—"

"Sit, Sydney, and finish your drink."

Sydney uneasily took a seat again. Ian poured himself a whiskey, studied the color of it in his glass, and sat upon the desk. He smiled somewhat grimly at them both. "Cheers, ladies. Now, Sydney, do go on. You're Alaina's best friend in the world, and you know all about her being in love with . . . ?"

Sydney sat very still, returning his stare in miserable silence.

"Well?" Ian pursued.

"Stop it!" Alaina told him. "You've no right to be cruel to Sydney."

"Sydney can take care of herself," Ian said sharply.

"I was madly in love with Peter O'Neill," Alaina snapped. "That's what she was about to say."

Sydney gasped, then quickly recovered. "Ian, you've been out all day; I thought someone should entertain your new *wife*—"

"Well, thank you, little cousin," Ian said huskily, studying his drink once again. His eyes fell firmly upon Sydney. "But I'm here to entertain her now."

Sydney flushed and came swiftly to her feet. She started out of the room and Alaina was furious, ready to go to battle against Ian over his curt behavior to his cousin. But before Sydney had reached the door, Ian called her back.

"Little cousin."

Sydney paused, looking back to him.

Ian rose and walked to her. He hugged her very gently. Sydney was stiff for a minute, then hugged him back, and Alaina realized at that moment that Sydney was probably almost as close to him as his own sister, and that there was something special that bonded all the McKenzies. No matter how good a friend Alaina was to Sydney, they weren't bound by blood. She remained on the outside.

Even as Ian's wife.

Sydney offered Alaina a grimace of encouragement behind Ian's back. "Good night!" she said softly.

And fled the room.

Ian closed the door quietly in her wake, slid the bolt, and turned. Back against the door, he crossed his arms over his chest and faced Alaina.

Posed by his desk, she returned his stare. "McKenzie, you've been gone all day. Under the circumstances, you're not welcome now."

"Really?" he inquired, amused.

"Indeed, sir," she continued, growing nervous at his presence despite herself. "You performed the great sacrifice of marriage—then went on to completely humiliate me before your family and my father."

"I was missed?" he inquired softly.

"I imagine my father noted your absence."

"Did you?"

"You were rude—"

"A social slight most assuredly punishable by hanging."

"A pity they can't hang you."

He smiled. "Ah, but society be damned, my love. Did *you* miss me? Had I known that you were yearning to spend time with me, I would have made every effort to be more available."

"Perhaps I should remind you that you were the one to force me to realize the gravity of the situation which brought our marriage about. Appearances caused this travesty. You could have made an appearance today!"

"Ah. Alas, my love, you insisted that I leave you be— but now you're angry that I did so."

She cried out her frustration. "Damn you! Go back and sleep in the hay!" she hissed.

"Ah," he murmured.

She moved around the desk, putting its bulk between the two of them. "I mean it, Ian. You've no right to torment me when you choose to . . . to . . ."

"Sleep in the hay?"

He left the door and started walking toward her.

"Ian, this is very serious."

"Indeed it is." He reached the desk. He'd been out somewhere, she thought. Drinking, though how much, she had no idea. Riding, she was certain. He carried the mingled scents of fine leather polish, brandy, and tobacco.

The desk remained between them. His eyes were very dark and sharp as he surveyed her, and his lip curled with a strange curve of amusement. She lifted her chin determinedly. "Ian, you're about to go back to the military. There's really very little time now that we need play out this charade. I can go home—"

"You are home—now," he said softly.

She ignored that. "There are places I'm quite certain you'd rather be—"

"I've already been many places."

"So I'm aware."

"There is nowhere else at this moment I've any desire to be."

"Fine. I've no idea where you've been or what was so important that you had to make such a pathetic fool of me, but I mean this with my whole heart; leave me alone."

"Madam, I suggest you quit dictating to me."

"Fine! Go back to the hay, go straight to hell. I don't give a damn where you go. . . ."

Despite her best efforts to remain calm and rational, she was losing her temper. But the arch of his brow and the sharp glitter in his eyes was suddenly unnerving. She had to control her temper and behave in a reasonable, dignified manner.

"Ian, this is becoming quite ridiculous. There is no reason for us to be enemies."

"I haven't come to fight," he informed her. But there was an edge to his tone.

He'd fight, all right.

"Ian, I've had a wretched day. If you come any closer to me, I swear by God, I promise that I will make you wretched, I will fight—"

"Fight your lawfully wedded husband?" he mocked, eyes narrowing.

"Ian, really, now . . ."

"Really, now, yes, indeed, my beloved—wife?"

He suddenly leaned across the desk; she found her wrist imprisoned in his grasp. Before she could protest or wrench free, he was around the desk in a lightning-swift movement.

He'd been drinking, yes. She was suddenly afraid of the volatility of his mood.

But he wasn't drunk. He wasn't drunk at all. She saw that in his eyes as he swept her up despite her sputtering protests. He held her tightly in his arms. She strained against his hold to no avail. He cast her down upon the bed, bracing against it, his palms flat upon the bed on either side of her head. He stared at her with a barely constrained anger, eyes seeming to rip into her as he spoke at last. "I'll be damned if I'm sleeping in the hay again. Tonight, I'm sleeping here, in my room, in my house, with my wife. Your current feelings on the matter are quite irrelevant to me; accept the situation or fight it—and me—it makes no difference."

He pushed himself away from the bed and seemed to tower over her. "There will be but one outcome for this marriage tonight. I will have my way—and my wife."

Chapter 9

She could be the most exasperating human being Ian had ever come in contact with: willing to fight when all hope of any purpose was gone, and never, never willing to accept defeat in any way, shape, or form.

And yet . . .

If he weren't still plagued with guilt regarding Risa, he wouldn't be entirely displeased. And if he didn't remain quite so infuriated with Alaina regarding the entire Peter O'Neill incident . . .

Then what?

She was beautiful. Gathering herself against the bedstead, looking up at him warily, Alaina was beautiful. With her cat-gold eyes, sun-silk hair, and slim yet curvacious form, she was stunning. He had married her with a prayer that she wasn't carrying O'Neill's child; he'd been almost ridiculously pleased to discover that she had been as innocent as any young woman in their society who might have been brought up in the strictest home under a careful mama's ever-watchful eye. And still . . .

She was accustomed to doing whatever she pleased, however dangerous it might be. And he was sick to death of hearing that she'd been in love with a swaggering, useless braggart like O'Neill. He still wanted to tear Peter O'Neill to shreds.

Perhaps it had been rude to stay away the entire day. But a streak of pained nostalgia had seized hold of him, and it had seemed important to spend the time with his kin—and away from the bride who played such havoc with both his temper and his passions.

Admittedly, he had spent a fair amount of time consumed with guilt because of Risa.

He was going to have to face her. What would he tell her? How would he explain?

Alaina had taken her place . . .

Alaina. Who was in love with Peter and ready to fight her new husband to the death for the honor he had fought to preserve!

They'd spent the day out in one of the old Indian cabins near Cimarron—Ian, James, Julian, Jerome, and Brent. Ian's father had joined them eventually and they had drunk brandy and talked and laughed about the old days. James and Jarrett had reminisced about the war; they had all laughed about fishing incidents, Ian's first encounter with a gator, the beauty of everything around them. The day had been good; but Ian still felt a strange pain, and it didn't help to have this shrew he had acquired—no matter how beautiful—telling him to go sleep in the hay.

Yet as he watched her, she intrigued him, for she began playing a new act. She scrambled up and sat rigidly as she stared at him, knees drawn to her chest, arms wrapped around them, hair billowing freely down her back in long, thick waves the color of a brilliant sun. That angelic shade framed her delicate face; her small chin was lifted high.

"Ian?"

"No."

"No, what?" she flared. "I haven't even said anything yet!"

"No, I'm not leaving. You can fight from here until the peninsula sinks."

"You don't understand. I'm really, really tired."

"Oh?" he queried with some amusement, turning away from her and sitting at his desk to pull off his boots. Her voice was no longer defiant. It definitely carried a note of hauteur, but it was somewhat pleading as well.

She nodded earnestly. "I mean, you must admit, it's been an eventful two days. Tired can't begin to describe how I feel. I'm actually exhausted. . . ." her voice trailed off with a slight catch as she watched him rise, doff jacket and shirt, and then breeches. Her eyes rose to his, faltering only once to take in the length of his naked body, widening, riveting back to his face. She was beautifully flushed against the pure white cotton of the embroidered nightgown she wore tonight, and he knew that she had ascertained in her quick sweep of his anatomy that he had come in definitely intending to keep her awake awhile.

And tonight, maybe she hoped not to have to fight him because she knew she couldn't win. She meant to use other tactics now—appealing to his sensibilities as a gentleman?

"Ian, you're not listening to me. Really, I'm so desperately tired," she informed him.

"Ah . . . vigorous physical activity helps sleep," he told her.

"I've had sufficient vigorous physical activity already, thank you!" she snapped.

He couldn't help but smile. Nor did he intend to let her off the hook in the least. "You're a newlywed, my love. Newlyweds never sleep until dawn."

If he hadn't seen the swift calculations going on in her mind, he might have been swayed by her sudden tears.

"Ian . . . it's been a difficult day. I'm . . . I'm hurt . . ." she said, forcing two liquid tears to pool in her eyes. "Last night was new to me, you must understand—"

He strode to the bed, arms crossed over his chest as he stared down at her. "You're in no physical pain— I'd say that's quite evident. And as far as your delicate emotional state, I thought you were suffering last night when I saw those sweet little tears on your cheeks. The next thing I knew—despite my warnings—you were crawling down a rose trellis to meet Peter O'Neill."

"I didn't go to meet him!" she cried.

"Right. You went to escape me—and this room."

She let out an oath of irritation, then met his eyes. He saw a pulse ticking wildly at her throat, and he was both startled and aroused to realize that she was fighting both him—and herself. She was afraid—not so much of what he would do, but of what she might feel. He brushed his knuckles against her cheek. "There's an old expression, my love, and I've told you it will hold true. You make your bed, you lie in it. Well, Mrs. McKenzie, this is the bed."

"And I'm a *small* pleasure."

He started to laugh, coming to another realization. He had offended her. He tilted her chin upward. "Mmm . . .

well, as you said, it was all rather new for you. I imagine you'll be an excessive pleasure this time."

She jerked her chin free from his touch. "Ian—"

"Alaina, you're not going to talk me out of sleeping with you tonight."

She scowled furiously, keeping her eyes averted from the length of him at her side. "There's a whiskey bottle on your desk," she said. "Are you sure you wouldn't like me to summon your kin up here for a few more drunken toasts to start off the night?"

"Are you sure you're not wishing I could summon Peter O'Neill up here?"

"Perhaps it would be better to have an adoring married lover than a bitter autocrat of a husband!" she told him, and made a move to leap from the bed.

He caught her wrist. "You have what you're getting," he told her warningly.

"I'm just getting the whiskey bottle."

"I don't need any whiskey. And I think it only fair to warn you that I am heartily sick of hearing about your mad devotion to Peter O'Neill."

"And I am heartily sick of you thinking that you can— that you have the right to walk in here whenever you so please and make demands. Let me go! Fair is fair. I need quite a bit of whiskey!"

He shook his head firmly. "What you need is to be very aware of the fact that you have *married me*."

She wrenched free from him and started to spring from the bed. She was very fast. So was he. He lunged across the bed and caught the sleeve of her gown. He heard the rending of fabric and became entangled in the gown as it tore from her torso and held fast against her limbs. He straddled her as she lay trapped, breathing far too quickly, her pulse hammering against her throat. A tiny blue vein was just barely visible in the ivory flesh of her breast. Her eyes were brilliantly gold in the room's dying firelight as they met his; like a cat it seemed she flexed her claws as her hands and nails pressed against his chest.

"Must we do this again?" she whispered.

He laughed softly. "We must."

"Why?" she demanded, eyes wide and flashing.

"Why?" The question gave him pause; she had voiced it in earnest.

"Because . . . making love is what husbands and wives do."

"Making love is more frequently what husbands and mistresses do, so it appears in life!" she exclaimed.

She was angry, he thought. Angry—because he had wounded her tremendous pride today. He hadn't done so intentionally, yet the fire burning in her now made her all the more tempting. He wanted her; he'd married her.

He'd be damned if he'd ever be such a fool as to sleep in the hay again.

He shook his head, and gently curled a tendril of her hair around his finger. "Sex is one reason men marry; it is a craving, a hunger, and I promise you, you will realize that it is so for your fairer—if not gentler—sex just as it is for us."

Her eyes clouded. "Ian, your hunger is not for me."

"You're quite mistaken. What goes on between men and women, husbands and wives, can be exceptionally beautiful. And yet . . . a weapon as well. We'll not use it so."

She shook her head, but stared at him and must have seen both the amusement and determination in his eyes. She threw her arms out to her sides with exasperation, eyes furiously defying his. "Fine. Fine. Just do whatever you so choose!" she cried out dramatically.

His smile deepened. "I intend to," he assured her.

Yet staring down at her, he suddenly remembered words Peter had used to describe her: ripe, lush. It galled him to think of Peter and Alaina.

Lush . . .

The valley between her breasts. He lowered his head and brushed her flesh there with his lips first, then the tip of his tongue, drawing a hot, liquid line between them.

Ripe . . .

Her breasts themselves. His mouth traveled to cover a dusky rose nipple, tongue sweeping around it, flicking the peak. His head against her chest, he could feel the thunder of her heart. She lay so perfectly still, not protesting, not moving. He rose slightly above her. Her eyes were squeezed shut; her face was pale, her lips just slightly parted, her breath sweeping quickly in and out. He smiled, pressed his lips to her throat. Cupped her breast into his palm, caressed it again with his tongue and the gentle edge of his teeth. He drew his hand down the length of her, so sensually enticed that he forgot for a moment who she was, and even that she was his wife. He savored the slim and so beautifully curved length of her, stroking, touching, moving against her. Her flesh burned as soft as silk against his own; he felt her vibrantly with his fingertips and limbs, felt each curve with the fullness of his body. He rose above her again, taking her lips. Her eyes were still clenched, but her mouth parted to his coaxing, and he hesitated just a moment as humor tempered the fever within him. He moved his mouth seductively upon hers; he eased his weight to her side to allow him the freedom to know her, kissing her all the while with a deceptively soft, slow, tender thoroughness while the questing touch of his fingers roamed as lightly over her body. His mouth grew bolder, tongue delving, raking, plundering, drawing a little whimper from her throat. His touch became far more invasive as well, palm rotating over the soft blond triangle between her thighs. A needful throbbing began within his own flesh. He slipped his hand between her thighs; she started to clench them together. He shifted his weight, forcing her limbs apart with the weight of his own body. His sex, fully erect, teased the tender flesh of her femininity and he heard a sudden, wild intake of her breath. Her eyes flew open with sudden awareness and defiance; she trembled fiercely, staring at him, then closed her eyes again, going rigid.

The dutiful wife. She didn't fight; she endured.

He smiled, watching her for long seconds. Her eyes remained closed, her breathing shallow. She lay so perfectly still. . . .

He inched lower, once again creating liquid trails of kisses against her throat and breasts. Fondling her flesh, suckling it. Inching still lower, cradling her breasts while drawing his mouth against her ribs, waist, and navel. Inching still. Lying directly between her thighs. Staring at her pale face briefly before parting her with his fingers and plunging into the most intimate kiss with the seductive caress of his mouth and the searing liquid impalement of his tongue.

Her eyes flew open; a desperate, stunned gasp escaped her. She wriggled to free herself, and did nothing but bring herself more tightly against him. He caught her hands, his fingers curling against them as he continued to caress and seduce, feeling the wild trembling and surge within her that created an explosive fire in himself. Her every twist and buck further inflamed him until he throbbed with an agonizing pain; still he persisted, drawing her as high as he dared.

He rose over her at last, thrusting into her with fevered passion. A choked sobbing sound escaped her; her eyes were open, dazed, unfocused upon his. Her palms fell against his chest, then her fingers curled into his shoulders. She lay shaking, then clinging to him as he wrapped her tightly against him, pressing ever more deeply into her. The sight, feel, and scent of her was intoxicating, scarcely bearable. He fought to control his pace until . . .

Her body tightened, constricted. Face pressed to his shoulder, she cried out and her limbs went limp; searing, liquid warmth gloved his sex as he moved deeply within her.

He thrust and shuddered violently, amazed at the explosive force her climax had drawn from him in turn. Wickedly delicious heat seared throughout him and he finished, moving again, and again, more gently within her, until she, too, was filled with the mercury of their lovemaking. He eased himself to her side, drawing her against him. She stiffened; he persisted. He inhaled the rich scent of her hair.

And remembered with sudden raw clarity that he had told Teddy he could take his daughter home when Ian's leave was done.

Could he leave her? Could he endure to do so, now, when he had just discovered the ferocity of the heat she could create in him? He stroked her hair. She tried to pull away, and he realized she was sobbing softly.

At a complete loss, he firmly pressed her to her back so that he could meet her eyes. "What? By God, I know that I didn't hurt you."

"Ian, please!" she whispered, cat-gold eyes shimmering. The sound of her voice was earnest; no play-acting now. "Please, just—"

He touched her cheek. "Alaina, I'm not a fool, and I'm not stupid, and I do admit to a certain amount of experience! I caused you no pain. In fact, I dare say that you enjoyed what passed between us."

"Oh, you will never understand!" she cried.

Puzzled, he allowed her to turn away from him. He leaned up on an elbow, stroking the length of her spine with the back of his hand. She trembled at his touch.

"You just take . . . everything!" she whispered to him.

He smiled, feeling the budding of a new tenderness for her rising within him. She wouldn't have been angry or hurt now if she hadn't responded to him.

"Alaina, you're my wife."

"It's still wrong; you don't . . . love me."

"Ah, and there it is! Well, dear wife, you don't love me, either," he murmured. He felt his body tighten with irritation, wondering if she hadn't dreamed of such feelings in the arms of a different man. That thorn in his side.

But she wasn't trying to be hateful; she was just young, and new to the games of love.

He rolled her back to him determinedly. For once, her gold eyes were open and vulnerable, her delicate face was simply beautiful, her cheeks were damp with tears. "We have married, Alaina, for better or worse. You are my wife. Circumstances were not, perhaps, what they should have been, but I am frankly pleased to have discovered what I have in this bed of mine you do so detest. Marriage is a commitment, and you are married to me. So I beg you, find peace with it. I have done so already."

Her lashes fell upon her cheeks. "Tell, me, was your peace found here—or in the hay?" she whispered miserably.

He hesitated, wondering how much power he dared give this woman over him. He touched her cheek, brushing her silken flesh ever so softly. "I slept with no companion other than Pye; most uncomfortably so. And I have spent this day with my kin, and my kin alone. Does that make what we've done any more acceptable?"

Her eyes opened to his again. "I . . ."

"Well?"

Her lashes fluttered again. "Yes," she said very softly.

Ian smiled, easing down beside her. He drew her close. The fire burned low; the night air cooled them. She reached for the covers. He warmed her again with his body. Touched her, stroked her.

Made love again. Rested, sated, for a time.

In sleep, she shifted against him. He cupped her buttocks with his hands, curved to her length. The feel of her brought him to a full hard erection again, and he slipped in her. Made love.

Dawn came, and with it, a heavy sleep at last. Full daylight filled the room when he awoke. She was just rising. He caught her sleepy gold gaze, shook his head, pulled her back. "Not yet," he whispered.

"Ian, it's late in the day!"

But her protest was weak.

And he did not allow her to rise.

James and Teela McKenzie, along with Brent and Sydney, left that afternoon. James had business in Tampa, then they'd be leaving for Charleston.

Jarrett McKenzie was sorry to see his brother, sister-in-law, nephew, and niece leave. It was a difficult parting.

Somehow, when they had been younger—half-brothers, one white, one Indian—they had managed to fight the rest of the world. Through the long years of the Second Seminole War, they had remained close. Not even the new flare-up of trouble in '58 had caused the least difficulty between them.

Now Jarrett discovered either himself or James growing quiet when discussions regarding the possibility of war arose.

And as they said good-bye on the river that day, they looked into one another's eyes. Oddly, James, the Seminole son, had their father's deep blue eyes. Jarrett's own were his mother's—as nearly black as those of any full-blooded Indian in the country.

Jarrett felt his heart slam against his chest. He was getting old. In his fifties. Much of life spent. Funny, he didn't feel old. The world changed around him, but he didn't feel old. And certainly they didn't look old. James hadn't seemed to change a bit in all these years. Not in appearance. His bronzed face showed little signs of age. Just a trace of silver was beginning to touch his temples.

Only James's eyes were old, and Jarrett was certain that same sense of age was reflected in his own.

If war came, they'd be on opposite sides. And Jarrett knew then with a sinking heart he'd be on the wrong side, according to most of his own people.

"Take care on your trip," Jarrett told James.

James stepped away from him, slipping an arm around Teela's shoulders. Jarrett thought that there was a trace of tears in his sister-in-law's beautiful emerald eyes. Teela was a strong woman; she'd been willing to brave any danger to be with James. After difficult beginnings for them all—he and Tara, James and Teela—they'd been blessed. For over twenty years, their lives had been good. They'd had children, and their children were healthy and strong. Friendships had formed between them to augment the closeness of their blood ties. No family had ever been more supportive of one another.

And yet . . .

The future loomed before them in a frightening manner.

"For once, brother," James told him with a trace of amusement, "I think that I can say I'm going to be all right. Jarrett, you have to be careful about voicing your philosophies."

Jarrett might have replied, but he chose not to in front of so many people. "As father liked to say: I'll do my best to behave—as honorably as I may."

Despite the fact that the family laughed and joked easily while they awaited the barge by the river, a strange pall seemed to lie over them all. Jarrett and James discussed the roads that had been cut through the northern portion of the state, making transportation in that region so much better than it had been when they had first been blazing their own paths via old Indian trails. While the south remained a wilderness—still mainly inhabited by Indians and gators—northern Florida was gaining quite a population and all the amenities of any civilized state. The McKenzies exchanged embraces before the barge left, and those remaining behind watched and waved until it disappeared into the sunlit day.

That afternoon, Jarrett McKenzie had at last the opportunity for a long talk alone with his eldest son. With the barge gone, the remaining group split up. Teddy McMann drew his daughter along the river, excitedly studying the plants there. Jerome and Julian went walking down the quay, discussing the merits of Brent having taken up a practice near Charleston. Jarrett suggested Ian might indulge him and take a walk out to the pool.

They strode out together, speaking of casual things until they reached the fallen log by the pool. Jarrett drew a silver brandy flask from his frock coat pocket and offered it to his son. Then he took a seat on the log, folding his arms across his chest in a determined manner. "It's definitely time we talked," Jarrett said, and watched his son as Ian sipped from the flask, studying the crystal ripples of the water.

"As you say, Father."

He was proud of his son. Jarrett had served in the military himself as a very young man, until Andy Jackson's Indian policies had driven him to a stand on his own. But throughout his life, he'd had close ties with many military men. A good friend, Tyler Argosy, promoted last year to lieutenant general, had seen to Ian's entry to West Point, and served as Ian's mentor for years. It had been difficult for Jarrett to watch his son struggle with his conscience and his duty. Ian was against the military's treatment of the Indians and would have resigned his newly gained commission if he had been assigned to Florida during the fighting of '58; thankfully, he'd been assigned elsewhere. It was only in the last few months that he'd received the rank of major and been given a position as a guide and liaison for the army cartographers and surveying teams in the south of the state.

Yet Jarrett was damned well aware that though his son might have spent a fair amount of time with his uncle James recently, he hadn't been near McMann's daughter—until his arrival home. Now, in civilian clothing, standing very tall and dark in breeches, shirt and frock coat, Ian was a striking figure, his features strong, combining the best of both himself and Tara, Jarrett thought. He awaited his father's questions with quiet dignity.

"I do believe that your mother and I are worthy of the truth—the complete truth," Jarrett said firmly.

"The truth is that we were caught in a compromising position," Ian said, then added quietly, 'and so went immediately to the Reverend Dowd's and were married."

"A compromising position?"

Ian smiled, shaking his head. He suddenly reminded Jarrett of James. "I didn't seduce her, Father. It was accidental . . ." He hesitated, then shrugged, aware that whatever he said to his father would go no further. "She is Teddy's daughter, raised a bit wild in the wilderness. She decided to go swimming at the pool."

"Lots of people have found themselves swimming in that pool. Swimming, in itself—"

"She was swimming naked."

Jarrett stared at his son. "Ah. You were naked as well."

Ian hesitated, but didn't lie or make excuses for himself. "I was."

"Looking for Mrs. Trehorn?"

"Father, I know that you never particularly approved of that liaison—"

"Indeed, I did not. But you're a grown man. Certainly old enough to choose your relationships. And to suffer the consequences they create. Thank God, however, that you didn't march to the Reverend Dowd's with Lavinia. I might have become immortal just to assure myself she never became mistress of Cimarron! And thank God that Alaina didn't march there with Peter O'Neill."

Ian arched a brow to him. "Lavinia would have thumbed her nose at scandal. She's quite fond of me, but much more fond of her money. And as to Alaina and Peter . . . she did think rather highly of him at one time, I believe," Ian said lightly. Jarrett was slightly amused. Ian had never had patience for Peter O'Neill. He considered him a blustery pretty-boy braggart who created hard times for others. But now, it seemed, Ian sounded just a bit jealous. And maybe it was well. Ian was far too accustomed to having women listen to him, pay him heed—and fall for his rugged good looks. Naturally, Jarrett was of the opinion that Theodore McMann should have taken his daughter over his knee years ago—but there was little to be done about that now.

Jarrett liked Alaina; she was a bewitching, vibrant little bit of baggage. But he was sorry for the marriage when another woman—who seemed so ideal—awaited.

Jarrett sighed. "Alaina might have thought herself in love with Peter, but I've lived a long time, son, and I've studied human nature. The most unlikely people can make magnificent matches—because they understand and respect one another, as was the case with your uncle James and aunt Teela. Alaina would have seen through Peter's stories very quickly; she would have realized that his words were nothing more than wind, and she would have hated him. Their marriage would have been hell."

"Well, Father, I pray you foresee something better for the two of us, then," Jarrett said, smiling wryly.

Jarrett shook his head, noting the grave look that came into his son's eyes. "Were things as they were ten years ago, I would have wished you every happiness. I haven't seen Alaina in quite some time myself, but she was always an enchanting child. She has grown into a vital woman, full of life, beautiful, intelligent."

Ian listened quietly. "Sir, it sounds as if you approve—those are wonderful qualities in a wife."

"Usually. But what of Colonel Magee's daughter?"

"Risa?" Ian murmured.

"You wrote as if you two had already discussed an engagement."

"There was nothing that we had actually discussed, Father. We spent time together; we were falling in love—we liked one another very much."

"You made no promises to her?"

"Not because I didn't intend to, only because I hadn't had the chance. I meant to talk with you and Mother while I was here, speak with Risa when I reached Washington this time, then ask her father for her hand. I had thought we'd make a good pair; we are excellent companions, she is accustomed to the military, and she is . . ."

"Young, lovely, and intelligent as well?"

"Yes," Ian said simply.

"She will be hurt in this."

"Yes," he said again. "I will see her when I go to Washington."

"There is no way I can help you there, son."

"Father, I'm a full-grown man who has faced some serious fighting in the West. I accept responsibility for all my actions, and will face them on my own."

"With honor," Jarrett said softly. "But I imagine you'd rather go back and fight a skirmish in the West than explain this to Miss Magee."

Ian inclined his head slightly. Jarrett studied his son, aware that Ian seldom let his emotions show.

"Well," Jarrett murmured, "under the circumstances that occurred here, I can understand you felt you must act. Teddy is a good man, and disgracing his daughter— with or without intent—would have shattered him. So you are now a married man. The deed is done. As your father, I congratulate you. And as your father, I also give you these words of advice: Bear in mind that Alaina is a passionate, independent woman who grew up creating her own rules as she went along. She can be strong, and willful as well."

A dark expression passed quickly through Ian's eyes, and Jarrett saw that he was already aware of those qualities in Alaina. "Father, I am capable of handling my wife."

Jarrett sighed deeply, wishing he didn't feel such a sense of doom regarding the future. "Are you capable of waging war against her?"

"What do you mean?"

"We're Unionists, Ian, you and I. The time hasn't quite come when sides must be drawn, but we have deep-seated beliefs in the sanctity of the Union, coupled with the fact that we have been living in a slave economy without slaves. If war comes, we will be at odds with our state. Teddy and Alaina live in the far south where the Federal uniform has long been despised for all the pain wrought on the Seminoles by the army. I don't think that Alaina will ever understand your determination to go against your state and remain with the army."

"I haven't made that decision yet," Ian said unhappily. "The decision isn't even there to be made as yet."

"But it's coming."

"There is no way I could make such a decision without weighing all the risks and dangers—to myself, to my family, and to Cimarron. But whatever decision I make, my wife will have to accept."

"I pray it's so. You are both proud, stubborn, and very determined to have your own way."

A sneeze suddenly sounded from a few feet away. Ian arched a brow to his father, then walked around one of the oak trees to find his brother seated at the foot of the oak, his back leaned against it. His boots, socks, and shirt were off; he'd obviously been at the pool ready to plunge in when Ian and Jarrett had reached it. Julian, so like Jarrett they might have been twins, rose unhappily. "Sorry. Truly. When you first arrived, I was about to make my appearance known, but Father's voice had that deep tone to it, and I didn't want to intrude. I thought I'd lie low and slink away after."

"The whole damned world should know all my personal business," Ian muttered darkly.

Julian stood impatiently, joining in the conversation, now that his presence had been discovered. "I'm hardly the whole damned world; I'm your one and only brother," Julian reminded him. "And quite frankly, I don't understand the difficulty here. In my opinion—"

"Julian, I don't recall asking for opinions."

"In my opinion," Julian continued with quiet dignity, "she is absolutely stunning, a whirlwind of grace and energy. Of course, she has no money—that's been held against her by a great many respectable families—but then we McKenzies have done very well. Naturally, of course, that is your doing, Father, though you have trained us with sound business expertise so that we are all quite good at managing property and money. We like to go against the grain—your doing as well, Father, since you taught us all that people are unique in themselves, and that society might dictate behavior, but never the honor within a man's or woman's, heart."

Ian smiled at his father as his brother seemed to be warming up to his speech. Jarrett smiled in turn.

Julian went on. "And since it certainly appears to be a customary marriage—they're obviously thoroughly enjoying their honeymoon—"

"Julian!" Ian protested, indignantly interrupting his brother. "What the hell do you know about my marital relations?"

"Well," came a deep drawl, and Jerome stepped from around another oak, clad only in denim breeches and still wet from a dive into the pool. He paused momentarily, facing Jarrett, who looked at him expectantly. "Excuse me, sir, I didn't mean to intrude; as you can see, I was just emerging from the pool and, like Julian, found myself awkwardly trapped here. This being the case, though . . ." He looked to Ian. "I believe that the entire household is aware of the pleasant normalcy of your marriage, largely due to the fact that the two of you didn't emerge from your room until my folks were afraid they'd have to leave without saying good-bye to you."

"Indeed?" Ian muttered darkly.

Jarrett McKenzie lowered his head, trying not to smile at his son's exasperation. Julian and Jerome, having found themselves in the midst of the conversation, meant to torment him to some fair degree.

"It bodes for a good marriage, I think," Julian said. "A very good relationship. Don't you think, Jerome?"

"I would have to agree."

"Though, naturally, Jerome, being intelligent and reasonable and civilized men, we're all aware that common ground must be found—"

Jerome set an arm about Julian's shoulder, nodding in amused agreement. "But then, entertaining sexual relations can create some damned good common ground," he said, his lip curled in a half smile. Then he remembered Jarrett, sitting on the log, studying them all. His bronze features flushed to a deeper shade. "Sorry, Uncle, I meant nothing, of course. Alaina is like a sister to me." He paused again. "Ian, we've been as close as brothers, and we'd have been friends if no family ties existed at all, but you have acquired a wife who is near and dear to my heart. Quite frankly, what hardship can be found in marrying a woman who is young and exceedingly beautiful? Now, then, looking at this from Alaina's point of view—"

"She's acquired a tyrant,'" Julian said with a mock sigh, eyes alight. "Trust me, I know—I came into the world a bit more than a year later, and paid the price for my tardiness!"

"So it's good that Alaina is a bit willful," Jerome murmured. "She'll need to be so to survive Ian."

"Are you both quite finished?" Jarrett inquired sternly.

"Indeed," Julian murmured.

"Well, then—what is done is done," Jarrett stated, rising. "Ian, we all wish you happiness."

With that, he left his sons and his nephew behind him and started back toward Cimarron.

Jerome, watching his uncle go, felt a shiver go up his spine—someone walking over his grave, as the expression went. He turned to Ian and spoke seriously. "We do all wish you every happiness," he said.

Ian nodded, smiling slowly. "I know."

The exchange seemed to be growing too earnest for Julian. "Ian looks flushed, sweaty, hot. Don't you think he looks hot?" he asked, gazing from his brother to Jerome.

"He does!" Jerome agreed gravely.

"Dammit, no—" Ian began, but he hadn't been expecting the attack, and between the two of them, his brother and cousin brought him crashing down into the pool. In retaliation, he set out after his brother; Jerome deserted Julian, and Julian was duly dunked. He was then pleased to join Ian for an attack on Jerome. An hour later, they were all three panting, lying on the embankment, gasping for breath, laughing, sharing the last of the little silver flask of brandy.

"What are your plans, Ian?" Jerome asked.

"I have to go back to Washington. Bring some of the new maps we've made."

"I can't imagine Alaina in Washington."

"I . . . won't be bringing her. Teddy has asked me to allow her to come home with him."

"What?" Julian demanded, rolling to his stomach to stare at his brother.

"You have acquired nights of heaven and you're going to leave your wife behind?"

"He has some explanations to make to the colonel's daughter, remember?" Jerome said lightly.

Ian sat up, staring at his cousin. "It isn't that. I told you, Teddy asked me if she could go home with him. I haven't even discussed it with Alaina yet, but—"

"But you know damned well that's exactly what she's going to want to do?" Jerome said.

"Can you argue that?"

"No." Jerome studied Ian's eyes. "But you're not happy about it."

Ian hesitated. "I'm afraid."

"My big brother, afraid? I don't believe it," Julian murmured, rising then.

"I do," Jerome said quietly, coming to his feet as well. "We're all afraid. But as to your wife, Ian, I'll be nearby. My folks will be home soon, and Jennifer and Lawrence and their baby are even closer to Teddy's islet than we are. I promise you, I'll look out for her."

Ian stood and clasped his cousin's outstretched hand. "Thank you," he said huskily. "I'll count on that."

They all started back to the house.

"Jerome," Ian said.

"What?"

"If Peter O'Neill comes near her . . ."

"Kill him?"

"That would be illegal—and if anyone kills him, it's going to be me. Just deck the hell out of him for me, will you?"

"It's a promise," Jerome assured Ian. Then a sudden shiver seized him.

"What's wrong?" Ian asked.

"Nothing, a chill."

But he wasn't cold.

He'd felt the oddest sensation again.

Footsteps walking over his grave. . . .

Chapter 10

There were, in marriage, moments of sheer delight, and in the brief time Ian was home, he came to discover them.

Time was at a premium.

Cimarron was not just a plantation, but a vast agricultural enterprise, and when Ian was home, he played his part in running it. One day Cimarron would be his, and he would be responsible for all the lives dependent upon it. Though cotton was king, the cattle raised at Cimarron were also important, and becoming more so. Central Florida plantations and farms were becoming immensely valuable in production, with Florida cattle feeding populations throughout the country.

That afternoon, Alaina was not deserted while he ran accounts and discussed business decisions with his father and brother. James's eldest daughter Jennifer—six years Ian's senior and always calm, poised, and in control of any situation, remained at Cimarron with her husband Lawrence, and their baby, Anthony. At the death of her mother, Jennifer had lived at Cimarron until James had remarried, and so Jen was quite comfortable with the house, and well versed in its functions. Jen and Lawrence planned to travel back south with Teddy McMann and Jerome at the week's end.

Tia was still home on a holiday as well, and among them they kept Alaina busy exploring the house and grounds.

And Ian began to damn himself for his promise to Teddy. Logically, it was probably the most reasonable solution for the moment. He didn't know how long he'd be required to stay in Washington; he'd most probably be sent back soon, and he would be sent to the far south for more expeditions into the Everglades—which would put him closer to Alaina there.

As dusk came, Jarrett reminded him that he was due to leave in the morning. "It's late; spend some time with your wife."

He found Alaina playing with two-year-old Anthony along with Jen and Tia. Alaina didn't see him as he arrived at the upstairs nursery where so many McKenzies had played before. She was laughing, rolling on the floor with Anthony and Jen, and he felt again the strange stirrings he had felt when he had first seen her fencing on the lawn. Her laughter was like music; her smile was captivating. The gold light in her eyes was purely seductive.

He cleared his throat. She jumped swiftly to her feet, almost as if she were alarmed by his presence. He arched a brow, reaching out a hand to her. "Come for a ride with me?"

"I was occupying the baby. Jen planned on packing a few things for her trip home."

"I'm fine," Jen said.

"And I'm here," Tia added.

"Come ride," Ian insisted.

"I'll . . . just change," Alaina said.

She did so quickly, joining him at the stables in a matter of minutes. He helped her mount, then leaped up on Pye. He kneed his horse quickly to a gallop, knowing that Alaina could follow easily—and perhaps pass him if she chose.

He showed her the way the McKenzies had divided their property, so much land given over to cattle and livestock, so much given over to the growing of cotton, and a few acres where they were now growing sugar cane. He loved Cimarron: the house, the land, the look of it, the feel of it, the life that was lived there. Though he didn't betray his emotions, he remained angry about her statements on the night of their marriage—that she hated Cimarron and detested his room.

But as dusk began to turn to dark, the wildness of their ride seemed to put her more at ease with him. She was flushed and happy, and complimentary of all that she saw. Watching her, Ian realized that she was glad to be out; Alaina loved to ride. She loved the wind, she loved to run, to feel the earth. He already knew she loved to swim. When she caught him staring at her, her coloring deepened.

"You're glad to be out?" he asked.

"I . . . I must admit . . ." she shrugged. She looked every inch the young lady in an emerald-green riding habit that perfectly highlighted her coloring. Her golden hair was swept up, delicate tendrils just escaping the blond coils beneath her plumed hat. "I admit that growing up far from civilization makes life quite different. Your family has been very kind. But I do usually ride every day. And the beach at sunset is always so enticing. . . . It's fun to run on the sand and play tag with the tide."

"You miss your home?"

"Everyone misses home—don't they?" she asked him, and there was a soft wistful sound to her voice.

"When I'm away long enough, I miss it terribly," Ian said.

"But that's the way of the military, isn't it? They send you where they need you?"

He nodded. "Luckily, I've been needed near home often enough lately." He watched her as she sat her horse, so elegant in her perfectly tailored riding habit, the wistful expression still playing upon her perfect features. "Let's head back, shall we?" he suggested.

Alaina nodded, and followed his lead when he turned Pye about to race across the fields. She was riding one of his mother's Arabian mixes, a fast little filly named Sable. Alaina rode neck and neck with him, delighting in the rapid pace he set. She was smiling happily when they reached the stables. Her hair had come free from its neatly pinned sweep, however, and tumbled down her back in a riot of gold beneath her plumed hat.

He helped her from Sable, then said, "Wait here a minute."

Ian left the stables and hurried to the house. He found his brother and Jerome intently involved in a game of chess. Julian informed him that both their parents and the rest of the family had left to have dinner with their nearest neighbor, Robert Trent, and his family.

"Do you need something?" Julian asked.

"Yes, I need both of you to stay out of the spring pool

for the next few hours," Ian told them. "No jumping out from behind rocks."

"Now, Ian, you know damned well we were accidentally caught there."

"Yes, I do know. But I'd appreciate some privacy now."

Jerome, staring at the chessboard, kept his head low and smiled. "I'm about to humiliate your brother by soundly thrashing him. Naturally, he's going to feel compelled to challenge me again and again until he can win a game himself. We'll do our best to see to it that you have absolute privacy."

"Interesting, though, don't you think?" Julian inquired, studying Jerome's last move gravely. He glanced up at Ian then. "You spent your first day home by the pool in order to spend your last evening there as well."

"Thank you, Julian, for your deep concern regarding my whereabouts. Jerome, thrash him slowly, will you?"

The two kept their attention upon the chessboard as Ian left them. He found Alaina standing outside the stables where he had left her, and slipped an arm about her waist. "Come on."

"Where are we going?"

"You'll see."

When they reached the pool, she kept her distance from him, standing perfectly still as he sat upon the log to pull off his boots and socks.

"What are you doing?" she asked him uneasily.

"Going swimming. We can't quite chase the tide here, but then, there's no salt. Easier on the eyes."

"You think—oh, you must be teasing, you wretch!" she exclaimed. "After all the trouble caused by this horrible pool—"

"The pool, my love, did not cause the trouble. People cause trouble. But since we're already in such trouble, doesn't it seem ridiculous to waste the pool?"

She shook her head. "Someone might come."

"No one will come."

"How do you know?"

"I've seen to it."

"Oh! How reassuring! You've seen to it that people *know* you intend to . . ."

He arched a brow. "Go swimming?"

She spun around, certain he was making fun of her. He leaped off the log, coming swiftly behind her and sweeping her up into his arms.

"Ian—" she protested, hands against his chest.

"You miss the water; you said so. You can go in with your clothes on—or off."

"Ian—"

"I warn you that this is my last night at my home, and I'll not be denied."

She trembled suddenly, a strange expression filtering through her eyes. "Clothes . . . off," she whispered after a moment.

He arched a brow, but set her down, working upon the intricate little buttons of her bodice. She was very still, accepting his assistance, until all of her clothing lay pooled at her feet.

The sun was setting. Its beautiful colors, bursting out over the horizon, fell upon her naked length in a dazzling glow. The sensual perfection of her slim young body assailed his senses anew, and perhaps something predatory ignited within his eyes, for she suddenly took flight, running from him to dive into the pool.

She was an incredible swimmer. She disappeared into the depths while he shed the last of his own attire and came diving in after her. She was fast; it took all his effort to catch her, and she was supple and sure, evading his reach several times before he took firm hold of her at last, fingers threading into her hair, mouth forming firmly over hers as his kick jackknifed them to the surface. The bare brush of her thighs and breasts against his flesh was so keen it was almost unbearable; he groaned deep in his throat while his tongue hungrily savaged the honeyed sweetness of her mouth, and he damned himself a thousand times over for the promise he had made Teddy.

His lips parted from hers at last. His fingers moved down the length of her spine, palms molding over her buttocks to press her ever closer to his growing erection.

"I thought—I thought we came to swim."

"We swam."

"It's your last night in your home," she murmured.

"It is," he said, but eased away a breath to determine

just where she was attempting to go with her conversation.

"Ian, we need to talk."

"About?"

Treading water, she inhaled, then spoke quickly. "Ian, if you are going to be moving about, I truly beg your indulgence in this: Let me stay with my father. I'm all that he has. He needs me."

He stared at her, glad that the setting sun, now crimson, was in her eyes and not his own. He remembered vaguely then that Teddy had said he wouldn't tell Alaina that Ian had agreed she should return home. Ian was to have told her himself.

He'd never done so.

Interesting

"Ah . . . you want to go with Teddy—because you don't want to be left at so horrible a place as Cimarron?"

She flushed, but held her ground "I don't hate Cimarron."

"You don't?" he demanded.

His gaze upon her was so demanding that she allowed her lashes to fall "I was angry when I said that. I don't hate your home, and your parents are charming."

"As you can be, when you want something," he murmured

He could see her temper stirring in the flash of her eyes, but she controlled it, and it was quite intriguing to watch the thought patterns race through her features. She hated the reality of it, but she had acquired a husband whom everyone seemed to consider had the right to dictate her future and whereabouts.

She lowered her eyes again. The water rippled cool around them in the pool.

"And you want this very badly," he murmured dryly.

Her eyes flew up to his, flashing gold. "Teddy is all alone without me," she said.

He gave her a sharp look. Teddy wasn't all alone.

"All right, not exactly alone; he has his fieldworkers, of course, and we have the household servants, but . . . he needs me."

Her hair was slicked back from her lovely face; her eyes were liquid gold. He studied the classic elegance of her features and felt his gaze sweep lower then, fixing upon the rise of her breasts beneath the water. Her nipples were a soft rose, hardened now by the coolness of the water to fascinating little peaks.

"What if I needed you?" he asked huskily.

"You don't need me. You don't even particularly want me."

His eyes flashed and it seemed that every inch of her skin from head to toe flushed crimson. "I definitely protest that statement," he told her.

She shook her head impatiently. "You *wanted* another woman; you got me. Since so many marriages are arranged, as you've informed me, I imagine that you most probably consider me quite interchangeable with any young woman with whom you might have found yourself bound. Except that, of course, you're Ian McKenzie, and nothing is usually arranged for you that you don't want. In this case, your sense of duty dictated your desires."

"Is that what you think?" he asked her, reaching out for her again, suddenly quite passionate. "Madam, you're wrong. You're not interchangeable in any way. And I'm not about to leave here worried sick about the affairs of state—and the affairs of my wife as well."

She gasped, startled by his sudden vehemence. "Ian, you know that I—"

"Were you in love with O'Neill?"

"No!" she gasped. Then, "Yes!" She shook her head unhappily. "I—I had thought so, but he behaved so despicably. Ian, I swear to you, before God, whatever I felt for Peter died the minute his engagement was announced. I never intended to meet him." She clutched his hand suddenly, pleading. "Ian, please, let me have this favor, and I will swear my loyalty on pain of death." Anger suddenly burned in her eyes. "Besides, you're going back to that woman you intended to marry. At the very least, you can let me stay with so innocent a man as my own father! Oh, this is so ridiculously unfair!"

"Indeed, but the way of the world, I'm afraid," he reminded her pleasantly.

"Ian, please, don't torment me now. Answer me."

"Let you return to the untamed wilderness . . ."

"Your uncle has gone to Charleston, but Jerome will

be very close. And the Malloys, your cousin Jennifer, and her husband are next door to my home, and . . ." She paused, then added with a strange bitterness, "They are all my friends, but they are your blood, so I'm quite sure that if I were to so much as sneeze in the wrong direction, you'd know about it instantly."

"Your father is an honorable man."

"Then what is the difficulty?"

He smiled. "I might have intended for you to travel with me. I've a wife now, and I've so little to remember you by."

She flushed again and murmured, "I'm in the pool, aren't I?"

"It's a start."

She exhaled on a gasp of impatience and started to swim past him. He caught hold of her waist, drawing her to him, her back against his chest and hips, her head beneath his chin. "I don't know what you want!" she whispered fervently. "We spent all of the nights—I never—I never once offered the least resistance—"

He laughed softly, intoxicated by her nearness again in the coolness of the pool, feeling the heat of her body against him. "If I remember rightly, there might have been just a hint of resistance there at first. But still . . . they were good nights. I just want . . . more."

"More?"

"Mmm. I want to go away feeling . . . secure. Feeling that my wife couldn't possibly be swayed by an ex-lover—or any other man—since she is so enraptured by all that she has in me."

"Ian, you're cruel"

"My love, I don't mean to be. And you don't sound enraptured."

"But I am!" she protested "Really."

"Really." He eased his hold upon her, turning her within the embrace of his arms. He caught her hand, powerful legs still knifing through the water to keep them afloat. He drew her palms and fingers down the length of his chest, bringing her fingers in a curl around the throbbing length of his erection. Her initial gasp— as if she had been handed something so loathsome as a poisonous snake—was not exactly an "enraptured" sound. But she quickly recovered. Her gold eyes met his briefly, incredibly wide with amazement and surprise, then she buried her head against his shoulder, trembling, and her body pressed to his as she . . .

Experimented.

Her hand rubbed over the length of him in an instinctive stroke. Her fingers feathered his flesh within the water. He groaned deeply, gutturally, as she reached lower, cupping and caressing his testicles, delicately hesitant, more and more surely. . . .

He forgot to tread water. They pitched downward. He caught her shoulders, drawing them both back up. A few hard kicks brought them to the embankment, and he swiftly had her upon her back. His kiss was nearly violent as his mouth found hers; his touch plundered the dips and curves of her body, savoring the heat of her flesh beneath the chill of the water droplets upon her. He began to kiss, caress . . . lick them from her . . . her breasts, the hollows at her hips, her thighs, between them. . . .

The harsh intake of her breath brought him over her again. Her eyes met his, dazed, golden, and somehow still challenging. Her fingers stroked his hair; her lips met and melded with his in a fiery explosion in which she gave all the tempest she received. Her fingers arched into his shoulders, stroked his back, his buttocks, his chest. Her nails raked, then her hand closed over him again as the searing sweet heat of her kisses rained upon his chest. . . .

An agony of desire shot through him; he pressed her back, surged into her. The sun falling from the sky became a blood-red passion that burned into the landscape, and into their flesh. Beneath him, she met the tempest of his rhythm, rode the lightning of his hunger.

The sun fell into the earth with a last burst of fiercely glowing rays. He felt a trembling within her, sweetly volatile, and cradled her hard against him, easing his weight from her, as the darkness came and the night blanketed over them. She lay very still against him, the heat of their bodies still warming them. He lay there, surprised by the tenderness he felt toward her as she lay so trustingly against him. He smoothed back her damp hair in a gentle, lulling motion, watching the night take over the sky.

Apparently, his motion was indeed lulling, he thought moments later, with a certain wry amusement.

He had lulled her right to sleep.

His last night . . .

It didn't matter. He was content, for the moment, to feel her length against his. Her hair, drying, blew softly against his chest in delicate tendrils.

He did his best to let her lie against him as comfortably as possible, trying not to disturb her. His arms gently encircled her.

The botanist's wild, wicked . . . innocent daughter.

His wife.

Alaina opened her eyes and realized that it was night—and that she was sprawled atop her husband.

He wasn't sleeping, she realized, but gazing into the night. She was suddenly grateful for the shadows that lay upon them.

Yet the night, in darkness, began to grow chill. Where his body covered hers, Alaina remained warm. Where it did not, she was cold. She still felt shaken, trembling inside. It was so frightening to feel such a violent, desperate sensation. She remained amazed by the way he could make her feel, by the strength of emotions awakened in her through this intimacy that still seemed so new, so strange. Each time he made love to her, she thought at first that he demanded what she didn't want to give, but she was wrong. Somewhere in the midst of it, things had changed. Now it seemed that the sound of his voice could stir a warmth within her, the lightest brush of his fingers could ignite a burning, and when he pressed her down against the earth, she was desperately willing to feel the heat of his desire forever. She didn't like the way she felt herself buffeted along. She didn't want to want him; she certainly didn't want to need him. Marriage had given her his name and salvaged her reputation; it had given her an amazing respectability. It had put her beneath his power in a way, forced this intimacy upon them both. But what it hadn't given her was his . . .

Regard. Affection.

Love. She shivered and sat up. "Ian—"

"We'll go back to the house," he said, rising with a swift, graceful speed that suddenly made her cold again. He had learned a great deal from his uncle's people in the Everglades. He could move in absolute silence, with a staggering agility. She knew firsthand that his ability with a sword was second to none.

He would certainly be a deadly enemy.

She wasn't his enemy, she told herself. She was his wife.

He'd planned on marrying elsewhere. Maybe that made her more of an enemy than she could begin to realize.

He returned with her clothing to where she had curled to a sitting position on the embankment. "You're cold. We'll hurry to the house."

She stood, slipping into her chemise, then letting him tie her into her corset. Her emerald-green riding habit was slipped over her head, and she suddenly couldn't help but smile.

"And what's that for?" he queried.

"For once, McKenzie, I feel the upper hand. I'm dressed—and you're not."

He arched a brow, grinning. "And you think that gives you an advantage?"

"It could."

"Under what circumstances?"

He stared at her with such arrogant, cocky male assurance that she couldn't possibly ignore such a challenge. "Under such circumstances that you should find yourself walking up to Cimarron . . . bare-ass!" she informed him gravely.

"What?" he demanded, his head inclining with curiosity and his tone deep with a warning note.

She laughed and sped by him, sweeping up his clothing, and turning to flee.

She could run.

With shoes, without shoes.

She was her father's daughter. She had learned to scamper over mangrove roots and wet sand, through shallow waters and thick brush and foliage. She was delighted to realize at first that she had left him in her dust.

"Alaina McMann, get back here with my things!" he called in warning.

She kept running, musing about the possibility of returning his clothing—once she had come to the end of the trail that broke out onto the lawn, of course. Then it occurred to her that he had called her "McMann." And just as that thought raced through her mind, she felt a breath of air close behind her.

And she realized, as well, that she knew her own skills, and she had even reminded herself of his. He was as fast as a wildcat, as sleek, sure, and well muscled. The end of the trail was in sight. She spun to see that he was indeed right behind her. "My God, you'd better dress!" she cried out, throwing the bundle of his clothing behind her.

It didn't cause him to waver in the least. He seemed to fly after her. She was suddenly swept from her feet and brought down beneath him, pinned to the earth, gasping. His dark eyes were above hers, warily assessing, but a smile curved his mouth and he was both panting and laughing. She slowly smiled as well, wishing then that he was dressed and that she hadn't stolen his clothing.

"I very nearly bested you—and left you in a most difficult situation," she informed him primly.

"Very nearly—but not quite. And, my lovely wife, take heed. You'll never best me. I simply won't allow it."

"Oh?" she inquired sweetly.

The way he was pressed against her, she could feel every nuance of change within his body. The warmth, the growth. . . .

She grew breathless herself.

"You're supposed to be charming tonight," he reminded her softly. "Bending me, forming me, manipulating me to your will. So far, you've been doing excellently, but since it is growing so cool, it would be nice to be bent, formed, and manipulated in front of a fire with sweet warm wine, wouldn't you say?"

Looking into the cobalt glitter of his eyes, she nodded. "Wine is always good," she murmured.

He gave her a bemused look. "To smooth the rough edges of life?" he inquired somewhat hoarsely.

She shook her head. "Because sometimes I still feel so awkward."

He smiled a deep, gentle smile. And she thought that when he smiled so, there could not possibly be a more striking man in all the world, with features both so ruggedly hewn and yet so handsome. He rose, and she felt a thudding within her heart, because he was so striking, so tall, hard-muscled yet sinewy, sun-bronzed so that muscle and sinew rippled in gold reflections beneath the moon with every movement he made.

He reached down a hand, helping her up, then turned away, gathered his scattered clothing, and dressed quickly.

They returned, unseen and unaccosted, to the house. In his room, he dragged the blankets before the fire, poured them each brandy, then slowly and meticulously undressed her again before drawing her against him. He seemed to be in no great hurry now. The fire crackled, the brandy seemed warm and delicious.

And it was good to lie against him.

"Don't fall asleep again on me," he whispered softly.

"Would it matter?" she asked.

He reflected on the question a minute. "No," he told her.

He eased her to the floor then and kissed her. Softly, deeply, hungrily, teasingly. His lips just brushed her flesh. His hands moved over her body before the fire, and he seemed fascinated just to touch her. The gold and crimson flames of the fire seemed to leap and dance, touching her, warming her, bringing a buildup of heat and sensation that quickly set something ablaze within her. She could not lie still, but reached for him, seeking his lips when he teased, trying to slow his hand when his touch became invasively intimate. Her breath grew ragged. She was entwined with him, careless where the blanket lay. Eager for his kiss, eager to touch him in turn, eager to fondle and stroke . . .

As he had taught her today.

She touched him, seeking his mouth passionately as she did so. The brandy burned away her inhibitions. Her body arched to his, her breasts rubbed against his chest.

Her lips broke from his and she tasted his throat, his chest, played the tip of her tongue upon him, moving against him all the while. Kissing, caressing.

She found herself quite suddenly lifted, staring down at him, and slowly, slowly being lowered . . .

Impaled. His eyes were on hers, narrowed, cobalt fire. The sensation, so slow, was excruciating. She cried out, her head falling back. He drew her more slowly still, down, down until she sheathed him completely. . . .

Later, spent, she lay at his side and shivered as the fire of energy that had burst between them ebbed and she was cold. This time, he simply wrapped her in his arms and carried her to his bed.

She curled against him, and he held her. Perhaps she dozed; she wasn't sure. She slowly became aware of a deliciously wicked sensation simmering within her . . . and the stroke of his kiss moving down the length of her spine.

They made love again.

Sometimes she thought she dreamed his touch, because each time she closed her eyes, she opened them to a new seduction.

The fire burned to embers.

The moon waned in the sky; the sun began to rise.

She awoke again—chilled.

He wasn't in the bed, he wasn't in the room. She leaped up, shivering.

The fire had died completely. Outside, the sun was beginning to rise high.

Alaina dove into a wardrobe and quickly threw on a chemise and dress. She started to run out of the room, then paused long enough to stand before the dressing table and smooth down the wild tangle of her hair.

She rushed to the hallway and down the stairs. The house was quiet. She heard a noise from the dining room and hurried there, only to discover her father contentedly reading his paper and dining on pancakes.

"Good morning, daughter!"

"Father. Good morning. You're . . . alone."

"It's a busy household. The McKenzies are all up and about, and you'd best get moving yourself, my dear. Jerome is escorting our little party, and he's anxious to get a move on."

"Our little party?"

"Home!" he said happily.

"Ian . . . is gone?"

"Well, of course he's gone. You knew he had to report back to duty."

"Yes, but . . ."

Her father was looking at her with concern.

She floundered. "I—I hadn't imagined that he'd leave so early. He didn't wake me."

"Ah, well, maybe he didn't wish to disturb you, since he knew that we wouldn't be leaving so early. I assume you said your good-byes last night."

"Mmm." She realized then that her father had known Ian had had no intention of having her come with him— nor had he intended to force her to remain at Cimarron. The decision had been made long before last night. Ian had simply been determined to torment her.

So much for his murmured words that he might need her! He had tricked her, used her, and the worst of it . . .

The worst of it, she thought miserably, was that she had spent the night ecstatically happy, glad to be tricked, used, and . . .

And falling in love with her husband.

"Are you ready to go, my dear?"

She nodded. "Yes, Father. Thirty minutes, no more," she said flatly. She turned away from the dining room, fleeing back up the stairs.

To *his* room.

She had thought that she wanted to leave. That she wanted nothing more than to be back home. But here . . .

The indention of his head remained upon his pillow, the scent of him imbued the sheets. The wardrobe was filled with his clothing, the desk held his papers, mementos, and other belongings.

He'd gone away without even waking her to say good-bye. Marriage had apparently been fun while convenient, but now he was back to a different life.

And back to the woman he had intended to marry?

Alaina held her breath for a moment's misery. Peter O'Neill had told her that no respectable man would marry her. If nothing else, she'd certainly had a subtle revenge upon Peter. Ian McKenzie had married her. She couldn't allow herself to wonder just what it meant to him.

She closed her eyes tightly and exhaled.

She needed to pack. And quickly.

She was going home.

Chapter 11

From the front porch of their home, a handsome, sprawling wooden structure that sat just center of Belamar Isle—which wasn't really an island at all, since at low tide it connected with the mainland of the south Florida peninsula just a few miles from the Miami River—Alaina could see her father working with one of his new lime trees, a small smile of perfect contentment curved into his mouth. She had to call his name another three times before he looked up.

"Papa!" she shouted at last with exasperation. "Papa, you must come in from the fields and eat! Now!"

He waved a hand in her direction. "Coming, daughter. Coming directly!" he returned cheerfully.

But he hadn't even looked up. She sighed. He probably wouldn't come in until she went after him and dragged him back.

"Men! He's as stubborn as the rest of them!" Jennifer said, laughing. She set down the last of the silverware on the table that sat out on the porch. It was a hot day, but beautiful, with a breeze coming in off the water. A wonderful day to have a midafternoon dinner outside.

Anthony already sat in a special child's chair that Teddy had carved for him. He happily banged his cup against the wood. Jen smoothed back his hair and came to stand behind Alaina and watch as Teddy McMann blithely ignored the call to supper. "But then again, Teddy at least is quite sweetly stubborn."

Alaina shook her head with exasperation as she looked at Jennifer.

"Indeed, my father is a sweetheart—but as hard-headed as a rock!"

"Well, it could be said that he simply has superb powers of concentration," Jennifer consoled her. "Want me to take a walk out and get him?" she asked.

"No, that's all right. You stay with Anthony. I'll go."

Alaina was glad of Jennifer's company. She might never see her husband—and at times, it did seem as if her marriage had been a bizarre dream—but since her return home from Cimarron, she had grown closer than ever with James, Teela, Jerome, Sydney, and Jennifer and Lawrence and their baby, Anthony. She'd been home nearly four months. In that time, she'd grown especially close with Jennifer. James and Teela made a point of seeing her and Teddy at least every few weeks. Sydney would drop by at least once a week with Jerome, but Jennifer, whose house was little more than five miles away, came every few days, and when she didn't, Alaina went to visit her.

Jennifer was about ten years her senior, and in days past, she had looked after her younger brothers and sister—and cousins as well—so naturally, since she had been a young child, Alaina had known a deep affection for Jennifer. Despite all the pain and bloodshed that had plagued her life when she had been young, living among her mother's people, and running from the white army, Jen had the ability to look on the world fairly. She never judged men or women by their race, color, or beliefs, but loved her home in the wilds because it kept her far from those who did.

And though she readily admitted to having friends in the military, she despised the uniform worn by Federal forces, and always would. Soldiers had nearly slain her when she had been very young; only Tara McKenzie's intervention had saved her life.

She did, however, love her cousin Ian very much—which she had told Alaina several times, lest Alaina make the mistake of bemoaning her marriage to Jennifer.

They had all been friends before—very close friends. But it was Alaina's marriage to Ian that had made her family.

Jennifer was tall, with strong, beautiful bone structure, exotic hazel eyes, and a long, heavy fall of lustrous dark hair. Her husband, Lawrence, was a salvage diver who had literally run—or swum—into her in Biscayne Bay.

Lawrence had originally thought of the area as an isolated hell, but through Jennifer's eyes, he had begun to
see things differently. Like Teddy and the McKenzies,
he now jealously guarded his privacy along the coast.
James had given them acreage as a wedding present, and
they now planted sugar cane to supplement Lawrence's
salvage income. The baby, Anthony, had his mother's
hazel eyes and olive-toned skin along with his father's
fair hair. At a little over two years old, he was not just
walking everywhere but running, and babbling a mile a
minute. Anthony was clever, precocious, cute, and entirely lovable. Alaina enjoyed him tremendously.

Especially now.

Now . . .

With a sudden swift shiver, Alaina grabbed her shawl
from a small wall post just inside the door.

"What is it?" Jen asked her. "Are you all right?"

"Yes, yes, of course," Alaina said quickly. "It's just
my father—you know!"

"Well, by the time you get your father, we might have
more company. Look, I think it's my brother coming."
Jennifer shielded her eyes from the sun, looking northward along the bay.

Alaina followed her gaze. She could see a small sailboat moving their way, the sail billowing in the breeze,
the vessel well piloted and seeming to fly over the water.

"I imagine it is Jerome," Alaina agreed. "He sent a
note with the last soldier who came through that he'd
probably be by today. He's going to sail to St. Augustine
soon, then up to Charleston, and he's going to bring
some of my father's fruit with him for the markets there.
I'm so glad he's almost here. My father is quite fond of
your brother—and masculine conversation! I may even
get him up here to eat!"

"Hmm," Jennifer murmured. She frowned. "Looks
like lots of company, maybe. Can you see—there, coming around those mangroves. There's another little boat
coming in. Look, it's even closer. No sails flying—it
seems to have come around into the bay from the little
inlet there."

"Maybe a couple of army men or sailors, heading
down to an outpost in the Keys or down to Fort Taylor,"
Alaina guessed. "Maybe a letter from . . ." She paused,

glancing at Jennifer. "Maybe a letter from Ian," she said lightly. "Perhaps we should arrange for more settings and warn Lilly and Bella that we may be feeding more mouths than originally intended." Bella was their cook, a wonderful Creole woman who had been with Alaina and her father as long as she could remember. Lilly had asked to accompany Alaina south from Cimarron. Being so fond of the young woman who had been so quick to champion her, Alaina had agreed that she would be a wonderful help to her and her household—as long as Lilly didn't mind the isolation.

Lilly didn't mind—in fact, she didn't feel isolated at all. She had been befriended by one of the families of Seminoles living nearby, and she felt as if she had come to the height of civilization.

"Maybe you should hurry your father in, then," Jennifer said. "I think I'll get his spyglass and see if I can't discover who's coming."

"What's the matter? You sound uneasy," Alaina said.

Jennifer glanced at her and gave her a rueful smile. "There's nothing the matter—not that I can see. I just got a chill, that's all."

Sighing with affectionate irritation, Alaina started down the porch steps. Her father! Indeed, he did take some care and concern! The renowned Theodore McMann was behaving just like a small child. Give him a new tree, and he forgot all about the fact that he needed to eat to survive.

And Alaina was ravenous herself. A wonder—since she'd scarcely been able to endure eating at all as of late. But then, recently her hunger patterns had been in nearly as great a maelstrom as her emotions. At first she had simply been unable to believe what was becoming more and more obvious. Then she had been incredulous, fearful, excited, resentful; then fearful, excited, incredulous, and resentful all over again. Jennifer had guessed what Alaina had been unable to believe.

And today it was time to talk to her father. He'd be excited beyond belief, ecstatic. Since she didn't know what she herself felt yet, she could at least be grateful to know that her father would be delighted.

She hurried across the spit of lawn between the house and the grove where Teddy worked so intently with his new limes. As always, when she watched him, her love for him welled deep inside her, and she was glad to be with him. He did need her, no matter how restless she felt now.

Coming home from Cimarron had at first been very strange. In a way, life had been so much the same; she had worked with Teddy, as she had wanted. Taken care of him. Things should have been just the same.

But they weren't. Things would never be the same again. She had married Ian. Still, so much time seemed to have passed now. She should feel as if it had never been.

But most annoyingly, she still lay awake at night, remembering her brief week of marriage. And when she fell asleep, to her horror, she dreamed. Vividly. Dreamed of his touch, his eyes scorching as they swept her, his hands . . . so talented.

To her absolute amazement, she missed Ian. She missed the sound of his voice, the feel of his eyes, when they burned into her, or raked over her. At times she actually ached for him, and it was torture to wonder what he was doing.

Everything she had felt for Peter O'Neill had died that day at Cimarron. Everything. It was as if she had worn blinders and they had been taken away. But with Ian, things were certainly quite different. He remained in Washington, where the woman he had intended to marry lived.

She tried to tell herself that she wasn't jealous, that it didn't matter. Society allowed men . . . to be men. It wasn't just acceptable that they did what they wished; it was expected.

So why did she spend her days in torment, seething, wondering? Was it so frustrating simply because she had no power whatsoever? And worse . . .

He might be anywhere. And she might be incredibly far from his thoughts, a nonentity to him. While the life they had created together grew within her.

He could forget her, but she couldn't forget him. The situation was almost laughable. She'd thought she'd had some kind of influenza at first; in fact, she'd thought for quite some time that she'd caught hold of some strange stomach malady she couldn't quite shake. It had actually taken a full two months for her to realize that she was sadly naive and almost incredibly stupid—her week with her husband might have been brief, but apparently quite timely.

There had been a time when all she thought she wanted was to come home here, unencumbered, and live the life she had led before. Well, she had what she wanted. But life had twisted on her. She wanted more. She had never thought of herself as isolated before. Now she felt as if the world were spinning away without her.

Ian hadn't been back in Florida in over four months. But for each month she'd received a letter from him, delivered by a different military man in transit to Fort Taylor at Key West.

But Ian's letters had been distant; polite and courteous—but nonetheless, distant. It was as if he had realized the folly of what he had done. Being Ian McKenzie, naturally, he wouldn't think of backing out of it.

But perhaps that couldn't stop him from regretting it. Especially now, with events across the country moving so fast and furiously. Alaina had received letters from Sydney, who remained in Charleston, where South Carolina politicians broadcast their intent to draw their state from the tyrannical hold of the Union should that upstart Lincoln be elected. President Buchanan, it seemed, was doing little to lessen the strain in the election year, and he seemed to be straddling the fence regarding the oh-so-touchy slavery question. Alaina had even received a pleasant letter from her brother-in-law Julian McKenzie, who entertained her with stories about St. Augustine's volunteer militia forces and with the lyrics to new songs being written. It was quite true that a good percentage of the officers who had come out of West Point and other military schools were Southerners—men who could ride exceptionally well and handle their arms with expertise, while Northerners were finding work more and more often in factories and offices. But according to Julian, Florida citizens were arming themselves for whatever should come. Indeed, the country was spinning rapidly into exciting and revolutionary times.

Teddy claimed they were lucky to be so far from all that was happening. While most people believed the country would split apart and both sides would accept it as inevitable since they could not agree on certain issues, Teddy thought there would definitely be war. He said it was the realistic view.

It seemed strange to Alaina that her father should be so certain—and realistic. Teddy was a dreamer. A scientist, but a dreamer, and his fruit trees were the center of all his work. He'd been experimenting with them for many years now, but his new little lime trees were his darlings. As she walked toward her father, Alaina reflected with a certain amount of humor that she was rather like one child competing with many others for Teddy's attention.

As she neared her father, she was startled by the sudden searing cry of a bird. Maybe it was the way it sounded against the crystal-clear summer's day; maybe it was the simple, sharp loneliness of the cry. But something within that sound suddenly chilled her despite the piercing heat of the day. She stopped walking and stared up at the sky, alarmed by the sudden sense of foreboding that filled her.

Jerome had warned them to be watchful. And they were careful. Her father posted two men on guard every night. But his workers were in the field now and the heat made them less alert. Even the household staff was moving slowly these days.

There were loaded rifles in the cabinet in the den. Alaina's French fencing swords were across from it. But she didn't dare take the time to return to the house. If there was trouble, Jennifer would go for the guns. Jennifer—who could aim like a sharpshooter.

The bird let out a shriek again. The breeze seemed to go still, then crackle with an air of danger.

"Papa?" she cried. It seemed critical that she reach him. She started running.

Someone else was running. Birds suddenly burst into flight above Teddy's lime grove, and two men bolted from the shelter of the trees, racing south toward the shallows between themselves and the mainland. Their movement was awkward and ungainly. They were dressed in dark, filthy, ragged clothing, and both had long hair and rough, scraggly beards.

Alaina stared at them in horror, realizing that their

flight was made so very difficult because they were in chains. They'd been chained at the wrists and ankles, but had shattered the links in the center, allowing them a certain freedom while they still dragged the weight. The chains clanged and grated as they ran, making a noise that was as threatening as the shattering cry of the birds. Alaina realized suddenly that she had come to a dead halt, staring at the men.

Then she heard shouts, coming from the direction of the bay. She spun around. The small launch she and Jennifer had seen coming toward the islet had made it in. Three soldiers stepped out of it, splashing into the shallow water, racing onto the land.

"Halt!" one of them cried.

She turned again. They were shouting at the convicts.

The men ignored the command and kept running.

"What in God's name—" Teddy McMann shouted out in a loud and angry voice.

But his words were cut off by a startling explosion of gunfire as the soldiers shot at the men in chains, who were armed as well. They instinctively ducked at the sound of the gunfire, then turned back and exchanged fire.

"Wait!" Alaina cried, incredulous. "Stop!"

But the soldiers kept firing. They were so intent in their pursuit, it seemed that they ignored the fact that she and her father were there in the middle of their cross-fire.

"What a perfect day," Ian said.

He'd stripped down to his breeches and stretched out in the rear of Jerome's small sailboat, *Windrunner*. The sky was cloudless. The breeze was just enough to fill the sails and caress his sun-heated cheeks without making the water choppy. They seemed to skate across the water.

Jerome was manning the tiller and guiding the sail. Ian had nothing to do but laze where he sprawled so comfortably. He'd made the trip from the Capital to Charleston via government packet, then taken a ride with a merchantman from Charleston to St. Augustine, where he'd looked up his brother, coerced him into a trip south, and found naval transportation for them both down to his uncle's dock. Like Ian, Julian was stripped down pirate style to breeches alone, and stretched out on the other side of the tiller.

"Perfect day," Julian agreed. He grinned at his brother and glanced at Jerome, who shook his head tolerantly. "Indeed, perfect," Jerome said wryly.

"You can stretch out and we can work for a while," Julian offered guiltily.

"Yes, it should work that way, shouldn't it?" Jerome said. "Stay where you are. The *Windrunner* is still new enough to me that I enjoy the feel of taking her through the water."

"She's your best work yet," Ian said, stating a fact rather than complimenting his cousin. The speed with which they were slicing through the water was truly impressive.

And being on the water was a good feeling for Ian. The wind against his face, the sun burning down on his flesh, the sky endless above him. It was good to be with his brother and cousin, good to sail, good to have the day. He missed the water when he was away, missed the sun. Summer's heat was already fading in the north, but here, the slightest cooling was just beginning to come at night. It was a beautiful day. The ocean breeze kept them from feeling the dead heat of late summer. There was nothing like the water on a crystal-clear day when the sun was bearing down in all its glory. The warmth seemed to ease out all the kinks and crimps in his joints and bones. More. It seemed to ease away the turmoil that continued to plague the world.

The presidential elections were just three days away, and the entire country seemed to be holding its collective breath, waiting.

Returning to Washington after his leave, Ian had found himself working part-time with the army cartographers and part-time with young recruits, drilling, training, teaching.

The nation was sluggishly preparing for war. For the most part, no one wanted to believe that there could be a war. To those hotheads on either side eager for the excitement, if there was a fracas, it would be dealt with swiftly.

Still, most military men waited. Waited for the elections, waited to see what their individual states would do.

Ian had worked hard, since work itself could be a tonic, exhausting him by nightfall so that he didn't dwell on the many situations that plagued his mind.

He'd seen Risa his first night back. She had come running down the steps from her father's house to throw her arms around him and kiss him. She'd smelled cleanly and sweetly of lavender, her dark hair soft as silk, her violet eyes shimmering with tears of happiness as she greeted him. Her kiss held a more evocative seduction than he had ever felt from her. A promise of passion that was sweetly tempting.

Somehow, he'd broken that kiss. And he'd tried to explain.

Naturally, she'd been shocked.

She never cried. Not in front of him. She had far too much pride. She told him that she understood—did she really?—and she said that she was glad that she'd never mentioned a word to her father, that she'd been waiting for Ian to do so. This way, she said with calm, rational control, no one else was involved, no one was hurt.

But she had been hurt, and he knew it. And he found that he was hurt himself in a way he had never imagined possible. The world had been so sane before. She had been his future. There had been a difference between love and lust. His casual affairs would have naturally ended once they were married, and he and Risa would have been all things to one another, friend, confidant, lover . . .

Except that it wasn't to be.

Risa really was the perfect partner for him. She was Colonel Magee's daughter, dignified, beautiful, knowledgeable, admired by the colonel's friends—and foes. Ian was afraid to analyze his feelings for her. Social situations continually threw them together, and it was difficult to keep his distance. He cared far too much for Risa to dishonor her in any way, or hurt her any more than he could avoid.

His affair with Lavinia now seemed such a petty, worthless enterprise, and though he could blame Alaina for what had happened, he was just as guilty. When Risa had rushed to him with such sweet passion, he wondered why, other than foolish male lust and ego, he had risked a future with Risa in so fanciful a form of play. He realized, seeing Risa, just how much he had come to love her, and yet oddly, at the same time, he realized that his feelings for Alaina left him in a tempest as well. He desired his wife; he felt responsible for her . . . and possessive. And though he was glad to have time alone with Risa to explain what had happened—truthfully, the whole truth, including his part in the affair—he was sorry that he had allowed Alaina to return home.

Risa was near him far too often, so beautiful and so impeccably well mannered. Speaking so intelligently in any company. Charming everyone near and far. And still attempting to be his friend despite the way her beautiful violet eyes clouded each time they met.

And all of it made worse by the temper of the country.

Drinking with friends at night in D.C. could quickly become far more nightmare than pleasure. Many men were quiet, waiting, worrying, wondering what they'd do when "the time came." Many still swore that there would be compromise. But longtime military men were already resigning. A number of states were arranging emergency legislative sessions to deal with the situation, should a situation arise, after the elections. Militia groups were forming right and left. Many men were brash and arrogant, swearing that they would "whoop" the other side in a single battle. It would be fun, it would be glorious.

It would all be over so quickly. . . .

"You commented that it was a perfect day," Jerome told him, eyeing the sail as he brought it down just a hair. Then he looked at Ian. "And not that I'm not glad to serve, but when we started out, you were smiling and content. I'll be damned if I'll stand here doing all the work while you scowl and brood."

Ian sat up, shrugging, then shaking his head.

"You're thinking about the elections?" Julian asked.

"I am."

Jerome stared ahead at the water. "There's a very good chance that an acceptable candidate will be elected."

Julian added, "No one thinks that Lincoln can possibly win. He isn't even on our state ballot."

"But," Ian said, "everyone is talking about secession and war anyway."

"There's nothing like being prepared," Jerome murmured.

"The towns are all forming militia units," Julian said. "I've already been asked to serve as a surgeon with a group of the St. Augustine boys. Retired commanders are becoming officers, and half the state drills constantly."

"If secession comes, there will probably be no shortage of able commanders in the South," Jerome said, staring at Ian again. "They'll resign from the Federal military and take up new positions. And they'll come in with nice high ranks. You could be Colonel McKenzie— hell, you could make up your own brigade with little effort and become a general in no time."

"So . . . you're for secession?" Ian asked him.

Jerome stared ahead at the water again. "It wouldn't matter if I was or wasn't—Florida is rearing at the bit to secede—I think that half the politicians in this state are hoping that we'll be forced to secede. I can promise you this—Florida may not be the first state out of the union if it comes to a division, but she'll follow the first cotton state out as quickly as she can manage."

"I didn't ask you about the state," Ian said "I want to know your feelings in the matter."

Jerome hesitated a long moment, looking out on the water. "Am I for secession? No, I'm not. I think that the founding fathers worked hard to create a new country, and both our independence and our growth made us strong. I think that the industries of the North support the agriculture of the South, and that our many diverse qualities and peoples are what make us unique. So am I for secession? No. I don't own slaves, and I don't think one of us could have possibly grown to adulthood without having the lesson of the importance of personal freedoms taught to us. I am Seminole, remember. I have always respected your choice to join the military, Ian, and even my father has very good friends among the army. But in my house, and among my grandmother's people, it's hard to forget that it was men wearing that Federal blue uniform who slaughtered the Seminoles so ruthlessly, considering them savages—*lesser* people than themselves. My heart is with my state. If Florida secedes, I am with her. If there is war, then I am on the side of my state."

Ian nodded slowly, watching the sun glint off the water, watching as his cousin expertly drew the sail to bring them closer to the shoreline.

"Julian?" he said to his brother.

"Ah, well," Julian said softly, "I'm not ready to decide the issue as of yet. Sometimes I feel like Jerome; my heart is with my state. Then I think about Father, and how firmly he has always stood for the belief that good and bad men come in all colors and races. I won't support slavery."

"I don't support slavery," Jerome argued, "but I do support the South."

"How can you do both?" Ian demanded.

Jerome shook his head, staring out at the water. "Gentlemen, supposedly the issue isn't slavery. The issue is a state's own right to make choices. Slavery isn't economical in the North—naturally, then, it is easy for Northerners to think that the 'peculiar institution' can be thrown right over. Believe me, Ian, I see all sides. I wish sometimes that I did not."

"If Florida secedes, she will have a rough road ahead," Ian murmured.

"In what way?" Jerome asked.

"You know as well as I—there is so much coastline! She will be vulnerable to attack, and her fellow cotton states—"

"Her fellow cotton states will need her support," Jerome said fiercely. "Florida is a food basket, with the amount of cattle we raise. And then there is salt—my God, salt will be invaluable in the event of war. There are important Federal forts in the state, which I imagine the state would take over immediately if Florida secedes. Personally, I'd like to see someone take charge of the remains of Fort Dallas."

Ian glanced at Jerome. "Has there been trouble?" he asked worriedly.

"No real trouble. But I imagine it's a matter of time. Drifters, riffraff, army deserters, all make their way there. The English owners seem to have no plans for the property, and so it is an open invitation to cutthroats and thieves. The army comes in now and then to attempt a clean-out. I dragged out three men I'm certain caused the wreck of a schooner they took salvage from. It creates a danger, that's certain."

"Maybe I should force Alaina to return to Washington with me," Ian murmured.

"Jennifer is almost always with her; Lawrence works the waters right off Belamar. We're close, and yet . . . well, Teddy has help on the islet, of course. They've rifles, a few handguns . . . but Teddy always expects the best out of people. He's only recently started loading the weapons he keeps in the house."

"Why has he done so recently?" Ian asked.

Jerome looked at him. "I suggested he do so."

"Teddy is a bit of a dreamer, but he's not a fool," Julian murmured assuringly. "Look, Belamar is coming into view."

Ian looked out across the shimmering water. He could see Belamar ahead of them now The northeastern section of Teddy's pleasantly sprawling wooden house was clearly visible from their angle.

Someone was on the porch. Someone dark-haired. His cousin Jennifer, he thought.

Where was Alaina?

Near. Very near.

He narrowed his eyes, startled by the strange heat and quickening that seized his muscles, spread through his torso and limbs.

He was anxious to see her. It had been a very long time. A long, uneasy, tormented time for him. Days when he wished that Risa would rage and condemn him. Nights when it seemed she hinted she still loved him, nights when it seemed almost inevitable that they would be together. Nights when he would go to bed thinking of Risa, her laughter, her convictions, eyes, voice, scent . . .

Yet he would sleep.

And in sleep, he found himself dreaming of being hotly entwined with another woman, the one he had come to know. His wife. He was damned anxious to hold her again—all but desperate for the night.

IIe frowned suddenly as their course veered them into a more northerly angle, allowing them a better view of the breadth of Belamar Isle. A small boat was drawn up to the beachhead.

A sudden barrage of gunfire exploded so loudly that they could hear it clear as day, even at their distance.

"Jesus!" Julian breathed.

More gunfire

Then . . .

A woman's high-pitched scream, carrying out to them over the water.

Chapter 12

"What in hell?" Ian demanded, balancing on the balls of his feet. He stood watching as the soldiers advanced, still firing. "Sweet Jesus, what in hell is going on there?"

"I don't know. On Belamar itself, it's been quiet as a cemetery. Ian, Julian, take the sail; we'll let her out all the way. We can be on the islet in a matter of minutes," Jerome said.

Ian and his brother took control of the sail while Jerome sat back against the aft of the boat, his full weight on the tiller to bring them into the wind. They seemed to skim above the water.

The scream echoed in Ian's head. Dread filled him, along with a desperate anxiety to reach Belamar.

He shouldn't have left her here!

He had to reach the isle, had to reach it now, this second, had to stop whatever was going on.

An inner voice mocked him. Oh, he had to reach it now? He'd been away for months! His heart seemed to be in his throat.

"There's surely some explanation; the military can't be shooting at Teddy," Jerome said.

"Right," Ian agreed. They were nearing the sandy shore side of the islet. They had reached the area with incredible speed, because the three of them needed no commands; they worked in silence. How often they had sailed together, worked together. Played together. In days gone past, as kids, they'd played soldiers and Indians, stalking one another. Escaping, discovering. Battling. Sometimes winning, sometimes not. Sometimes arguing, with Ian and Julian wanting to play the Indians, while Jerome and Brent had to be the soldiers. And upon occasion the girls, being headstrong creatures, would insist on being part of the games as well. Searching each other out in hidden lairs, letting out their war cries on the air. Arguing, exploring, playing . . .

Banding together when it was necessary.

"Anyone have weapons?" Jerome asked.

"I have my medical bag," Julian said.

"My Colts, there, with my jacket," Ian said.

"Colts—two of them? Toss one over—I only have my rifle."

"Give me the rifle," Julian said.

Jerome tossed him the rifle. Ian went for the Colts, tossing one to Jerome as they beached the sailboat.

There was another barrage of gunfire as the three of them leaped from the boat into the water and began running to the beach and then across the scraggly, sand-spurred lawn to the groves that grew toward the mainland.

"Alaina! Get down, Alaina!" Teddy shouted to her.

She met her father's eyes across the distance that still separated them. They were clear and blue and sharply on her; she had his undivided attention now. "Down, Alaina, get down now!" he repeated.

"Papa!" she shrieked back. "You get down, do you hear me? Get down."

The army men were running toward them.

The chained men were closer.

"The old man! Get the old man as a shield!" one of the convicts called. He was darker, ruddier than his companion, older perhaps.

"Papa, run to me, we've got to get out of the line of fire!" Alaina cried.

Teddy tried to run.

He wasn't fast enough.

The younger man came hobbling up quickly behind her father and locked an arm around his throat. He dragged Teddy against him, then stared at Alaina, his eyes growing wider. She realized that the men hadn't seen her until that moment; her father had blocked their view of her.

"The old man!" the young convict snorted. "By God, get the woman!" he shouted.

Teddy's throat was in a death lock. His face was growing crimson.

"You let go of my father!" Alaina shouted furiously,
so frightened for her father that she couldn't allow herself the luxury of personal fear. She burst into motion.

Her actions were foolhardy; but at that moment, all
she saw was blood-red fury and the danger that threatened Teddy.

She raced like a madwoman toward Teddy and his
attacker, throwing herself against the man and hammering him furiously on the back.

"Thayer, get her!" the young man shrieked.

The older man grimly obeyed, clamping his arms
around her. She kept fighting like a tigress, swearing.
Then she heard a *click* and saw that the younger man
had brought his gun against her father's temple.

The fellow wasn't just tattered and dirty. He had a
lean, starving look about him like a fox that hadn't eaten
in far too long. His teeth were broken and tobacco-
stained; his eyes were a strange, pale blue, far more un-
settling than his words. "Quit, bitch," he said simply,
"or I'll splatter your pa's brains all over your fine white
dress. She's a might pretty one, eh? Out here on this
hellhole. She's a better hostage, I'd say. Wouldn't mind
having her with me tonight at all, no, sir."

"You let my girl go," Teddy said. His voice was calm.
He seemed impervious to the steel against his skull. "I'll
protect you all the way back into those mangroves yonder. A hundred men could search a week and never find
you there."

"Papa, I'm fine, and I can take care of myself," Alaina
assured her father. Could she? Against these filthy, mur-
derous fools? Yes. She turned to the convicts. "All right,
you scurvy bastards. You let him go! Can't you see that
you're strangling him? Leave him be, and I'll get you
out of here myself," Alaina promised, "but you step
away from my father—now!"

The pale-eyed convict smiled. The sizzle of light in his
eyes made her feel ill, but it didn't matter. She had to
get the men away from Teddy.

"The girl comes with us," he said.

But then the day was newly shattered by another barrage of gunfire. The convict holding her swore.

"Damned idiot army!" he cried. "Shooting at us while we're holding hostages! Move, girl, move!"

"Papa—" Alaina began.

But she didn't see Teddy because the older convict had her elbow and viciously jerked her along with him, taking her about twenty feet toward the eastern shore.

The water looked shallow. It seemed as if the mainland might be a walk away through thigh-high water.

But the tide was rising. When it did so, it rose fast. Right now, a nonswimmer could walk through the shallows. Halfway across, though, the water would rise over their heads.

Alaina was as familiar with the rise and fall of the water about their small islet as she was the rise and fall of the sun. But the convict prodding her along with his merciless grasp probably didn't understand a thing about the isles, the reefs, or the tides.

Alaina let him drag her to the water.

She had little choice.

Yet his escape route could be her best chance. She hoped that the men would decide that they didn't need her father. And if Teddy was taken in to the water behind her, well, he was an excellent swimmer, too.

Their captors' accents were Northern; she prayed that they never had the opportunity to learn to swim.

"Well, I've the better part of this deal," the man shoving her along muttered. "You can show me how to disappear into those mangroves—and survive there. You might even find out you like old Ned all right, eh, little lady?"

Ned was disgusting. She'd kill him before she ever discovered if she liked him.

But she had to know that Teddy was safe first.

She tried to look back and make sure that her father was all right. The convict pulled her with such a vengeance—his gun shoved hard against her ribs the whole way—that she couldn't even twist around.

"You don't need to do this. If my father is safe, I'll get you across without protest!" she cried.

"Just keep moving. Fast. They're right behind us."

They reached the water.

The convict shoved his gun against the small of Alaina's back. "Move! Now!"

Alaina started into the water.

They ran hard across the islet. The distance from the northeastern beachhead to the grove was no more than a quarter of a mile, with another half mile of grove crowding into an area of good growing soil before the sparse green grasses and spurs gave way to sand beach again, dipping into the cove that flooded with high tide.

Ian, Julian, and Jerome moved across the distance with such speed that they arrived at the spit of lime trees along with the three uniformed soldiers.

And Jennifer.

"Where's Alaina?" Ian demanded of his cousin.

"In the grove, toward the beach, I don't know!" Jennifer said desperately.

Ian started to run. A shot was fired over his head. He spun back around.

One of the soldiers had fired over his head. He felt his temper soar.

"What in God's name is going on?" Ian demanded. He didn't know any of the three very green and very young men who were tentatively edging through the trees.

"And who the hell are you to ask?" The oldest of the trio—a cocky boy with a scraggle of whiskers on his chin—demanded in return. "McKenzie. *Major* McKenzie," Ian informed them, his eyes narrowing. He strode quickly toward the boy, wrenching his gun from his hand. "Now answer me!"

"We're after two men," the boy said quickly, chastised. Ian was not sure if the boy had been intimidated by his rank—or by the sight of himself, Jerome, and Julian bearing down on his awkward trio. "Two deserters; they made their way to old Fort Dallas, robbing a few good citizens in the Keys along the way. Armed, dangerous, desperate men. We have to stop them."

The boy himself sounded desperate then. There was something like the sound of a little sob at the end of his words.

Ian glanced to the grove and saw why.

One of the convicts was down.

And Teddy atop him.

"Oh, God!" Ian's stomach knotted. He ran forward and knelt by his father-in-law.

"Alaina," Teddy whispered in a labored breath.

"I'll get her, I promise," Ian said.

He stood, his every muscle seeming to constrict with fear. "Where's my wife?" he demanded.

"Who?"

"The woman!" Jerome bellowed.

"The water," the soldier said.

Ian turned and ran.

Alaina tried to take her time, allowing the water a greater chance to grow deeper.

The convict shoved her from behind. The water became deeper and deeper as they moved across it. The convict began to swear. "What's going on here? You trying to drown me, girl?"

"The tide is rising; I have no control over it."

"You knew it was going to rise!"

"The tide always rises."

"You meant to drag me out—and drown me!"

"I haven't dragged you anywhere!"

"If I die, you die. If I go down, you go down with me!" he promised her.

"Bastard! I didn't attack you, I never threatened you!"

"Blame the bloody army, ma'am!"

His head went down suddenly as a wave washed over them. Salt stung their eyes.

The convict inhaled raggedly when the wave was gone. "Get me out, get me ashore, now!" he commanded her. His eyes narrowed. "I'd sure like to have you around tonight, girl, but you'd best take care. I'll kill you if you try anything, I swear that I will!" he warned.

His gun jammed against her ribs. Was his shot still any good? His powder would be soaked.

She had to do it carefully, had to do it right—but it was time to take her chance and wrench free.

For a full minute she moved along as docile as a lamb, leading him, as commanded, through the deepening water toward the mangrove-laden shore.

Then she jerked against him with all her strength.

He swore; he reached for her again, and lost his grip upon his gun. It went drifting down into the rock and sand and seaweed.

"Bitch!" he roared, and though she nearly escaped him, his fingers bit into the material of her white day gown, pulling her back. They began to struggle in the water. Alaina knew that her strength lay in eluding a solid grasp by his fingers. All he had now was material; she had to find a way to rip free.

She managed to inch back beneath the water, just avoiding his groping fingers each time.

Then, quite suddenly, he realized he was drowning and he panicked.

He no longer attempted to kill Alaina; he was clinging to her. She was nearly free, but he had her gown. She tried desperately to rip and tear at the fabric and make her way back up to the surface.

She kicked him hard in the chest. His grasp eased, but she couldn't move swiftly enough in the bulky, voluminous weight of her clothing. She needed to rid herself of the skirt before he regained his strength and grasped hold of her again.

She worked industriously at the fabric, trying with all her strength to rip free.

Then she screamed, nearly inhaled, nearly died, as she felt another set of arms coming around her. A moment's panic seized her.

There was a hand before her.

Wielding a knife.

The knife caught the brilliant light of the sun, even through the water, and flashed silver.

Dear God, they were going to kill her, slash her, slit her throat.

No.

The knife flashed once, then again and again.

Cutting fabric. Freeing her from the drowning bulk of it. She kicked hard, surfacing. She inhaled deeply, treading water. Five feet separated her now from the two bodies that were thrashing in the water. She swam hard, backing away, watching the churning water all the while.

Then a head broke the surface, and she thought that

she was dying after all, and hallucinating in the process.

It was Ian.

"My God!" she breathed.

"You're all right?" he demanded, eyes hard on her, as cobalt as the water. Hair pitch black and water-slicked. Bronze shoulders naked.

"I'm fine. My father—"

"You're not hurt?"

"No, but my father—"

"Let's get back," he said, cutting her off huskily. There was something strange about his face, his eyes. Or was there? She hadn't seen him in so long. Naturally, he would appear strange. Months had passed. He had more or less deserted her on this islet to pursue his own life.

She had wanted to be here, she reminded herself. She had been willing to bargain and barter to stay with her father.

She simply hadn't thought about how hard the separation would be.

"I can swim!" she protested quickly as a few strokes brought him to her side. Warmth seemed to come along with him. Strength, which she seemed sadly lacking at that moment. He was very close, very solid, bronze muscles glistening in sun and water.

Alaina realized then that she was deliriously happy to be alive, but so shaken to see him. She wasn't ready, wasn't prepared. And now he would think this too dangerous a place to leave her. He would want her to come away. Not with him. He would want her back at Cimarron, so far away from Teddy.

Dear God! What foolish things to be thinking about when the isle was still all but crowded with military men, and a man intent upon her murder still lurked in the water not at all far away.

"Ian, that man is desperate. He'll come after us again. He'll—"

"He'll not."

"But he—"

"He is dead," Ian said flatly. "Come on."

Dead.

Her eyes riveted to a spot ten feet beyond Ian.

There, the attacker drifted. Body submerged, just the tip of his head floating above the water. Indeed, he was dead. Life and death, both so fleeting.

She was relieved; she was chilled. Death was terrifying, especially as she had just escaped from its clammy grasp.

"Alaina, let's get to shore," Ian insisted firmly.

"I'm all right, I can move on my own."

Despite her protest, he was by her side. He slipped an arm beneath her breasts, towing her along with his powerful strokes, as it didn't seem that she moved quickly enough for him.

When they reached the shallows, he drew her up against him. They stumbled together through the water and sand. She was glad. Even the shredded and tattered remains of her soaked petticoats and skirts were incredibly heavy. Her knees wobbled.

His arms around her were supportive, reminding her again how she had missed him. She stood within his embrace, shivering despite the heat.

He was a stranger after all this time, but she was glad to see him. Warmed by his very presence. Yet she felt that she had to explain, though nothing that had happened was her fault. "I was almost free, you know, Ian. I'm grateful, of course, that you came in so timely a manner. Naturally, I am quite glad of the assistance. But we're not careless, Ian. This was just so sudden."

She was shivering violently. She had to stop. She had to get herself under control. She was safe; they were all safe. He had come.

She gazed at him, her eyes widening then with amazement that he could really be there, but still disturbed by the look in his eyes. She had been chattering, talking just to talk. "How can you be here?" she demanded now. "How can you have been gone so long, and then be here . . . in the water?"

"I came by way of a navy packet that left my brother and me at my uncle's house last night. We were on our way here with Jerome when we saw the other boat beaching," he told her. "I thank God I was here," he added softly.

"Who—who—where did those men come from?" she asked.

"They were convicts who had taken refuge in the deserted fort," he said.

"And the army—"

"The army came after them."

They had reached dry land. Alaina stumbled; he held her up. She smiled ruefully, clinging to his arm as they walked over sand and spurs toward the lawn. "My father will be so glad to see you! You certainly do have good timing. I'm still not at all sure I understand what was happening, though. I swear to you, I don't know what is going on elsewhere, but we haven't had the least speck of trouble anywhere near here since . . . since the last Seminole uprising, which, of course, didn't affect Teddy and me. You must believe me. The islet is really quite safe. . . ."

Alaina broke off. He wasn't angry.

She had expected a lecture, at the very least. She was too sure of herself, she never realized the danger she could be in, she was far too reckless.

She'd once made the mistake of trying to convince him that she was quite capable of taking care of herself. And once, of course, she had been confident that she would be all right in any circumstance.

But Ian taught well, and she learned quickly.

And she would never forget the night by the pool when he had determined to teach her the lesson that she wasn't invincible.

But he wasn't lecturing.

He was uncannily quiet.

He didn't seem impatient at all with her insistence that the islet was safe. He looked pained; his strong, dark countenance far more sorrowful than irate.

"Ian?" she murmured worriedly.

He was gazing past her, and she realized why. Ahead, in the grove, a group had formed in a circle.

The younger convict lay facedown next to one of Teddy's fine lime trees.

Flies already buzzed above his body. He was dead, and Alaina did not need to be told that it was so. And under different circumstances, she might have cared.

And she might have cared more deeply that the older man floated dead somewhere in the sea. She might have cared, simply because she had been taught that all life was precious.

But no life was more precious than that of her father.

And Teddy was down on the ground as well. Soldiers stood awkwardly nearby.

Jerome and Jennifer knelt at Teddy's left side. Jennifer was industriously ripping the hem of her skirt and petticoats into bandages. Julian, with his medical bag opened at his side, was working over Teddy as well, trying to stanch the flow of red that seeped into his shirt and spilled into a puddle atop his chest.

Julian ripped open Teddy's shirt to better put pressure against the wound.

"Papa!" Alaina screamed. "Papa!"

She broke free from Ian and tore toward her father, her heart in her throat, choking her. She fell to her knees at his side.

His eyes opened. Soft, beautiful, kindly, gentle blue. They focused upon her. He smiled. She grasped his hand. Drew his knuckles to her cheek. She felt the slightest movement in his fingers. "Papa, it's going to be fine. We're going to get you inside, we're—"

"Alaina. You're safe," Teddy mouthed.

"I'm fine, Papa. And you'll be fine, too. Julian is here, and Ian. Jennifer, Jerome. You know how very good Julian is, Papa, how he always wanted to be a doctor. Julian can keep you alive, Papa. He'll make you well, just listen to him, save your strength, do as he says."

He didn't seem to hear her. His eyes seemed to be clouding over. "Alaina. Thank God, thank God."

"You have to hush, Papa, save your strength."

She looked anxiously at Julian, but he was looking at his brother. She realized that Ian had asked Julian a silent question.

And Julian was shaking his head.

"No!" Alaina gasped, staring from Ian to Julian. "No, Julian, you must—"

"Alaina," Teddy breathed. For a moment his fingers squeezed tightly around hers. "Thank God. Love you, daughter. Love you."

"Papa, hush, please, you have to save your strength!" Alaina said, smoothing back his white hair. "Papa, I have to tell you—"

"Ian?" Teddy cried suddenly, his gaze shifting wildly about until he focused upon Ian.

"Sir, I'm here."

"Keep her safe," Teddy whispered. "Keep her safe."

"Papa—"

Once again, his fingers curled around hers. Tightly. Then his grip eased. He closed his eyes. And died.

Chapter 13

Alaina was inconsolable.

In all his life, Ian had never felt more helpless.

He tried to say the right words to her; it didn't matter, she didn't seem to hear him. He couldn't tell her that things would be all right; they would not. Teddy was dead.

Alaina hugged her father's body, at first refusing to accept that he had died, then refusing to let him go. She begged him to breathe, and she told him that he couldn't leave her.

Not even Jennifer could reason with her.

Alaina sat in the grove, Teddy's head in her lap, shaken by endless silent tears that streamed down her cheek. Ian hunched down by her side, arms around her shoulders, looking at Julian as the violent tears shook her.

"Julian?" he murmured.

"Just let her hold him—and cry for now. She has to cry, it's a part of grief, Ian."

A part of grief . . . She was going to hurt herself crying so hard, Ian thought. Her shoulders convulsed beneath his touch. He looked past her and saw that Jerome had taken charge of the green soldiers who had brought about such disaster. He had dragged in the body of the man Ian had killed in the shallows. The man's corpse, with the chains rattling, hung over his cousin's bronzed back as Jerome strode to the soldiers' boat to deliver it there.

The convicts would not be buried here.

Ian watched as his cousin spoke angrily to the soldiers, standing on the shore until the men were back in their boat and leaving Belamar.

"Alaina, Teddy is gone, you must come away," Ian urged.

And still Alaina couldn't be talked into giving up her father's body.

"Give her time," Julian suggested.

But the minutes ticked by into more than an hour, with all of them still there in the grove, watching helplessly.

"Maybe it's enough time," Julian told his brother quietly.

Ian met his brother's eyes and nodded. He had never seen anyone cry so hard, or so long. Her golden eyes were rimmed with red; her delicate features were drawn and white, her cheeks wet. She didn't seem to see or hear anything; she just kept whispering Teddy's name, cradling his head, stroking his cheek.

"Alaina, you must come away." He wrapped his arms firmly around his wife's waist, lifting her.

"No! No, no!" Alaina shrieked out.

"Take Teddy, for the love of God. Julian, Jerome—take Teddy!"

Ian had to grasp her hands to force her to release poor Teddy's blood-soaked body. She fought like a tigress to hold on to him, shrieking, sobbing, thrashing out.

The day was hot, and under the scorching sun, a body wouldn't last long.

Even drawn away from her father at last, Alaina continued to sob in such a way that Ian grew genuinely frightened for her health. Once separated from Teddy, she ceased to fight. But she continued to sob brokenly. He lifted her up and carried her into the house, following Jennifer to Alaina's room. Once there, he laid her upon her bed and sat beside her, stroking her damp hair.

"Alaina, please, please, don't cry so hard. Alaina!" He stroked her cheek, staring into her eyes.

She barely seemed to recognize him.

Or to care.

He sat with her while the shadows in the room drifted and changed. Her sobbing began to quiet.

At last, a soft rustle of skirts could be heard and Ian saw that Jennifer had come in. "Jerome and Julian need to see you on the porch," she told Ian. "I'll stay here with Alaina."

Ian nodded. "Thanks," he said, shaking his head, at a loss, staring down at Alaina. "I don't seem to be much help to her."

"Probably far more than you realize," Jennifer assured him. She squeezed his shoulder gently and he gazed up at his cousin. Her hazel eyes were red-rimmed as well, and he knew that Jen had cared about Teddy very much, too. Jen always had a quiet strength about her, learned through bitter lessons as a child, he thought. She had been one of his first teachers; he had looked to her often for advice as a boy—and as he grew up. He was very glad to have her here now.

"Thanks again, cousin," he said, standing, drawing her close in a quick, tight hug, then leaving her with Alaina.

He found Julian and Jerome with Teddy's body out on the porch.

Night had come at last. With it, cooling breezes. Julian had bathed away the blood, Ian saw as he approached his father-in-law's body, feeling the weight of sorrow encompass him. He touched Teddy's white hair, remembering the many times they had talked, the things the man had taught him, and especially the conversations they had shared since spring. How strange that they should have discussed Henry Perrine then—a good man caught in the cross-fire of others.

Teddy, it seemed, had lost everything the same way.

"I don't understand why the convict killed him," Ian mused quietly. "He would have made far better use of Teddy as a hostage."

Julian looked at his brother. Then he wiped his hands on the surgeon's apron he was wearing and turned to pick up a small bowl on the planked wood table where he had brought Teddy to dress him for burial.

Ian looked into the bowl, then at his brother.

"It's a bullet. The bullet that killed Teddy."

"That's right," Julian said.

"Look at it, Ian," Jerome advised.

Ian picked up the bullet, smashed from contact with one of Teddy's rib bones, and stared at his brother again. "Army issue," he murmured.

Julian nodded.

"Well, the convicts were deserters, naturally—"

"The dead man in the lime grove was carrying an elaborate Sharps single-shot pistol."

"So he didn't kill Teddy," Ian said. Anger seemed to wash over him in giant waves. Teddy's death had been a complete waste. Trigger-happy green recruits had killed a fine, decent man in their pursuit of a pair of deserters. He felt sick, wishing that Alaina didn't have to know.

For a moment he wondered if the truth could die right there, with him, Jerome, and Julian.

But it couldn't. Teddy was dead, and he had a right for the truth to be told. And there had to be a hearing as well; the army didn't have a right to kill the citizenry. The duty of the armed forces was to protect the citizens.

He inhaled deeply. "If Alaina is willing, we'll bury Teddy tomorrow afternoon, in his lime grove. His favorite place. What am I talking about? Alaina will have to be willing; with this heat, well . . . There's a good stack of pine boards in back; Jerome, if you don't mind, you can help me make him a coffin tomorrow. Once Teddy's buried, if the two of you would do me the favor, I want you to take the bullet down to Fort Taylor. I'm afraid to leave Alaina right now, but there's going to have to be an inquest into this tragedy."

Jerome, arms crossed over his chest, features tense, nodded. "This should never have happened."

"Never," Ian agreed. He hesitated. "I'm really worried about Alaina. Julian, have you anything we can give her?"

"Of course," Julian agreed quickly.

"She adored Teddy," Jerome said. "This must be unbearable for her. I'll finish here. There's nothing you can do for Teddy now, Julian."

Ian led the way through the back kitchen to the long hallway, through the house, and to Alaina's bedroom. Oddly, tonight was the first time he had ever seen her private sanctuary, the room that had been hers since she'd been a child. Like the rest of the house, it was as open as possible to the breezes. Mosquito netting lay over her high-canopied bed. Sleek, handsome cherrywood furniture filled the room: two wardrobes, a dresser and dressing table, and secretary. Bookshelves lined one wall; doors opened onto the porch across from them. Two wing chairs in a deep blue brocade sat before the fire. The room was feminine—*Godey's Lady's Book* fashion magazines were stacked on a trunk—but Alaina's reading material was as varied as that in her father's main library. She had histories on the various European countries, books on Washington, Jefferson, and Jackson, underwater salvage charts, descriptions of ships and sailing. She also had all manner of books by authors as varied as Molière, Shakespeare, Thoreau, and Poe. Mystery, adventure, romance, classics, and newer, more avant-garde works.

Manuals on fencing; histories of firearms. Alaina had always been intent on taking care of herself, and she wasn't a simpering little fool; she was quite capable, intelligent—even cunning. She might well have escaped her attacker this afternoon whether he had made an appearance or not. She was very, very hard to break.

Yet now she seemed shattered.

Jennifer sat on the side of the bed. Alaina was curled into a ball away from her, still in nothing more than the tatters of her white clothing. The sound of her ragged breathing, punctuated here and there by a sob, could still be heard. Jennifer helplessly rubbed her shoulders, looking at Ian and Julian, shaking her head.

"I'm going to give her something," Julian said.

Jennifer nodded, but stood up, approaching her cousins and whispering softly. "You should know . . ."

She broke off, looking at Ian.

"I should know what?" he asked.

"Ian, I hate to tell you this way. . . ."

"Jen!"

"Well, I doubt if Alaina will think of it at the moment, but you two are expecting a child."

"A child," Ian repeated, staring at Jennifer. At first the words didn't sink in. Then emotions twisted through him in a tempest. A child. He wanted children, had always known he wanted children, had expected children from marriage. Yet his marriage had been so brief, and he had been away so long. . . .

And she hadn't thought to write him. To let him know. Actually, she hadn't written to him at all. Not a single word, not an acknowledgment of his notes to her. Anger rose swiftly within him as he wondered what games she thought she was playing. Then a sob racked through her labored breathing again, and he was torn between his desire to shake her and his desperate wish that he could do something to ease so terrible a pain.

Julian whistled softly through his teeth. "A babe, Ian. You're going to be a father. Congratulations."

Ian nodded. "Indeed, a child. . . ."

It should have been a time for celebrating. Champagne, the best cigars. Laughter, claps on the shoulder. He calculated quickly. The babe would be born at the end of January; she was very nearly halfway along. And now this.

"Julian," he murmured uneasily, "this violent emotion can't be good for her, but I'm afraid of what sedatives can do. When I was at Fort Taylor years ago, an officer's wife was given a fairly large dose of laudanum for her headaches, and she had a stillborn child the following week."

"And yet she needs something, poor dear," Jen said.

"I'll be very careful in dosing her," Julian promised. He glanced at Ian. "Perhaps a brandy would be the best medicine. If she could only sleep. . . ."

Ian nodded.

Jennifer walked across the room to the secretary, where a crystal decanter of brandy sat on a silver tray. She poured a small measure into a glass, handed it to Ian, and set a hand on his arm. "We'll leave you," she murmured.

His brother, too, touched his back, then the two departed. Ian stared at his wife for a moment, holding the brandy. Her soft blond hair was in wild disarray. Her back shook. He approached the bed, touching her gently on the shoulder. She shuddered, twisting away from him.

"Alaina!" he said firmly, forcing her around.

She stared at him blankly.

"Drink this," he told her.

Her eyes flickered from him to the glass, back to him again. They filled with tears.

He sighed, set the brandy down, and reached firmly for her. She resisted. He dragged her into his arms, picked up the glass of brandy again, and brought it to her lips, forcing her to swallow. She shuddered again, then went lax in his arms.

And began to cry softly again.

He rocked with her, smoothing back her hair. They stayed together as time passed, as the night slipped away. Her clothing, after all this time, remained damp. It was the heat and humidity, Ian thought—nothing could dry. Not the seawater in her clothing; not the tears she continued to shed.

With evening, the breeze coming through was pleasant, cooling. How strange. It was a perfect night. The perfect night he had imagined on his way here. A perfect night for lying with his wife, burning in the heat of desire, cooling beneath so damp and luscious a breeze. It wasn't to be. His father-in-law was dead, and though he needed to get his wife's clothing off, it was only so that she could be warm and dry. How strange what the heart knew, and the body refused to accept. But she was in his arms, soft, shapely, and he realized with a rueful poignancy that he wanted her no matter what. He'd resisted the temptation of another woman he had loved for a long time; indeed, he'd resisted the temptation of Washington's darker underside, and he hadn't really known why himself until now. He was married. An honorable life with Risa was out of the question, and as to any other . . .

No one else could compare with the woman who was his wife. Who still held so very much of herself away from him.

Who cried now in his arms with such desolation and despair.

"Shhh, shhh, Alaina, you must stop now," he told her very gently, smoothing back the tangle of her hair again. "It will not be good for the babe."

Another bout of sobbing seized her, and she was suddenly choking out words. "I—never told him. He would have been so glad. I meant to tell him. He never knew, I didn't have a chance. I meant to tell him today . . . at lunch, but he wouldn't come in, he wouldn't come when I called. And now he is dead today. . . ."

Ian bit into his lower lip, refraining from mentioning to her that she hadn't seen fit to tell *him* about the child, either.

And that she'd had months to tell Teddy.

"He knows now, Alaina," he told her. "He knows now."

"How can you say that?" She looked up at him at last; really seeing him, her beautiful gold eyes swollen with her tears. Whatever his own anger or resentment, it would wait. He eased his knuckles over her cheek, feeling the dampness of her tears. "Because there is a heaven, and Teddy is there, and he lived his whole life as a very good man, and God has let him know that his seed will live on."

Her eyes remained searchingly on his for a long moment, then her lashes fell. She gave off a tremendous shudder, then lay shivering—but silent—in his arms.

"Alaina," he said after a moment, "you have to get this ruined clothing off. You're cold."

"This is south Florida," she said tonelessly. "It is impossible to be cold."

He laughed softly. "We both know that it's damned possible to be cold. The night breeze is very chill, and you're wet. Alaina, for the love you bore your father, cherish his grandchild and let me help you into something warmer."

At last it seemed that something he said got through to her. She was still listless, barely movable, but he managed to strip her of the remnants of the gown, petticoats, and stockings. She hadn't been wearing a corset, just a chemise, and when he at last slipped it over her head, he felt a new, sweeping range of emotions.

She remained beautiful. Yet there were subtle changes in that beauty. Her breasts were swollen, her nipples had enlarged and grown dusky. And what he hadn't seen while she was dressed was that her abdomen had swollen as well. The curve of their child already rounded her stomach, if only just slightly. Her body was still incredibly sensual, perhaps even more so, and perhaps, despite her now obvious condition, it would have been all right to fulfill the functions his own body so heartily required. Yet something more powerful tamped down hard upon him. He set her gently upon the pillows. She stared into space, unaware of him, unaware or uncaring that she lay naked and shivering. He dug through drawers until he found a soft cotton nightgown, and helped her into it. He realized his own breeches were still damp, shed them, sat back against the pillows, drawing the covers over his lap, then pulling her stiff body back against him. Again, he did nothing more than soothe her with his touch, smoothing her hair from her face in a slow, lulling motion.

She lay very still. Only occasionally did a sob rattle through her now.

"Ian?" she asked softly at last.

"I'm here."

"Why did it happen?" she demanded, in a voice so soft and broken that he might have cried aloud himself.

"I don't know, Alaina."

"Why my father? Why did those wretched men have to come here? He was so good, such a good man, he tried to feed people all the time, he tried to grow plants that cured wounds and ailments, that eased boils, that helped children, that saved lives."

"Alaina, there has never been an answer as to why, sometimes, the wretched live and the good die. He knew that there was danger here—"

"The Indians loved my father. He treated everyone like a human being, and he was scoffed at for it. Oh, God, I pray that at least he never knew that—"

She broke off suddenly.

"That what?"

Still she hesitated.

"Alaina?"

"He never had to know what Peter O'Neill told me."

Despite himself, Ian felt his arms tightened in an angry constriction. He tried very hard to control his voice.

"And what did Peter O'Neill tell you?"

"That—that no respectable man would ever marry me, because I was botanist's daughter."

Ian was silent a long time, wondering how now, in these present circumstances, he could want so badly to kill Peter O'Neill—or at least break and bloody his face.

He weighed his answer carefully.

"Peter O'Neill is an arrogant, social-climbing fool, and Teddy would have had the good sense to ignore anything he might have said."

"But I think it was true. People admired my father,

but they thought that he was an eccentric, and that he raised a young hellion.''

"He did raise a hellion.''

"Yes, but nothing bad about me was Teddy's fault.''

"Alaina, I have told you, Peter is a fool, and Teddy never did know anything about your relationship with him. Teddy saw you married, Alaina, and safe and cared for in his eyes. Marriage might not have pleased you greatly, but you can take comfort in knowing that Teddy believed it best.''

He felt her nodding against his chest. "Yes. He thought a great deal of you.'' She choked on another sob. "And at least those awful men are dead!'' she whispered vehemently.

Ian winced inwardly, wondering how she would feel when she discovered that Teddy had died from army bullets.

Tonight, however, wasn't the time to tell her.

She started to cry again.

But softly this time.

He sat in silence, still soothing her. There wasn't much he could say. He murmured her name, assured her that Teddy had died without pain, stroked her hair, her nape.

And at long last, she slept. He lay awake much, much longer, staring at the mosquito netting cast back upon the canopy of the bed.

He'd lied to her, he thought. Oh, Teddy had liked him, he knew that. But Teddy had been worried. Alaina was like the South, Teddy had said, Rebellious, independent, proud, determined. Anxious to have her way. Well, it could not always be so. She was his wife; she was going to have his child. And under these sad new circumstances, she was going to have to see life in a new way . . .

His way.

He eased himself down within the bed, cradling her gently into a softly curled position against him. A shudder swept through him. He kissed her forehead, overwhelmed suddenly by the desire to shelter and protect her.

He closed his eyes, holding her.

And still he lay awake.

*   *   *

Waking the next morning seemed to be the hardest thing Alaina had ever done.

At first she just felt the sun on her eyelids.

Then the events from the previous day came rushing in on her.

And she tried to tell herself that it had all been a nightmare, that she could awake, run out, and find her father on the porch, drinking his coffee, perhaps chewing on his pipe stem, reading his latest botanical periodicals.

But such a prayer didn't live long in her breast. A dull thudding seemed to fill her heart, her mind, her head. Teddy was dead. The pain was terrible. And it would never go away. She didn't want to move; she didn't want to get up. She wanted to go back to sleep and dream that it had never happened.

At her side, she felt Ian stirring. She kept her eyes closed as he shifted, rising very carefully, trying not to awaken her if she still slept.

She opened her eyes just barely, watching him through the shield of her lashes. She watched his naked back as he rose, observing the taut bronze ripple of muscle and flesh as he moved. He looked very good, she thought, as if from some very distant place. She felt oddly removed from herself, objective in her observations. He was long-limbed, beautifully proportioned. And oddly enough, at this of all times, she found herself jealously wondering whom he had been with since he'd left her, if other women had stroked their fingers down the length of that bronze back, if they had watched the hardness of his buttocks and the structure of his legs as he walked, moved, slipped back into breeches.

Shame filled her. Her father was dead and she was staring at her husband's naked body, wishing she could allow herself to forget and feel something other than the pain.

Breeches back on, he turned suddenly, as if he sensed her watching him. She edged herself back against the pillows, wondering if her eyes could be anything more than slits, they felt so very swollen and sore. How strange. She didn't feel like crying at all anymore. She felt empty. A void. Teddy was gone. She had taken her own life so seriously before. Now it seemed that her life didn't matter at all. Teddy had been her life, all of her life, and he was gone.

Ian walked back to her, sitting on the edge of the bed, eyes anxious as they swept over her. He touched her cheek. "How are you doing?"

She nodded. She didn't trust herself to speak. He'd been very kind, she thought. Whatever life he'd been living before he arrived here, he was certainly taking the role of her husband as gently as might be imagined now.

Naturally, she thought. Her father had just died.

And he knew now that she was expecting a child. Their child.

"I'm . . . fine," she said. But as soon as she spoke the words, she felt tears welling back into her eyes. She blinked furiously, then lowered her head, burying it into her hands. "I'm fine, really," she said, her voice muffled. She managed to sit up straight, her head high. "I will be fine," she amended softly. She looked at Ian then. "Where is my father?"

Ian hesitated. "We have to bury him this afternoon."

"We can't bury him so quickly; we need a minister."

"We have to bury him, Alaina. As soon as we can bring a minister, we'll have a service for him."

"Oh," she murmured, fighting the urge to cry again. Her father was going to rot if they didn't move quickly. He would bloat, smell horribly, attract bugs. The thought of flies buzzing around his body made her shudder.

"Will you be all right for a few minutes?" he asked. "I'll get Lilly or Jen in here."

"I—I don't need anyone," she told him.

"Alaina, it's—"

"I'm really fine. I'd like some time alone," she said.

He stared at her, blue eyes so sharp and yet so unfathomable, then he turned and left her.

Alaina sat in her bed. She had to get up, had to move, had to function.

"Miz McKenzie!"

Before she had quite managed to move, Lilly came in. Lilly, bustling about in her no-nonsense manner. "Now, missus, you stay where you are for a minute!" Behind Lilly came Delby and Jean, two of the freemen of mixed blood who had worked with her father in the groves. They were dragging in the hip tub, which had been half filled already, apparently in the kitchen. The men were huffing and puffing in a manner that would have caused Alaina to laugh at a different time.

"You wash the seawater away, you wash away a little bit of the pain. Soak in the water and forget yesterday, and the clean will bring you fresh memories, those of special times, love and laughter. Come, you must feel better."

The men nodded to her sorrowfully, sun hats in their hands, then they left the room. Alaina hesitated just a minute, but she had done nothing but cry since she had come upon her father's body; she was still encrusted in salt and seawater. The bath, only half full but with steam issuing from it, beckoned.

"A bath would be nice," she said. "Thank you, Lilly. You are very thoughtful."

Lilly smiled complacently. "Come. I'll wash your hair. Let the water heal you. You are a child of the water. Your father's child. He is not really gone, for he is within you. And the little one. Come, now. Yesterday was for pain. Today, already, you must begin the healing."

She was never going to heal, Alaina thought. But for now, hot water would feel good. She shed her nightgown, stepped into the tub, and let Lilly work her magical fingers through her hair.

The bath worked wonders. When she stepped out, dressed, and dried her hair, she regained her composure. She told herself that she wasn't going to cry again.

And she did not.

Not even when she came to the parlor and discovered that Teddy had been dressed in his finest white shirt and frock coat and laid into a hastily built coffin lined with folded cotton sheets. She sat by him, holding his cold, stiff hand. She smoothed his soft white hair, touched his beloved cheek. And she silently promised him that she would love him all her life and never, ever forget him. "Nor the islet, Papa. I promise, I'll never let Belamar go; I'll save it for your grandchild, for all the time to come."

She stayed with him throughout the long day.

They buried Teddy early that evening, right after the sun set, in the midst of the trees he loved so very much.

Jerome had sailed earlier in the day to bring his parents down to bury Teddy, and luck was with him. An old friend of his mother's, Colonel Harrington, was visiting along with an Episcopal priest who had recently taken up duty with the army in the Keys.

Teddy was buried with touching reverence. The young priest spoke from the Bible, then invited the others to talk. James McKenzie came forward first and spoke about Teddy, the man, his friend, who'd had the courage to come to a wilderness and make a home there, a friend to men and women of every color and creed. Ian stepped forward next, saying that Teddy's enthusiasm and knowledge were a light against the darkness. Jerome, Julian, Jennifer, Teela, and Lawrence Malloy came forward as well, all adding something special about Teddy. Alaina was grateful to them all. The priest had spoken from the Bible; the McKenzies and Malloys had all spoken from their hearts.

Teddy was lowered into the earth. Alaina tried to take comfort in the fact that he had lain in the parlor he had dreamed of and designed himself, in a coffin built for him by men who had honored and admired him. Now his final resting place was in the grove he had loved so dearly, and he was lowered there with the greatest tenderness.

When the coffin lay in the ground, Ian led her forward. She held a wild orchid, and let it drop down on the coffin.

Then Ian led her away.

But she heard the sound as his brother and cousin shoveled earth back into place, and the sound of dirt falling upon the pine box had a finality about it that was terrible.

Death had claimed Teddy.

Ashes to ashes; dust to dust.

Chapter 14

Alaina had sworn to herself that she would cry no more, and she did not. Sometimes it was easy. Her eyes were dry; it seemed there were no more tears.

And the night passed swiftly. She was numb, and not functioning, but it didn't matter. Ian remained at her side. Jennifer and Teela McKenzie took charge with Bella and Lilly in the kitchen, and supper was laid out. Again, the McKenzies were wonderful. They were strong in their support; united, it seemed, in all things. They talked about everything, politics, the weather—and Teddy. When the meal was finished, James took the *Windrunner* and sailed Colonel Harrington and the young priest back to their own launch where it was berthed at the McKenzies' dock. The remaining men adjourned outside with tobacco and brandy while Jennifer and Teela stayed with Alaina.

She sat in a chair, staring at the McMann coat of arms, which hung over the mantel.

Teela McKenzie came to her, taking her hand and perching upon the arm of the chair. She silently squeezed her hand.

"I'll never forget him," Alaina whispered.

"You must never forget him," Teela told her.

"I'll miss him so much."

"You will always miss him," Teela said quietly. "But you'll come to cherish all the memories, and all the time that you did have. I lost my father when I very young, and on top of that, I was cursed with a heinously cruel tyrant for a stepfather." She smiled at Alaina. "At least you will be spared that!"

"How did you bear it?"

"Not well," Teela murmured. "But because of my stepfather, I came to Florida, and met James. There is

a certain justice in the world," she said, a sparkle in
her eyes. "My stepfather came to murder the Indians. I
married a half-breed. Alaina, this is so very hard. Teddy's death was a tragic waste, and there is no way out
of that. You have to remember the good. He was a
happy man. He lived as he chose to live. He adored you.
All things do come full circle. Your father will live with
you, and beyond you. Naturally, my children have a
great deal of their father in them, but sometimes I'll see
Jerome or Brent sitting in a certain light, move in a
certain way, and I see my father again in them."

Jennifer came over with Anthony clinging to her
waist. "It is an awful agony, Alaina, and time doesn't
take away the loss, but it does soften the pain. I was
barely five when my mother and sister died." A teasing
grin played upon her face. "And then, you see, there
was this stepmother in my life—"

"Oh, dear! Are you about to call me a tyrant?"
Teela demanded.

Jennifer offered Teela a quick hug. "She was absolutely wicked!" Jennifer said with a wink. "She made all
our lives whole again."

"Thank you." Teela's eyes, a dazzling green, were
on Jennifer.

Jennifer playfully wrinkled her nose. "Then she gave
me a few little hellions as half-siblings as well!"

At last, Alaina had to smile. Anthony was reaching
out to her. She stretched her arms out in return. The
little boy crawled to her, hugging her. His face against
her neck, he curled his fingers into her hair and held
fast. She cradled him tightly. She loved holding Anthony, feeling his baby softness and sweetness. He was
so trusting, so quick to smile. He made her wonder what
it was going to be like to hold her own child, which
stirred her somewhat from her desolation. It was incredible at first to realize that another life could be created.
It was scary, hoping and praying that everything would
be all right. And it was exciting to wonder if the child
within her was a boy or a girl, and if it would be born
with hazel-gold eyes like her own, or a dark cobalt blue
like Ian's and so many other McKenzies.

But even allowing herself to wonder about the babe

now brought regret; Teddy would never hold his grandchild.

Teela rose from her seat on the edge of Alaina's chair, patting her knee. "You must always remember your father with love, but you need time away from all that has happened as well. You mustn't worry about anything here. We'll take care of Belamar for you."

Alaina shook her head. "I—I'm sure I can manage."

Teela glanced quickly at Jennifer, who grimaced uncomfortably.

"Oh," Teela murmured softly.

"No, no, please, talk to me. What's going on? Jen, Teela, please. Why will I need someone to care for the place for me?" Alaina insisted.

"You need to speak with Ian," Jen said.

"Well, I will speak with him, I assure you. But you can't begin something like that and then not follow through. It is my property and my life we're discussing."

"Except that we shouldn't have been discussing it. I'm so sorry, I'd simply assumed . . ." Teela began. "I've spoken out of line. It's Ian's place to tell you his decisions."

"His decisions? Tell me what his decisions are," Alaina demanded. "Please, Teela, Jennifer, this isn't fair in the least. Someone must tell me."

Teela still looked unhappy. "Well, naturally, after what has happened, Ian plans to take you back to Washington," she said.

Alaina stared at her blankly. "Washington?" she murmured.

Ian had decided she was going to Washington.

She couldn't go. It was that simple. She couldn't go, not when Teddy had just died, not when some small piece of him might still linger here in the air, the sun, the groves.

"I have to admit, Alaina, I'm not so sure myself that it would be good for you to stay on here alone," Jennifer advised her hastily.

"I'm not alone. You and Lawrence are here. James and Teela are just up the coast. Sydney will come home eventually, Brent will probably return here—"

Teela gently interrupted to remind her, "Ian only

agreed that you should come here to be with your father. Naturally, a man wants his wife with him."

Did he? Alaina wondered. She could still vividly recall the night before he had left her.

Yet he had gone away, without looking back. And he had stayed away a very long time. He had written; she had not. She'd been furious to realize that he'd made arrangements to leave her behind long before they'd discussed the matter—and perhaps just a little wounded to realize that despite his words and passion, he had easily taken leave of her and gone on with his own life. She wondered if she had kept the news about the baby from him hoping to hurt his pride in some small measure in return. But she hadn't really said anything to anyone, except for Jennifer. It had taken her so long to realize herself. . . .

"Personally, I think you'll like Washington," Jennifer advised. "A change of scenery will be good. Washington can be a fascinating place. People from everywhere, all the politics—and parties."

"Alaina, you must see, under these circumstances, he can't just leave you alone," Teela said.

"But . . ." Alaina began. Her voice trailed away. She didn't know what she felt. Things that had mattered so much had ceased to mean anything. It didn't matter where she was. When she wasn't feeling the dreadful hurt, she was numb.

She didn't want to think about it. She wanted to sleep and escape the pain for whatever hours she might.

And when she had her chance, she would accost Ian with what she had been told.

"I think I'm going to go to bed and get some sleep," she said, rising carefully with Anthony. "He's sleeping, Jen. I'll put him in the guest room—you and Lawrence will be comfortable enough there, won't you?"

Jennifer took the baby from Alaina, saying, "Lawrence and I can just go home—"

"No, no, please don't. Not yet. The house is empty and it—it feels good to have the house so filled with people. Teela, you and James don't mind my father's room, do you? It's probably the most comfortable."

Teela smiled. "James and I have slept out in the open often enough. Your father's room will be very comfortable. And don't you worry about anyone or anything. You do need to go on in and get some sleep. You don't want to endanger your baby."

Alaina swallowed hard and nodded. She kissed both Teela and Jennifer on the cheek and practically fled down the hall to her room. She undressed quickly, slipping into her nightgown. She lay down. She had wanted to sleep so badly; she had wanted to be alone.

Washington.

He meant to take her away. With him. And she didn't know if she wanted to fight to stay here, or if she was glad he meant to have her with him. In his world. With the woman he had intended to marry.

She closed her eyes tightly, willing thought away. It didn't work. Her thoughts merely refocused. She kept hearing the dirt fall on the coffin.

She got out of bed. The balcony door was ajar, letting in the night breeze, and she stepped outside, looking toward Teddy's grove.

Then she realized that she could hear the men talking. They were speaking quietly enough, but their voices were carrying on the breeze.

"I imagine we'll stay about a week," Ian was saying. "Time to tie up whatever needs to be done here, leave the isle functioning and everyone working here set. And I want to be here after you've been to the base at Key West, Jerome. I should really go myself; I just don't like the idea of leaving Alaina now."

"Don't worry, I can argue well with the military," Jerome assured him. "Maybe it's best that I'm going; you are still a part of the army, and you do have a quick temper."

"Does Alaina know yet?" James asked quietly.

"No," Ian told him. "I'm not sure when will be the right time to tell her."

"There's not going to be a right time to tell her," Lawrence said.

"That may be true," James said, agreeing with his son-in-law. "You could just forget what really happened, Ian. Spare her any further misery."

"I can't, Uncle James. It wouldn't be right," Ian said.

"No, it wouldn't be right. But you are the one to make that decision."

Alaina hadn't realized that she'd been walking around the porch to accost the men until she reached them, her hands clenched into fists at her sides as she came to them at last. James was by the door, Jerome and Julian were in the rockers, Lawrence Malloy was on the steps. Ian was leaning against the railing.

He was the one she needed to face.

"What are you all talking about?" she demanded hoarsely. "If there is something that has to do with my father—"

Ian was angry. He moved away from the railing, setting his hands on her shoulders. "If you'd wanted to be a part of the conversation, you should have made yourself known," he told her. She felt the power in his cobalt gaze, the heat and strength in his hands.

She felt, as well, that his anger was directed almost as much at himself as it was at her.

She pulled free from his touch, spinning around to Julian. "What is he talking about?"

Julian looked at her helplessly.

Jerome stood and walked to the far end of the porch.

"Alaina," Ian said, turning her back to face him, "your father wasn't killed by the convict. He was killed by the soldiers' fire."

Alaina inhaled sharply, stunned.

"My God, the *army* killed him!" she exclaimed.

Ian shook his head. "No, Alaina," he explained patiently, "the army didn't kill him—he was killed by reckless men."

"One and the same," she cried.

"No, you can't blame an entire army for the misdeeds of three frightened young recruits who were pitifully trained."

"They have to pay!" she insisted.

"We intend to see that there is an inquest."

"An inquest!" she exclaimed angrily. "An inquest! Those men should go up for murder."

"Alaina, you must understand. There was a situation—"

"You're excusing them!" she cried to Ian. "They killed my father, and you're excusing them!"

"Alaina, please! You're misunderstanding. You're distraught—"

"Distraught! Teddy is dead, my father is *dead*! And you don't know anything about it because your parents are both living, your great, wonderful family is all alive, and you can't begin to imagine what this feels like! You—"

"Alaina, please," Ian said, catching her shoulders, his grip firm. "I'm trying to explain the law—"

"The law!"

"We can demand an inquest; the soldiers will surely be reprimanded, perhaps dishonorably discharged. But no matter how you're hurting, you can't go about this like a foolish child—"

He was interrupted as she slapped him—a sudden, reflexive movement she immediately regretted.

But it was done.

The sound of it echoed on the porch.

Every man there was quiet. Dead still.

Including Ian. Who simply stared at her, his cheek bearing the imprint of her palm.

She wanted to apologize. She wanted to tell him that he and his entire army could go to hell.

He reached for her. Her eyes had been dead dry; she felt tears welling against her lids. She wasn't going to cry anymore. She backed away from Ian, stricken. "You'd defend the army over my father!" she charged him. She was filled with anger at Teddy's death all over again. She was afraid of Ian, afraid of what she had done, and so angry that she couldn't begin to control herself. She had backed away from him; suddenly she leaped forward again, slamming her fists furiously against his chest in a wild, desperate fury.

"Alaina!"

His arms came around her with force, drawing her to him so that she could no longer pull back to strike. "Alaina!"

His voice was softer.

She went limp against him.

"They killed my father!" she whispered.

He picked her up, striding around the porch to the balcony doors to her room. He set her down upon her bed. Sobs shook her, dry sobs. No tears came to her cyes. It had been bad before. It was anguish upon agony now. The army had been so determined to kill deserters that the men had killed her father along with the convicts.

She gasped, drawn back up as Ian came to her side, firmly taking hold of her wrists and forcing her to face him. He took a seat beside her on the bed, staring into her eyes. "What do you want, dammit, Alaina? Should I have shot the three of them on the spot? Would that have avenged Teddy's death?"

"They should be charged with murder!" she cried. "You're defending the bloody military!"

He shook his head. "If they were soldiers, if they were civilians, lawmen—it wouldn't matter. There was no intent to kill Teddy. He was caught in what happened. The men were negligent, they were at fault. And yes, they must accept blame. But you won't be able to bring a murder charge against them. They were scarcely boys sent out in the line of duty to bring back two cutthroats who had deserted and robbed and killed one man already out on Indian Key. Do you really want those three men to hang for your father? Would your father want that "

"Yes! No! I don't know, I just can't let it go, something has to be done, those men must pay in some way, maybe I do want them to hang—"

"And me along with them?" he interrupted wearily.

"Ian—"

"Why didn't you tell me, Alaina?"

"Tell you . . . about what?"

"That you were expecting a child."

That *she* was expecting a child.

"Alaina?"

"You weren't here to tell."

"I wrote letters. You could have done the same."

"You wrote letters that said "I'll be assigned in Washington indefinitely" and not much more. You knew where I was, and there was no question about it, so there seemed little sense in responding to your letters."

"Indeed, perhaps it was rather definite that you were remaining at Belamar, but I do consider the fact that you're expecting to be something you might have considered important enough to write to me."

"I didn't know at first. I wasn't certain. I would have written eventually."

"Would you? I'm not so sure. But I imagine someone would have told me when the child was born," he murmured dryly.

"I imagine—if you were somewhere to be told," she replied sweetly.

"You knew exactly where I was."

"With the army! And what can this matter now?" Alaina whispered. "My father was murdered by that same army."

"It matters, because the child has to be first in everything now," he reminded her. "Alaina, my God, I understand your grief, please believe me. I respect your pain. But you can't change what happened with your fury. You won't be able to—"

"You won't even try!" she accused him.

"Alaina, I've already written a letter to the commanding officer at Key West. The matter will be handled. But for now, you have to forget about it."

"Forget—"

"Not your father, Alaina. You should never forget your father. But you should forget what happened, because the wheels of justice can be slow. And your father died, you did not."

"Damn you, Ian, you can't possibly expect me to simply forget that my father was killed by the men who should have been protecting him. You can't—"

She broke off, gasping suddenly, her features going very pale. She'd never appeared quite so delicately beautiful and fragile before.

So vulnerable.

"What? What is it?" Ian demanded harshly, frightened. He stood, drawing her to her feet along with him, staring at her anxiously. "Alaina! What, what now?" he persisted.

"The baby . . ."

"My God, what's wrong?" He swept her back off her feet, laying her down on the bed, even as she protested.

"I'm all right, I'm all right, it's just that . . ."

"What? For the love of God, what?"

"It moved, Ian. It moved. I've felt—well, little wiggles before, but never, never something like this! So very strong."

Her palm lay over her stomach. His hand curled over hers. She shook her head. "Can you feel it? Oh, he is refusing to move again now that I am anxious for him to do so."

He could feel nothing as yet except for the tightness of her abdomen.

"Children, at any age, seldom do as their parents wish," he reminded her.

She offered him a brief smile. "Oh, God, Ian, he is alive. Definitely alive!" she murmured in wonder.

Ian stood in the shadows. He doffed his boots and shirt, then lay down upon the bed at her side, drawing her against him.

But she stiffened against his hold. "Ian, you can't defend the army!" she insisted.

He refused to reply. His hand moved low again, over the curve of her stomach. The warmth of his breath burned damply against her forehead as he held her to him.

"The babe is alive. For the love of God, Alaina, let's keep him so," he whispered vehemently.

She closed her eyes. She felt the ripple of movement— so fascinatingly, wonderfully strange!—within her again.

Life!

And how sadly ironic. Teddy's life was gone, yet new life quickened. Teddy's grandchild.

Ian's babe as well, she reminded herself. Ian's babe, and she'd not told Ian, he'd found out when he'd come here, found out from someone else.

She felt the strength of his arms around her, and wondered briefly when he would cease to pity her—and allow the anger he was surely feeling to erupt.

And now, to make matters worse, she'd slapped him in front of his family.

Why was she suffering so now over her own actions? Did they matter?

"Something must be done," she said stubbornly.

"Something will be done. Alaina, quit fighting me. Let's get some rest."

She bit her lip, but did as he bid her, feeling the warmth and power of his body as she rested against his chest, far too weary to fight any more that night. With a twinge of guilt, she realized that she was glad he had come and was with her, and she wondered what might have happened had he not arrived. She had nearly escaped the man in the water, and yet, if she hadn't been able to put enough distance between them . . .

Yet it all seemed so cruelly ironic. Had Teddy just come in when she called him, they'd have been safely at the house when the convicts and army came through. She felt a moment's fierce anger with her father for being so obsessive, then she felt guilt along with that anger, and again the frightful pain of loss.

Ian's fingers moved through her hair, stroking so very gently.

Despite her best resolve, she was shaken by another trembling, dry sob.

"Alaina . . ."

She shook her head against him, feeling the sleek warmth of his flesh, breathing in the scent of him. "I'm all right. I was just . . . Ian, you've such a huge family. You have your folks, your brother, your sister, aunt, uncle, cousins . . . Teddy was all that I had."

He was quiet, still stroking her hair.

"Well," he murmured after a moment, "you do have me."

She found herself rising up against him, trying to read his eyes in the night. "Do I, Ian? Do I have you?" she whispered softly.

"Ah, now, Mrs. McKenzie, that works two ways!" he reminded her softly. "Do I have you?"

"How could you not? I am nearly four months along with child, too pathetically shattered to have my wits about me, married to you, and therefore apparently at your whim and mercy."

"Mmm," he murmured, and she felt the strange sweep of his gaze touching her in the shadows. "I wonder, my love, if I will ever have you exactly at my mercy," he said, and the sound of his voice was dry, but not without a certain tenderness.

"It seems that you are the one who will dictate where I will live," she reminded him.

"I'm in the army; I go where I am assigned. I will not leave you alone here, Alaina."

"You could send me to Cimarron."

She felt him watching her. "I could."

"But?"

"But I've decided that you're coming with me," he said with some exasperation.

She wanted to go with him, she realized. Very much. She had spent far too much time when he was away brooding about his possible activities—and his proximity to Colonel Magee's daughter.

But she'd never, never let him know.

And so she replied to him gravely with another question. "And what if Florida secedes?"

"Florida has not seceded. We don't even know the results of the election as of yet. Besides, you are at my mercy—didn't you just say so? You'll just have to abide by whatever decisions I might make."

"Ah."

"You will do so."

"Naturally, I will—assuming you make the right decisions," she murmured.

"Trust me, they'll be right," he said firmly. He reached out, cradling her head gently, drawing her back to lie against him. "Let's get some sleep, Alaina," he said softly.

She closed her eyes. He hadn't answered her when she had asked if she really had him—he'd turned the question on her. But he was here with her, and for her, now. And in her present circumstances, she was rather at his mercy, even if it was a good thing that he didn't realize just how much.

"Ian?" she said, curling her fingers where they lay against the crisp dark hair upon his chest.

"Yes, Alaina?"

"Will you mind that I am with you?"

"Alaina, you're my wife, expecting my child. I'll certainly not mind in the least that you are with me. It was your choice to stay with your father, remember?" he asked.

"You'd intended that I should stay with my father before I asked," she told him.

"Your father had asked that I leave you," he said. "Get some sleep, Alaina."

She wanted to sleep.

Perhaps, even, to begin to heal.

Maybe she didn't want three young men hanged. Their deaths would not bring her father back to life for her. But she did want justice.

She was sorry; she couldn't just forgive . . .

And she'd never forget.

Never.

Chapter 15

The air was definitely taking on a cooler measure, especially in the early morning. And still the sun beat down through the cool, damp air, striking Ian's bare back as he worked splitting the slender pines he'd hauled from the mainland to the islet, preparing to leave the place in the care of his family.

Teddy had been buried four days. Jerome and Julian had yet to return from the base at Key West; Ian hoped they'd return soon, because he had only two weeks left before reporting back to duty. And if he was bringing Alaina with him, he'd need time to make proper travel arrangements.

The time he had spent here now seemed like a very strange waiting period. For Alaina, it was a time of deep mourning. He had offered what comfort he could, and she seemed to be coming to an acceptance of her father's death. Sometimes she was very quiet, staring into space. Occasionally she gave way to a single dry ragged sob. Then sometimes she just wanted to be left alone, and so he had decided to give her what distance he could.

The last two nights, he had found himself staying very late with his uncle and Lawrence on the porch. It was easier to come in later, when she slept already. They didn't argue, and neither did he suffer quite so keenly with the desire to remind her that he was alive, very much alive, that he had been gone a very long time, and very much wanted his wife.

He raised his arms, bringing his ax down so hard that the pine shattered rather than splitting. Swearing, he moved the wood chips to begin again.

Ian wasn't quite sure why they should be trying to hang on to Teddy's islet—except that it was Teddy's islet and Alaina's inheritance. The real estate was not worth a great deal; had they decided to sell, it was quite unlikely that they'd find a long list of buyers. The far south remained mostly a haven for wreckers, salvagers, downright pirates, Seminoles, runaways of all makes, colors, and creeds—and eccentrics like Teddy. Perhaps his McKenzie kin could be classified as eccentrics, too, despite the fact that his uncle James assured him constantly that the time would come when the south Florida beaches would be worth the gold they resembled. Perhaps, but not in his lifetime. Still, his own father had held onto his property here, clearing a few acres, leaving a great deal of heavily wooded swamp and foliage as well. Ian knew that he would never sell McKenzie property himself, and he wondered if, at heart, he wouldn't rather be a runaway himself. He'd spent so much time growing up prowling through the hammocks, mangroves, pine isles, and pure swampland. He loved the sunsets, maybe that was it. And the sunrises as well; mornings like this, when the air was cool and still, such a radiant warmth could work its way into his bare back. . . .

He paused, his foot upon a log, leaning on his ax as he saw Alaina come to the porch. She looked very pale, thinner than when he had arrived, a childlike waif. She was in a simple off-white cotton dress, wearing no petticoats, no corset—not even shoes. He reflected that in parts north they'd both be quite indecent—he was barefoot, wearing breeches, nothing more. A bead of sweat trickled over his chest. Yes, in such a remote square of primordial Eden, it would seem quite indecent to be fully dressed. And Alaina appeared entirely arresting in her natural beauty, her hair free, rippling down over her shoulders, falling past her waist, as delicate and angelic as a lost sea sprite.

She waved to him; to his surprise, she started walking toward him. Not that she'd actually been distant, but she'd never, not once, sought him out in the time that he'd been with her.

He waited, feeling the morning air cool his shoulders, as she approached him. She came down to him, perching atop his pile of pine logs, wrapping her arms around her chest, shrugging, and smiling ruefully. "The house seemed so very strange when I awoke! It's been so full . . . and this morning, there's no one in it. No one at all."

"My aunt and uncle left early; they didn't want to wake you," Ian told her.

"And Jen and the baby?"

"Packing to come stay here."

"Where is Lawrence?"

"Back to working the sea." He still leaned against his ax, watching her.

"Oh," she murmured. "Well, what about Bella, Lilly, and my father's workers?"

"Bella and Lilly are giving Jen a hand; your father's men are learning to become salvage divers."

"Oh!" Alaina said, startled. Her long lashes swept her cheeks. She looked off toward the sea then. "It's so strange, isn't it? Last week, at this time, it was still Teddy's islet, and now, Teddy is . . . gone. He loved his lime trees, and they'll just become overgrown."

"Jen has promised to take special care of the limes," Ian assured her.

Alaina watched him, and nodded after a moment. She shivered slightly. "It seems so strange, so silent," she mused, then flashed him a quick smile. "I suppose it's part of what I do love so much about Belamar. If you look in one direction, the sand and sea seem to stretch forever, into eternity. But when you turn a corner, you're into a mangrove cove, and it's as if you have a spit of the world all to yourself with just wind and warmth." She hesitated. "Ian, perhaps I should stay awhile—" she began, then broke off, frowning, as he suddenly approached her, hands on his hips. "Ian, what—"

"What is this, Alaina? Pleasant conversation, sweet smiles—because you want me to change my mind?"

"Well, I was just thinking—"

"And I was just waiting to find out how damned far you are willing to go for your own ends!" he said. He was ready to reach for her, grab her, shake her. His frustration was at an agonizing level. He tried very, very hard to remind himself that she had just lost her father.

He let out a furious oath and turned away. He walked a few steps, then began running.

The stretch of sand she had spoken about was just

before him, and a sea view that seemed to stretch forever. He ran along the sand until it curved out of sight
before striding out through the waves and then diving
into the ocean.

The water was as crisp and cool as the morning air.
It was good against his flesh, and he swam hard for a
long time, then turned onto his back and stared up at
the sun above him, narrowing his eyes. With his periph-
eral vision, he realized that she had followed him around
the islet to the cove and stood staring into the water
after him, perplexed.

He swam toward the shallows and stood.

"What?"

"Nothing. I was just worried," she murmured.

"About?"

"Your . . . behavior."

"It's a hot day, I came swimming. You should try it."

"Ian, I'm in mourning. I couldn't possibly—"

"Do you suppose Teddy might want you out in the
water?"

She flushed. "You don't understand."

"No, Alaina, you don't understand," he said quietly.
"But it doesn't matter. Not now. Go back to the house.
I'll be along shortly."

But she didn't move. She stood on the shore, tall, slim,
gold eyes caught by the sun, the roundness of her abdomen barely visible, blond hair waving sensuously with
each soft brush of the breeze, and he wondered again if
she hadn't come here to seduce him into promises to
leave her here.

He wasn't quite sure what he was doing when he began
to move; her grief was real, and he had no desire to hurt
her. But he reflected, too, that it was easy to dwell on loss,
and the only way to find life again was to live.

He walked through the water to the sand with purpose. She stared at him as if he had lost his mind. When
he was nearly upon her, eyes still locked determinedly
on hers, she cried out, "Damn you, Ian, what . . ."

She backed away, then turned as if she would run. He
caught hold of her wrist, drawing her back, swinging her
into his arms and carrying her into deeper water. She
struggled fiercely, staring into his face, apparently finding
no answers in its hardened contours. "Ian, what is the

matter with you? I said that I could not . . . You're supposed to be a gentleman, my father has just died—"

"But *you* haven't, *I* haven't, and you can't spend the rest of your life trying to make a shrine of his home and burying yourself in it."

"Ian, damn you—"

"We're going swimming!"

He dropped her into chest-high water. She sputtered to the surface, glaring at him. "I didn't want to come swimming."

"No?" he demanded. "Then we'll do something else."

She stared into his eyes incredulously, then cried out furiously, "You're an oaf! Can't you see, don't you know, don't you *feel*—"

She broke off, backing into the water with a cry, then turning around to swim, and swim hard. Despite the encumbrance of her skirt, she moved quickly, slicing through the waves with the speed and agility of a damned shark. He saw a length of long wicked limb slicing through the water, and he knew that she wore nothing more than the day dress, and she wouldn't be too heavily dragged down by its weight.

Indeed, it was all he could do to keep up with her, keep her moving, keep her in the surf. When she tried to rise or elude him, he drew her back. She surfaced, gasping, sputtering time and again. When they reached the depths and she escaped beneath him in a cloud of seaweed, he nearly lost her. She had almost reached the shore again when she turned back, triumphant . . .

Laughing.

He found his feet, and with a burst of speed, he raced for her. Alarm touched her eyes and she turned to run again. But she had taken flight too late, and he tackled her, bringing her crashing down into the surf. She shrieked, swearing wildly at him, half laughing, half angry, hands pushing against the wall of his chest.

He ignored her protests. Pressing her back into the wet sand, he kissed her. Cupped her cheek, kissed her, kissed her hard and deep until something of a little whimper echoed in her throat.

And then he felt her arms curling around him.

Felt her fingers, teasing through the hair at his nape, working into his shoulders, drawing him closer, holding him. Her mouth parting sweetly; accepting then meeting the fevered urgency of his hunger. Cool salt waves washed over their limbs. The sun beat down in a burst of searing rays. He continued to kiss her, hand stroking down over the length of her. The water molded her dress to the contours of her body, and he felt supple curve and hollow and mound beneath it. He found the wet hem of her dress, drew it up her thighs, stroking her bare legs, her buttocks, cupping her firmly and close to the muscles in his thighs, straining against the fabric of his breeches, the hardness of his sex. She still clung to him, meeting the urgency of his mouth, seeking, finding. He broke from her lips at last. Her eyes were closed beneath the rays of the sun, lashes wet with water droplets, dancing like prisms against her cheeks. Her mouth was slightly parted, lips damp, sensually swollen. At her throat, her pulse leaped and raced. . . .

He lowered his head with a hoarse and desperate groan, pressing his lips against the fragile blue vein. His hand lay upon the bodice of her dress, rounding the fullness of her breast beneath. He thumbed her nipple through the fabric, closed his mouth upon it. Her thighs parted under the gentle pressure of his weight, and his fingers stroked between them. A soft moan escaped her, creating a soft whisper at his ear; she was supple and pliant to his will, with a sinuous undulation beginning to stir within her at his touch. She was warm, wet. . . .

He tugged at the buttons to his breeches, freeing himself. Yet as he shifted with the sudden urgency of an all-but-depraved madman, he felt the very subtle rise of her abdomen.

His desire was not diminished, yet it was tempered. He shifted to his side, capturing her waist, drawing her with him so that he would not burden her with his weight. He meant to take the gravest care, yet when he would have moved with slow precision, she cried out, shifting against him, and the startlingly tight and sweet enclosure of her body upon him seemed to awaken every primal urge within him. He struggled mentally for control . . . yet surrendered the physical battle within minutes, for his wife had seldom clung to him with such a desperate passion and yearning of her own.

She moved with a wickedly graceful rhythm that

sheathed and aroused him again and again, and he fell back upon her with greater ardor, rising to a precipice, falling back, only to immediately rise again. Finally they reached a peak where he could bear no more, and a climax burst upon him with all the fiercely burning heat of the sun. And then, only then, as the convulsions ripped through his body, did he remember the tender state of his wife and draw away, alarmed at the volatility with which they had made love. He stretched by her side, eyes raking over her now with concern as he readjusted his clothing.

But she lay on the sand, seemingly quite well, the water washing over the beautiful length of her bare legs. Her eyes opened at last. She was trembling slightly, her heart pounding furiously, her breath still causing a hectic rise and fall of the lushness of her breasts. Her nipples remained hard, peaked against the fabric of her gown; yet somehow she appeared as pure and untouched as an angel.

"Oh, Ian . . ." Her eyes looked stricken.

"What?" he asked quickly. "Sweet Jesu, what? The babe, we've hurt it, have I hurt it?"

"No! No!" she protested quickly, eyes wide and golden.

He leaned over her, brushing her cheek with one hand, sheltering her body from the hot sun and chill breeze with his own. "Alaina, unless you want my heart to abruptly cease beating, please don't frighten me so."

She smiled, but it was a tremulous, fragile smile. "Ian, it can't be right to feel so vigorously alive! To—to take such pleasure . . . in life! I mean now, under these circumstances."

He was somewhat startled to realize that she felt guilty. She'd allowed herself to enjoy making love— when Teddy lay under the ground.

He sighed and spoke to her gently, his thumb brushing lightly over her cheek and lips. "Alaina, the only sin in life is not living it when we are blessed to have it, and I swear to you, Teddy would tell you the same."

"Would he?" she asked softly.

Assured of her health, he leaned back upon an elbow. "Indeed, he would. By God, though, you very nearly scared the life out of me."

She actually smiled, a swift, fleeting flash of real amusement.

And happiness.

"I'm sorry. The babe is fine, and Jennifer said that it's fine to—"

She broke off, her cheeks suddenly a flaming red.

"Ah. You've discussed the intimate details of your marriage with Jennifer?" he queried with a feigned note of indignation.

"No!" She protested, still flushing furiously.

"Yes, you have!"

"You're mistaken."

He lay against the sand, trying not to laugh, studying her face. "I see. You asked Jennifer if physical intimacy would harm the child when I was hundreds of miles away. Interesting."

"Well, I did assume you'd come back eventually—to visit your kin, if not your wife. And you, sir, were footloose and fancy free, while for me . . . I am . . ." she said, and her voice trailed away.

"Burdened with child?" he heard himself query with more than a note of anger.

She shook her head. "Would you have come back sooner, had you known?" She asked him softly.

He hesitated just slightly. Could he have come back any sooner?

His hesitation was a mistake, an answer unwittingly given her.

"Is it me—or your child—you're so determined to have with you in Washington?" she queried then.

"Alaina—"

She started to rise, ignoring him.

He would not allow her to do so. He straddled her carefully, pinning her arms to the sand, meeting her eyes.

"I will have you, and my child. You're my wife, and if you haven't noticed that I want you very much, you're quite blind. Are you seeking compliments? Reassurances? How strange, for I'm damned certain that you are well aware of your own abilities and beauty. I promised you the day of our wedding that this would be a real marriage, and nothing less. Teddy wanted you with him; at the time, I had no logical argument to keep you from him, as I assumed I'd be traveling here with great frequency. As events would have it, my assignment remained in the North! Now, let's see . . ., you wanted to remain here. You wanted to remain here so badly that you were willing to use all your charms and feminine persuasion to . . . hmm . . . what's the right word? Bribe! Right, bribe me into letting you stay here with Teddy. And if I'm not mistaken, you came out this morning with the intent—perhaps consciously, perhaps not—to, er, *bribe* me into allowing you to stay again. It's not going to happen."

She stared up at him, her eyes flashing amusement, anger, then amusement and anger once again. "Ian McKenzie—" she began, her voice deep, husky, and filled with the warning that she was about to start out on a tirade of her own.

But she did not, because Ian didn't give her a chance. The breeze brought the distant sound of voices to his ears and he leaped up with a swiftness that brought a startled cry to her lips. He reached down to help her to her feet, explaining quickly, "Someone's here."

Alaina looked at him questioningly; it was clear she hadn't heard the voices as yet.

Inwardly he was calling himself every manner of fool. He hadn't forgotten what had happened here with Teddy; he'd even brought one of the Colt six-shooters with him to the woodpile.

But he'd left his gun there when he'd run for the water, and left he and Alaina unprotected.

"Alaina, stay here until you hear me call out that it's all right," he told her.

Her eyes were very wide, but before she could reply, Julian's voice could be heard, loud and clear, calling out toward the house. "Ian? Alaina? Is anyone here?"

Ian exhaled with relief. "It's all right. It's my brother and Jerome."

"It's not exactly all right. My God, we're soaked, we're indecent, we're—"

"We're married this time, and it's not the enemy who has come upon us," he told her dryly. "Besides, you've managed to remain rather decently clad. It's only going to look like we were swimming. But we should let them know where we are."

He reached a hand out to her. She met his eyes,

smiled after a moment, and took it. He led the way back around the mangroves and toward the beachhead. Jerome was in front of the house, hands on his hips, calling out their names again, while Julian was just heading off toward the lime grove to see if they were among the trees.

"Hello—we're here!" Ian called.

Julian stopped, turned, and started back. The four met just in front of the house. Ian's brother and cousin had their formal frock coats over their arms and had opened their shirts, but they both smiled with obvious amusement at the state of dishabille in which they found Ian and Alaina. Julian's brow arched as he stepped forward, shaking Ian's hand, then loosely embracing a sodden Alaina. "Nice morning for a swim. . . ."

"Never mind," Ian told him, shrugging to Jerome and asking, "What happened?"

"Should we go in?" Julian suggested.

"Alaina is shivering," Jerome advised.

"Am I?" she murmured. "It's not really cold at all anymore."

It wasn't cold; the sun was now high in the sky, its rays growing hotter. "Yes, let's go in the house," said Ian. "There's coffee on the stove, I believe. Alaina, you need to get into something dry." He set his hand upon the small of her back, propelling her up the porch steps, into the house, and toward her bedroom.

He lifted a hand, indicating the back porch to Julian and Jerome, and then followed the two of them out. Jerome perched upon the railing, Julian in one of the rockers. Ian angled himself upon the railing, waiting to hear what had happened.

"There will be a disciplinary action," Jerome said.

"What will the action be?"

Jerome shook his head. "I don't know."

Julian cleared his throat. "We tried to wait around and see, and naturally, under the circumstances, I threw Father's name at them, your name, and every other name that occurred to me—including that of General Winfield Scott. I inferred a great friendship, so I hope you do know the man, Ian. But it didn't matter. We were still informed—politely and properly—that whatever was done would take time because it was such a delicate situation. The whole trip was hell, Ian—but you know damned well Jerome went in with the temperament to take a few scalps if that would help, so believe me, aggressive pressure was applied. So there's a possibility that the men may face a court-martial. A possibility. When decisions are made, they'll let us know. Oh—and of course they send their deepest sympathy on the death of Teddy McMann to you and his daughter. I have a letter from a Colonel Talbot for the two of you."

Ian rubbed his chin, watching his brother and Jerome. He'd never known anyone capable of being as fierce, determined, and stoic in his resolve as his cousin Jerome. No one walked over any of the McKenzies, but still Ian should have gone himself. He was a military man, and it was a military situation.

"So—there are infinite possibilities!" he heard Alaina say sarcastically, and he looked down the length of the porch, startled to see that she had chosen not to change after all, but had gone through the house to her bedroom just to slip silently out to the porch to hear their conversation. He should have expected as much from her.

Her gold eyes were on Jerome. "They're not going to do anything, are they? They just put you off with a lot of excuses."

Jerome sighed, lifting his hands in the air somewhat helplessly, and looking to Ian for a lead.

"Alaina, I warned you that there was clearly no intent to harm your father—"

"And I didn't expect them to be hanged, and I don't think I wanted anything so drastic," she said angrily. "But I did expect more than a sympathy letter!"

"Alaina, there will be disciplinary action. Were you really listening? Julian said that there will be disciplinary action."

"Right. They *may* face a court-martial. Oh, Ian! That was a lot of talk just to get the McKenzies off their backs! Nothing will be done; we'll be put off and put off until the worms have eaten my father to the bone, and that will be that!"

"Alaina, this is going to be a difficult time for the military, and yes, I imagine, under the circumstances, matters that aren't entirely critical will be put off. With all the fury going on around the country—"

"What fury?" Ian interrupted, frowning.

Jerome and Julian looked at one another, then back at Ian and Alaina.

"You haven't heard?"

"Heard what? I don't know what you're talking about."

Jerome exhaled on a long breath. "Well, then, you can't realize what an uproar is taking place." Jerome stared at his cousin. "Lincoln was elected to the presidency."

Alaina gasped. Her fingers wound tensely into the palms of her hands as she walked across the porch to Ian.

"Lincoln—president! Ian! You can resign from that detestable army right now!"

"What?" Ian demanded.

"You can resign—"

"Are you trying to punish me—or the army?" he inquired, feeling his temper begin to burn. He'd known it was coming. Somehow, he'd known it was coming. He'd made a point of getting leave now, so that he'd be in his home state for the elections.

Saner heads would still prevail! he told himself.

But they would not. The South was outraged, and he could imagine that even as they spoke, most of the cotton states were calling for special legislative sessions.

To discuss secession.

"Ian, I don't understand why you're being so stubborn and angry," Alaina insisted. Her cheeks were flushed, but her flesh remained very pale. Her eyes looked like true gold fire. She had twisted her hair into a knot at her nape, cleanly displaying the elegance of her classical features. Her damp gown hugged her figure, and it reoccurred to him that—despite the slight bulge of her abdomen, or perhaps more visible because of it—she had grown thinner in the last few days.

"Ian," she persisted, "what I'm saying makes perfect sense. Florida will form her own armed forces—"

"Oh, really?" he interrupted sharply. "Since when are you running the state government? Excuse me, Jerome, have I missed something? Has Florida seceded from the Union as yet?"

Jerome shrugged. They both knew that Florida was most likely to secede and that the state would begin making preliminary preparations for a split from the Union.

But it hadn't happened yet. And it might take time. Ian might be one of the few people in the South not surprised that Lincoln had been elected, but just the same, he had dreaded this happening.

And it was bad enough without Alaina harping at him.

"*Have* we seceded?" he demanded again.

"No, not that I know about," Jerome said. "The election results are really just out. This has all just happened, of course."

"But Lincoln has been elected!" Alaina cried. "And Ian—"

"If and when Florida actually secedes, Alaina, I will make my own decisions regarding my military commission."

"Ian! You must resign!" she informed him, as if there was no question regarding the matter.

His head was pounding. He had expected it; he had feared it. And it had come.

He stood, suddenly furious. He walked directly to where she stood, lifting her chin so that she was forced to look into his eyes. "Do you know, my dear, that I have really tried in every way to be as courteous to your feelings as I was able? Pay heed to me now, Alaina. I will be damned if I will ever allow you to tell me what I must or must not do!"

She stared at him, her face growing even more pale, except for the crimson flush that flowered at her cheeks.

"Indeed!" she whispered. "Then you pay heed to *my* words. You must—understand me—you must go straight to hell!" she cried out, and with a wild fury, she tried to push past him.

"Oh, no, Alaina!" He informed her.

He gripped her shoulders and dragged her back around in front of him.

"Alaina, dammit—" He broke off suddenly, feeling the amount of heat that emanated from her. Her shoulders were on fire. Naturally, she was flushed with anger, but . . .

She opened her mouth as if she would argue with him again. Her eyes were dazzling, seeming far too dilated, too dark. "Ian, Ian .. damn you!" she cried. But then the tone of her voice changed, touched with confusion and alarm. "Ian, Ian, please . . ."

But she didn't finish. Her lashes suddenly closed over her eyes.

And she collapsed into his arms, dead weight.

Chapter 16

She was sicker than she had been in her entire life, and there were times when she knew it.

At other times, she didn't know anything at all; life was nothing more than a strange series of visions, some real, some hallucinatory.

She saw her father. They were someplace where the background was a soft whitish blue, as pale and gentle as Teddy's eyes. She kept asking him how he felt; she was very worried. She vaguely knew that he was dead, and she wondered that he could seem so well and at peace. "I've never felt better, daughter," he told her indignantly. "And pay attention now, Alaina, see what I've grown from that little seedling I showed you?"

Then Teddy was gone. Soldiers marched across a field of white, in line, in a row, growing in number, one after another. They marched and marched. A sergeant called out "Ready, aim, fire!" and a thousand guns seemed to explode in a riot of gunfire. . . .

She was hot; she was cold. She saw Ian's face, bronzed, gaunt, eyes fierce and blue and grave; she felt his touch, heard his voice. "Drink this, you must drink this."

"No . . ."

She couldn't drink, couldn't swallow.

He made her drink.

She was hot. So hot. She didn't want to be touched. He kept putting wet towels on her. She couldn't bear them touching her, and she cried out and tried to fight, pushing the towels aside. He put them back and barked her name sharply, and she met his eyes again, so fierce upon her own. "Leave them be; you must cool down."

Ian was gone, Jennifer was there. Jennifer, who smiled, and was so gentle. Alaina closed her eyes, and

Jen was gone, and Ian was back. Julian came, Jerome, and when she opened her eyes once again, she found that Teela was there, and hers was the most gentle and practiced touch of all.

Alaina walked in clouds of lime trees with Teddy once again. It seemed they walked through hills, and she knew, of course, that there were no hills on Belamar Isle.

"Drink," she heard, again and again.

A dozen voices.

Ian's voice.

And then, in the lime field, Teddy was urging her to drink as well, and she did so.

The soldiers marched . . .

But finally the sounds of their footsteps faded, and they began to blur and meld to black.

She was dying, she thought.

"Alaina!"

His voice, so sharp. His eyes, so blue, piercing into her. He forced liquid between her lips, forced her to drink again.

By the third night of Alaina's illness, Ian was in a haggard and dangerous state himself. When Julian told him at last that her fever had broken, he was exhausted.

He'd stayed at her bedside through most of the long hours when she tossed with fever, leaving her only briefly to the care of the family he trusted so much. When his aunt arrived, he slept a few hours, leaving Teela and Jennifer to continually douse her with cool well water to keep her fever from getting too high.

"She's young and strong, and she'll fight this instinctively," Julian assured him all along. "We've just got to help her; we have to keep her fever down."

There were times, naturally, when Ian did wonder about the child she carried. And his brother was honest when Ian asked him if the babe could possibly survive. "All things are possible. Babies have survived through their mothers' incredibly severe illnesses. Alaina is fairly far along now, which is good. But I don't know. It's still to be seen."

When the fever broke at last, and Julian assured Ian that Alaina had fallen into a peaceful sleep, he came out to the parlor, grateful, numb. Weary and unshaven, he sat before the fire, damning himself for her illness. She had been too fragile with Teddy's death. He had dragged her into the water, he'd let her get cold, he'd made love to her too soon. Pure terror had tugged at his heart when he thought she had slipped from life, lying still as a marble angel, tangled sun-blond hair spread about her delicate features like a radiant halo. She had come to mean more to him than he wanted to imagine; in his days here, he'd discovered far more about her as a person, though he'd known almost instantly that he craved holding her, having her, like a man craved air to breathe, water to drink.

If it killed him, he silently swore, he was going to keep his distance from her. Until she had come to peace with Teddy's death; until she had healed herself.

Until their child was born.

"You know, Ian, however you sit there blaming yourself, you didn't cause this!"

Startled, he looked around. Julian had come out of Alaina's room.

"She's—"

"She's doing well enough. But quit blaming yourself. God, Ian, if any of us could actually understand what causes these awful fevers, we could revolutionize medicine. Many doctors believe that fevers are carried on the air, and that the only defense against them is to cease breathing. Naturally, that's a joke, since even we in medicine are aware that man must breathe to live."

Ian shook his head with a weary sigh. "If I didn't make her ill, I certainly contributed to the low spirits that made her so very vulnerable! There's the matter of Teddy's death, and now . . ."

"Now, Lincoln."

"Yes."

"And you're disturbed because you're not ready to resign your commission."

Ian shook his head. "The most hot-blooded of my friends, fellow officers, and acquaintances are all treading carefully here. Virginia will lead the South, I think, and the talk in Virginia now is for moderation. But Florida—Florida hasn't a moderate rock within the state! You know that as well as I do. When we left St. Augustine, your friend John, the state senator, was saying that some men were quietly going about beginning the preparations for a special legislative session to vote on the matter of secession just *in case* the elections came out badly!" He shook his head uneasily. "I keep telling myself that I don't really know what I'll do if Florida secedes. And yet, I can't help it, Julian, I believe it is wrong for one person to own another, no matter what their differences in color, race or creed. No man should have the power to sell another's wife—or child. And I do believe in the sanctity of the Union."

"Your beliefs did not make your wife ill."

"Mmm, but they won't help her recover, either."

"I've yet to see either of you cowed by any argument," Julian pointed out. "Trust me, she'll be ready to fight you again quite soon."

Maybe. Ian rose, anguished by what he was about to say, yet certain that Alaina needed some time without him. "Julian, can you stay awhile longer?"

"Certainly. But—"

"I have to report back to duty, and Alaina can't possibly accompany me now. I thought that perhaps in a month or so you and Jerome could bring her as far as St. Augustine, put her and Lilly aboard a steamer, and send her to Charleston. I'll meet her there and we can spend a day with Brent and Sydney. A few days' leave for me down to Charleston is far easier than getting extra time here. . . . I don't want to take any more chances with her life, or that of the child."

"As you wish. I'll do my best."

"Thank you, Julian. You're quite an exceptional brother."

Julian grinned wickedly. "Indeed I am. Thankfully, you didn't beat me too mercilessly as a child."

"I never beat you at all," Ian protested.

"Well, there was that time you whacked me over the head in the yard with the oak branch."

"You were two, I was three, and you had just bitten a chunk out of my calf! I still have the scar."

Julian grimaced. "Well, all right, perhaps that's a good point." His grew serious once more. "When will you leave?"

"Tomorrow morning. Jerome plans on sailing his

mother home; I'll get a chance to say good-bye to her and Uncle James, since I don't know when I'll be back again."

"Do you intend to at least say good-bye to your wife? By morning she should awake with a clear mind, rested at last."

Ian nodded gravely. "Indeed, yes. I intend to say good-bye."

Alaina came awake very slowly, aware of a bird singing from somewhere outside the house. She opened her eyes. To her amazement, they were no longer heavy, nor was it painful to open them. She blinked only briefly at the light that filtered in through her windows, spilling over the soft white cotton sheets on her bed and the embroidered gown she wore. She shifted her vision and saw a dark head bowed over a St. Augustine newspaper.

"Ian?" she mouthed.

"Alaina!"

The newspaper went down; the man stood. The eyes were the same—but he wasn't Ian.

"Julian?" she murmured.

He sat by the bed, immediately feeling her forehead, her cheeks, her hands. He smiled with obvious pleasure. "Not a speck of fever left! Thank God my brother decided to trust me. . . . You have come around wonderfully."

"What happened?" she asked him.

"You had an influenza. Exactly what it was, I haven't the faintest idea—but please don't go repeating that! What caused it, I cannot say; what aggravated it was your state of desolation and the fact that you hadn't eaten much at all in the days preceding the onslaught of your illness. Then there was the babe. . . ."

The way he said the words sent her heart into a quiver. She could scarcely believe the wave of anguish and regret that washed over her and she clutched his hand quickly. "Oh, dear God, I've killed it!"

He shook his head, squeezing her hand in turn. "No, no, Alaina. To the very best of my knowledge, your babe is coming along just fine. I felt movement just this morning."

"You felt it . . . moving?"

He nodded. "Yes, of course. You're halfway through now, Alaina. The young lad—or lass—is becoming quite strong. It's fascinating, really, what we're able to learn in medical school through deceased fetuses. Such a pity they are often in such abundance—"

He broke off, suddenly aware of the thoughtless direction of his chatter. "Sorry, Alaina, sorry. Naturally, of course, you were our primary concern. And now that you are beginning to look me directly in the eyes and make sense, I can tell you quite frankly that right up until last night, we had our doubts about your future! But you are a fighter, little sister-in-law. I'm quite grateful."

"Apparently, Julian, I must be very grateful to you—and your family."

"Ah, but it's your family as well, isn't it?" he queried her gently.

"A borrowed family," she agreed.

"Not borrowed, for you are never to give us back," he teased, smiling with good humor. "And you are carrying my blood relation inside you, Alaina, so therefore, at this moment—we are blood relations ourselves. How's that?"

"Probably far kinder than I deserve, Julian," she told him, trying to rise against the pillows. She was out of pain, but she felt she had no more strength than a newborn kitten. Julian saw her intent, though, and quickly rose to help her set up the pillow so that she could lean against it.

"Julian, how long have I been sick?" she asked him.

"Three days. Long enough to scare us all heartily."

"Did anyone else become sick? Is . . . is Ian well?"

"Fit as a fiddle," Julian assured her. He stood, pouring a glass of water from her bedside table. "Sip this slowly; we'll work on Lilly's island soup next—that will certainly give you your strength back." She swallowed the cool, clear water and he took the glass back.

When Jen came in with a basin and washcloth and a hairbrush, Julian left the two women alone. Jen sat on the edge of the bed, eyes alight as she bent down to kiss Alaina on the forehead. "Good as new! You look wonderful."

"Jen . . . I can't possibly look good."

"Ah, but you can. Alive is good," Jen advised her gravely.

Alaina smiled. It did feel good to be alive and so well cared for. "Thank you so much—for everything," she told Jen. "You were here through everything. You're a wonderful nurse."

"I had a great deal of help. I have a brother and a cousin who are doctors, and I grew up with Teela, who is all but an herb-goddess; however, she claims that she learned all about the properties of plants from a good friend during the Seminole War. I'm still quite certain myself that half of what she accomplishes is magic from her soul."

"There is magic in her soul—and in yours," Alaina told her.

Jennifer gave her a fierce, quick hug. "Don't underestimate yourself, Alaina. You are so very much Teddy's daughter. And there was never a kinder man."

There was a quick tap on the door, then it opened. Alaina was surprised to feel the way her heart quickened when she saw that it was Ian.

He was dressed in uniform. The blue of the United States army. The hesitant smile she had wanted to offer him failed. She remembered the rows and rows of soldiers in blue, coming toward her, rifles aimed.

Like the men who had killed Teddy.

She lowered her eyes quickly, trying to be rational herself before arguing with Ian. The entire army had not killed Teddy.

But Lincoln *had* been elected. Unless that was part of the terror of her nightmare as well.

"Alaina," he murmured, coming to the bed and sitting on the opposite side from Jennifer. He seemed exceptionally striking to her that morning, so tall in the uniform and frock coat he wore so well, features cleanly shaven, very strong, dark hair still slightly damp as if he had just bathed and dressed in the last hour. He smelled pleasantly of soap, and of leather and good polish. His boots were shiny, his shoulders appeared incredibly broad, and she felt a strange tremor within her, a strange wanting . . .

And odd sense of jealousy, and of . . . possessiveness.

His eyes were sharp, searching, sweeping over Alaina,

looking to Jennifer for confirmation that his wife was as well as she looked.

"She's indeed out of the woods!" Jen said pleasantly, rising. "Well, I'll leave you two." She quietly walked out, closing the door behind her.

Ian reached out, touching Alaina's cheek. There was something very gentle in the gesture—and something that made her uneasy as well.

"Ian."

"You're back with us," he said quietly.

She nodded, not trusting herself to speak for a minute. He had been with her constantly, she knew.

A tyrant. Making her take the steps to live.

"But now you're leaving," she whispered.

"I know that you want me to resign, but I'd rather not face a court-martial myself. When you're in the military and instructed to report to duty by a certain date, you do so. I have to go back, Alaina, and you won't be able to travel for some time; you have to regain your strength."

She willed herself to look at him and do nothing more than nod, even though she hadn't felt quite so bereft since she had first realized that her father had died. They had married, become lovers, and were expecting a child, and she knew that she would always be inextricably entwined in his life.

But he had removed himself somehow this morning. He had taken a step back and erected a wall between them, and she wondered if he had grown weary of her. Or if he pitied her, and simply determined that she had become so fragile that he didn't dare touch her.

She looked down at her hands. "I'm sorry I've been such a nuisance to Julian. He has a medical practice in St. Augustine."

"Julian is glad enough for any opportunity to come south. He likes fishing off the coast, and he is exceptionally fond of hot water for swimming," Ian said, his fingers closing over hers. "In another few weeks, you'll be fine to travel. He'll bring you to St. Augustine at the beginning of December and send you on a steamer northward."

"Ah. Northward to . . ."

"I intend to meet you in Charleston."

She felt almost ridiculously relieved. He hadn't
planned on abandoning her entirely.

"Well," she murmured, determined that she wasn't
going to cling, "it will be wonderful to visit Charleston.
And see Sydney."

"I thought you'd enjoy that."

"I do love Charleston; it was one of my father's favorite cities. I've never been to Washington, though I'm not
so sure this will be the time to visit."

Ian was quiet a moment. "It will be some time before
Lincoln is actually sworn in, Alaina. You'll reach the
Capital while Buchanan is still in the White House."

"Does that mean we'll be ready to leave by the time
Lincoln is sworn in?" she asked softly.

"It means we'll be in the city during a time of great
upheaval—and excitement, I imagine."

He rose, and she was alarmed, wishing that she had
never spoken. She hadn't wanted to fight.

But if she didn't fight . . .

She lowered her lashes quickly. Ian just didn't want
to see the truth. His state was going to leave the Union.
When his state actually did so, Ian would accept the
fact that there was going to be a split. And he would
resign then.

He was going to leave her. And she didn't want him
remembering her as harping like a shrew. She forced
herself to smile. She stroked the back of his hand with
her fingertips, eyes downcast. "Then I will be anxious to
reach D.C., except that . . ."

"Yes?" he inquired.

"Ian, our child could be born then . . . in the North."

"It will be born in the North."

She shuddered slightly, and he laughed. "If two cats
were to reproduce on the moon, my love, they'd still be
cats. Our child will be a Floridian, no matter what."

"Are you a Floridian no matter what, Ian?"

"Yes, my love, no matter what—and no matter what
anyone thinks," he added quietly. The last words
seemed ominous.

She didn't want to argue! she reminded herself. And
still, she would have challenged him, except . . .

"Ian!"

"What?"

"Now, Ian, now. Oh, Ian, Julian is right! He—or she—is alive and . . . strong! Feel, Ian, feel!"

She drew his hand against her. To her delight, the child within her quite agreeably gave another mighty kick.

Ian held very still, his hand upon her. Then he jerked away quite suddenly, almost as if the babe's movement had burned him.

"Ian—"

"Indeed," he said huskily, "He—or she—lives."

Tears of relief and happiness stung her eyes. She blinked quickly and furiously, hiding them.

Ian leaned over her then. She felt his warmth, breathed his scent, wished that he would hold her.

He kissed her chastely on the forehead. Then he straightened, touching the brim of his plumed slouch hat so that its angle shadowed his eyes. "Take care of our child—and yourself. Take care, my love," he said.

And before she could reply, he turned and left her.

Chapter 17

"**I**an!"

Through what seemed like a solid mass of humanity, Ian saw his cousin Brent. Thankfully, Brent was tall enough to stand above most of the chattering men and women who milled about. Ian waved in return to his cousin's call and moved through the crowded public room of the Thayer Inn, an establishment directly across from the Charleston battery. He wondered now if he hadn't been a fool to plan on meeting his cousins and his wife here. He'd never seen the city so crowded. The hotel itself was very old and most customarily a reserved place frequented by the same families throughout the generations. Today, it might as well have been the Fourth of July.

He made his way to Brent at last, who embraced him quickly and drew away, smiling wryly. "It's madness here, isn't it? Come on over, I've maneuvered a space at the bar—and we've already secured our rooms. The minute Sydney heard that they were bringing the legislative council meeting here from Columbia because of the fever there, she saw to our rooms. Naturally, we could have gone to the plantation, but with the excitement in the city, it seemed that we should stay. Did you hear what's happening?"

Of course Ian had heard. South Carolina's legislature had called a convention in the state's capitol to form an ordinance of secession; smallpox, however, had caused the members to move the convention to Charleston.

The first meeting had taken place at Institute Hall on December 17. Now the Convention had been hammering out details for several days. Ian had learned all this on his way to Charleston. It was far too late to stop Alaina from coming here, and so there was nothing to do except hope that her ship had arrived without incident.

Not that he sensed any hostility at the moment. The mood in the streets was jubilant. People felt as if they were part of a second Declaration of Independence—which, in essence, they were. And it didn't matter in the least that so many men were wearing the uniform of the United States army. Everyone waited. Timing was everything.

December 1860 had been a time when many had desperately sought compromise. The Congress of the United States had worked feverishly. The Virginia Legislature had called an unofficial "Peace Convention."

Ian could have told them all, however, that very little would happen in Washington now. President Buchanan was a good enough man, but a man sitting on a fence. Biding his time until Lincoln should take over the presidency.

"I just heard on the docks that they're expecting the convention to break today," Ian said. "It seems there will be a meeting at Institute Hall with state and city officials."

"And the bands will all play!" Brent agreed with a touch of sarcasm. Brent was against secession, Ian knew, but he was a Southerner, with deep convictions. Still, he hadn't resided in South Carolina long enough for it to be his state. What Florida did in the next months would matter to his cousin, but no member of James McKenzie's immediate family was ever going to wear the uniform of the United States army. At best, most of Ian's own family would remain neutral.

"A wonderful place to have arranged to meet my wife," Ian said unhappily as he and Brent wedged their way to the old oak bar. Brent had apparently become well acquainted with the bartender in the last months, because he did nothing more than lift a hand and shots of whiskey were set before the men.

"Actually," Brent said with a trace of amusement, "she's enjoying it tremendously."

"She's here?" Ian said startled. "But her ship wasn't due in until tomorrow afternoon!"

"It seems they had favorable winds," Brent said, lifting his whiskey. "Cheers. Alaina disembarked last eve-

ning; but don't worry. Sydney and I were there when
the ship came in, and your wife wasn't alone anyway.
She was accompanied by Lilly and and a man of mixed
blood called Samson."

"One of Teddy's laborers," Ian murmured, glad that
Samson had traveled with his wife. Julian's doing, no
doubt. Samson's Indian blood was strong, but his mother
had been a mulatto slave in St. Augustine. Teddy had
purchased both mother and son years ago and freed
them, and the family had worked for Teddy on Belamar
ever since. "So where is Alaina now?"

Brent grinned, looking past Ian. "Coming down the
stairs with Sydney right now."

Ian turned toward the elegant stairway that led to the
second floor of the establishment and the guest rooms
there. Sydney was first, very lovely and quite proper in
a deep lavender taffeta day dress, laced at the bodice in
both black and white trim. She saw Ian, smiled, waved,
and turned to Alaina, who was just behind her.

Alaina remained in mourning, wearing black from
head to toe. Against the severe ebony of her gown and
the black velvet of the cloak she wore atop it, her hair—
swept into a chignon with only a few tendrils artfully
escaping—seemed to burn like the rays of the sun, a true
gold. Her face held a trace of new maturity that somehow added to her extraordinary beauty. Though she was
pale, she was obviously well, smiling in response to a
passerby on the stairs, then turning in Ian's direction.

Her eyes met his, as gold as her hair, glittering with
pleasure and warmth. Her lips curled into a slow, only
slightly hesitant smile, and she held very still, watching
him.

The buzz of revelry in the room seemed to fade, and
he made his way quickly through the throng of people
to reach the foot of the stairs. He offered Sydney a quick
smile, kissing her cheek, then reached for Alaina's hand,
drawing her into the fold of his embrace.

It was only then he realized that despite the slender
appearance of her face, she was . . .

Quite simply huge.

He frowned, instinctively worried that such a small
woman should be carrying such a large child. He quickly
readjusted his stance, slipping an arm about her shoul-

ders and kissing her cheek almost as chastely as he done
with his cousin. Crowds seemed to press around them,
even as he led the two women back toward Brent's position at the bar. "I'm sorry!" he shouted to Alaina. "Had
I known of all this mayhem, I'd never have had you
come here!"

She turned slightly in his arms, face alight with laughter. "Ian, I'm fine. It's fascinating! There's so much going
on! South Carolina's secession is going to be announced
today, there are going be bands playing, parades all over
the city—fireworks. Ian, it's quite amazing to be here
for this!"

He was irritated with her enthusiasm. He didn't know
why no one was worried about the loss of what had been
the great experiment of the United States. And in truth,
he wasn't at all certain she should be up and about in
her condition.

"Amazing," he agreed dryly, studying her.

She had made enormous progress the last two months.
Though she was pale, she did have a touch of color to
her cheeks. Her lips were as deep as wine, her vibrance
gave her an enchanting appeal. She seemed truly pleased
to see him—unless she was simply so pleased to be here
to see the states begin to secede.

"Ah, ladies!" Brent said as they reached his side.
"Now that you have maneuvered all that . . . perhaps
we should go back up. We've a balcony room overlook-
ing the streets. We'll see most of the festivities from
there."

"Quite right," Ian heard himself saying firmly. "Brent,
as a physician, advise Alaina that this mob is not good
for her condition."

Brent ever so slightly arched a brow; in his practice,
he'd noted that women who went best to childbirth were
those who had kept active up to their time of confinement. But he went along with Ian's ploy.

"Sorry, ladies, but Ian is correct. Shall we go on up?"

On their way back through the crowd, Ian was startled
to hear his name called. He turned to see Andrew
Tweed, his great-uncle. Andrew was nearly seventy,
straight as a rod, with a headful of rippling white hair.
Ian gladly clasped the man's hand, greeting him warmly.

"Ian, my good fellow, what are you doing here?" Andrew demanded. "I had last heard that you were working in Washington with the Army Corps of Engineers."

"Something like that. I was actually with the cartographers for quite some time. I'm here to meet my wife." He drew Alaina before him and introduced them.

"Wife and child, eh?" Andrew teased, greeting Alaina with a polite brushing of her hand with his lips. "Brent! Good Dr. Brent! You neglected to tell me your cousin was on the way," Andrew accused, looking past Ian.

"Andrew, I've scarce had a moment these days, what with everyone fearing the smallpox."

"Ah, of course. Well, people will be heedless of an outbreak in Columbia today. All hell has broken out on the waterfront. How intriguing it all is! As of today, it seems I will no longer be an 'American.' I'm not quite sure just what I shall be."

"A Rebel!" cried a slim, dandified young drunk from the bar. "A Rebel. Watch it, ah, there's a Yank in the crowd. Just waiting for word to damn the old eagle and take flight with the new South, eh, Major?"

Ian ignored the drunk. "We're moving upstairs with Alaina and Sydney, sir," he said to Andrew. "Please, come up if you've a mind to do so."

"What's the matter, *Yank*?" the stranger called out, irritated at Ian's lack of response. He pushed his way between Andrew Tweed and Ian. "You're in a free state here, so that uniform means nothing, less than nothing. You're wearing dirt!"

He spat, aiming for Ian but hitting the floor between them. He took an angry step toward Ian then, his arm swinging.

Ian easily avoided him, and to his own dismay, he acted before thinking. He punched the man with a rapid-fire right hook, and the drunk went down on the ground. People were milling everywhere then, hooting in derision to the fallen man, hailing Ian. "It's Major McKenzie, out of Florida! A Rebel soon enough, eh, Major?" came another cry.

To Ian's surprise and fury, Alaina determined to answer for him. "When Florida takes action, so will my husband!" she cried out, laughing.

He could have throttled her then and there, despite her enchanting enthusiasm and beauty—and profoundly rounded abdomen—and the light in her gold eyes as they touched his.

"Uncle, forgive me," he said simply, stepping over the drunk, securing Alaina's elbow, and propelling her up the steps.

Alaina knew that Ian was angry, and yet she felt exasperated and at a loss.

She'd been so glad to see him. So anxious at home, gaining strength each day, sometimes so eager to see him she could scarcely bear it, and at times, so worried as to what he might be doing that she grew furious that she could allow herself such foolishness. But she had fallen in love with him; and she couldn't help but be plagued by jealousy. And even today, her thoughts when she had dressed had spiraled in a mad fashion, for she loved the child it seemed that she had carried now almost forever—loved it deeply, sight unseen. The baby's movements were as familiar to her as her own. Yet this morning, she wished fleetingly that the babe might be born.

Because she did resemble a house, and because . . .

She wanted Ian to want her.

All that had brought about their marriage failed to matter now, and all that did matter was that she loved him. She loved him not just for holding her, but for holding his own temper when she was hurt. She loved him for his manner with Teddy, for his pride, for his dogged determination, for his sense of honor. More. She loved the sight of him, the feel of his hands, the way he moved, the way his eyes burned when he was angry or filled with desire.

He was simply entirely unreasonable, and it was his fault, not hers today. She was disappointed not to stand in the midst of things as Institute Hall was crammed to the gills at nightfall and South Carolina declared her secession from the United States of America. They did see and hear the shouting and mayhem in the streets after the proclamation was made, from the vantage point of the wrought-iron balcony that opened from the parlor of their suite. Young men from a military academy paraded to the blaring music of an able band; dancers and acrobats played in the streets. Fireworks were set off, filling the night sky. The atmosphere was electric.

Ian sat by her, watching the festivities, commenting—mostly to Brent—on the music they heard, on the youth of the men marching, on the beauty of the fireworks. He was perfectly courteous through the evening, but subdued, his cobalt eyes very dark despite the light tenor of his words, and Alaina was afraid that something was simmering in him that would eventually explode.

She refused to let his mood dampen her own evening. She watched wide-eyed, laughing and cheering with Sydney, enjoying the music and the spectacle.

It was long, long after midnight when the festivities at last died down.

And it was very late when she and Ian retired, saying good night to Sydney and Brent.

She felt awkward disrobing, and wished that she hadn't excused Lilly to go about and enjoy the city. Her velvet cloak hid her condition; her mourning dress did not. Still, she was startled when she felt his hands upon the tiny buttons at her collar. Insecurity gripped her as she couldn't help but wonder how she could possibly compare with another woman now.

Her buttons undone, she held the gown to her breast, murmured a thank-you, and slipped behind the dressing screen to put on her encompassing nightgown. He didn't seem to notice. When she emerged from behind the screen, he was already in bed, hands folded behind his head, and he gave her little heed as she took her hair down, brushing it out at the dressing table.

"It's not exactly my fault, you know," she said softly, "that South Carolina has seceded."

His eyes shot to her, and she froze uncomfortably, wishing she hadn't spoken. 'No, it's not your fault. But I fail to see the joy in something being destroyed. Something that will probably mean the deaths of thousands of young men."

Alaina sighed impatiently. "Ian, you're being entirely unreasonable. You're simply assuming that there will be war. Most of the North is anxious to let the 'erring sisters' go, if that is their choice! Ian, you can't be so blind. I promise you, Florida will be right behind South Carolina. Our senators are already composing demands to the War Department regarding Florida officers. They are making plans to seize Federal installations—"

"Oh, really?" he demanded. "And where do you get your information, madam?"

She hesitated just slightly, recalling just where she had gotten her information.

Peter O'Neill.

Not that his letter of apology had actually changed her mind at all regarding his disdain for propriety or his total lack of honor, but he had written and had profusely apologized, and then he had gone on to describe the many important changes taking shape in the state. He wrote with passion and patriotism, and Alaina couldn't help but think that this great divide might force out the best in Peter—and she wished heartily that she could even begin to understand how Ian failed to see which way his state was leaning.

"Ian, I read the newspapers," she said, then added, "and I am acquainted with other people in the state—despite Belamar's isolation."

"So you are all eager for secession!" he said heatedly. "If it is the state's choice, it will be a great pity. It's an ill-advised rebellion that will cost dearly in the end."

"Rebellion? Yes, it is rebellion! Ian, it was rebellion when the thirteen Colonies broke from England. Tyrants were dictating to the Colonies, and the Colonies refused to accept rule by others. The South is doing no less now, Ian. This is no ill-advised rebellion; it is a quest for independence and self-rule."

"So you would be a rebel, too," he intoned coolly.

"You're a Southerner, Ian," she persisted, setting down her hairbrush. "Apparently, we're not going to come to terms on this—"

"There are no terms to come to, Alaina. We're not negotiating anything here."

She stood. "Ian, you don't understand. I won't accept remaining in the North when Florida does break with the Union."

"You won't?" he said heatedly. He rose suddenly, walking over to her, and she saw that he had chosen to sleep in warm long johns that covered him from waist to ankle. He braced his arms against the dressing table, pinning her there, eyes a deep blue fire as he told her,

"You won't accept living in the North because there just might be war. But you know what, Alaina? If there is war, the South will lose. It will not be a ninety-day affair—which hawks are claiming on both sides. Let's see, the population in the South is estimated at about eight million—there are nearly twenty million living in the North. Of the eight million living in the South, about three million are slaves. Southerners fear slave rebellions as it is, so that not only cuts the population of the South down to about five million rebels, it adds an element of danger. There are almost no machine shops, and no manufacturers in the South. What else? As of now, no government! An army must be raised, a treasury created. While this is all going on, the North will blockade the Southern ports, cutting off essential supplies."

"They'll never be able to blockade all of Florida."

"Right. Neither will the South be able to defend it," he returned quickly. "Trust me, the cause is doomed before it is born."

"I don't see it your way!" she cried softly.

He stared at her angrily, touched and lifted her chin. "But you're my wife, Alaina. You'll have to see it my way."

"But Ian—"

"Wives support their husbands," he informed her, his voice even harsher.

She tried very hard to control her temper, but could not.

"Not when their husbands are behaving like idiots!" she exclaimed.

He moved so swiftly that she cried out softly, expecting some violence from him.

But he did nothing other than pick her up and deposit her in bed, and she realized that he'd never offer her any real menace now.

She was carrying his child.

She was suddenly tired, and felt very keenly just how ungainly she had become. She wanted to curl up and sleep with his arm around her. She'd wanted to see him so badly, and they were together and . . .

He turned down the gas lamp on the bedside table and lay down beside her.

And turned his back to her.

She curled up to sleep, turning her back to him as well.

And she lay awake forever, it seemed, completely uncomfortable, unable to find a position that allowed her any rest.

He didn't move.

At last she tossed and turned so that she curled against his back. Almost immediately she felt the baby begin to kick. Ian felt the movement as well, for he turned to her. His long fingers extended over her abdomen, and he didn't pull away. "Through everything, this little one has intended to survive," he murmured softly, and with a sigh, pulled her to him at last. He was quiet then, and she was so glad to be held that she kept her peace as well. She thought that he slept, but he added after a moment, "The Union is going to survive as well, Alaina."

She pretended she slept herself.

It wasn't an argument she could win tonight. Time was going to tell.

And time was against him.

They had met on December 20, and since it was so close to Christmas, Ian decided that they should spend the holiday in Charleston with Brent and Sydney.

Secession excitement remained high in the air, and the city continued to surge with revelry, people coming and going.

Ian spent some time on Christmas Eve with old army friends he had come upon in the city. Men who were already planning on resigning their commissions.

He wondered how in God's name they were all going to go to war against one another.

But it was going to happen.

After his first rather sleepless night, he managed to avoid further argument with Alaina, mainly by avoiding her, which seemed incredibly ironic. He wanted to be with her. Worse. Lying beside her night by night, even feeling his child kick and squirm, he felt the most painful urges to make love to his wife. The scent of her hair, the feel of her flesh, the entanglement of her limbs with his own . . . all seemed to taunt and tempt his senses, but he had sworn to himself that she was going to bear a healthy child and completely regain her own health before he touched her again. And although he respected both his brother and his cousin very much as physicians and knew that they both believed childbirth was a very natural activity and that many of the restraints put upon women came from old wives' tales, Alaina was very far along now—so much so that he decided they must go to Washington immediately following Christmas day. No matter what he had said to her, he would have been happiest if their child could have been born at Cimarron; the house he had rented in Washington was going to have to do instead. Although she wasn't actually due until after the middle of January, Ian didn't want his child born on the road between North and South.

He awoke early on Christmas morning, rose quietly, dressed, and left Alaina sleeping, to wander down the battery at Charleston Harbor. It was early, very crisp and cool. Ships moved lazily on the horizon, and he could see the various forts in the harbor standing sentinel to the city. It was a beautiful scene, extremely peaceful, and Ian wondered just how long it could last.

He leaned a foot against a rock and drew from his pocket the letter he had just received from his brother last night. Julian was practicing in St. Augustine again, and according to him, the city seemed to be as electrically charged as a lightning storm.

> Hello, brother!
>
> Just a quick letter to advise you that I am resituated, that your wife has convalesced exceptionally in my *learned* opinion, and that Jerome reports everyone safe and well in the southern section of the state. There's a flurry about, though, as you can imagine.
>
> As you're well aware, both Governor Perry and Governor-elect Milton are ardent secessionists, and our senators, Yulee and Mallory, are becoming more and more overt in their determinations that Florida bases must be wrested from Federal hands with all speed. It's as if a secession ordinance has already been passed—of course, it will be so.
>
> Saw Mother and Father last week. Neither is pleased with the state of affairs, and Mother is trying to keep Father's roar—and damned honorable hon-

esty!—down to a low level. They are somewhat removed at Cimarron, being fairly far along the river
from Tampa Bay, and we can only hope that whatever
comes to pass within the state will leave our home
untouched. You cannot imagine, however, how news
of South Carolina's secession was celebrated here;
when the state does leave the fold, I can only say that
there will be mayhem.

How does my fair sister-in-law do without me? Tell
her I miss so lovely a patient—my most recent medical
prowess has been to extract a bullet from a hopeless
young militiaman who shot his own foot. Hope all is
well there; Alaina is in good hands with our cousin
Brent. Assure her that Jennifer tends Teddy's lime
grove with love and care. We eagerly await the news
of a nephew or niece—and of course, any decision you
may make regarding the military.

Julian

He tapped the letter against his leg, folded it, and
returned it to the pocket of his frock coat. Another man,
dressed in a lieutenant's stripes, walked by him, started
to salute, hesitated, then did so. "I imagine, sir, that your
rank will remain higher than mine in the new army!"
the fellow said, smiling and passing quickly by.

Ian stared out at the harbor again, then closed his
eyes, as if he could imprint the peace and beauty of the
scene on his mind. Then he turned away from the water
and started back to the inn.

His cousins and wife were there, and had ordered dark
roasted coffee to the balcony along with biscuits and
gravy and scones. They were seated at the table. Alaina
looked troubled, but she offered him a smile as he came
around the table to join them. He stood behind her for
a moment, lifted the heavy fall of hair, and kissed her
nape gently. "Merry Christmas," he told her huskily.

"Merry Christmas," she told him gravely in return.

"Services are in forty-five minutes," Sydney advised.
"We should hurry along, since I'm quite certain, being
Christmas, every erring sinner in all Charleston will be
seeking entrance."

"Sydney, how cynical!" Ian teased.

"Ummm, we're bringing you, aren't we?" she murmured sweetly.

Alaina laughed, and the sound was sweet.

But she maintained a strange expression as she watched him that morning, and even as he slipped his arm through hers, escorting her as they walked the distance to the Episcopal church.

The sermon was on revolution. The priest spoke constantly on the subject of "If thine eye offend thee, pluck it out," saying if the Union had become offensive, then it must be thrust far from them, their stance must be strong against the forces that might oppose freedom in South Carolina. There was a great deal of cheering; Christmas services, Ian reflected dryly, seemed to have very little to do with the birth of Christ, and everything to do with an extension of the secession celebrations.

As they walked back to the hotel, Alaina asked him, "Ian, how can you begrudge these people their enthusiasm for freedom and self-rule?"

He hesitated; it was Christmas. He wanted it to be a day of warmth and goodwill. To all men. And women.

Including his wife.

"I'll answer you that, Alaina, and then I'm going to refuse to argue with you. There is a fault line in all this; a schism. The whole of the civilized world is seeing the barbarism of slavery. If the states' rights of the South are centered around the right to hold another man as a slave, then the South sits upon an archaic and decaying institution from the start. I begrudge no one, though I differ with the priest's assertion that God will be on the side of freedom—God will turn from this fratricide. You know my mind, and that is that."

"What of my mind, Ian?" she asked him softly.

"You're my wife, Alaina. Support me," he suggested broodingly.

Surely she noted his tone. But her eyes were suddenly downcast, and she didn't reply.

"You do remember that you're at my mercy, eh, my love?" he queried.

That brought a quick, fiery gaze from her. "Perhaps not for so very long to come!" she informed him.

"Oh?"

"The babe is nearly due, Ian."

"Ah. So that's it? You need only be obedient to my will if you're expecting a child?"

"Of course not—"

"Hmmm. You never intend to be *obedient* to my will at all; you only find yourself at my mercy at such times as these!" he said, and laughed softly, but he wasn't so certain he was truly amused. "I'll have to keep you with child at all times in order for any hopes of sanity in my household, so it seems."

Her eyes flashed again, but before she could reply, Sydney swung around. "Alaina, are we walking too quickly for you?"

"Not at all," Alaina returned.

And she quickened her pace, catching up with Sydney, but Ian drew her back.

"Behave. It's Christmas."

"But Ian—"

"It's Christmas."

She was silent.

"Well?"

"Merry Christmas, Ian," she said sweetly. And he laughed, drawing her against him once again and allowing her to choose the pace as they walked.

When they returned to the inn, they sat in the public room for dinner, listened to the traditional Christmas songs performed by a talented group of musicians, and talked idly among themselves. It might have been an extremely pleasant day, a beautiful Christmas.

Except that a cloud hung over the city. Ian wondered if he was the only one who felt its malevolent presence.

When they were alone that night, Ian presented Alaina with his gift to her. It was a wedding band, delicate, with beautifully etched gold and small topaz insets. She sat before the dressing table, brushing out her hair. He took her hand, and the brush from it, then took the oversized ring he had placed on her finger at her wedding and replaced it with the delicate new band, which slid perfectly into place.

She stared at it for a very long while, then into his eyes, and her lips trembled slightly, and her voice was soft and shaky as well. "It's . . . beautiful. Thank you."

She came to her feet, attempting to kiss him, and rather awkwardly doing so, with the babe quite prominent between them. Still, the whisper of her lips against his was evocative; as always, her scent was equally tantalizing to him. As if somewhat dazed, she looked from his eyes to her finger, and back again. "Ian . . . thank you."

"The jeweler told me that I should use diamonds, and if not, emeralds or rubies. I told him no. The topaz was just like your eyes."

"The topaz is perfect!" she whispered, then spun away, digging into her drawer. She brought out a box with an English packing insignia on it, handing it to him. "It's not anywhere so beautiful or valuable," she told him, those eyes which he had compared to topaz so brilliant upon his own. "But I did make it."

He arched a brow, then opened the package and pulled out the soft folds of plaid wool in it to discover a large and handsomely hemmed scarf.

"It's the McKenzie plaid," she told him. 'And very warm, so I've been told. If you must spend time in the North."

He couldn't help but smile and appreciate the thoughtfulness that had gone into the gift. He wrapped it around his neck, noting that the colors in the plaid would go very well with the dark blue of his uniform. He refrained from mentioning that fact to Alaina.

"Very warm," he said huskily. "And greatly appreciated." He smiled. "Naturally, my father would appreciate such an appropriate gift as well."

She started to smile, but her smile faded, and he remembered suddenly that it was her first Christmas without her father, and probably her first Christmas away from home as well

Her first Christmas as his wife.

"Thank you, my love, very much. Thank you," he told her softly, and he suddenly swept her off her feet, carrying her to the wing chair before the fire. Her arms slipped around his neck, but she protested. "Ian, I'm far too heavy—"

"Alaina, you will never be too heavy," he protested impatiently, and sat with her.

And she allowed her head to fall back against his shoulder, and sat trustingly against him, her fingertips delicately fallen against his chest. Her hair smelled clean, intoxicating with its subtly floral scent. He thought that if the country were not coming apart at the seams, he might be a completely contented man. His wife was very beautiful, capable of being wild, impetuous, opinionated—and yet so gently sweet as of this moment. If he was plagued at all, it was by the wanting of her, a condition that would simply have to wait. Yet even in that, they were both young, vital, wealthy, and expecting a child any day. The perfect son, perhaps, and if not, a daughter, and years before them to complete a family.

"Ian," she said after a moment.

"Hmmm?"

She hesitated, then murmured, "I wanted to thank you for—for everything when Teddy was killed. I'm still bitter about the army men, and I do pray that some justice is done. But you were very patient and kind, and I know that I never said so at at the time, and I just wanted you to know that it meant a great deal to me."

"Alaina, Teddy was my father-in-law. You're my wife. Naturally, I would have done anything in my power for him, or for you."

"Really?" she murmured, and a skeptical tone was back in her voice. Their differences regarding North and South always seemed to come between them. If he would do anything in his power, she was certainly thinking, why wouldn't he resign his commission?

"Within reason, my love," he told her.

"Is that true?" she whispered softly.

"Within reason?" he queried.

She looked up at him, smiling wistfully, gold eyes touched by the flames of the fire. "No, I meant . . . I meant . . . I suppose that's exactly what I meant. Within reason, of course. And I'm not always within reason."

He shook his head, wondering what she had really been about to say.

She shivered suddenly.

"You're cold," he said quickly. "I'll get a blanket."

"No, no . . . please, just hold me," she said very quietly, and he did so. Her knuckles stroked his cheek, and he sighed, somewhat despairing to realize that all the logic and reason in his mind were doing little to keep him from wanting his wife. And yet it was good just to feel her warmth, the brush of her fingers against him. . . .

He felt the sudden movement of his child against his hand where it lay upon her abdomen.

Perhaps he wasn't entirely content, but he was, indeed, at peace.

A calm always came before a storm, so Jerome had told him once, and so he thought it would be.

But for that Christmas, though . . .

There was peace.

Chapter 18

Ian had taken a house in the center of the Capital.
They arrived at night, but even in the darkness, D.C.
seemed to be extraordinarily alive. Carriages rattled
down the streets; the clip-clop of horses' hooves could
be clearly heard. Alaina didn't particularly want to enjoy
anything about Washington; despite herself, she liked it
from the moment they first arrived. The place seemed
so very vibrant. Vendors sold nuts roasting over open
fires, calling out to passersby in singsong voices. Boys
hawked newspapers and circulars even by night; messen-
gers seemed to be going and coming busily no matter
what the hour.

Houses were ablaze with light.

The journey had been rough. Despite the fact that the
rail system had brought them almost all the way from
Charleston to the house, traveling had not been easy for
her. Alaina could feel the strain of the baby's weight
easily now, and she found sleep very difficult to acquire.

The carriage ride from the station to the house was
wretched, with winter weather making bogs of the road.
Alaina thought she'd be exhausted and anxious to retire
when they reached the house. She had come a long way
from the fever that had so nearly killed her after her
father's death, but she hadn't entirely recuperated from
the illness, which added to her weariness.

But the city made her feel alive. And she was pleased
to discover that the house Ian had taken was very near
the Capital itself, near the Mall, and in the bustling center of everything. It was quite cold and damp the night
they arrived, but when they alighted from the carriage,
she didn't really notice. She spun around, fascinated,
then realized that Ian was watching her, and that he

looked weary as well, and was trying not to be impatient with her.

"Would you like to see the house?" he suggested.

"Of course."

The walkway was slippery; he held her elbow carefully, escorting her up the stairway to the porch. When they reached the porch, the door opened automatically, and Ian called out a greeting to the very tall and slender man standing there ready to welcome them.

"Henry, I've brought my wife," Ian said. "Henry serves as my butler here, and much more."

"Indeed," Henry said pleasantly. He was so tall and slim, he reminded Alaina of a stork, but he had a surprisingly pleasant smile to go with his wild white hair and thin wrinkled face, and she liked him immediately. "I am master of whatever trade is needed, Mrs. McKenzie," he added, greeting her with an inclination of his head. "Welcome, Mrs. McKenzie. I am delighted to serve you in any manner that I may."

"Thank you, Henry," Alaina told him.

"Henry, if you would be so good as to show my wife's cook and maid to their lodgings, I'll bring Mrs. McKenzie through the house."

"As you wish, sir."

The architecture of the house was stoically Federal in style; the entryway was fashioned in a half-moon shape with a fashionable marble-toned wallpaper and a very high ceiling with a handsome chandelier. A curving staircase rose immediately from the entry, while the downstairs rooms branched off from either side of it.

"To the left," Ian said, leading her forward while Henry led Bella and Lilly up the stairs. "The formal dining room—naturally, no one will expect you to entertain in your present condition, but in time perhaps we'll have guests. Beyond here, the ladies' parlor, and beyond that, the grand salon. And next to it, the library, and my office." Rooms led into one another in a neat pattern, the grand salon being directly behind the curving stairway. Next to it, the library had a very definite masculine appearance with its dark woods and leathers, and the office beyond seemed to state that it was off limits to the female gender as well.

She studied the library and connecting office, then

turned to Ian. "It's very grand—for a place to stay while you're assigned here. One would think you intend to stay awhile."

"I took the house several years ago, which has proven to be a wise decision," he said simply. "Come on, I'll bring you upstairs. You must be completely exhausted."

"I'm really fine—"

"But you don't want to become overtired," he said firmly, leading her back the way they had come and then upstairs.

"The servants' quarters are all on the third floor," he told her, pushing open a doorway just down the hall from the landing. "I've had this prepared for you."

Alaina stepped into the room. It was extremely pleasant, with a large bed covered in a thick white quilt in the center of the room. The furnishings were pine, the wallpaper was in a delicate blue pattern, and the crown molding about the ceiling had been edged in the same blue.

"It's quite nice," she murmured. But her heart seemed to be pounding in her throat. It was her room. Her room alone. Not his.

She glanced at him. "And where . . . do you sleep in Washington?" she asked politely.

"I'm the next door down the hall," he told her, his gaze sweeping over her. "It's best for the time being. I crowd you and the baby."

"That's not really true."

"Well, then, my love, I've gotten very little sleep as of late, and I need some," he said softly. "There's a washstand there, a hip tub behind the screen, and a kettle to heat water on the bracket above the fireplace. There's a bellpull by the bed; if you need anything at all, Henry has a staff of three, and of course, we've more help now with Bella and Lilly here. I'll leave you to get some rest. Would you like Lilly to come help you?"

"No, thank you, I'm fine."

He came to her quickly, as if he had suddenly become quite impatient. He kissed her forehead. "Get some rest!" he murmured, and left her.

When he was gone, she sank suddenly to the foot of the bed, perplexed, uneasy—and hurt and lonely as well. Certainly they argued about state of the country, but she had been very glad to be with him in Charleston. She had felt secure sleeping at his side, comfortable in his arms. It seemed, however, that he was adamant about not having her in his room here, and she felt as if he were creating another of his walls between them. She couldn't help but feel a certain jealousy and wonder if he didn't crave something different from her here in Washington.

His freedom.

To spend time with the colonel's daughter?

Still, she was very tired, and not at all sure of how to approach him, and far too proud to insist that he should be with her. What if he absolutely refused her? She didn't think that she could bear such a situation.

Someone had already brought her trunk from the carriage to her room, and she struggled out of her traveling garments and into a nightgown alone, dismissing Lilly when she came to help her, with the explanation that she had already changed clothing and was mercilessly tired. Which she was.

She lay on the quilt-covered bed, staring into the night.

She did fall asleep, but it seemed that she had just barely done so before voices drifted up from the porch below. She walked to her window, carefully drawing back the thick brocade draperies. Ian stood on the steps with Henry, talking so quietly that she couldn't make out what was being said. Then he started down the steps, and she saw that Pye had been brought around from the stables by a young groom, and Ian was mounting his horse.

He didn't look back to the house; he rode out the gate and down the street, into the night.

And with both anguish and anger, she wondered just where he really intended to spend his night.

Alaina was determined that she could be every bit as withdrawn as her husband—which was not terribly difficult, because he was continually out of the house. Congress still battled for compromise, the newspaper assured the citizens. But Alaina knew as well that Florida's representatives remained in Washington, demanding information from the Secretary of War regarding military installations in Florida, Florida officers, and enlisted men in the United States military. Likewise, South Carolina had sent representatives regarding the military bases in that state.

The first few days of January seemed very cold indeed.

Ian was extremely polite and solicitous, in the few hours he came home. And so remote, she longed to slap him nearly half the time she was near him. The baby was due very, very soon, but she couldn't help the miserable feeling that she had been set inside a clean, decent cupboard—and then had had the door firmly closed on her. She wasn't to be seen or heard. She was certain of this because, though Ian never failed to be out of the house when she woke in the morning, he did come home for a late dinner, which they ate together. When she tried to talk about the state of the country or demand to know if he was aware of anything else happening, he replied shortly, then changed the subject. When she suggested that she'd like to see something of the city, he reminded her that it was winter, there were patches of ice all about, and she should be concerned with her health and that of the child. She'd be out and about soon enough.

Alaina thought that he was slipping away from her in some intangible way; she knew that he didn't talk to her about the country's schism because he had determined that he wasn't going to fight with her. In order not to fight, he avoided her. He left the house frequently at night. He kept his distance, barely touching her. Impatience and anger simmered within her, and it was more frustrating to know that she had to control her temper— or hear that she was distraught because of her advanced condition. She longed to lash out with fury, and at the same time, she was afraid.

She didn't want to lose Ian. In truth, she didn't know if she'd ever really had him, but there had been times when she had felt as if all was well, as long as he held her. She'd never intended it; she had fallen in love with him. And now he had picked her up and set her as far away from him as he could manage, so it seemed, and it was unnerving to her not to know how to fight. Once, when she had wanted something, she had known the way to go about getting it. Now she was quite uncertain.

She didn't dare give vent to her feelings. She tried to keep her distance—and maintain a fierce hold on her temper.

She'd been in Washington a little more than a week when Henry brought her a message from Ian saying that he wouldn't be home for dinner, he was going to attend a social they'd been invited to at the home of a Mrs. Rose Greenhow.

"Though, naturally, I had previously declined," Ian wrote,

> Colonel Magee has suggested strongly that I attend. Mrs. Greenhow is probably the premier hostess in Washington. Mr. Greenhow passed away several years ago, and Rose is the mother of four, but as she has recently lost her daughter Gertrude, she has not been entertaining much of late. Due to the fact that Mrs. Greenhow is such a remarkable woman and manages to bring all sides together, and far more is being achieved through private friendships than more formal, diplomatic means, I shall attend for a short time. I won't be late, but please don't wait up.

"Would you like dinner in your room, perhaps, Mrs. McKenzie?" Henry suggested.

Alaina tapped Ian's message thoughtfully against her chin, then said, "No, I think not, Henry. I think I will go out for a while myself."

Henry wasn't quick enough to hide his surprise. "But Mrs. McKenzie—"

"Yes, Henry?"

He looked like a very unhappy Ichabod Crane. She smiled sweetly.

"Mrs. McKenzie, the baby . . ."

"The baby needs air," she assured him.

"But—"

"Send Lilly up, please, will you, Henry?"

Henry clamped his mouth shut. When he had left her room, Alaina hurried to her dressing table. The invitation from Mrs. Greenhow had come addressed to her; she had opened it and told Ian about it at dinner, but he had brought up the baby, the severe weather—which she wasn't accustomed to in the least—and her own recent bout with fever.

Despite the fact that she'd grown up in the wilderness, her wilderness had been in the South, and she was very aware of the proprieties and the fact that women did avoid social commitment when they were so near their confinement.

But she couldn't bear being locked in the house anymore. She avidly read the newspaper from front to back, but the news was biased, and she was anxious to hear what people were saying. Washington remained filled with diverse opinions and she was quite certain she could find a Southerner more willing to talk about the state of affairs than her husband.

And she could no longer bear waiting to meet Colonel Magee's daughter.

Lilly, usually her staunchest supporter, helped her dress with blatant disapproval. "It simply isn't proper," Lilly informed her. "Your first concern must be—"

"My baby. My baby is very well."

"If you fall—"

"I won't fall. Lilly, I'm going mad. I'm locked up in the North all alone—"

"You're not locked up."

"Fine, then, if I'm not in prison—"

"He might well be furious." Lilly was referring to Ian.

Alaina met Lilly's eyes in the mirror. "I imagine so. But he will have to live with it, as I have learned to do," she said simply. "Lilly, you can't argue me out of this, so please, make my hair look as attractive as you can."

Lilly let out a loud sniff, but went to work on Alaina's hair.

Thirty minutes later, Alaina was ready.

She studied herself worriedly in the mirror. She had gained some weight back; but it refused to fill out her cheeks and the hollows about her collarbone. She gnawed lightly on her lower lip, wishing she dared try a corset. Her gown was black, for no matter how much she longed to make her best possible appearance, she remained in mourning for her father. She told herself that black in itself somewhat concealed her size. Jennifer had helped her adjust the gown, and it had an old-fashioned look to it, with a moderately low bodice, ribboned just below the breasts so that the gown streamed out in a soft, full line beneath. She told herself with a sigh that she simply wasn't going to look at all alluring, but she was, at the very least, quite decent.

As she came downstairs, slipping her encompassing cloak around her shoulders, and asked Henry to call the carriage, she felt a moment's panic. Ian was going to be furious. What if he was there with Risa Magee?

She bit into her lower lip. The invitation had been addressed to her. And she was going, she determined.

The hell with all else.

Risa Magee sipped sherry and pretended to laugh and smile and pay heed to her father's good friend Colonel Montgomery as the old man went on and on about an Indian attack in the West.

She wished that she were in the West herself—or even in the wretched South, for that matter. Anywhere but here. But Risa's upbringing had entailed the military all the way. Her father had wanted her here, and she was here—because it was her duty. She could hide the unpleasantness of almost any task. Not that the gathering should have been unpleasant; the room was filled with glittering, intelligent, fascinating people. People who would surely play important roles in the unfolding drama of the country. Colonels were plentiful, as were majors—and there were even a few generals, as well as politicians, writers, businessmen, and clergy.

But among the majors was Ian McKenzie, and as hard as she tried, Risa found it almost impossible to pretend that there had been nothing between them, that she hadn't assumed she'd be engaged to him by now, perhaps married already, or at the very least contemplating marriage. But then . . .

Ian had married elsewhere.

Naturally, he had come straight to her with the fact, even though rumor had reached her before she had heard the awful truth from his own lips. And she knew how it had hurt him to come to her; she believed with all her heart that it had been incredibly painful for him. And she knew, as well, when she felt his eyes on her, that he still found her more than attractive, and she had felt at times that he actually wanted her. . . . Naturally,

his wife was back somewhere in the jungle frontier of
Florida, and, she convinced herself, there was nothing
between him and his wife except for their marriage—a
forced marriage, which propriety and circumstance had
demanded. She'd convinced herself as well that Ian had
married a pathetic, leathered crone of a girl, completely
ruined by the heat of the tropics, undoubtedly ugly as
sin. And to her dismay, she wished that she hadn't spent
nearly so long flirting—nor been anywhere near so sure
of herself. But growing up in a sea of men, she'd matured with a great deal of confidence in herself. She'd
naturally had numerous suitors and been exposed to the
most intelligent, courageous, and intriguing men in the
nation. She'd dissuaded a number of fascinating young
men before determining on Ian. Except that she'd done
so too late. And now, to her horror, she found herself
wishing upon occasion that she'd had the good sense to
seduce the man without delay. Then she could be the
one with him now, expecting his child—and supporting
him in his love for the Union, rather than bringing that
pained expression of mixed loyalties to his eyes she saw
there now! There had to be so much bitterness between
Ian and his wife.

However, she'd had to accept, of course, that there
was some kind of a relationship between the two, once
she'd learned that Alaina was with child.

Naturally, she'd offered her most heartfelt congratulations. Naturally.

She was living on pride.

When Risa and Ian had first spoken once he'd reported back to her father after his leave back home,
she'd been disturbed to realize that she hadn't managed
to fall out of love with him. He had stood in her parlor,
so tall and handsome in his blue coat and plumed hat,
staring into the flames that burned within the grate. He
had appeared weary and thoughtful, his handsome features taut, his eyes betraying the depths of his feelings.
She knew he had been deeply concerned for some time.
He had anticipated Lincoln's election when everyone—
not just the slaveholding Southerners—had thought of
him as nothing more than a country bumpkin of a law-
yer. Ian had told her once that south Carolina was itch-

ing to secede, and that many more cotton states would
follow suit.

And he predicted war.

Not that they were anywhere near anything so serious.
Tonight, men who argued in Congress were laughing and
congratulating one another on marriages, births, and
promotions. Soldiers from the far reaches of the country
were pouring drinks for one another. It was a wonderful
place to get together. Mrs. Greenhow was considered to
be one of—if not *the*—finest hostesses in Washington.
She had a sympathetic ear for everyone. President Buchanan had come and gone, preaching peace, assuring
men and women from both sides that time would heal
the wounds between them. Risa was aware that many
men were condemning the president for not taking action, but what could the man do? Lincoln would become
president next month, and the world would change anyway. Buchanan fought just to hold a steady course—and
keep the hotheads from firing upon one another.

A few feet to her left, Risa saw Ian. He looked exceptionally striking tonight, in full dress uniform, the cobalt
of his eyes so grave and enhanced by the color of his
uniform. She felt a new twist in her heart as she watched
him. His every movement held a natural grace. His
shoulders were so broad, his hair so sleekly dark.

He was at her father's side, conversing with one of
the generals who reported directly to Winfield Scott. If
there was war, the Union might well be in trouble. Winfield Scott had served his country very well. He had the
ability to listen to the commanding officers beneath him,
and because of that, he had brought a brilliant victory
in the Mexican War. But he was getting very old now.
And looking around the room, Risa wondered to whom
the Union would look to guide an army into battle now
against their own friends and kin should shots be fired.

A young man with frazzled brown hair and angry eyes
approached Ian suddenly. Risa strained to hear the conversation and realized that the man was a Alabamian
who had just resigned his commission to go home in
anticipation of Alabama leaving the Union. He was annoyed that Ian hadn't done so yet as well. Ian replied
to him in an even, well-modulated voice, not arguing—
and not agreeing. Standing his ground.

Risa decided that she could actually go to Ian and touch him.

Rescue him.

She had a good excuse for doing so.

"Colonel, if you'll pardon me?" she inquired of her father's friend, watching his white brows shoot high on his forehead. "I believe a friend is in distress," she continued, flashing the older man a brilliant smile.

"Of course, dear, of course!"

Risa set her punch cup into his hand and quickly turned toward Ian. The musicians had just started playing a waltz, which aided her nicely.

"Gentlemen!" she said, sweeping in among the men with a vibrant enthusiasm. "Will you be so good as to indulge me? Ian, I know that I shall make a poor substitute for your wife, but perhaps you'll allow me this waltz?"

His eyes met hers with amusement, relief—and, as always, something just a little bit pained and uncomfortable. But he responded quickly and gallantly.

"Miss Magee," Ian murmured, "I'm quite sure that you could never be a poor substitute for anyone; indeed, I believe you must be aware that your beauty surpasses itself with each new day."

"Father, you do manage to draw the very best from your officers!" she exclaimed in return, addressing the colonel but smiling at Ian. The light banter drew laughter from around them. And Ian took her arm, leading her to the polished floor, where they began immediately to move to the music.

His eyes touched hers. There always seemed to be a brush of blue fire to them. Despite herself, she felt a vicious pounding in her head. She wished again that she'd defied convention and propriety and seduced him when she'd had the chance.

"Thank you for the rescue. It was brilliantly achieved."

"Was it?"

"You did seek to rescue me?"

"I did."

"I wonder how much longer you will be able to do so," he mused, affection in his voice.

Well, they had long been friends. They had seen so

many things that were important the same way; they knew the games in Washington, and in the military. They both loved life, new places, adventures, and . . .

She loved the warmth of him. Dancing. What a wonderful idea. She could come close, feel him, feel his strength, his breath, his scent . . .

Twist ever harder on her heart.

"Mmmm . . . why do you say that?" she asked, forcing herself to remember that to all outward appearances, she had simply asked an old friend to dance—a married friend.

"At any time, we will hear that Florida has seceded."

"Perhaps they'll vote against—"

"Not a chance in hell."

"What will you do?" Risa asked.

"I still don't know," he said, then his eyes touched hers again. "Yes, I do. I'm not resigning. I think secession is insane and slavery is wrong. If the country splits peacefully enough, maybe I'll eventually resign and return home and be a proper planter. That's my ultimate plan. But if war breaks out, I suppose I'll become a complete outcast."

"Not here, Ian!" she assured him in a fierce whisper. "You'll never be an outcast here."

He offered her a slow, crooked smile, looking down into her eyes as the two of them swirled around the floor. "Not here. But that's the sad part of it, Risa. I love my home. Passionately. And that's where I'll be an outcast. Not to mention—" he began, then stopped abruptly.

Risa didn't know what could possibly be driving her to such brash behavior, but she searched his face. "Not to mention the fact that you'll be an outcast from your own bed?" she inquired.

His hold tightened around her waist. His eyes were very cold, very hard, and she didn't know if the look was for her . . . or for his absent wife. "My wife will have to be tolerant of my choices. My mind is made up," he told her.

Then they swirled around the room again to the sweet strains of a trio of violins. And as they turned, Risa saw that the front door had opened. Rose Greenhow greeted an exquisite petite blond who was encompassed in a black velvet cloak.

Risa didn't know how she knew, but she *knew*.

Ian's Southern wife had come to survey Northern society for herself.

A tall, dark-haired woman answered the bell when Alaina arrived. Alaina had been ready to flee the minute she reached the door, but she chastised herself and nervously determined that she had come so far, she must now go in.

The woman's taffeta skirts rustled, a sweet whisper of perfume touched the air around her. She was, Alaina thought, perhaps in her forties, an extremely handsome woman with a special vibrance about her face and eyes. Her eyes were very dark as was her hair. She had a wonderful smile and appeared impressive in every way.

The woman swept her gaze over Alaina and apparently decided she must be among the invited. "Good evening, do come in," she said with an engaging smile. "And pray do tell me—whom have I the honor of meeting?"

"I'm Alaina McCa—McKenzie," she corrected quickly. "Mrs. . . . Greenhow?"

"Oh, indeed, yes! I am Rose Greenhow," the woman said delightedly. "And naturally, you're Ian's wife! How foolish of me, I should have known, it's just that—well . . . my dear, in that lovely cloak your condition isn't at all apparent, and it's my understanding that you're expecting your confinement quite soon?"

"By the end of January, I imagine," Alaina told her.

"Ah, yes, well, it seems we do like to make such a hush-hush thing about the beauty of human life, eh? So many women behave like silly ostriches themselves, hiding away when they should be up and about. Children are a gift from god."

"You have children?"

"I had four daughters. I'm afraid I've recently lost one. Please, do come in. It's absolutely marvelous to see you here. I'm sorry; I didn't expect you. Ian had originally sent his regrets for you both, then he was apparently influenced to attend. . . . I believe his senior officer specifically asked him to be here tonight for a few informal discussions. However, he should have warned me that you would be here!''

Alaina wasn't sure how to respond; she was glad not to have to do so, for Rose Greenhow didn't wait for an answer, but swept her into the room.

Alaina's heart sank. For there was her husband dancing with the most beautiful woman in the room.

The colonel's daughter?

She was tall and slender, but her wasplike waist appeared all the more perfect in comparison to the more than adequate cleavage that rose from her bodice. She was dark, her hair as soft and sleek as deep sable. Her face was a perfect oval; her eyes were light green. A shade that changed even as they lit upon Alaina and seemed to darken to a deep aquamarine.

She noticed Alaina when the rest of the people in the room were still too preoccupied to do so. They were quite possibly living on the eve of destruction, Alaina thought, yet the place pulsed with life. She could hear bits and pieces of conversation as she entered the room. Men who might well soon be enemies met and mingled in the home of this society matron, smoked cigars together, bragged as to why the cotton states would secede and win any skirmish, or why the North would stomp out such ill-advised rebellion.

"Come, dear, let me find your husband and introduce you about," Rose Greenhow said, adding in a whisper, "People have been just dying to meet you, dear. They'll be so pleased that you've made an appearance."

Alaina doubted that Washington society women would be glad to meet her; they would surely condemn her presence, and she might well be fueling the gossips for some time to come. But then, that wouldn't be something new for her.

Still, now that she was here, she longed to run away. Especially now that the colonel's daughter was watching her with her perfect green eyes while Ian's hand rested upon her waist.

The colonel's daughter whispered to Ian, and he spun around.

Startled. Truly startled.

Ian was good at concealing his thoughts and emotions. He betrayed very little. But Alaina knew him. And she saw the pulse ticking at his throat, and the quick darkening of his eyes, and she knew that he was angry. She suddenly wanted to hide, but she could not. A servant came for her cloak, and she was left in her black lace gown, forcing a smile, extending her hand as Rose Greenhow propelled her toward a handsome older couple and made introductions.

More and more people came forward, men and women. Alaina fought the temptation to tremble, smiled graciously, and responded as well as she could. Then she found that Mrs. Greenhow was introducing her to the colonel's daughter, the young woman with the velvety dark hair, beautiful green eyes, and perfect, minuscule waist. "Ah, there you are, dear Risa! This is Alaina, Ian's wife. Risa is Colonel Magee's daughter, so naturally you two must become great friends!"

Alaina and Risa stared at one another with wooden smiles.

"It's a pleasure, Miss Magee," Alaina managed.

"The pleasure is mine," Risa responded courteously. "Ian has been so much a part of our lives—my father and I have been most eager to meet you."

"But my dear!" exclaimed one of the older matrons to whom Alaina had just been introduced. Mrs. McNally, Alaina thought. Her husband was in Congress. "There's no need for you to hide away! There's always such a busy social scene here, and you simply must be a part of it! Such a shame that you haven't been about before!"

"Now, Clara, Mrs. McKenzie was ill last year, and you musn't demand her time," Risa said politely.

"I was ill—but I'm quite well now," Alaina assured the other woman. "Well, other than . . ."

The very beautiful Risa was watching her, waiting courteously for her to continue. Then the strangest light in the other woman's eyes let Alaina know that Risa had just realized her situation; that Ian was obviously having little or nothing to do with her now.

Alaina closed her eyes, suddenly feeling ill. She was the one wearing his ring, the one having his child, bearing his name, she told herself. And surely that hurt the other woman.

The woman he had *intended* to marry.

"I'm really feeling extremely well," she said. "I could . . . climb mountains!" she offered sweetly.

"Ah," Risa murmured, arching a brow suddenly.

Alaina turned slightly realizing that Ian stood behind her. With her cloak.

A tremor ripped down her back. His eyes appeared nearly black. "My love," he said, in a tone that indicated she was anything but. "I've not been able to reach you—you're quite surrounded. It was so good of you to come out, but I think it's been quite long enough, don't you?"

She fought the flush that threatened to engulf her cheeks, feeling like a child being reprimanded. In front of Rose Greenhow, Risa, and Mrs. McNally—the sum of Washington society.

"I'm really quite fine," she insisted mildly.

But suddenly she wasn't.

She was . . .

Drenched.

For the first fraction of a second, she didn't know what had happened. But Jennifer had warned her about all the stages of childbirth, and she knew what had happened as her skirts became soaked, even while she tried to deny that fate could twist around this way: Her water had broken.

The baby was coming.

She hadn't felt the first hint of pain . . .

Except that she did then. A sudden, awful pain. Like a knife right across her back.

Panic filled her; she felt the blood draining from her face. Oddly enough, it was Risa Magee's flashing green eyes she saw touch upon hers with realization. They held her gaze for what seemed like an endless time, yet it was just a matter of seconds.

She spun around with perfect precision, knocking a large amber beer from the hand of a nearby politician. "I am so sorry. Oh, look at the spill I've created!"

"Alaina, dear, don't be distressed, we'll get it picked up," Rose assured her calmly.

And though Alaina was grateful, she was humiliated as well when Risa leaned across her, suggesting softly, "Ian, I think you might want to get your wife home now. Quickly."

Chapter 19

Florida officially seceded from the Union on January 10, 1861, the third state to do so, following Mississippi's secession on January 9.

Alaina was blissfully unaware of those events, however, for Sean Michael McKenzie finally made his appearance at precisely noon on the tenth of January. Despite the fact that Alaina's water had broken and her pains were almost instantly severe, her son chose to take his time coming into the world.

With an immediate understanding of the situation, Ian had enwrapped her in her cloak, swept her up, and carried her outside to the carriage. By then, she was shivering fiercely, and already learning the meaning of the combination of the words *labor* and *pain*. He was anxious, angry, and called her a little fool, but then, in retrospect, that was nothing considering some of the things she called him as the night progressed to morning. The doctor Ian summoned was a kindly sort, but of the firm belief that a fair amount of suffering had been dictated upon women by God himself—and who was he, as a mere mortal, to intervene?

It was almost good to have Ian to argue with as the hours wore on. Despite the fact that the doctor suggested he be about his own business, have a drink in his library, go for a midnight ride, Ian remained with her once Lilly—who had the most irritating "I told you so" manner about her—had gotten her out of her soaked clothing and into a clean gown and her bed. Stroking her head with cool cloths, Ian demanded irritably, "What on earth possessed you to do such a stunt?"

"I had to get out," she told him. "I was bored, I was—"

"More concerned with politics than your child, madam," he finished angrily for her.

"No, no, I . . . Ian, really. He or she is just a bit early here."

"There was no reason for you to be out."

They were in the room alone at the moment. She closed her eyes and whispered, "I needed to see the reason you were out."

"Oh really. Well, you did manage to bring me home, didn't you, my love?" he queried softly.

Her eyes flew open as she searched his, but they were fathomless, and when she would have spoken again, she was seized by so wretched a pain that she nearly screamed aloud. She wasn't going to allow him to see her suffer, however, and she clenched down on her teeth, fighting the rush of tears that burned at her eyelids. "You should . . . leave!" she gasped.

"I think not. I am responsible for the current situation," he said thoughtfully. "I was there for the beginning of this; I'll see it through to the end."

So he wouldn't leave her. Even when she very viciously told him what he really should be doing with himself. And as time passed, she became glad he had stayed, nearly breaking his fingers upon occasion as she clutched his hand. Through the hours she listened to the deep tenor of his voice as he soothed her through the worst of the pains, feeling the gentle pressure of his fingers as he rubbed her temple or her nape, helping ease her tension.

Even when the babe was actually born, he refused to leave, and he was the first to take his son from the doctor, studying him even before Lilly could scoop him up to be bathed and wrapped in a towel. And there was something very wonderful, in all her exhaustion, about hearing the pleasure in Ian's voice as he told her, "A boy, Alaina, a boy with a mop of hair, ten fingers, ten toes, perfect in every way. I did tell you it would be a boy, didn't I?" he added, and not without a certain amount of arrogance. Yet at that moment, it didn't matter. She smiled. She'd never felt so tired and worn or so dazzlingly happy at any time in her life. She reached for her son, who wailed in indignant protest at the new world. She examined him quickly and saw that Ian was

right: He was perfect in every way—large and well
formed, ten fingers, ten toes—and an amazing amount
of dark hair for an infant. His eyes were blue, like his
father's, yet she wondered if they would stay. She felt
an amazing surge of emotion within her then, for the
child, and his father. She had known that she loved Ian
despite the difficulties between them; but until that moment, she hadn't realized how deeply.

"Your eyes," she whispered softly to Ian.

"Mine, or maybe Teddy's," he said quietly.

Alaina glanced up at him. He smoothed damp hair
from her forehead, and she caught his hand and kissed
his fingers. "Thank you for that," she said softly.

He leaned down and pressed his lips to her forehead,
and then her mouth. "Thank you for my son," he told
her. She smiled, looked at her son, who was now gravely
observing her, and then allowed her eyes to close. Someone took the baby away. Ian, she thought. She had never
felt quite so much at peace.

And she slept.

The following days passed quickly. She was tired and
slept frequently, because it didn't matter. All that she
wanted to do in those first few days was see the baby
and marvel at him. She didn't even notice the hours that
Ian was gone, because he came to her room every evening, and sat at her bedside and studied the baby with
her. He didn't sleep with her; he remained in his own
room. But it seemed that he was always close, and for
the time being, she was content.

She was glad that he didn't dictate their son's name,
but consulted her. "I'd like to name him Sean Michael
McKenzie, after my grandfather," he suggested, looking
down at his son. The baby gripped Ian's thumb tightly
as he studied his father. Ian continued, "I suppose you'd
like Theodore, but I'd prefer to use a McKenzie family
name first, if you agree. If you wish, we can name our
second son for Teddy."

"What if we don't have another son?"

"Theodosia? Theodora?" Ian said, looking at her
then, and her lashes fell, because she didn't want him to
see how glad she was that he seemed so certain they
would have other children.

"I like Sean Michael," she said simply. "And actually, I rather like Teddy for a girl as well."

"Then Sean Michael you shall be," Ian informed his son.

Sean was just a few days old and Alaina had been sleeping with him by her side one morning when she heard a slight tapping at her door. She awoke drowsily and clasped her nightgown together, as she had dozed off while the baby was nursing. She looked to the door and started, realizing that it was Risa Magee who stood there. She nearly jumped, remembered the baby, and more carefully sat up, trying to smooth back her hair with some facsimile of dignity. She wouldn't have traded the baby for anything in the world, but neither could she help but feel a twinge of jealousy. Risa was elegant. Slim, yet so curvacously so, her beautiful dark hair swept up into a perfect chignon, her eyes brilliant against her dark coloring.

"Congratulations," Risa said very quietly, tiptoeing into the room and around the bed to look down on Sean. "He's gorgeous."

"Thank you," Alaina murmured, watching the other woman. She hesitated. "And thank you, too, for covering for me so swiftly the other night."

"You certainly did manage to be dramatic," Risa smiled.

"It was not my intent," Alaina said, "and I am grateful to you." She paused. "I'm not at all sure why you would want to be kind to me."

Risa seemed startled, then laughed softly. "Why, indeed? I don't know, actually. Maybe we share a sisterhood as women, or something of the like. But you're right; we might as well be out in the open between us. I can't begin to understand why I would want to help you in any way. Sean's a beautiful baby—and he should have been mine. Except, of course, that you stole Ian."

Alaina gasped, sitting up. "But I didn't—"

"It's not really your fault. I should have slept with him myself."

"I never—"

Risa laughed, looking pointedly at the baby. "You must have."

Alaina shook her head, determined to make her point. "I didn't sleep with him before—"

" 'Sleeping with' . . . what an expression! Were people merely to *sleep,* so much mayhem could be avoided. Nevertheless, all right, a fine point. I should have jumped naked into a pool with him."

"I didn't jump naked into a pool with him!" Alaina protested.

"He lied to me?" Risa said politely. Alaina flushed, unable to believe they were having this conversation; but then, she had actually brought it about. She winced inwardly, realizing that Ian had most probably been painfully honest with Risa about everything. He no doubt shared much more of his heart and mind with Risa than he ever had with her.

Suddenly some of the enormous contentment she had felt at the baby's birth was jarred. Even now, Risa seemed to mock herself far more than Alaina, yet the honesty of her manner made Alaina uneasy.

"I don't know if Ian lied, because I don't know what he said," Alaina informed Risa. "But I assure you, I meant no ill to you—or him. I never set out to entrap Ian, I didn't intend what happened, and I didn't actually *want* to marry him at all!" she said, beginning quite evenly, but feeling her temper rise as she spoke. Then, to her horror, she realized that Ian stood in the doorway.

Risa didn't see him. "Well, it doesn't really matter now, does it?" she asked softly. "You are married, and you have a beautiful child, and congratulations are in order."

Ian stepped into the room, and Risa spun around, startled. Alaina wanted to sink into the bed and disappear. She was painfully aware that Ian had heard her words, she felt the coldness of his stare.

"Ian. He's absolutely beautiful," Risa complimented again. She was so smooth, so composed, so poised. Alaina felt ill, yet she desperately wanted to be dignified.

"Thank you, Risa. Alaina, is the baby dressed?" Ian's tone was smooth, smooth as silk. "I was anxious to have him baptized, and Colonel Magee and Risa have agreed to stand as godparents."

"Now?" Alaina whispered, stunned. Then she didn't know why she was surprised; parents were naturally anxious to have their babes baptized as quickly as possible, simply because life was so very fragile for a little one.

But he hadn't even asked her about having Risa and her father stand as godparents. Colonel Magee had often served as Ian's commanding officer, so it wasn't at all unusual that he should stand up for the child, but . . .

Ian strode to the bed, gently scooping up Sean, placing him in Risa's arms. She laughed with soft delight, holding the babe gently.

"He is just adorable!"

A tremor of unease swept through Alaina, and she wanted to snatch her baby back. Ian, Risa, and the baby were extremely handsome together.

Risa looked over at her and seemed to notice her pallor. "We'll have him right back," she promised. Alaina bit into her lower lip and forced a smile.

"If you could just give me a few minutes, I'll come with you," Alaina said, ready to slide out of bed and dress.

"You shouldn't be up," Ian said flatly, "and the reverend only has so much time. It isn't necessary for you to be there."

Alaina smoothed her hands over the sheets, willing herself not to fight or argue—she was determined that she wasn't going to be humiliated further in front of Risa Magee. She had never quite understood why poor women were expected to bear their babies and go right back to work while ladies of society were confined to their beds for days after the fact. But she didn't have her strength back, and she wasn't going to risk falling on her face.

"He's got quite a temper and he may not take kindly to baptism," she said, smiling at Risa. "I hope he'll behave."

"We'll be fine," Risa assured her and left the room.

Ian stood in the doorway, staring at Alaina. Then he closed the door.

Alaina wanted to jump up and call him back. She felt so alone.

What else? she mocked herself. She had just told the woman he'd intended to marry that she hadn't wanted to be his wife at all. She might as well have written out a permission slip for the two to commit adultery.

*   *   *

Despite Alaina's fear, Ian couldn't have been more courteous in the days that followed—though he kept a distance from her. The doctor had warned her that there would be "Ahem! No, er, intimate marital relations" for some weeks to come, and so she couldn't argue with Ian's determination to keep separate rooms. Besides, her pride wouldn't allow her to insist that he come sleep with her. Still, she did her best to be amiable, and it was easy, because they were both so fascinated with being parents. They spent many hours with Sean laid out on the bed, assigning his various features to family members, then laughing and agreeing that he looked like Sean, and that was that. Sean Michael McKenzie.

Sean was a little more than three weeks old when an invitation to another of Rose Greenhow's soirees arrived. Alaina realized that she had been living in a clamshell, in a greater isolation than ever. She had been so preoccupied with the baby and her own troubles that she hadn't given a thought to the world around her. She hadn't even glanced at a newspaper—her only reading had been the letters she had received from Ian's family, congratulations from James and Teela, Jerome, Brent, and Sydney, and Jennifer and Lawrence. And since the day Risa and her father had been to the house, Alaina and Ian had received no visitors. She was aware that Ian had made a point of being home, and despite the warmth they shared regarding Sean, in other matters he had smoothly erected a wall of reserve toward her. Alaina was suddenly extremely anxious to get out and discover what was going on in the rest of the country.

Ian was working in his library, poring over charts and maps, when the invitation arrived, hand delivered by one of Rose Greenhow's maids. Alaina brought it to him, hesitating in the doorway as she watched him work, then knocking softly. He glanced up quickly. There was a newspaper at his side which he folded and put aside, indicating she should come in. Wordlessly, Alaina handed him the invitation. He read it and handed it back to her.

"It's too soon for you to be going to parties," he told her.

"Ian, it's not. Please, I'd love to get out for just a

few hours. I've not left this house at all since the baby was born."

He looked back to his work. "Alaina—"

"Please, Ian?"

"And what about Sean?"

The baby was a serious and legitimate consideration, since she had refused the services of a wet nurse. "Ian, we're but a few blocks away from Mrs. Greenhow's. I'll feed him right before we leave." He didn't answer right away, and she thought that he was looking for excuses.

"Please, Ian!"

He hesitated a moment longer, then shrugged, as if this evening was going to be an unpleasantry he was going to have to face sooner or later. He turned back to his work. "As you wish," he said simply.

Ian had never seen his wife more beautiful than when she came down the stairs that night. She still wore black, in Teddy's honor, and he knew she would do so for a full year. But she wore black very well, her hair appearing like spun gold against it, her skin like porcelain. Her breasts were enhanced from nursing, and her waist appeared more slender than ever. She wore her hair swept up, with a few tendrils falling in evocative curls down her nape and over her shoulders. Watching her come down the stairs with her eyes flashing a brilliant topaz and her cheeks flushed, he felt his senses go into a spin. She reached him, and the scent of her perfume was completely intoxicating. But it would be several more weeks before he could touch her again, and he didn't dare brush her cheek with a kiss or reflect too long upon her cleavage. For a moment, he wryly envied his son her breasts. Then he thought again with weary resolution that by the time it was medically prudent to make love to his wife again, she wouldn't want to feel the least brush of his fingers.

"Shall we go?" he inquired, making no comment on her appearance. She nodded, and he noted that her eyes swept over the length of his uniform—with distance, he thought. She hadn't liked his Union uniform since her father had been killed.

She caught him staring at her in the lamplight that

trickled into the carriage, and she nervously looked to her lap, smoothing her skirt.

"Is there something wrong?" she inquired.

"On the contrary. You look dazzling."

She looked toward the window. "I adore Sean, and you know it. I am delighted to be with him. But I am not accustomed to such inactivity."

"And naturally you never did want to be married to me and dragged to the wretched North," he reminded her softly, wondering why the words she had spoken to Risa still disturbed him so. They were no surprise. And he didn't know why he was creating war between them now. It had been painful to keep his distance from her as her waist slimmed and her breasts swelled, but the time they had spent together had actually been quite domestic. Happy.

That was about to change. With or without his desire to make war.

Alaina continued to stare out the window. "I was merely trying to explain to Risa that I hadn't intended to destroy her life."

"I can't see how you've destroyed her life," he said flatly.

She looked at him with a peculiarly wistful smile, her eyes a shimmering topaz. "Really? Surely you are aware that she's still in love with you?"

He didn't mean to be cruel in any way; he just knew that she would be damning him before the night was over. "Do you think so?" he inquired politely, as if concerned and surprised, yet a raw pain seemed to tear at his heart. Yes, Risa cared. And he cared about her as well. But he had become consumed with his wife, and no matter what barriers he tried to erect around his soul, she slipped through them.

And as of tonight . . . well, he wouldn't worry about it now.

"Ian," she said huskily, her hands folded in her lap, her eyes upon them. "You are no fool. You are well aware of Miss Risa Magee."

"We're here," he said as the carriage came to a halt in front of Rose's handsome home. He stepped down, reaching for her. He should have told her more about his plans, he thought fleetingly. But he craved peace, as long as he could have it.

When he escorted her to the door, he felt as if something had lodged in his throat. He was going to choke on his own damned desire for peace.

As they entered the foyer, Alaina offered him a grateful smile—she was so glad to be out. She felt a sweet rush of excitement to be involved with life again. So many people greeted her like an old friend; everyone was concerned for her and the baby. Risa was there, naturally, as stunning and poised as ever in royal blue silk. Colonel Magee was grave and kindly, concerned with Alaina's welfare, and quite solicitious. Yet after she had exchanged pleasantries with a number of people, she found herself becoming part of conversations that weren't pleasant in the least.

"Major McKenzie, just what is the world coming to?" Jill Sanders, the wife of a young naval lieutenant, demanded. "Can you just imagine? They've gone off and formed a new country—the Confederate States of America!"

"What?" Alaina asked, startled.

"Oh, my dear, of course, you've been busy with your precious little one and all—so soon after a babe, and you've got a waist like a my pinkie ring already! Ah, but domesticity does take one out of the news, eh? The cotton states have formed a government—there are seven of them now, though Texas didn't manage to get a delegate to Montgomery in time to be in the forming of it all. Texas just seceded on February first, you see, and their mockery of a government was formed on the fourth. Major! Had you heard that Jeff Davis was provisional president? Why, the man was a senator, a soldier! He was Secretary of War for President Pierce, and now . . . and that Alexander Stephens! Why, I heard him say myself that he was dead set against secession, and just look at him—vice president of the Confederate States of America!"

Alaina stared at Ian, feeling as if a fire had been set inside her stomach. Not a word. He knew all this. And he hadn't said a single thing to her.

"Stephens argued eloquently against secession," Ian responded to Mrs. Sanders. "But Stephens is a Georgian.

Apparently he felt obliged to follow his state despite the fact that the vote went against him."

"Tell me," Alaina interjected, "which of the Southern states have seceded so far? I'm afraid that I have been so very isolated in the last few weeks!"

"Well, now, you couldn't have missed South Carolina's secession!" Jill exclaimed, shaking her head. "Those rabble rousers! Then, hmmm, Mississippi, your own Florida, dear, Alabama, Georgia, Louisiana—and Texas! Yes, that's it—and in the right order. Isn't it, Ian?"

Alaina felt the blood drain from her face as she stared at Mrs. Sanders, then at Ian. His expression was impassive; there was an edge to his eyes, a cold glitter as he returned her stare. Yes, he had known all this. No, he hadn't felt it necessary to inform her. She started to move away from him, but a waltz was playing, and before she could protest he excused them and had her out on the floor among the other couples dancing. She stiffened in his arms, staring at him with hot contempt.

"Do I have this correctly? The state of Florida has seceded, and you have done nothing? *Nothing?*"

His cool blue eyes assessed her in turn. "My dear, you do have it correctly. The state of Florida has seceded— and I have done nothing—*nothing.*"

She inhaled sharply. "But Ian—"

"You've long known my opinion of secession," he said curtly, cutting her off.

"But—but what is your intent?" she demanded.

"I have no particular intent at the moment," he said. It disturbed him—and irritated him—that her anger brought such a flush to her cheeks and such fire to her eyes. More than ever, he wanted to hold her. Drag her against him, tell her that they did not have the force to prevent the winds of war that were beginning to blow.

But she was shaking in his arms. Shaking, because she wouldn't tolerate his words.

Or his ideals.

"I don't wish to dance with you," she said icily.

"What a pity."

"Ian, let me go," she told him.

"Alaina—"

She was surely going insane, she thought, because she didn't want him to let her go. She wanted him to hold

her, and tell her that yes, this was all horrible, it was
breaking his heart. But Florida, his state, had seceded,
and he was going to be loyal to his state, he was going
to resign. And they would go home. To Florida. To the
Confederate States of America.

But he wasn't going to say that.

"You're a traitor, Ian!" she cried. "A traitor to your
state, to your own people."

"Alaina, stop."

"No, I can't stop! Let me go. I don't want you touching me. Ever."

"You're my wife, Alaina—"

She shook her head. "I want to go home!"

"Alaina, you can't—"

"I've got to go. I *am* going home!" she informed him.

He tightened his arms around her. "If you ever walk
away from me and humiliate me in public due to your
views, I will drag you right back. And if you decide to
leave me, my love, you leave your son. If you think you
can kidnap him and run to the swamp and hide, remember that I know your state far better than you ever will.
If you think you're going to take my child, be aware
that I'll hunt you down wherever you go, and in the end,
I will win. You married me, Alaina. For better or worse.
You're my wife, and I will never allow you to forget
that fact."

She had never heard him speak so coldly. Nor with
greater warning and conviction.

"How can you turn your back on your state, your own
home?" she demanded furiously.

"I'm not turning my back on Florida; it will always be
my home. But I am against secession. There will be war,
and it won't be over in ninety days, though eventually
it will end and the North will be victorious, and the hard
path will be to see the state back into prosperity when
the bleeding is over."

She shook her head, staring at him as if he had quite
clearly lost his mind.

"I won't walk away from you, but Ian, let go of me!
In my eyes, you are a traitor. Don't touch me!"

He released her then so suddenly that she nearly
stumbled back from him.

"They called you a Yankee in South Carolina," she

reminded him suddenly. "An enemy. That's what you are. A *Yankee!*" she hissed. "You're a Yankee, and your wretched army did nothing about my father's murder."

"Your father died by accident."

"Negligence."

"Be that as it may—"

"You're a part of their horrid bureaucracy."

"You're refusing to see, Alaina—"

"I refuse a Yankee!"

"Ah. But you're married to a Yankee," he said politely. Then he bowed briefly to her, turned, and walked away, pausing to smile as someone stopped and spoke to him, answering another man, laughing with a friend. Mrs. Greenhow tapped him on the shoulder and he turned, flashing his handsome smile to her as well, then drawing her out to the dance floor.

Alaina turned in dismay, feeling almost blinded as she blinked back tears of confusion and frustration. She tried to make her way to the door; she had wanted to come here so badly tonight. Now she wanted only to escape.

She wasn't allowed to walk away from him, but he had managed to walk away quite easily from her.

She tried to escape, but people stopped to speak with her, congratulating her, asking her about Sean. They were kind; they were pleasant, worried that she was warm enough here in the Capital in such wicked winter weather. She smiled; she had to be as easy and nonchalant as her husband.

She made it to the door at last. A maid brought her coat, and she convinced the free black man Ian had hired as their driver to take her home; she was afraid the baby might need her.

That much was true. Her breasts were full, aching, sore. She hoped that Sean was hungry.

When she came in, she could hear Sean fussing, and she hurried upstairs to the bedroom, trying not to let Lilly see the misery in her face. But Lilly shook her head, *tsk*ing out a warning even as Alaina reached for the baby, taking him into her arms and quickly loosening her gown so that the baby could nurse.

"You're upset, you'll upset the little one as well."

"Don't be ridiculous. I won't upset the baby."

Lilly sniffed. "You're in a tempest—you'll make sour milk."

"Oh, Lilly, please."

"Now, you knew that it would happen, that Florida would secede. It has happened. What goes on in the world isn't your concern. You're a married woman. You support your man."

"He's a blind man!" Alaina hissed.

Sean began to cry. Lilly was right; she was upsetting the baby. She had to calm down.

"Shhh, shhh!" she whispered, rocking back and forth with Sean. She laid him down on her bed, struggling to get her clothing off. "Lilly, please. Just help me get out of this and into a nightgown—the beige one with the buttons down the front."

Lilly sniffed and helped her.

"Thanks," she told Lilly. "I'm fine now—I—I'd like to be alone with him."

"You remember what I say," Lilly warned.

Alaina wanted to remind Lilly that she was a servant, except that of course she was much more, and Alaina didn't particularly want to make an enemy out of Lilly. Lying next to Sean, she closed her eyes, wishing she could find some rest from the misery that plagued her. But there was just so much she could endure! The United States army hadn't done a thing yet to chastise the men who had killed her father. She couldn't possibly support that same army now when her home state had decided that Florida would have no more of it!

She lay awake, nervously looking toward the door, wondering if Ian would come barging in, furious that she had left him at a party she had insisted that they attend.

But Ian didn't come to her room.

She heard him come home about midnight.

And she heard him ride out again less than an hour later.

And she lay in tortured silence then, remembering that she had commanded that he not touch her.

And she knew that there were those who did not mind his touch at all.

Chapter 20

Abraham Lincoln was sworn in as president of the United States of America on March 4, 1861.

Ian wasn't in the city for the inauguration.

Alaina didn't see him after she left Rose Greenhow's party; Lilly told her later that she had still been sleeping when he had come up in the morning, spent time with Sean, and then departed. He had left her a note; he had gone "to fulfill my orders," and he assumed he'd be back within a month. She wondered if he had asked for orders that would send him away.

She wondered if he had decided he really didn't want a wife after all.

But he did want his child.

She considered leaving Washington herself, making arrangements to travel home. But he had said that he would come after her. And she knew that he would. He might not want her, but he did want Sean.

And so, for the time, she waited. And watched. And read the newspapers, and the various letters she received from Ian's family.

By the middle of March, the Confederate states had taken over most of the military bases and strongholds within their borders. Fort Sumter, in Charleston Harbor, remained in Union hands, as did Fort Pickens, and the forts at Key West and the Dry Tortugas. Alaina wondered if Ian had been sent to Fort Taylor at Key West, a place where he had often been based in better times. He had left her no information at all, which he had surely seen as for the best, but which made her believe that he was already involved in military operations against his own homeland.

So she waited, watching, as forces brought the North and South swiftly toward war. General Beauregard—late

of the United States army and a Mexican War hero—
had fortified Charleston Harbor. At Fort Sumter, Major
Anderson pleaded for reinforcements to keep his men
in rations as he awaited further orders. Every day, he
faced the armaments Beauregard had amassed on the
harbor.

In the midst of all this, Alaina was glad to know that
though Ian was not in Washington, Risa Magee was.

As was Mrs. Greenhow. Alaina found herself invited
to luncheons and teas at the woman's house, and she
was glad to go. Mrs. Greenhow was fascinating. So were
the people who came her way. And in her household,
men talked excitedly about the preparations for war.
Men talked about troops and brigades, and the numbers
and expertise of certain men as sharpshooters, engineers,
and more. Mrs. Greenhow never appeared bored at their
talk of warfare. She raptly listened to all they had to say.

It was strange, for Alaina knew Mrs. Greenhow remained in deep pain for her daughter Gertrude. She had
two older married daughters, and a little namesake
Rose, who lived with her now, and was the delight of
her life. Rose Greenhow seemed to appreciate the good
friends and family who supported her against her loss.
She showed Alaina her daughter's room one day; Rose
had not changed a thing since the day her daughter had
died. She handled her grief very well, fighting it with
living. Alaina admired her very much and felt her love
for Sean Michael grow ever fiercer. She learned that
though it had been agony to lose her father, there would
be no pain on earth like that of losing a child.

The days passed.

Ian's cousin Sydney wrote her that the situation in
Charleston was growing extremely grave and that it
seemed something would happen very soon. She was
anxious to go home to Florida and begged Alaina to
keep her informed of all the news from the Capital of
the old U.S..

Alaina also received a letter from Jen—written under
circumstances that greatly aggravated Alaina, for she discovered that Ian had been to her home in the *Confederacy* while she had been left behind in Washington. "How
odd!" Jen wrote.

We had heard that we were now a part of the Confederacy, and a Union officer takes his chances in the South these days, but it was so wonderful to see Ian. He brought news, which we crave. We're so far from the rest of the world that it is terribly difficult to know what is going on. We knew, of course, that the Federals are still holding the forts at Key West and the Dry Tortugas, but it's quite terrible to think that soon, we may have to dread Federal ships out at sea, and fear any arrival, lest it be a *foreign* attack! What a situation! My mother and father were here, and Lawrence, Ian, and I discussed the coming difficulties with them. It's very strange, because Father and Ian are on opposite sides, but they both see the same fate for Florida—it cannot be defended, but then again, how to blockade so very many miles of coastline? Ian told Father that he was sorry Florida was so quick to secede and join the Confederacy, for he thinks the Confederacy will have no choice but to throw Florida to the wolves if and when war does break out. Ian says that the Confederacy will have to strip Florida of her men to fight farther north, leaving Florida vulnerable to all manner of attack. Father might well agree with him, but he asked Ian what in God's name would the North want with our swampland. One way or the other, it will be a strange war on the peninsula. We will grow food and supply manpower. Salt, cattle, and men!

Your husband was well, bragging about your baby, whom I long to see, of course. I was terribly sorry to see Ian go; God knows when, or under what circumstances, we will meet again. Take the greatest care in these dark hours. My love,

                                                              Jen

The letter had been written several weeks before Alaina received it, which left her feeling more frustrated than ever. She didn't want to be here. Her heart was in the South. She longed to see Belamar again, to run on the beach. Spring was coming to D.C., but not quickly enough for Alaina. She belonged in the Far South.

While the nation crumbled, Sean thrived. Alaina delighted in him, and learned to maintain her sanity in

Washington—all the while growing increasingly furious with her husband's absence. She was restless, brooding over the newspapers, wondering where Ian was—and what would happen. Thank God for Rose—and even Risa, whom she saw occasionally at Rose's home. Risa had a gift for matter-of-factness, and whatever resentment she bore toward Alaina was open, and often tempered by her quick humor. One afternoon the two of them determined to make cookies as guests at Rose's house. Quite accidentally, Alaina had let slip a cup of flour, and it had spilled all over Risa's dress. Risa, in turn, had set down a bowl very heavily, and the flour naturally floated over Alaina. After that, they both picked up the flour—and let fly.

Rose's kitchen was a disaster, but they were laughing uncontrollably until they both sobered at the sound of Sean suddenly waking and bellowing out in hunger. "I think your son is calling you," Risa told her.

"Is it safe to go get him?" Alaina inquired.

"Is it safe?" Risa inquired innocently.

"Dare I turn my back, lest there be another barrage?" Alaina demanded.

Risa smiled very slowly. "You're safe. You're quite safe from me." Risa dusted off her hands. "Of course, I understand there's a widow living outside of Tampa who might not be quite so safe."

Alaina inhaled so sharply that she breathed in a cloud of flour and began to cough. Risa pounded on her back. "Sorry—I mean, you do know her, I assume, and know about her?"

"Yes, I know her—and you were condemning *me* for being naked in a pool. Well, your dear honorable almost-fiancé was only in that pool because of the widow to whom you now refer."

"Ah!" Risa said softly, her dark lashes sweeping her floured cheeks. Then she looked to Alaina with a shrug. "It just goes to show you that a woman behaves honorably, as she has been taught all her life—and pays for that nobility. Had I not heeded propriety, I'd probably be married to Ian now."

"You really did love him," Alaina said quietly.

"I really did. But I also promise you, as long as you

don't throw your marriage away, I'm no threat to you. I'm the honorable one, remember?"

Alaina smiled, looking at Risa. "I'm not afraid of Lavinia—the widow Trehorn. She amused Ian, and nothing more. *You* are a threat to me, because he cares about you. He may still be in love with you; I don't really know."

Risa stared at her, hands on her hips for a long moment. "You two are married, and you have a beautiful child—with a bloodthirsty scream. Please, go attend to him!"

Alaina smiled. To her amazement, she reached for Risa and gave her a quick hug before hurrying off to clean herself up and tend to Sean. Strangely, she felt that she had found a good friend.

While Risa was decidedly pro-Union, Rose Greenhow was not. She was amazingly truthful about her sympathies for the South, while maintaining wonderfully proper but flirtatious relationships with Union officers, cabinet members, and congressmen. Alaina, who was far more quiet in her convictions, nevertheless enjoyed Rose tremendously.

Yet no matter what friendships she formed in Washington, she wondered how long she could bear to remain, because every day brought new information about the great divide splitting the country. Everywhere, militia groups formed, horses and arms were counted, the United States army began to arrive en masse in Washington, D.C. Despite Ian's threat—or promise—that he would hunt her and the baby down if she were to leave him, she longed to find a way home—to his family, if need be. Surely, going to her in-laws could not be considered desertion! Besides which, Ian had no right to threaten her, when it was he who had left.

One evening in early April, Alaina was invited to a "casual buffet supper" at Rose Greenhow's home, and Alaina determined to ask for her wise older friend's advice, if not assistance. She had been surprised to discover—through Rose herself—that Rose, who was extremely friendly with many high-ranking officers and officials, was also an ardent anti-abolitionist. Rose's father had been murdered by a black man who had risen against him when Rose was just a child.

Alaina didn't know exactly what had happened, but Rose had been very young, and she didn't carry reason in her breast, merely hatred. Many people hated for different reasons; she knew her own hatred for blue uniforms might not be entirely just, but it was there. She recalled a letter from Julian regarding the special legislative session in which Florida had decided on leaving the Union; apparently, one of their neighbors had proclaimed that it was a pity Harriet Beecher Stowe hadn't died as a child—that way, *Uncle Tom's Cabin* wouldn't have been written, and the entire country might not be up in arms!

Rose Greenhow's strange conflict of feelings seemed to make her all the more an interesting person, and Alaina thought that if she was able to make it back home, she was going to miss Rose. But she *was* going to escape Washington. For home. Soon.

On the night of Rose's buffet, Alaina dressed carefully, wearing one of the new black mourning dresses she'd had made since the baby's birth. The neckline was lower than those she had worn lately, and the bodice was laced and closed with a series of tiny buttons. Her sleeves were short, and she'd had a beautiful shawl made that fell gracefully from her arms. She felt in an exceptionally reckless mood that afternoon, and when she reached the Greenhow house, she was glad she had come. The house was filled with laughing men and women, and even if the soldiers were sounding like braggarts, they were all in a high state of excitement—everyone in the country seemed to be waiting, for what, no one was quite sure.

"Alaina! How delightful that you've come," Rose told her, greeting her with kisses on both cheeks, then added in a soft whisper, "You do your husband very proud, you know. From senator to soldier, the men find you quite charming, and my lady friends are taken with you as well! Be a love, I need you to help me entertain. There's a group of young soldiers on the porch who have just been stationed here, and they're quite lonely, in need of sweet, feminine advice. Let me introduce you."

Rose led Alaina out the back door where four handsome young soldiers lounged against the railing. At the ladies' appearance they all quickly straightened. "Boys!"

Rose drawled with her delightful accent, "you are at ease here. I've brought you Major Ian McKenzie's wife to meet, just in case you find yourselves riding with her husband somewhere in the future! Alaina, the boys are all recent graduates of West Point—there you have Charlie Litwin, Harold Penny, William Mony, and Nate Dillon. Gentlemen, Mrs. McKenzie."

Alaina smiled, acknowledging them all. The men greeted her enthusiastically, caps in their hands. Charlie slicked back his hair nervously.

"Punch, ma'am? I'll just bring you some punch," William offered.

"Why, thank you," Alaina said, smiling. It would have been impossible not to enjoy their attention.

William brought her punch. Harold ushered her to the porch's largest cushioned rocker. "Well, gentlemen," she said, lifting her punch cup. "To the future."

"To the future!" Charlie said.

"Whatever it may be," Harold added a little glumly.

"You sound upset, sir," Alaina said.

"I am. I'm from Maryland, ma'am, and I'm not quite sure yet whether I'm North or South."

"Really?"

William explained. "Harold and I are both from Maryland. Charlie and Nate are Virginians."

"Ah."

"Maryland isn't going to secede. It just isn't going to happen. Geographically, the North can't let it happen," Charlie said.

"But if Maryland chooses—" Alaina began.

"Ma'am, it ain't always what we choose!" Nate said, and drew a map in the air, explaining what it took to move large groups of men, and how armies worked with cavalry, infantry, artillery, reconnaissance—and spies. Their conversation intrigued Alaina, as did the fact that they seemed so willing to tell her so much. A certain amount of flirting was natural and in order, and after her last encounter with her husband, it felt very good indeed.

"Now, Virginia, ma'am," Nat was saying, his wheat-colored eyes bright and his manner charming, "is not a brash lady. No, ma'am. She'll not get hot under the collar, get her dander up—lest some great fight takes place and she is called to take up arms against her friends. No, sir, she'll balk like a mule!"

"And if Virginia secedes, Lieutenant Dillon?" Alaina inquired. She was quite comfortable; Rose's punch had assuredly been spiked with a bit of whiskey. The rocker moved back and forth, the breeze was pleasant. The sun was beginning to set as they talked, the moon to rise. Nate and the others leaned against the railing in a semicircle around her; it was almost as if she was holding court.

"Ma'am, I don't know. I do love Virginia, mightily. But I know some good men who just can't see clear to what is happening. Right now, I'm just praying that Virginia stays in the Union. But everybody is preparing for bloodshed. If old Virginia secedes, they lose some of the finest men in all the military."

"Yes, of course," she said, smiling at Lieutenant Dillon. Then her smile faded.

There was someone standing in the doorway to the porch, standing very still within the frame and shadowed by the coming of night. Yet she knew the stance and the build.

Ian was there.

Her heart began to tremble. She felt the strangest weakness sweeping over her.

She blinked quickly, thinking the twilight was playing tricks on her. But it was Ian, and she wondered just how long he had been standing there watching her. Listening to her conversation.

"Ian!" she gasped.

"Hello, my love," he murmured, moving into the misty light of the early evening.

Lieutenant Dillon sprang to attention, the other young men following his lead. "Sir, Major, sir!" he said.

"Sir, Lieutenant, sirs, all of you—at ease," Ian teased lightly in return, his smile crooked as he strode to stand behind Alaina's chair. She tried to rise; his hands upon her shoulders kept her down, and he leaned to kiss her quickly on the cheek. She felt herself stiffen against his touch, despite the fact that her heart continued to pound wildly.

It was only the presence of others that kept her manner calm, her voice level, as she spoke to him. "What a . . . surprise," she murmured. "When did you return to Washington?"

"Quite recently."

"And you came straight here!" she exclaimed, her tone so light that the edge to it was barely discernible. "The perfect officer and gentleman, seeking the company and enlightenment of his fellow officers even before seeing to the welfare of his own wife and son."

"But I've found my wife here—how very fortunate," Ian responded smoothly. "It's so good to see that you haven't pined away during my absence. It's a relief to see you entertained by Union fighting men, and it seems you admire the Union uniform when worn by these young men. Ah, but then again, gentlemen! You must learn to take greater care in the company of Southerners! My wife is a Floridian—she could be seeking military secrets from the lot of you."

Lieutenant Dillon, who had appeared very nervous and uncomfortable, laughed—apparently finding himself at ease at last since Major McKenzie joked with him so. "But, sir! She's your wife."

"Indeed," Ian murmured. "Well, gentlemen, I thank you for entertaining my wife, and I bid you good night. Alaina, my love, I must admit, I am weary, and ready for my home."

Alaina longed to say that he'd been getting about on his own quite well for some time now—he was welcome to continue doing so. But the pressure he applied to her shoulder was such that she could let out a shriek or rise, and she chose to rise.

Ian was in a foul humor indeed, for he was very nearly brusque with Rose Greenhow when they said good night, and he didn't have a single thing to say to her when he set Alaina into her carriage. He didn't join her, but rode behind the conveyance to the house. Alaina didn't wait for anyone to help her out; she opened the door, set down the step, and exited the carriage quickly, hurrying into the house. In the foyer, Alaina found Lilly waiting. "Major McKenzie is home, directly behind me, Lilly, if you would see to him."

She ran up the stairs to her room then, closing the door, leaning against it, gasping for breath. After a mo-

ment she went to the crib where Sean slept, and saw
that he was not in his little bed.

"Oh, my God!" she cried in sheer panic. She spun
around, racing back to her door, but it opened just as
she reached it, and she plowed straight into Ian. She
brought her hands up against his chest, striking him
wildly with her fists. "Where is he? Where is the baby?
You—"

He caught her wrists, stopping her. "Safe," he said
flatly.

She wrenched free of him, backing away, so very
afraid of his touch. "But you've taken him."

A deep, dangerous look in his eyes stopped her cold.

Despite her firmest resolve, she found herself shaking.
"I had no idea where you were. You chose to leave
without saying a word to me. It's true, I meant to leave,
before it became impossible to do so. I waited here a
long time."

"Other women wait."

"Other women's husbands have the good sense to be
loyal to their home state! I was just going to go to your
parents' home."

"Were you?" he inquired skeptically.

She moistened her lips, painfully aware of her growing
fear. He'd been gone a long time. He was leaner.
Stronger. Meaner, she thought. Far more ruthless than
ever. Solid as steel, as inflexible as rock. Hotter than fire.

"What difference does it make? I want nothing to do
with you, Ian. I told you, if you must persist in being a
traitor, I don't want you touching me. Now, I don't know
what game you're playing, but I want my son."

She lifted her chin and started to stride past him. He
caught her arm, swinging her back before him.

"Oh, no, Alaina, I don't think so. You're not walking
out of this room now."

"The hell I'm not!" she said, furious, shaking. She
started past him again, this time trying to circle around
him for her freedom. It was a futile effort. One long
step brought him to her.

"Ian, I—"

She broke off with a shriek, for she found herself
lifted and thrown down on her bed. Before she could

draw breath, he had pounced upon her like a jungle cat and straddled hard and furious atop her.

"You aren't going anywhere. Not today."

"I despise you in that uniform!" she cried out.

"Ah, but what a little hypocrite you are, my love! I come home after endless weeks on duty to find you laughing away, the loveliest little belle in all D.C.—flirting with a circle of young men in uniforms of the United States army. Would flirting describe the situation? Hmm . . . yes, I think so. But to what end—when you so despise those uniforms?"

"Mrs. Greenhow asked me to help entertain her company," Alaina said, grating her teeth. His eyes flashed cobalt fire. His thighs were tight about her hips, strong, warm. His hands pinned her wrists to either side of her head, and she wanted very desperately to hate him.

But she didn't. She just . . .

Wanted him.

"Ian, leave me be!" she pleaded.

He shook his head slowly. "I've never been anything but honest with you. I've never made promises I could not keep. And you can shriek and scream that I'm a traitor until the end of time, but I'm your husband, and I'll be damned if I'll spend my time watching you flash your smile and laugh and flirt with other men while you seek to deny me!"

"You're pigheaded and arrogant and you've no rights when you simply leave—" she began, but this time her words were broken off by the force of his lips upon hers. She forgot what she had been saying. His mouth was all-consuming, covering, devouring hers. The passion of his kiss momentarily stunned her and all she could do was taste the wonder of his mouth, feel the brutal but sensual plundering of his tongue, demanding, thirsting, taking, arousing, eliciting. The feel and scent of him were so unbearably sweet that she could scarcely believe he was with her again, the weight of his body so hard against her own. His hands stroked her cheeks, held her face to his kiss. His knuckles brushed her throat . . . his fingers . . .

Plucked one by one the tiny buttons of her bodice until her breasts were free, and his hands and lips were upon them, cupping, kneading, massaging, teasing, tasting, taunting. . . .

Her fingers threaded through his hair. Her breasts were swollen; she'd been away from the baby several hours. And she told herself that Ian's touch should hurt, but it did not, she wanted more.

"No . . ." she whispered softly.

He paid no heed.

But then, just then, from somewhere below in the house, she heard Sean begin to cry. She jerked, trying to rise.

"Ian, the baby!"

"We have a good staff who will see to the baby!" he exclaimed in exasperation.

"But Ian—"

To her amazement, he rose suddenly, shedding his boots, his uniform jacket, and shirt. She stared at him for a minute, then tried to clasp her bodice together, rolling swiftly to the side of the bed.

She never made it. He was back, stripped down to his breeches, and she was pinned beneath him. "Do you really want me going elsewhere?" he inquired softly.

She inhaled sharply, staring at him. "Oh! You really are a bastard!" she hissed.

"Do you?"

"Perhaps—"

He cupped her face, stroking it with his palm, staring into her eyes. "Can you really say, my love," he demanded very softly, "that you don't want me? If you can say so . . ."

She gasped, spun about suddenly as he impatiently maneuvered the dress from her. "You're going to rip it!" she cried.

"Good. I should rip all your clothing. You'd be forced to stay inside."

"Ian, I've just had it made."

"It's far too revealing."

"It's a mourning gown!"

"Indeed."

The gown didn't rip; still, she struggled against him as she found herself stripped of her linen chemise, pantalettes, petticoats, and shoes and stockings. She shoved against him, only to linger on the hot sleek feel of his flesh. It was impossible not to feel his nakedness against her own, his chest pressed to her breasts, the proof of his arousal, still caught within the tautness of his breeches. . . .

"My love . . ." he whispered, fingers smoothing her hair into a fan on the pillow, breath fanning her cheeks. His hands moved over the length of her nakedness, demanding, subtle, barely brushing her flesh, then pressing insistently against it . . . his lips against her. Hot. Kisses, searing, falling on her throat, her breast, belly, thighs, and then between. . . .

Molton lead seemed to shoot through her, unbearably sweet, so sensually intimate after so long a time that she shrieked, fingers tearing into his hair. She felt herself shudder with a flood of instant, searing sensation. She tried to curl into the covers, embarrassed by the swift violence of her response in the midst of her denials. But he was up with her, his arms around her, forcing her to face him, and his lips covered hers again, the taste of their intimacy between them, and the stroke of his hand upon her then was tender and light, amazingly awakening the stirrings of hunger deep within her again.

His lips broke from hers. Pressed against her cheek. Nuzzled her ear.

"Should I leave now?" he whispered.

She tensed, longing to hit him, but he was suddenly over her, challenging her with his eyes, and parting her legs with the sudden hard shift of his body. She closed her eyes, shaking again, as he came very slowly into her, apparently aware, despite whatever emotion lay between them, that she needed gentleness this first time after the baby's birth . . .

And yet . . .

Oh, God . . .

It was easy. Easy to want him. Easy to feel the rise of longing, aching. Needing . . .

Easy to feel the fire, and become captured within the golden flames of its fury. Everything about him seemed as fuel to that fire, the friction of his bare flesh against her own, the hardness and heat of his muscles, the feel of him, inside her, a part of her, touching, stroking, inside, impetus rising, the cobalt of his eyes impaling her own, his every thrust driving her upward to a hunger like insanity, wanting, seeking, reaching that incredible surcease. . . .

She lay then, gasping for breath, feeling the sweetness steal throughout her again, quaking in its elusive pleasure. She felt the last shudders rake through his body as well. She was deliriously happy; she wanted to cry. And she wondered if their marriage, no matter how ridiculously begun, might have been wonderful if not . . .

If not for the world around them.

He lay beside her, stroking her back, evoking a last convulsive shudder from her as she curled into his shoulder, glad to just have him by her side. She didn't want to, but she loved the feel of his flesh, the sight of his muscled arms, the structure of his hands. She loved his face, handsome features, searing eyes; his mouth, so generous, sensual, quick to curl in laughter . . . in anger.

His fingers moved into her hair; his lips pressed against her forehead.

"If this is how you hate me, my love," he whispered, "you must continue to do so."

She raised a fist to pummel his shoulder; he laughed, yet it had a hollow sound, and he caught her hand before she could strike, easing out her clenched fingers, stroking the center of her palm.

Lying beside him, cloaked by his warmth, she felt a shudder rip through her again. "You're wrong, Ian!" she said miserably. "I don't hate you." She hesitated briefly. "I love you."

He was dead still. Then he rose on an elbow to stare down at her. Before he could speak, she added quickly, "But I hate the way you treat me; I hate what you're doing. I want to go home."

He was silent a moment. Then he leaned toward her and kissed her lips very slowly and sensuously. "Don't hate anything tonight, my love. Don't hate at all." He pulled her into his arms, drawing her hands against the breadth of his chest and cradling her tightly to him. "Feel me, Alaina. Abide with me. Tonight, we are home."

Quick tears stung her eyes. She buried her head against his shoulder, trembling. He started to make love to her again, and sensation swept into her, robbing her of all thought except for the certainty that she did love him.

And in his arms, she was happy. She longed to be at peace. She could almost . . .

Feel the sun.

It was good that the next few days went well, and that they had time together.

Time in which they didn't talk.

Because Beauregard's troops had been ordered to fire on the Union men who had refused to surrender Fort Sumter. Major Anderson had gallantly held on, but in the end it had come to a test of arms.

It was war.

"What will you do now?" Alaina demanded, finally putting the unspoken question squarely between them. "What will you do? It is war, real, bloody war, and your army is firing on your people." She turned her back on him as they stood in the parlor, the newspaper lying on the floor between them.

He was quiet for a long moment, then he sighed. "I will do what I have been doing. I will stand fast for the Union."

She spun around. "Then I will hate you!" she promised him.

He stared at her a long while, cobalt eyes unfathomable. "I've made my choice; I suppose you must make yours. So, my love—hate me," he suggested, and spun on his heel, leaving her there.

She wondered bleakly if he had gone to Risa, who stood as staunchly for the preservation of the Union as any soldier who might ever fight upon the field.

Alaina sank into a chair, trembling, praying, wondering how she could endure either staying or leaving. She was trying not to cry, but at last a sob escaped her.

Chapter 21

On April 19, President Lincoln proclaimed a blockade against all Southern ports from Texas to South Carolina. As the month progressed, so did the flurry of secession—and the clamping down on the border states such as Kentucky and Maryland. The Confederacy became solidified and those who had been calling for peace no longer felt that there could be any compromise.

In the midst of the schism, personal tragedy struck near and dear to both Ian and Alaina, for another of Rose's beloved daughters sickened, and died. Rose was devastated; Ian and Alaina did their best to sustain and comfort her—and both realized how dear their own child was to them.

In this, they found a special, silent comfort in one another as well. To ease Rose's sorrow, her friends all kept her involved in lively political discussions, and with Rose, it was certainly true: Argument and activity helped assuage her anguish and sorrow.

As war preparations on both sides continued, Ian found to his surprise that he had been summoned not to the Capital or War Department, but to the White House for a meeting with the chief executive himself.

Ian met with Lincoln in a small, private office. Though he had briefly shaken the man's hand a few years earlier after witnessing one of his debates, he found himself newly impressed not just by the president's height—Ian was two inches over six feet himself and Lincoln seemed to tower over him—but by the character written into the man's features. Lincoln had a look of melancholy about him, and Ian had heard that he often suffered from ill health. He was a very thin man, surely no more than one hundred and eighty pounds for his six-foot-four-inch frame. His eyelids drooped slightly, adding to his sad-hound look. He had a slow way of speaking—a slowness that lulled and charmed. Yet what impressed Ian most was the absolute faith Lincoln had in his own convictions—and the deadly seriousness and sorrow with which he looked upon the war.

Lincoln greeted Ian with a handshake, indicated a chair, and poured the tea himself. Then he sat back in an upholstered rocker facing Ian, studying his features. "So, you have remained with us, Major McKenzie. Do you intend to do so in the future?"

"I do, sir."

"What of your state?"

"I'm deeply distressed about the course of events."

"You're well aware of everything happening there?"

Ian nodded. "The Union soundly holds Fort Jefferson, Dry Tortugas, and Fort Taylor, Key West, and Fort Pickens. That the Rebs quickly and easily managed to seize the naval yard at Pensacola is a pity, because there is excellent anchorage there, armaments and tools—and a railway directly into Alabama. But the state continues to suffer, arguing over state versus Confederate authority over troops. The Florida legislature was at one time happy to disband the militia—save taxpayers' money— but then they had to reinstate it because they were desperate for defense."

"Discouraging, I would think, to Floridians."

"Yes, but don't underestimate their loyalty to the Confederacy," Ian warned.

"I try not to underestimate any power," Lincoln murmured. "And still, there are so many divided loyalties. Jeff Davis and I were both born in the state of Kentucky, and now we face one another over a great divide," Lincoln said with quiet irony. "Were you aware that I had informally offered command of all Union forces in the field to an old teacher of yours—Colonel Robert E. Lee?"

"Yes," Ian said.

Lincoln smiled, a slow, sad, wry smile. I'm terribly sorry he turned me down. I believe I have lost one of the finest soldiers in any military arena. He was most ardently against secession, and he served the Union brilliantly and loyally for a very long time. This is a bitter decision for him indeed, for his home, Arlington, sits upon a hill just across the river. He chose to resign and will most certainly accept a position with the Confederacy. . . ." Lincoln shrugged, lifting his large hands in a helpless gesture. "You, sir, are well acquainted with the strategy of warfare; we could not allow a hostile power to hold property from which cannons could annihilate Washington. Yet my heart was heavy for him when he left here. The poor man went home that night to a wife who is the grandchild of Martha Washington. And her father— stepson of *the* founding father of our country—built their home. A home where he has raised his family, watched his children grow, where Mary Custis Lee has cared for many historical artifacts left us by President Washington. What a terrible decision Lee had to make. But that will happen to us all. It is my understanding that you come from an exceptional home in Florida."

"Yes, sir."

"Your wife has a home in Florida as well?"

"She does, sir."

Lincoln nodded, as if with an understanding far deeper than he could ever explain. "My own Mary hails from Kentucky; if there is war, it is most likely many of her kin will fight against the Union."

"I'm afraid, sir, that this will be an unbearably painful situation for many a man—and woman."

"I pray with all my heart for God's guidance," Lincoln said with such a tremor to his voice that Ian wished he could reach out to the man and somehow ease the burden he saw for the future. So many people—on both sides—had taken the prospect of war lightly. Not so with this strange, thoughtful giant of a man.

"Well!" Lincoln said suddenly. "It's my understanding, Major McKenzie, that you are an expert in the terrain of your state."

Ian arched a brow. "Well, I'm familiar with the peninsula, but so are many men."

"The south of it?"

Ian frowned, and Lincoln smiled suddenly. "Surely, Major, you are aware that I have announced a blockade. Not that it is much in place as yet—it seems we Americans have a talent for getting into wars before planning for them—but I do feel strongly that the only way we will ever bring those rebel states back into the fold is to tie a noose around them—constrict them so tightly that they'll have to give up. So, I intend to assign you to one of my men here in Washington, and you will be responsible to him, and no one else."

"I'm afraid I still don't understand—"

"I want to set you ashore in enemy territory, Major. You'll have a small group of men; you'll choose them and train them yourself. And when the runners break through the blockade and enemy spies make landfall on the peninsula, Major, you will stop them." He stood suddenly, walked to the room's desk, and spread out a rolled map that lay upon it. Rising, Ian quickly saw that the map included Florida, and parts of nearby states of Georgia, Alabama, and Louisiana, as well as the Bahamas and Cuba. "Major, if you'll bear with me . . ."

Ian nodded, coming to stand beside Lincoln as he spoke. "Major, Florida's inner transportation system can be called primitive as best. I've learned that one path planned by the blockade runners is here—Mosquito Inlet. Supplies will then be hauled by wagon to the St. Johns River, then taken by small steamer up the Oklawaha to Fort Brooks. From Fort Brooks, they'll be carried again by wagon to Waldo, from Waldo to Baldwin by rail, then again by wagon from the Florida rail system at Madison to Quitman, on Georgia's railway system. I tell you, Major, that is a complicated journey. Hauling heavy materials . . . it's estimated it could take a month. Through poorly guarded country. A small party of specially trained men could strike quickly and without warning and do severe damage—either confiscating supplies or seeing that they're destroyed. Here—another route I've been shown. An even slower route! Biscayne Bay— a fine place to anchor, since seaman say there are places where fresh water can be obtained through the salt. And here, coming in by the Miami River—you have miles and miles of nothing—except for old Indian trails. Goods obtained from Cuba or the Bahamas might readily be brought here—then north." Lincoln looked up at Ian again. "That's where you come in. Your home state is little more than a massive coastline. With your knowledge of the marshland and swamps, we'll be making use of your special talents."

"Are you asking me to spy?" Ian inquired.

Lincoln shook his head. "On the contrary. You will wear a uniform at all practicable times, Major. I mean to be prepared for what will come. There might be very little action for months . . . and it may all be over quickly. God knows. I don't think so. We've a long way to go to create a sound military system, but our difficulties are not as great as those faced by our sisters in rebellion." He said the last with a wry smile. He wasn't going to say the word *enemy*.

Ian was quiet for a moment. It was not what he had expected. He wasn't just going to fight his state; he was going to fight from within it.

"May I trust you with this mission, Major, or is there a possibility that you might choose to fight for the South? I assure you—there are many who will still be leaving the Union service as the days go by. There is certainly no dishonor is stating such a wish now."

Ian hesitated for a long moment. The time had come; he had known it was coming. He had always known that he would reach this point, and he had known which way he would go. When he'd recently been sent down to Fort Taylor, he'd seen Jen, Jerome, and his aunt and uncle. He'd also gotten a message home, and spent time back at Cimarron with his mother, father, Tia, and Julian. His father would never condone the war, but he intended to sit tight, and not desert Cimarron. Tia had decided not to return to school, but to stay close to home. Julian had become attached to a St. Augustine militia group and been commissioned into military medical service as a lieutenant. Though they would go separate ways, they would do so without bitterness. They would all have to pray that Cimarron would survive.

Ian and Julian embraced long and hard before parting, the thought of which now disturbed Ian deeply. He was cavalry; he had assumed he'd be assigned to fight with the main branch of the army. He had hoped for, and assumed he'd be given, a command far, far from home.

"This is, of course, an informal request," President Lincoln continued. "Your orders will come down to you from General Brighton, who will also see to it that you, your men, and whatever supplies you need are transported as necessary. Sir, will you accept your assignment?"

Ian nodded slowly. "You are, sir, the commander-in-chief."

With a heavy heart, he stood, shook hands with the president, and left.

He heard a rumbling in the sky as he stepped out on the lawn. He looked up. There were no visible storm clouds. And still the rumbling continued.

He didn't want the damned job he had just been given. Didn't want it at all. Yet even as he started toward home, he was making plans on exactly how to carry it out.

Thank God for Alaina. For the amazing relationship they had come to share. He had thought that the actual outbreak of war would have driven them completely apart. Yet not so. Since the shelling of Fort Sumter—and especially since Rose had lost her child—Alaina had been quiet, but loving and supportive. The night he had first come home, she had said she loved him, and nothing could have surprised him more—nor so swiftly and completely captured what remained of his heart. He admitted to himself that he had been falling in love with her ever since he'd seen her all grown up—dueling on his lawn, since the night of their marriage when he had first taken her into his arms. If only . . .

It didn't seem to matter now.

After his talk with Lincoln, he returned home to find that she was entertaining Rose Greenhow and several other women in his parlor. "Excuse me, ladies, please, don't let me interfere," he said, but Alaina had risen, and at her cue, the other women rose as well. Ian left them, going upstairs. Since he'd come home last, he'd slept with her in her room every night. But now he came to his own room. He was delighted to see that some good soul had managed to prepare a hot bath in anticipation of his return home, and he gladly stripped and sank into it.

He had scarcely slipped into the water and leaned his head back against the tub's rim when he heard his door opening. He didn't open his eyes; he didn't need to. He could sense her presence. But long minutes passed, and he opened his eyes, turning.

She had slipped silently out of her own clothing and walked toward him now, naked as Eve, her long hair streaming behind her in a golden cascade. He stared, fascinated. She came to the tub, knelt by it, leaned over to kiss his lips—long, lingering, seductive. He felt himself harden in the warm water long before she slipped her hand into it to soap and caress his sex. He rose slightly, slipping an arm around her, dragging her down with him. Water sloshed over the tub. Heedless, he returned the wet, openmouthed passion of her kiss, running his soapy hands over the length of her body, caressing her breasts, hips, thighs, and mound. She moaned against his kiss and he rose, lifting her in the tub, and again the water sluiced from them and over the rim, onto the floor. He carried her to the bed and laid her down. But she was instantly upon her knees, meeting him, her lips on his again, then showering kisses over the matted dampness of his chest. Her hands stroked down his backbone, over his buttocks. Her caresses slid lower and lower until she took him completely, driving him to something near frenzy, desire so hot and vivid that the threat of war faded away, and life was a burst of brilliant white fire and flash. His body constricted as tautly as a bowstring, the pleasure in him so exquisite that it was sweet agony. When he could bear no more he captured her, forcing her down into the depths of the bed, finding himself in the very depths of her, and making love with a fever both violent and tender. When surcease came, he climaxed so volatilely that it was long, long moments before he could feel again at all, breathe—hear the world again despite the still raucous beating of his heart.

And she remained with him. Golden hair tangled all about him, one knee cast against his thigh. She was curled against him, sleek with the dampness of their lovemaking, her scent hinting erotically of that most recent bout, and still carrying a sweetly feminine hint of roses.

He pulled her even closer to him, sighing softly.

"Thank God for you," he told her.

She trembled suddenly, but smoothed a lock of his hair from his forehead.

"I thought that you seemed depressed," she murmured.

"Orders."

She sat up then, golden eyes on his with grave concern. "What orders, Ian? Talk to me, tell me what's going on, let me share it all with you."

He stared up at her. God, she was beautiful, strands of her glimmering hair falling over the fullness of her breasts, her body sleekly lovely, her eyes filled with concern. He reached out and touched her face, and the slightest little twist of guilt gripped him, then released. He might have married Risa, and he would have loved her, and they might have shared such moments. But he had married Alaina—and even if the circumstances which had seemed so crucial then paled now before the onslaught of war, he couldn't help but be glad of Alaina now, of her petite beauty, of the passion with which she could make love and ease his spirit. Yet even as he opened his mouth to talk to her, some strange intuition kept him quiet.

He drew her back into his embrace. "Just the situation, my love," he said. And he told her a bit about the many troops from different states filing into Washington. He gave her careful bits of information, things that the general populace might easily learn, and wondered how, when she had suddenly come around so magnificently as a wife in the midst of all else, he was just so damned . . .

Uneasy.

"Naturally, dear, the most important information we need now has to do with the immediate movements of the troops," Rose Greenhow told Alaina, playing with Sean as she spoke.

The woman was absolutely amazing, Alaina thought. Since Rose had first suggested there might be some good she could do for the Confederacy in Washington, things had moved rapidly along.

Rose had become the center of a spy ring.

Rose was first approached by a Captain Thomas Jordan, who had been serving as an assistant quartermaster on the War Department staff. Though Captain Jordan had served the Union, he had been covertly planning an intelligence system long before the shelling of Fort Sumter, and Mrs. Greenhow—who was admittedly an anti-abolitionist and pro-South, but a true matriarch of Washington society and friend and confidante to many in high places—had seemed the perfect woman to have in his

network. Captain Jordan had now joined the Confederacy, but he had left a cipher with Rose, and she would
communicate information to him through enemy lines.

It was frightening. It was fantastic.

It was for the rights of men. The Confederacy had the
God-given right to independence, just as the thirteen
Colonies had had the right to rebel against England all
those years ago. The Rebs were the patriots now, acting
like their forefathers.

Bankers, socialites, doctors, maids, and even soldiers
were all part of Rose's secret ring. Many people in
Washington were for the Southern cause—despite the
fact that it was the Northern Capital. Alaina was glad
to help Rose in any way she could, especially since her
assignments were generally quite simple. Rose spent
most of her time charming two men in particular: Colonel Keyes, who was secretary to General Winfield Scott,
general-in-chief of the army, and Senator Wilson of Mas-
sachusetts. As Rose's guest, Alaina drew certain men
into conversation, gaining from them every little bit and
piece of military information possible. It was easy; and
Rose was quite pleased with her.

Alaina felt passionately about her task: The better information the Southern commanders had, the more quickly
it might all be over. Rose had taught her what a good
spy learned: description and destination of forces; quan-
tities of artillery, cavalry, and infantry; dates of intended
departures and arrivals.

Sometimes it frustrated Alaina to realize that many a
dazzled man was eager to tell her all about his day, while
it seemed that Ian managed to say nothing to her at
all—no matter what the heat of their passion. She wondered why he kept quiet, but sometimes she was glad
he said so little to her, because it was one thing to spy
for one's country, and another to betray one's husband.

As spring turned to summer, the situation grew increasingly hostile between North and South.

At the beginning of July, Alaina came home from an
afternoon tea to find that Ian was in the bedroom with
Sean, almost six months old now, sleeping peacefully in
his arms. He held his son with such a tender closeness
that Alaina felt an aching in her heart—and a sudden
fear.

"Ian?" she questioned nervously, hurrying to his side, falling to her knees, and placing her hands upon his knees. "Shhh," he murmured, smiling sadly as he eased up, placing Sean in his cradle. He came back to Alaina, stooping down to draw her to her feet. "I sail out tomorrow," he said.

She inhaled sharply; there were no troop movements that she knew about as yet. The army had been amassing in Washington, but according to Rose's best sources, they weren't due to leave until the middle of July.

"Oh, Ian!" she whispered.

He said nothing else to her, but slipped a hand beneath her knees to pick her up. She clung to him. He had left her before, but this time . . . there was something very wrong with this time.

They left Sean sleeping in her room as Ian carried Alaina down the hall to his own. The shades were drawn; the afternoon was dark. He set her down without a word. She removed his sword and scabbard, feeling the blue fire of his eyes on hers. He shed his jacket and shirt and then had her in his arms, kissing her, holding her, tasting her, ravaging her mouth with a fierce hunger.

Somehow they both knew that this time together must be branded in their hearts and minds for a very long time. He removed her clothing with patience . . . and impatience. Some buttons were undone. Some were torn from the fabric. He kissed her flesh everywhere, as if imprinting himself upon her, as if taking her taste and feel and the scent of her into him to have for now, forever. She made love as wildly, with every bit as much abandon, close to tears many times, wondering how it was possible to feel such heartache even as she felt such pleasure and sweet, aching, spiraling happiness. She wanted to memorize him so badly. The breadth of his shoulders, the texture of his skin. The taste of his lips, the fire in his eyes, the supple length of his back, the feel of him, inside her, part of her. She clung to him, and kissed and teased and tasted in return, and, even when exhausted, so sated she could scarcely move, she held him still, her cheek against his chest, and she couldn't stop a sudden flow of tears that dampened them both.

"I'll come home," he whispered to her.

And she could only reply, "What is home, Ian?"

"Home is with you."

"This is war—"

"I won't be shot," he promised.

"You can be bayonetted. Or hanged," she whispered.

"Hanged! Spies are hanged, my love. I'm not a spy."

A chill went through her. "But then—"

He rolled over, taking her tenderly into his arms. "I love you, Alaina. I say that with all the heart and power and passion within me, and how very strange, for we were such strangers, so at odds, and still . . . I love you. Deeply, with all my heart. And I can never tell you how sorry I am that my pride and honor demand I not take the role in this conflict that you wanted for me. I can't, Alaina, but I do love you, and I swear, I will come home. To you."

"Oh, Ian!" Tears spilled from her eyes again. He kissed them away. Kissed her tenderly. Made love to her again, until she lay against him, utterly spent.

She slept.

And when she awoke, he was gone.

And she didn't actually understand the dread that filled her, but in her heart, she knew. For them, the war actually started that day.

Ian was the one betraying Florida, the Confederacy, their families, she thought.

So why was it that she felt such terrible guilt . . . such pain . . .

Such fear?

Chapter 22

A laina was pleased when she very quickly learned to correspond in code. She greatly admired Rose, for the woman hadn't blindly formed her opinions, but had spent time at Congress, listening to the senators and representatives debate; she could speak several languages, and she had frequently attended Supreme Court hearings. Following Rose's example, Alaina determined to learn Spanish, a language with which she was already familiar because of the many Cubans who traveled the waters off Florida, and the many Indians who spoke Spanish. Rose had assured her that languages could be superior weapons in any field of war.

Yet, not long after Ian had gone, Rose told Alaina that they had to escalate their operations. It was imperative that they get certain information across the Potomac. Rose sent Alaina south through Union lines, where she was to meet with an undercover agent, Captain Lewes, who would be waiting just outside Alexandria. The information was so critical that it mustn't be taken or confiscated. General McDowell of the Union army planned to launch a surprise attack on Beauregard's twenty thousand men stationed at Manassas Junction near Bull Run Creek, just thirty miles from Washington.

Alaina, traveling with one of Rose's maids, was easily able to reach Alexandria. She found Captain Lewes, a young man in plain farm clothing, buying laudanum for his wife's headaches. Alaina quickly slipped her message to him, and he thanked her.

It went so smoothly, but when she returned home that night, Alaina was shaking. She spent the entire evening holding Sean, even when he didn't want to be held. She told herself that the Confederates would swiftly whomp the Yankees—after all, they had gotten so many of the good Union fighting men!—and Southern independence would be accepted. The South could be as friendly with the North as the United States had been of late with Canada!

But the Battle of Manassas, or Bull Run, was fought just four days later.

Half of Washington society rode out to see the spectacle.

Alaina did not. She sat home, so nervous she was nearly sick.

After the battle, she came out and stood on the street, incredibly torn as McDowell's troops, routed by the Confederates—mainly because the Reb army was so well prepared for the "surprise" attack—came back into the city.

Maimed, filthy, bloody, bleeding. Soldiers dragging other soldiers with their own last reserves of strength. Alaina, Lilly, Henry, and the day maids came to the fence, handing out water to the broken, exhausted men. Alaina looked into their faces—grimed with dirt, hair plastered with blood—looked into their eyes and saw the horror of warfare. These Union soldiers became individuals to her, and she couldn't help but be devastated by all that she saw.

She wept that night and stared up at her ceiling in the darkness. But when it was nearly midnight, she heard pebbles hitting her window. She looked out and was startled to see Captain Lewes, in his young-farm-lad clothing, hiding beneath an oak tree. She slipped into a robe and hurried outside to meet him. "I've just brought a letter of thanks," he told her, brown eyes grave and earnest. "Mrs. Greenhow is greatly responsible for the Southern victory today—Mrs. Greenhow . . . and others."

Alaina nodded, feeling ill.

"You should be proud," he told her.

"I saw the men return from battle. It was awful."

"Ah," he murmured, and nodded. "Well, ma'am, you can take comfort in this: It is better that more Union men should be among the dead and wounded than our Rebs. It's war, Mrs. McKenzie, and we must take sides."

He tipped his hat to her and disappeared.

As she lay in bed that night, Alaina tried to find peace.

She hadn't created the war. She could only do her best, as the captain had said, to save Southern lives.

In the days that followed, she brooded at first, but then returned to Rose's frequently.

About ten days after the battle at Manassas, she received stunning and painful news when a woman at Rose's, the wife of a Union general, slipped her a letter.

It was from Jennifer.

Lawrence Malloy, filled with revolutionary fever, hadn't signed on with a Florida unit. He'd gone north, and from Charleston, he'd joined up with the Confederate army under Beauregard as a captain of cavalry.

Now he was dead.

Killed at Bull Run. His bullet-riddled body had been brought back by his admiring men.

Jennifer's letter wasn't just filled with grief, it was consumed with hatred. For Private Doby, who wrote Jennifer with the bad news, told her that the Federals behaved in a most despicable fashion—a hundred of them gunning down her poor husband even as he gave the order for his men to retreat! "May all those wretched Federal bastards rot and die in this war!" Jennifer wrote. "I tell you, Alaina, from this day forth, I will do my very best to see that they are brought low. I will risk anything, for there is no life without Lawrence."

Alone that night, Alaina grieved for Lawrence, handsome, dashing, always kind. He and Jennifer had been her best friends. Jennifer had grieved with her, and now Jennifer was alone. Not alone, of course. Her brother was near, her father, her stepmother. She had precious little Anthony. She had her aunt and uncle, and her cousins, Tia, Julian . . . Ian.

Ian, the Union soldier. The enemy.

It was only at Rose's, when Alaina saw Risa, that she felt a twinge of guilt once again for helping the South. Risa talked to her with the greatest sorrow; she'd gone to the hospital to help care for the wounded Union men. "I heard about Captain Malloy. I never met any of Ian's family, but I know they were close. I'm very sorry."

Alaina thanked her. "Jennifer is . . . devastated."

"And Ian?"

Alaina shook her head. "I don't know. I haven't seen him. I don't know where he is. Do you?"

"I'm afraid not."

"I know nothing at all," Alaina told Risa nervously.
"Can't your father—"

"Ian has been reassigned. My father is no longer his
commanding officer. Everything is shifting. My father led
men at Manassas—without Ian," she said softly. "I'm
just grateful my father survived. And I'm afraid he
knows nothing about Ian."

Alaina thanked her, wishing that she could hear something from Ian.

Anything.

He could pause, and listen, and imagine the world like
it always was. It was summer, hot, the sun beating down
relentlessly, only the deep green foliage of the Everglades sheltering men and beasts and all manner of
swamp creatures from the deadly heat. Closing his eyes,
listening, he could hear the flight of a great blue heron
from the nearby water, the rustle of leaves with the
slight breeze. When he listened the way his uncle had
taught him, he could even hear the slither of a snake
within the grass.

Once upon a time, it had been a playground for them
all. Now it was no longer play.

"Well, Major, what do you think?"

Ian opened his eyes and turned around. Jake Chi-
coppee stood just a few feet away from him, waiting.

Jake was a half-breed Seminole, a man happily living
with his wife's family in one of the hammocks deep in
the swamp. He and Ian had known each other since they
were boys.

Jake hadn't entered the Union army—he wasn't going
to go quite so far against an organization his people had
so recently fought. But he couldn't support the South
either because he did not believe in slavery.

Ian wished that his uncle saw the war that way, but
James did not. Hunkering down to survey the terrain
around him, Ian felt as if fingers clamped around his
heart and held tight. He'd heard about Lawrence's death
at Manassas. It was only when he was deep in the
swamp, as he was now, that he missed communications.
Usually he heard what was happening quite quickly, because he was using Key West as his main base, and ships

came and went with a fair frequency, bearing both news and supplies. Now, though, he'd been isolated in the swamp for several days. With Jake, he'd established a makeshift encampment in the midst of enemy territory— so sheltered by what most people saw as the deadly misery of the swamp that it would never be found. It was a high hammock, filled with pines and surrounded by water on three sides, its one entry naturally guarded by thick rows of trees. It was near enough to the water; it was large enough to accommodate several cabins and a barn for horses. Ian had to have horses here, if he was to be effective moving throughout the peninsula.

"Well?" Jake inquired again.

Ian looked around him once more. The trees were so dense, they could even hide buildings—and he just wanted a few cabins. The terrain would be extremely treacherous for anyone not familiar with it.

He nodded, looking at Jake. "It's perfect. I'll bring my men the day after tomorrow, and we'll start building."

"Why not tomorrow?"

Ian shrugged. "I've a few personal matters."

That night, under cover of darkness, he left the mangrove shoreline in a small rowboat. He left alone. He was stripped down to just his breeches, barefoot and bare chested, not because he wanted to discard his uniform, but because of the heat.

He made his way to Belamar. Even as he came near the beach, he heard a furious female voice call out to him.

"Stop!"

He frowned and kept coming.

"Stop, or I'll shoot your bloody head off!"

It was Jen's voice.

"Jen, it's Ian."

His rowboat grounded against the beach. He saw her standing there in the moonlight, a shotgun aimed at his heart. Pity seized him. She was still beautiful, but she was thinner and pinched, and her eyes had a wild look about them. She wasn't wearing a dress, but an old pair of men's breeches, tied up with rope, and a man's shirt and boots. A mangled slouch hat was pulled low over her forehead.

"Jen, it's Ian!"

"You bloody, despicable Yank!" she shouted at him.

"I came to see you because I'm sorry. I'm so sorry."

His cousin's hazel eyes glinted in the darkness. "Go away, Ian."

"Now, come on. This is my wife's property—"

"And your wife can come here whenever she wants. Go away or I'll shoot you. You're a Yankee. I hate Yankees."

"Jen, I'm your cousin Ian!"

She kept the gun pointed at his heart. Ian chose to ignore it. He stepped into the wet sand from his rowboat.

"Ian, damn you, I'll shoot!" she cried out.

He caught her eyes, her beautiful, red-rimmed hazel eyes. He thought of her gentleness, the way she had been with him when he'd been just a babe, and he thought of her tenderness when she had comforted Alaina at Teddy's death. He kept walking toward her.

The rifle butted against his chest.

"I'll shoot you, Ian."

He paused just another second. Then he pushed the rifle aside. "No, you won't shoot me, you won't because I love you, Jen, and I'm sorry, so very, very sorry."

She allowed the rifle to fall as he took her into his arms. And she sobbed.

Soon more people spilled from the house.

"Jen!" his aunt Teela's voice, filled with concern.

"Jennifer!" James, calling to his daughter.

"Jen!" Jerome, coming behind him.

And then all of them, staring at Ian.

After a long while, his uncle sighed deeply. "You've got to go now, Ian. You're the enemy here, you know."

He felt Jennifer clinging blindly to him, and he hugged her tightly in return.

"He's not the enemy, he's my nephew!" Teela said stubbornly.

"Mother," Jerome informed her quietly, "Ian is an enemy soldier." Jerome's eyes, as darkly cobalt as his own, pinned Ian. "Ian knows that he has to go. Sweet Jesus, there are Rebs all about in these waters now. . . . Ian, you fool, you're in danger here!"

"He's safe enough tonight in this house," Teela insisted. She spun on her husband, tears in her eyes. "He's safe enough," she repeated.

James exhaled on a long note. He looked at his daughter, still sobbing in Ian's arms. He lifted a hand helplessly. "You've got to be out of here by morning's light, Ian. I'll be damned if I'll see my brother's oldest son gunned down on his own property. And I'll be damned if I'll help the Union, you understand?"

"Yes," Ian said, and with his arm still around Jennifer, he walked to the house with his kin.

After Teela gave him a bowl of her rich conch chowder, she told Ian what she knew about his folks. Tia and Julian were living life like usual at Cimarron, though there had been some talk that Cimarron could be confiscated.

"What?" Ian demanded hotly.

"It's not going to happen; we still have laws in this state," James said.

"It was just talk," Jerome agreed firmly.

"Talk," Teela said quietly, and hesitated just a moment, "instigated by an old acquaintance."

"Who?" Ian demanded harshly.

"Teela, it isn't going to help him to know," James said, aggravated with his wife.

"I'm sorry, James," Teela said, "but he should know. It's that Peter O'Neill, who is naturally still bitter about the fact that you married Alaina."

"Why? He married Elsie Fitch, didn't he?"

"Yes, of course, but . . . he's an arrogant young fool, and always has been, and he's taken his father's money and made himself captain of a cavalry unit."

"So Peter is out to destroy Cimarron—to somehow even a score!" Ian exclaimed angrily, slamming a fist on the table.

"Nothing is going to happen to Cimarron," James said firmly. "With Julian McKenzie officially attached to Southern forces, no one would touch Cimarron. Julian is already acquiring quite a reputation—as a magician, as well as a doctor. They had a measles outbreak and all his patients survived. And he hasn't lost a man to injury yet—" Looking at Ian, his uncle sighed with exasperation. "We shouldn't have told you."

Ian smiled wryly. "I don't mind taking a few chances,

Uncle James, but I think I'd be certifiably insane if I went riding off through the interior to find Peter O'Neill and call him out for a private duel. Damn him, though! The man is such an idiot!"

"Ian," Jerome said, "Peter O'Neill isn't worth your anger. Nothing is going to happen. We've still got laws in this state!" Jerome faced Ian squarely, and Ian saw a countenance very much like his own. Jerome was darker, his complexion more bronze, and in the light, his hair carried a hint of his mother's red. But even the contours of their faces were similar, and in facing Jerome, Ian felt that he faced other forces within himself.

"If they took Cimarron, my father would—"

"Don't underestimate your father," Teela interrupted. "No matter what happens, he's a strong man."

"My mother—"

"May even be stronger," James mused with a touch of humor. "Hell, it's war. It's bloody war. And there's not a damned thing you can do here, Ian, fighting for the Union the way you are." James stood and paused before Ian. "I'll pray for you." He left the kitchen. Teela rose, paused, kissed Ian on the head, and followed her husband.

Jerome picked up a brandy bottle, indicating the porch. "I've got some good Cuban cigars," he said.

Outside they sat, passing the brandy bottle back and forth. "We've all known our feelings for a long time," Ian began. "Your family has known I would stay with the Union, even if trouble came. Yet tonight, somehow . . ."

"There's blood between the North and the South now, and that changes things," Jerome reminded him.

"Yeah, I suppose. Jesus, Jerome, don't let that bastard O'Neill get to Cimarron."

"O'Neill won't get to Cimarron. He may have bought himself a captaincy in the state militia, but he's still a braggart, and most men will pay him no heed. And trust in this: Your brother is as much a part of Cimarron as you are. And there are too many men who respect your father too much to threaten him. Cimarron will be safe. But there's something else I should tell you." Jerome exhaled after a long moment, then stared at Ian again. "I've accepted a commission into the Confederate navy."

"As . . ."

"Captain of the *Mercy*."

"The *Mercy* . . . the schooner you designed that was built out of Richmond."

"That would be the ship," Jerome said lightly. He puffed on the cigar, watching the smoke rise in the night. "I pray to God that we don't meet in battle," he said simply.

"Pray to God!" Ian concurred, lifting the brandy bottle. He consumed a long swallow and passed it to his cousin.

They drank until it was late.

That night, Ian slept in Alaina's bed. He remembered holding her, stroking her, and he missed her . . .

Ached for her. Longed for her.

Prayed for her.

For his family.

And for himself.

He left Belamar at the first hint of light, embracing each member of his family.

In the days that followed, he built his camp. He'd selected eight men as his company, and he was pleased with each of them, especially a man named Sam Jones, who had served at Key West a very long time and was familiar with both Florida history and terrain.

They constructed their cabins well off the ground, a lesson learned from the Indians, to discourage snakes and other predators. They used pine that matched the trees hiding the camp.

"No one will ever find you here," Jake said admiringly when the camp was half finished. "Hell, Osceola couldn't have found this place!"

Ian, staring at his camp, silently agreed. He hunched down, plucking out a blade of grass to gnaw on. "There's only one person who could possibly stalk me here," he murmured quietly.

"Who?"

He looked up at Jake with a rueful smile. "My cousin Jerome McKenzie. But then, he doesn't know yet that he should be looking for me. Maybe we can avoid one another for the duration of this war."

*   *   *

As they passed through August, Alaina grew alarmed when Captain Lewes began to make more frequent visits to her oak tree. She was still committed to helping the South win the war as quickly as possible, but she also wanted to do it with her marriage intact—if that was humanly possible.

"My husband could return," she informed the captain.

"Well, no one ever said there is no danger in being a spy." He smiled. "But Mrs. McKenzie, I don't think you need fear anything. Surely you could charm your way out of any situation."

Alaina refrained from telling him that he obviously didn't know her husband.

"Just like a snake!" he added admiringly.

"I beg your pardon?" Alaina said indignantly.

"A moccasin!" he told her. "A Southern moccasin, so very beautiful and yet so deadly." With a strange smile he turned and left her.

Two nights later, Alaina was awakened by the sound of stones crashing against her window again. She leaped up, expecting to see Captain Lewes. She gasped to see that Risa Magee, dressed in black, was standing by the oak, motioning to her wildly.

Alaina rushed down the stairs and outside as quickly as she possibly could. "Risa, my God, what—"

"You have to get out of here."

"But what—"

"They've arrested Mrs. Greenhow. They're searching through her house and papers now."

"Why—why have you come here?" Alaina asked, feeling a tightening in her throat.

"Oh, Alaina, I'm not an idiot! I've suspected both of you for quite some time—"

"Did you turn Rose in?" Alaina demanded.

"Alaina, Allan Pinkerton, the detective Lincoln hired, has been on her trail nearly from the beginning. Men can be such idiots! A few of Lincoln's own Cabinet members were giving her information, along with Scott's own staff! They are still so appalled to take action against ladies!" Risa said scornfully, then added, "No, Alaina, I never did anything about any of my suspicions. If I had, I might have prevented the deaths of some of our men who died at Manassas."

"Risa, you've got to understand," Alaina said, suddenly anxious that Risa should see things from her point of view. "You might have prevented Union deaths, but thousands more Southern soldiers would have died. Risa, I can't change what I am, or the way that I believe. People have the right to self-government. I am a Southerner. My country is foreign to me now."

"You've got to get out of here, Alaina, before they associate you with Rose and come to arrest you. I pray to God they won't do anything but just hold women and try to keep them from dangerous activities, but . . . there has been discussion that spies should be hanged. Even female spies. For the love of God, Alaina, pay attention to me tonight. Hurry. Get yourself and the babe dressed and ready. I have a friend—Captain Murdock—who is sailing down the Potomac tonight. He has just recently resigned his commission and has a pass through the Union lines. You and Sean can go with him as his wife and child."

Stunned, Alaina hesitated. She'd never been a fool; she had known what she risked. She had believed deeply in the Cause of the South, and she still did. But the very thought of hanging . . .

"My God—Ian . . ." she murmured.

"Alaina," Risa told her bluntly, "if they decide to hang you, there won't be a damned thing Ian will be able to do—assuming that he got the news before the deed was done!" Then she added softly, "If I see Ian before you do, I'll explain to him that I urged you to leave. Any friendship with Rose is cause for concern right now; Ian will understand that. And you can't be faulted for befriending her; Ian has known and liked Rose for years."

Alaina lowered her head, wincing. She believed that Risa would actually defend her to Ian. But still, neither was Ian a fool, and when he found out about her activities . . .

He would think that anything she had ever said to him was a lie, that she had come to him, seduced him, only for information. Which was true . . . and not true. It was such a fine line there! And it didn't matter. When Ian discovered what she had been doing, he might well want to hang her himself.

Risa threw up her hands. "Alaina, for the love of God, I didn't want to tell you this, but if it will cause you to hurry, then it's news you must know. Captain Lewes is dead."

"What?" Alaina gasped.

"So the man *was* your contact!" Risa mused.

Alaina ignored her blunder, feeling absolutely ill. Lewes had been so young, so brave. He'd had so much life ahead of him. "He was . . . hanged?"

"No, no—he was shot; he refused to respond when a picket demanded to know his purpose. He tried to run. He was killed."

"Oh, God!" Alaina breathed, reaching for the tree to steady herself. Poor Captain Lewes!

"Alaina, please understand. I'm sorry, but I am telling you this so that you will realize the seriousness of this situation."

Alaina inhaled sharply, studying Risa. "Why did you come? Why are you helping me?"

"I—" Risa hesitated. "I don't know. Maybe I respect your loyalty to the South. Maybe I've acquired a certain affection for you." Her eyes narrowed slightly. "And maybe I still care about Ian, and know that your death or incarceration would wound him beyond measure. What difference does it make? I've got a carriage down the next road. I can't be seen here. Get the baby—and Lilly. You can travel with a maid. Keep her quiet, though, and *hurry.*"

Alaina briefly bowed her head; she had never known so great a misery. It was war; it was no game of flirting and spying. Ian had probably been right that it would last a very long time and they would all be bathed in blood.

"Alaina!"

She raised her head, squared her shoulders, and nodded. Impulsively, she hugged Risa, and Risa hugged her tightly in return.

Alaina hurried into Ian's bedroom, pulling writing paper, pen, and ink from his desk drawers. She agonized in the seconds she dared take, wishing there were words that could explain how she could love him—and the

Confederacy as well. There were no words that could
begin to suffice. She wrote simply:

> I'm so sorry. So very sorry. I need to go home. I do
> love you.
>
> > Alaina

She left the note on his desk.

She turned and studied the room. She hadn't wanted
to come here. But now, she didn't want to leave. She'd
learned here just how much she loved her husband. Her
baby had been born here. It had become their home.

She closed her eyes, fighting the threat of hysterical
tears.

She hurried back to her own room, gently cradled her
son in her arms, and, with Lilly silently at her side, left
her home.

Left the North.

And her husband.

Chapter 23

By the end of September, Risa received a letter from Alaina assuring her that she and the baby had made it safely from Washington to Richmond. She went from there, via the railroad, to Charleston, where she was welcomed by the cream of Confederate society. She wrote with enthusiasm regarding the kindness of those she met—and with renewed patriotic fever for the Confederacy. Alaina had actually come out of the situation quite well and Risa could assure herself wryly that she had been a good friend to both Alaina and Ian.

Risa had suspected that Alaina might stay in Charleston for quite some time. Although Brent had so far refused to accept a commission with either a Florida or South Carolina volunteer unit or the Confederacy itself, he and Sydney could certainly be construed as Rebels—but they were McKenzies. However, Alaina didn't stay with them. In the last letter she had managed to get friends to smuggle through Union lines, she told Risa that, after stopping in St. Augustine, she was going home. She wanted to be with Jennifer, at Belamar.

It was November when Ian finally returned to Washington. Risa had been out at the home of a friend, working on a flag for a newly formed Maryland home guard—and feeling absolutely restless with her mundane part in the events shaping the country.

She rarely saw her father now; he was with the Army of the Potomac under the man Lincoln had brought in from a previous acquaintanceship in Illinois—McClellan. McClellan was dashing and charismatic, inspiring to the troops, but Risa had already heard from her father—who complained privately, but with great aggravation—that McClellan was like an old woman in many ways, exaggerating the number of enemy troops, no matter what the intelligence reports. He would wage far too careful a war, a defensive war, when he was supposed to be bringing ambivalent Southerners back into the fold of the Union.

More men were dying. There had been action at Ball's Bluff, Virginia, and skirmishes east and west. Risa prayed that winter might stem the flow of blood—and cool down some very hot heads.

As she came back to her house that early evening in November, her maid, Nelly, came rushing out to meet her. "Major McKenzie, ma'am, Major McKenzie is here!"

Risa stared at Nelly, then quickened her footsteps.

Ian's back was to her when she hurried into her parlor. His shoulders were very broad, trimming to the leanness of his hips, and with his dark hair, he wore his uniform very handsomely. His hands were on the mantel; his head was just slightly bowed in thought. She was so very tempted to run to him, to put her arms around him and lay her head against his back, to whisper some gentle words to ease the strain of war. A war in which he fought his own kin, his own wife.

She opened her mouth to say his name, but no sound came. She gently placed a hand upon his shoulder. He didn't turn immediately, and she realized he had known that she was in the room from the time she had first entered it. He turned at last, eyes very dark, face leaner, sharper than ever.

"Ian. It's good to see you," she said, moving back just slightly.

He smiled. "You, too, Risa. You look as well as ever. Very beautiful."

"Thank you," she said softly, then paused. "I assume you know that Alaina—"

"Oh, yes, I know that she left Washington. You know, it's amazing how slowly military orders can move about the country and how quickly the affairs of men and women can travel. I had actually been right off of New Orleans with my men, chasing a Southern sloop from Pensacola, when I met up with an officer who had recently spent time here. He was saddened by Rose's arrest, and anxious to find out if I knew how deeply it had disturbed others of the Southern persuasion in the area, including my wife. The officer seemed to think that Alaina left in protest regarding Rose. But I don't think that's true. I think she left because she had been in league with Rose. What do you think?"

Risa stared at him, hesitating. "I—well, of course, you know that I'm a Union patriot all the way, so it would be unlikely that anyone would share their thoughts on the matter with me. . . . Tea, Ian? A whiskey? What can I get for you? It is good to see you, even if being here is not all that you had planned. Let me get you something to drink."

She started to walk away from him. He reached out, gripping her arm. His hold was firm but not hurtful, and it felt as if his cobalt eyes penetrated right through her. "You know more than what you're telling me."

"She's written to me," Risa said quickly. "She knew, of course, that you'd be furious with her decision to go South, but . . . I think she wanted to go home, to Belamar, though I would assume that she'd still be in St. Augustine now."

"The baby?" he demanded, and Risa bit her lower lip, suddenly hearing the pain beneath the anger in his voice.

"Sean is doing well, thriving," Risa said. "You haven't heard from Alaina—at all? Well, I suppose it would have been difficult. . . . I'm not sure I would be able to reach you, Ian, if I needed to."

"Alaina left a note on my desk from three months ago, and that is the last I have heard from her," Ian said, and the steel note of deadly anger was back in his voice.

"I'm sure that she would have contacted you if she had known how, Ian. She loves you."

"Perhaps."

"I would have contacted you if—"

"If you should ever need me in the future, for anything, go to General Brighton. He knows how to find me."

Risa nodded. "You really shouldn't be too angry; all she did was go home. I think that you must see her position."

His dark look betrayed his doubt.

"Ian, she is a Southerner. Her home is in the South."

He turned away from her, staring into the flames of

the fireplace." And I should be a Southerner, too?" he inquired lightly.

"Oh, no, of course not . . ."

"There are but two issues here: The Union must be preserved, and slavery is morally wrong. Alaina knows that!" His aggravation and confusion mingled in the deep anguish of his voice.

"I'm sure she knows that slavery is morally wrong," Risa said. "In fact, very few enlisted men in the Confederacy actually own slaves. Many Southerners don't believe in slavery—they just feel that they have the right to be free and independent." What in God's name was she doing, defending Alaina? "Oh, Ian, if the two sides just tried to understand each other there wouldn't be a war," she insisted. And, hoping to slip from the conversation, she asked quickly, "Can you—can you stay for dinner? I doubt if we'll see Father; he is constantly drilling with the army and meeting with McClellan and his generals. Father is being promoted to brigadier general himself—had you heard?"

"Yes, I hope to see him and offer my congratulations. And yes, I'd love to have dinner, thank you."

"Fine. I'll tell Cook, and get you a drink. Please, make yourself comfortable here."

His eyes were on hers, and he smiled warmly. "I always have, Risa," he said.

She smiled, feeling a strange slam in her heart, and hurried away to see about dinner.

"Are you in Washington long?" Risa asked him in the course of the pleasant meal.

His eyes darkened; his mouth tightened, and she felt a little chill streak through her. "I'd had a little time, but now . . . I think I may head out on a mission of my own."

Risa convulsively curled her fingers into her palms and stood, nearly knocking her chair over. Ian stared at her in startled surprise. "Don't you go getting killed over her, do you hear me? And I don't mean that with any evil intent—believe it or not, Alaina is my friend. But you are my friend as well, and she is the enemy, and you shouldn't go getting killed for her!"

He smiled, rising as well, walking around the table to

her. He took her by the shoulders and kissed her forehead. "Risa, I am continually *ordered* into enemy territory. I know what I'm doing, and I don't take chances. But I thank you very much for your concern, and I swear to you, I will be careful."

Risa looked up at him. She felt as if her heart were pounding a staccato beat that he couldn't help but hear. Her flesh felt as if it were on fire. It would be so easy. Damn convention, and society. He was married, but his wife was the enemy, a thousand miles away, and he had been hers first, and he should have been hers now, and they would have understood one another perfectly, and these moments could have been a balm for them both. . . .

He was touching her. She could feel his breath against her face. It would be so easy to slip into his arms, and she was certain that he felt it as well.

"Ian . . ." she murmured.

"Oh, God, I wouldn't hurt you, Risa, I wouldn't hurt you," he said.

Again his lips brushed her forehead.

"What if you weren't hurting me, what if I wanted just a memory, what if . . ."

His arms tightened. He lifted her chin. She felt his lips on hers. Grinding down on them with an openmouthed fever and passion that inflamed her senses, set fire to a longing that was as yet only imagined.

Then suddenly, with an oath, he released her.

"I've got to get out of here, Risa!" he told her hoarsely.

"Because you love your wife," she said softly.

He was quiet a moment. "Because I love you both," he said.

And then he was gone.

Alaina had always loved the city of St. Augustine, with its handsome and impressive fort standing guard in the harbor. The fort—called Fort Marion now, in honor of the Revolutionary War hero Francis Marion—had originally been built by the Spanish as the Castillo San Marcos. The British, who had held Florida during the Revolution, had called the edifice Fort St. Marks, anglicizing the original name. Whatever it was called, it was beautiful and looked indomitable, like an ancient medieval castle.

Alaina arrived in daylight, in December 1861, and alighted almost directly in front of the fort with Lilly and Sean. Lilly was delighted that it wasn't even a chill day—Lilly hated the cold of the North, and had accompanied Alaina south with little protest. Alaina was happy to be there. She was still well over two hundred miles from home, but they were Florida miles, and it felt good. If thoughts of Ian didn't plague her continually, she might well have been content. Of course she had tremendous support for her position once she was in the South, and it was encouraging to feel that she was right, that she was part of a great revolutionary cause.

But her nights were torture.

She had left Ian, and she didn't know where he was, nor how he would feel, if he would ever forgive her, if she would ever see him again. . . .

"Warm is good," Lilly announced with a happy sigh. "Warm is good."

"Yes, nice."

"The street is nice. When Major Ian comes home, then it will all be nice."

"Lilly," Alaina murmured, "I'm not so sure he'll be home—for quite a while." But she, too, looked up and down the street and managed to smile. The city was charming, with its ancient Spanish architecture blending in with the growth that had been continuous since the mid-1500s. It had always amused Alaina to think that St. Augustine was the oldest permanent European settlement in the United States—especially when so many people still thought of Florida as being such a wild and new frontier.

Standing in the street where the coach had left them, Alaina stared up at Fort Marion. She felt a small, sweet thrill of excitement just to be here. She had enjoyed her stay in Richmond and Charleston, and she had experienced a wave of patriotism for the Confederacy in those stalwart Southern cities unlike any she had known before. The seat of the Confederate government was in Richmond, and she had even attended an evening's soiree at the White House of the Confederacy, where none other than the gaunt, intriguing President Davis himself had paused to thank her for her loyalty to her people. In those two cities, it seemed impossible that the South would fail in its mission for sovereignty. It had been wonderful to see Sydney and Brent, and frighteningly easy to lie, telling them only that Ian was so seldom in Washington, she felt it a dangerous city in which to be alone—the same story she intended to tell Julian when he met her.

She closed her eyes for a moment, listening to the clip-clop of horses' hooves, feeling the sun, the sea breeze, and the warmth of being home.

"Alaina!"

She swirled around and saw that Julian was leaping down from the driver's seat of a small carriage. A little tremor streaked through her, for he looked so very much like his brother. She hurried forward to hug Julian, to be lifted up and swung around, and hugged again. But then he let her down in front of him, and his eyes were grave. "All right, young lady, just what are you doing here? I know damned well my big brother didn't give you permission to leave Washington!"

Alaina exhaled a breath of irritation. "Well, your big brother wasn't in Washington, and it was becoming a very dangerous place for Southerners."

"Oh? For Southerners—or *guilty* Southerners?"

"Julian, don't be cruel—and don't forget that Ian is a Yankee when you . . ." she stepped back, surveying him from head to toe. He was very handsome in a uniform-gray frock coat with his medical and military insignia upon the shoulders. "You're a Reb," she reminded him bluntly.

"Fine. Let's not argue. Let me take you home. Lilly, welcome! And this . . . is Sean! He's so big already. I can't wait for my folks to see him, their first grand-child—they'll be so very proud!"

Alaina smiled. It was good—and strange. She felt that she was indeed welcomed home. Welcomed warmly by her husband's family.

When her husband was the enemy.

Alaina wrote a letter to Ian the first night at Julian's. Though she tried to pour her heart into it, her words seemed lame. She wrote again that she loved him, but given her escape and the rumors of her spying that must be all over Washington, he wasn't likely to believe her. Still, Julian took her letter, and she hoped that it would reach her husband.

She began working with Julian. He spent most of his days at the barracks, tending to the ills and injuries of the men. In the evening, he saw to the civilian population of St. Augustine. She enjoyed the feeling of working with the soldiers; it gave her a sense of usefulness and kept her from dwelling on her own situation.

She had been there about a week when the men from the Confederate States ship *Annie May* came in. The *Annie May* had been a blockade runner, and she had been destroyed at sea by the United States navy. Most of her seamen had been taken prisoner, but some had escaped. Many were seriously injured. Following Julian around from bed to bed, she was appalled by the bloodshed and the anguish of the men. At the beginning, she nearly passed out. Then, coming upon an already infected and pus-laden saber wound, she nearly threw up.

But she steeled herself to the carnage around her; she sopped up blood so that Julian could see clearly enough to suture. She applied pressure upon wounds when told to do so, she bandaged and bathed. When the ten survivors had been patched back together due to the skill of Julian and the other doctors, she wrote letters for the men.

That night, Julian and Alaina and a Dr. Reginald C. Percy dined together at an inn near Fort Marion.

Percy was perhaps sixty, a dignified man, ramrod straight, who had served in the Union army before secession. He told Alaina that in all his years, he'd never worked with so fine a surgeon as Julian McKenzie. He hadn't joined up with the Confederate forces, feeling that he could better assist in Florida's war effort by remaining a civilian.

"There was no reason for any of this last, tragic round of death!" he complained, slamming a fist against their dinner table. "From what the boys told me, they knew they were outmanned and outgunned, and they were surrendering their ship. The wretched Northerners killed those boys on purpose. They know that they haven't got the sheer gumption of the South—but they can keep replacing their own dead men, so they figure the only way to beat us is to kill us all!"

"Now, Dr. Percy, not all Yankees—" Julian began.

But Percy pounded the table again. "Damned blockade! This war isn't over like they said it would be—it's far from over. And it would be one thing if the enemy just went after the arms that were being shipped in, but when they take our laudanum, our morphine, our quinine—"

"It's war, Percy, and there's very little we can do about that fact," Julian told him.

A few minutes later, as coffee was being served, Julian was called back to the hospital. When both Percy and Alaina began to join him, Julian protested. "The fellow has a Christmas-is-coming croup, and I can manage on my own. Enjoy your coffee."

When Julian left, Percy sat back, still disgruntled. His dark eyes were very soulful, and with his collar-length thick gray hair framing his gaunt face, he looked both very old, and very sad. "More . . . we need more. Always more." He looked at her, then leaned his elbows against the table, studying her eyes. "It's my understanding that you're from the wilds of the south, Mrs. McKenzie."

"I grew up on a little islet—"

"In Biscayne Bay."

She nodded, curious that he should know her background so well.

"So, Mrs. McKenzie, you know the waters down there. You know the deep water, and you know the reefs. You know the trails through to the northern section of the state."

"Yes, of course, but—"

He leaned back. "I've already lost a nephew to this war," he told her, dark eyes suddenly seeming to burn.

"I'm sorry, sir."

"I'm sure you are. You knew him."

"What?"

He smiled slowly, bitterly. "Captain Lewes was my sister's boy."

"Oh, God!" Alaina breathed. "Oh, I am sorry. He was a fine young man, truly—"

"He spoke highly of you as well," Percy interrupted bluntly.

Alaina sat back, hands in her lap, staring at him uncomfortably.

"He called you the Moccasin."

"Did he?"

Suddenly Percy was leaning across the table, gripping her hand tightly with his own. "We may need you again, Alaina. And, oh, Lord, but it upsets me to ask such a delicate little woman to do her part, but . . . it upsets me more when those boys die and I know that I can do something about it!"

"I'm not quite sure what I could possibly do at this particular time—" Alaina began carefully.

"But I do," Percy whispered fiercely. Again he leaned closer. "Moccasin. No other name need ever be used; few people need ever know how you're aiding the Cause. . . ."

"But what—"

"On the right night, I slip you out of here, ostensibly to go home. Except that you sail to Freeport first, you pick up supplies from a friend of mine, a British subject, Dr. Bellamy. St. Augustine is usually ringed by Union ships, hungry, wary. You go into your Biscayne Bay, the captain lets you off with your medical supplies and whatever other contraband you've picked up, the captain brings in himself as best he can. Madam, you are perfect! You'll be in little danger! If your ship is taken at sea, you identify yourself as the Panther's wife."

"What? Who?" Alaina demanded.

Percy arched a brow and looked as if he were about to spit with fury. "Your husband, Madam, has been tearing up the coast. He comes in, attacks, steals our weapons, our supplies, and is gone again. He prowls the damned swamps and forests; no one ever sees him until it's too late, no one ever seems able to follow him. He moves like lightning. He and his men have hit from South Carolina to Texas; they've slipped in to survey fortifications and report on the number of troops and their exact locations. He's been dubbed the Panther by the boys trying to hold some sanity in this wretched and abandoned state! But don't you see—as his wife, ma'am, you would be sacred cargo to any Union officers who accosted you. And you need be guilty of nothing more than going home. You'll be invaluable, too, in negotiating with those foreigners willing to quietly help us."

Alaina looked down at her hands, feeling numb. They had to have medicines. She couldn't bear seeing the horror she had seen as a result of the attack on the *Annie May*. Death and dismemberment were terrible enough without added deaths because the right medications couldn't be had.

"Does my brother-in-law know about any of this?" she asked softly.

Percy shook his head. "No. And you do, of course, have every right to refuse me. But you won't, will you?"

That night, she dreamed about soldiers dying. She heard a woman crying, sobbing her heart out. A grieving mother.

She opened her eyes and cried out.

She jumped out of bed and hurried to Sean's crib. He was sleeping peacefully. She woke him up and he howled in protest in her arms. She would die if anything ever happened to Sean.

At the hospital the next day, she told Percy that she'd be glad to do whatever she could.

"So the Moccasin is born!" Percy said softly. "You will have nothing, nothing to fear."

She didn't protest, nor did she tell Percy that his nephew had once told her the same thing.

And that was exactly why she was so very frightened.

Chapter 24

Right before Christmas, Julian was given leave, and he, Lilly, Sean, and Alaina made their way across the state to Cimarron.

It was an interesting homecoming, for Jarrett was absolutely against secession and the war, and despite the fact that his beloved home sat in the Deep South, he was a profound Unionist.

Alaina was aware that Julian, usually so confident and self-assured, was quiet as they crossed the river by ferry. He stood watching his father, who stood with Tara and Tia at the dock. She realized that he was actually shaking.

But when they stepped from the ferry, he was instantly engulfed by his mother's arms. Tara's hug was brief, however, and then she was kissing Alaina's cheek and sweeping her first grandchild from Alaina's arms. Alaina stepped back and saw the way that Jarrett and Julian looked at one another. But then Jarrett McKenzie opened his arms and embraced his son. Both men were shaking then, and she thought she heard a sob of relief escape Julian, and she turned away, afraid that she might burst into tears herself. When she composed herself, Julian and Tia were hugging one another tightly, and she felt a bit like an intruder. She wasn't a real McKenzie.

But a minute later, Tia was embracing her just as warmly as any blood relation, and a minute after that, she found her father-in-law studying her with his mahogany eyes intent. "Well, daughter, I suppose I must accept your Rebel status as well, though I fear you have sorely wounded my son. Come here, Alaina, I am delighted to see you so well!"

His hug was fierce and warm, and she blinked furiously so as not to cry. Then she found herself in her mother-in-law's arms and she was able to ask softly, "Have you heard from Ian?"

And Tara nodded solemnly. "We have friends, you know, who get letters through. He is well, though I live in terror for him daily. He plays such a dangerous game! But then . . . well, you are here now, my dear, and we cannot be happier. Two of our children home for Christmas, our daughter-in-law—and grandson! My God, Jarrett, we're grandparents! How did we ever get so old?" she queried, at a loss. Jarrett smiled at her and assured her, "We're not old, my love, merely experienced."

Tia sniffed, they all laughed, and they went to the house, where Jarrett, Tara, and Tia inspected the baby, delighted, from head to toe. Sean, being nearly a year old and well up on his own feet, was somewhat indignant, but he seemed to recognize his own family, so he quickly made himself at home at Cimarron. Alaina realized that should they all survive the war, one day Cimarron would be her child's inheritance. One day, in fact, it should be her home.

She closed her eyes. It would never be. Life would never be the same again, because her husband was not just the enemy, he was the Panther. And coming to breakfast one morning, she heard her father-in-law tell Julian that the only reason Cimarron hadn't been burned to the ground was that he had his own excellent crew of men to protect the property—and because Julian was known as one of the few Reb surgeons who could really save lives.

After a lovely Christmas day of laughter and exchanging gifts, Alaina and her mother-in-law were alone together in Ian's room—a strange place for Alaina to sleep without Ian, for she kept remembering the night of their marriage, so long ago now—a different time, a different world.

"I wish you'd stay with us," Tara said.

Alaina didn't look up. She kept her eyes carefully concealed. "I need to go back with Julian. I think I'm helpful to him. And I want to go home, I need to see Belamar."

"I believe your husband might think that you were safer here," Tara said with just a touch of reproach.

Alaina inhaled, then looked at her mother-in-law at last and exhaled on a long note. "I'm sorry, but there are so many things . . . I believe in the South's right to be independent. And I can't forget . . . I can't forget what happened to my father. And since then there's been more. I can't be a Unionist, but like Julian, maybe I can just help the injured. And I'm sorry, so sorry about Ian, and I—" she broke off and sat by Tara, clutching her hands. "Did he say anything about me? I tried to write him; Julian said that he could get a letter to him. I haven't heard back, I don't know—"

"He's very angry with you," Tara admitted.

"But—"

Tara smiled suddenly. "But I think he loves you. And when I see you now, I think you love him, too." She reached out and stroked Alaina's cheek. "Love has a way—even in the face of war," she said softly. "I wish I could convince you to stay, but I can't. So we'll all just pray . . . we'll pray for peace," she said.

The women hugged one another warmly.

It was difficult to say good-bye but eventually they were on the road back across the state. Florida had built up enough so that they were able to stop at small towns along the way—and pass through militia encampments. Just after New Year's, their carriage brought them back to St. Augustine.

Within two weeks, just after Sean's first birthday, Percy came to see Alaina. A Confederate ship had slipped into the coast south of the city, and she would be able to take it home.

Both Julian and Tia were against her decision to take a trip home to Belamar. "Alaina—you will be on a blockade runner!" Tia reminded her.

"If the ship is taken, nothing will happen to me," Alaina assured them.

"I'd sit on you like a mother duck if it would keep you here," Julian told her.

"Please, Julian, I need to see my own home. I want to see Jennifer, and your aunt and uncle, and Jerome. Please understand."

"Well, I don't understand," Julian said curtly.

"But you can't stop me."

"I just might try," he warned.

In the end, Alaina had her way and left Sean with Tia and Lilly. Julian and Tia escorted her to the ship, and the captain, a fine old seaman named Nasby, promised that Alaina would be escorted all the way to Biscayne Bay; she wouldn't be alone or in danger for a minute. Instead, once they had traveled an hour due south, the ship turned and headed for the Bahamas.

They were steam-powered, and despite the blockade, they reached Freeport within forty-eight hours. At her rendezvous with Dr. Bellamy, Alaina discovered that she wasn't just to procure medicines. Nearly eighty years old if he was a day, Dr. Bellamy was a good Southern gentleman residing in Freeport. He insisted that she stay for a dinner he was having for some British diplomats. She wore a dark wig as disguise, but dressed for the occasion, and did her very best to persuade the men that their country must recognize the Confederacy, and furthermore, they should come to the aid of Rebels, showing the Union that world opinion was with the South.

When she was due to leave the next morning, Dr. Bellamy was delighted with her. "My dear, the gentlemen have done nothing but talk about your beauty and passion." He winked. "They all wanted to know who you were, but they will never find out! We have assured them that you are a patriotic Rebel and that we can say no more. Ah, my dear Moccasin! I do look forward to a long and illustrious acquaintanceship! Take the greatest care."

When she left him, she carried leather satchels filled with important medicines, and a tremendous feeling of satisfaction.

On the way to Nasby's ship, she and her guard, in civilian clothing, stopped by a dockside tavern while the men purchased produce, whiskey, wine, and supplies for the voyage back. Alaina, in her overcoat and dark wig, sat at a back table sipping coffee. She was startled when she realized that the men at the table behind her were Union navy—and that they were talking about an attack that was to made on *her* ship. They knew that a Reb schooner was in the vicinity, and they meant to catch it on the open water.

Alaina rose at a leisurely pace and slipped from the

tavern, hurrying to warn Captain Nasby. He was startled, but pleased with her information.

They postponed their sailing for a night, then started back across the sea, free of Union gunboats.

Alaina was still flush with her victory when she was set down in the bay off Belamar Isle. When she came ashore with her escort, she was instantly challenged by a harsh voice: "Who is it?"

"Alaina McMann McKenzie!" she called out.

"Alaina?"

Her boat slid into the sand on the beach. She stepped out and was instantly engulfed in Jennifer's arms. Her escort quietly rowed back to his ship, and she accompanied Jennifer back to the house.

Alaina's first night home, she sat with Jennifer, James, and Teela—and lied. She didn't say a word about her own war efforts. She told them that she was going back to St. Augustine, but planned to come back and forth frequently.

Jennifer couldn't stop describing the battle that had killed her husband, and Alaina realized that James and Teela were here with her because they must still be worried about her state of mind. Jennifer wanted to know all about Washington, Richmond, and South Carolina. How were they doing in St. Augustine? The South *had* to win the war.

The next morning they were out on the beach, entirely alone. Jennifer looked around carefully before telling Alaina excitedly, "I'm so grateful to be doing my part. By this afternoon, a company of militia will arrive on the mainland. They'll take you—and your contraband!—back to St. Augustine."

"Oh, my God!" Alaina breathed. "You're—you're my contact?"

Jennifer laughed. "Of course! Of course! Oh, Alaina, what did you think? That I could just sit back and watch the war after what happened to Lawrence? I'd die before I'd be helpless! And now you're part of it all, too! Oh, Alaina, I'm so happy, so pleased. Isn't it wonderful to be doing so much for our fighting men?"

Alaina was carrying morphine, quinine, and laudanum. Her ship had brought in arms as well, but she

didn't want to think about that. She had to remember
Captain Lewes, and that he had died. She had to remember all the other noble Confederate soldiers. She had to
force herself to forget the man who had surely come to
despise her by now.

Her husband.

Alaina had been back in St. Augustine about a week
and was on her way from the general store when she
was startled to find herself hailed by soldier in a plumed
slouch hat.

She stood still, frowning, feeling just a shade of unease,
as she watched the man rush over to her. "Alaina,
Alaina!"

"Peter!" she cried in return, startled, but not alarmed
to see him. With the war, everything that had happened
at Cimarron that long-ago day now seemed like child's
play.

"Captain Peter O'Neill," he said, offering her his best
smile and sweeping his hat from his head.

"Yes, of course, Peter. You look well. Congratulations, I'm happy that you seem so . . . pleased."

He smiled, reaching for her hands, pulling her close
to kiss her cheek, then drawing away to study the length
of her. "Oh, Alaina! You do grow more beautiful every
time I see you!"

"Thank you, Peter. You look fit, and seem to be in
fine humor as well."

"Ah, yes, I am in good humor. I'm Florida cavalry—
and quite proud of it. We're the most dashing, you
know—but the governor complains that every man in
the state who owned a pony wanted to be dashing and
daring at the state's expense. However, my dear Alaina,
your friend here is among the finest horsemen in the
state. You'll have to forgive my lack of modesty, please!
And besides, my father and I have put a great deal of
money into financing our own company, and thus we are
in high demand."

"I'm so glad."

He smiled, staring at her wistfully. "So you have left
your husband?" he asked her hopefully.

She stiffened. Peter's eyes instantly filled with alarm,
and he murmured quickly, "I'm so sorry, Alaina, I'm

trying to be friends, it's just that . . . well, I admit to a jealousy of him. I was wrong, so wrong where you were concerned, and still . . ."

"Ummm," Alaina murmured. "How's Elsie?"

Peter grew more somber. "You hadn't heard?"

"Heard what, Peter?"

"Elsie passed away about six months ago. Typhoid fever."

"Oh, Peter, I'm so sorry." She was sorry, truly sorry. Poor Elsie, who had been so terribly young!

"Thank you. So was I," Peter said, and he sounded quite earnest.

She couldn't help but feel a surge of pity for him. "Healing takes a very long time. I know."

"Yes, of course, you lost your father. Well, I do fear that if this war keeps up, the entire country will know the pain and devastation of loss."

"I'm afraid I have to agree. I saw the Union soldiers returning to Washington after Manassas, and—"

"Don't think about it. Not now. You're home. In the Confederacy." He hesitated, then smiled broadly, with a tremendous amount of pride, as if she were somehow his creation, and said very quietly, "Rumor is that you were part of the mechanism that helped save Southern soldiers at Manassas."

Alaina shrugged uncomfortably. He shook his head, moving closer to her. "Alaina, you can't begin to imagine how your talents are appreciated!"

"Peter, I don't—"

"Alaina, you are home because you love your country, aren't you? Because you want the South to win this war, quickly, with as little death as possible on either side?"

"Peter, I'm home because . . . it's home, but—"

"You're loyal and you're brave, Alaina. You've never minded standing on your own two feet, and you've never been afraid of any man."

That wasn't exactly true; she was afraid of her husband. It was strange, of course, for Ian would never really hurt her. Not physically. But he could hurt her . . .

Because she loved him.

And then again, this was war. God alone knew what anyone would do.

"Alaina," he said in a rush, "any Southern man would lay down his life for you if needed!"

"Thank you, Peter, but—"

Suddenly he stepped forward, gripped her shoulders, and kissed her cheek. "If I can ever be of service to you in any way, you must promise to let me know!" he said passionately. Then just as suddenly he left her, walking quickly away down the street.

She watched him, feeling peculiarly uneasy again. Did he know what she was doing now? She bit her lip, realizing how dangerous her involvement in the war effort really was.

In her bedroom in the guest cottage that night, a single candle burned on the desk, casting the corners of the room into darkness and shadow. She needed no more light, and wanted no more light. Sean was sleeping in his crib.

Alaina sat at the foot of her bed, easing off her boots.

She rose then and walked to Sean's bed, anxious to see that her son slept well. He did. Beautiful black hair splayed upon the pillow, little thumb near his mouth, something of a smile curled his lips. She adjusted the light blanket over him.

Then she thought she heard a sound.

And felt . . .

A chill. Some sense of danger creeping along her spine.

Even as she spun about, she assured herself that everything had to be well. St. Augustine was filled with soldiers, all guarding the coast. There was a massive fort right out in the harbor. No one could have come in here; she could be in no danger. There were several Confederate ships at anchor nearby.

But as she turned, she saw that she was not alone. A man leaned against the far corner of the mantel.

He waited.

Comfortably.

He waited in silence, in the shadows of the night. But even as she turned, she felt the rippling chill streak along her spine again, and she realized, disbelievingly, that it was Ian.

"Hello, Mrs. McKenzie," he said gravely.

The moonlight suddenly touched his eyes, and they

glittered blue fire against the hard, dark cast of his face. She was suddenly certain that she could feel his anger— wrath that had simmered for months. It came rippling off him like heat waves.

Foolishly, she turned to run.

Yet before she could take two steps, his arms were around her like prison bars, and his whisper was against her ear. "Indeed, my beloved Rebel, are you seeking an army to bring me down?"

"Ian—"

"Don't scream," he warned her icily.

Then he plucked her up by the arms and threw her. *Threw* her with an ungodly force . . .

And she flew as hard and fast as an arrow until her flight was stopped as she landed, stunned and gasping, against the quilt-covered bed.

Chapter 25

A laina rallied quickly, inching away from him to a sitting position against the headboard, staring at him all the while. As he approached her with long, swift strides, she tossed back her hair nervously, so very glad to see him, yet so terrified of him.

"I should scream, and I should turn you in to a Reb army." She leaped off the bed, but he caught her arm, drawing her back, and she faced him, crushed against him, feeling the power of his hold, and that of his eyes. "I should scream," she whispered again, "loudly enough to wake Jeff Davis up in Richmond! Ian, please, you don't understand, you don't—"

"Shut up, Alaina. I don't have forever."

She broke off, not because of his words, but because he silenced her with a kiss. Mouth consuming hers, tongue tasting, plundering, savage with fire and passion. He was like a tempest, a sudden firestorm out of the night, his fever so electric it charged throughout her instantly. She wanted to protest his violence; she could only match it. His subtle, masculine scent seemed to overwhelm her senses with temptation. She had dreamed of him so many times; she breathed him now. Felt him. His hands on her face; his mouth, liquid fire. And it was good. Engulfing, overwhelming, sensation so sweet she couldn't think to protest. An alarm within her warned that she should be asking questions, protesting, *talking* first, but . . .

It had been one thing not to know love. But now she had known him, lived with him, loved him, ached for him, and he was here, and that was all that mattered. The feel of his lips, even angry, hungry; the touch of his hands, even rough with the same desire. . . .

His hands moved and buttons seemed to melt away.

Clothing fell, his lips barely breaking from hers. She was more awkward, her hands tugging at Union wool. She wanted to tell him that he was a fool for being here in Union wool.

He was definitely better off naked.

Yet it was she who stood naked first, and finally his lips left hers, trailing against her throat. Her fingers knotted into his hair as he found her breast with his tongue, teased her nipple to a hardened tip, then licked, sucked, and bathed that tip until it seemed that the sensation streaked right through her body, bringing a red-hot hunger. She whispered his name, tugged at his hair, but he ignored her, kissing her belly, dropping to his knees, drawing her abdomen flush to his face and planting tiny kisses lower and lower.

Her hands gripped his shoulders; her knees buckled. She came down before him, shaking, seeking his lips and shoulders with her kiss, eager to touch him, taste him everywhere, lay her face against his chest, feel the smoothness and fire of his flesh. Arouse him, excite him, torment him as he tormented her. Her fingers closed fully around his sex, stroked. . . . His mouth crushed against hers, and she was suddenly off her feet, flat on the bed, and she felt the half-discarded wool of his uniform scratching against her thighs but it didn't matter; at that point every touch seemed like just another tongue of fire.

She met his eyes just as he sank into her, very slowly at first, watching her all the while. She couldn't close her eyes, couldn't look away. She gasped slightly as she shuddered with a sudden convulsion. With a swift thrust he went deeper still, and she came alive, writhing to the thunderous rhythm that gripped him and swept them up together. Reckless, wild, desperate, she clung to him, seeking and knowing what she sought, reaching and feeling the ecstasy take her at last, exploding into a climax that kept her trembling and convulsing with little aftershocks long after she felt the fierce constriction of his body shuddering throughout her own. . . .

They lay together in silence for long moments. She felt his heartbeat, her own. His head lay against her breast; she moved her fingers through his hair. "I'm glad to see you, Ian," she finally said in a worried voice, "but what are you doing here?"

She was glad to see, when he turned to her, that he was smiling. "I might ask you the same question," he reminded her.

She answered gravely, "Ian, I swear, I did not mean to desert you. It's just that I'm not a part of the North—"

"And I think I warned you once that wherever you went, I'd come after you," he said softly.

A sizzle of fear swept through her. "I really did have to leave Washington. And they've been exceptionally wicked to Rose."

"Under the circumstances, they've been tolerant of Rose. She's still living, isn't she?" he demanded wryly. "They have begun to execute spies, you know—and your precious Confederacy started it with a hanging in Richmond."

Alaina lowered her lashes. "It seemed prudent that I leave Washington. I'd been too friendly with Rose. Whom you introduced me to, if you remember."

"If I remember correctly, you introduced yourself, coming to a party on the night you were about to give birth."

"Well, I didn't know I was about to give birth, Ian!" She gasped suddenly, sitting up. "You're in danger here. How in God's name did you get here?"

Lacing his fingers behind his head, Ian leaned back against the pillow. "There are ways—naturally."

"Ian, it's dangerous. You can't stay."

His eyes seemed to slice right through her.

Alaina swallowed hard. "Did you see Sean when he was awake?"

He nodded.

Sean was never left alone; when he wasn't with Alaina, Lilly looked after him. "So Lilly knows you're here?"

He nodded again.

"Can we trust her?" Alaina whispered.

Ian rolled toward her on an elbow, arching a brow, studying her eyes. "I imagine I can better trust Lilly than you. Wouldn't you consider that a true statement?"

"I don't know what you mean," Alaina murmured, eyes downcast. She eased away from him, resentful, despite the fact that she was every bit as guilty as she appeared in his eyes. "Am I screaming?" she demanded. "Am I trying to have you seized and imprisoned?"

"No. But then, God knows, maybe you're waiting to see if the Panther can give you any information," he suggested coldly.

She was acutely uncomfortable. Nervous denial immediately sprang to her lips. "Ian, I don't know what you heard, and—" She broke off, then added softly, "I don't know where you've been, or with whom. But if Risa told you anything—"

"Risa," he said bluntly, "told me nothing but that she thought you should leave as quickly as possible, that it was simply a dangerous city for Southerners."

His hard, steady gaze gave away nothing of his own emotions—or his relationship with Risa since Alaina's departure. She longed to ask him, but too much time lay between them—or perhaps she was afraid to know.

"So you have seen her."

"Of course I've seen her."

"Ian, if you just understood—"

"You know, Alaina, I don't want to understand; I don't even give a damn anymore."

She gasped as she found herself pulled beneath him again, and the world and the war went away. His lovemaking was passionate and his fever bordered on violence, but it had been so long, so very long, that she couldn't care, she could only tremble in return, meeting and matching his ardor once again. She had almost forgotten how wonderful it could be in his arms, how unbelievably exquisite to be held, made love to with such demanding passion.

Yet this time, within minutes after she lay spent against him, he rose, reaching for his clothing.

"You're leaving?" she murmured.

"Do you suggest I stay and announce my presence to the good folks of St. Augustine?" he inquired.

She sat up slowly, drawing the sheets about her as she was suddenly chilled, and shook her head. "No, of course not. I just—"

"Ah. You were just waiting to see if I was going to make an attempt to abduct you back to Northern territory in the darkness of the night?"

Alaina flushed. "Ian, I'm assisting your brother, for God's sake! And—"

He kissed her lips suddenly, breaking off her speech. "I think that St. Augustine is a fine place for you to be. You're in Florida—which is where you belong, right?"

"Yes, of course."

He bent a knee upon the bed, his hands imprisoning her face, and his eyes were suddenly frighteningly intent. "I don't know what went on in Washington. Risa refuses to tell me, and Rose will do nothing but proudly admit her own guilt."

"It isn't guilt if—"

"I'm not arguing sides. I'm not going to drag you out of here. But I want your promise that you'll stay here."

"In St. Augustine?"

He nodded gravely.

She felt a grateful and relieved fluttering in her heart. She loved the Confederacy—and Ian. And it suddenly seemed possible to love them both.

"I promise I'll stay in St. Augustine. I wouldn't dream of moving away. I—"

"And you will behave."

"I don't know what you mean."

"I think you do."

"Ian, I assist your brother in surgery, I see to his troops—tonight I helped deliver a baby." She rose to her knees, hands against the rough blue wool of his jacket. "I came to *your* family. I—"

He nodded, and actually smiled, his fingers closing gently around her hand where it lay against his chest. "Promise me you'll behave, that you'll be careful, that you won't risk your life or that of our child."

With his eyes seeming to project their blue fire into her soul, she nodded. She stared up at him in turn, hot tears burning behind her eyelids with the knowledge that he would leave her again. Her hair tumbled down her back, her body crushed against his.

"Ian . . ."

He groaned. Then he exhaled suddenly and she found herself swept up, and down beneath him one more time.

"Ian, you've got to leave!" she protested.

"Yes," he whispered against her flesh.

"Ian, please—"

"Alaina . . ."

She forgot that she wanted him gone before he could be discovered, before he might have to try slipping away in the morning light. She forgot, for too quickly she was engulfed in the intoxicating passion of his kiss, the feel of his warmth, the texture of wool creating sensation against her flesh, the feel of his naked erection set free against her. . . .

She clung to him when it was over, loath to let him go, yet whispering, "Ian, it's dangerous for you to be here, dangerous for you to try to leave."

"I know what I'm doing," he assured her, rising, adjusting his breeches and buckling his scabbard back into place.

"Right. You're a man, a McKenzie. Bullets will bounce off of you!" she murmured miserably.

He walked back to the bed, cupping her chin so that she looked into his eyes. "The bullets won't bounce off me; I won't let them hit me."

Alaina suppressed her irritation. He was so wrong! "Ian, think of what you're saying. You're telling me to be careful, while you walk out into the war."

"I'm telling you—warning you—not to get involved in spying activities!" he stated with flat anger. "Because if you do, my love, you may prefer to have Lincoln himself arrest you, rather than me coming upon you. And yes, I went to West Point, Alaina, I am an army officer, and I have little choice but to go to war. And I am sorry for it; God knows, I am sorry for it!" he added fiercely.

"Oh, Ian," she said miserably.

He came to her one last time, holding her, brushing a kiss against the top of her head.

"Behave," he said softly.

She lowered her head. She knew that she couldn't promise him she would behave. If there was something she could do to save Confederate lives, she would have to do it.

"If only you could enter the city and come to me every night. . . ."

"I am good," he said with a certain dry amusement, "but not even I can come that often, madam."

She pulled away from him. "No, I don't want you to

come. I don't want you to be in danger. Ian, you must
stay away."

He smiled. "And you must stay here," he reminded
her, pulling her back against him. He kissed her lips then
released her and walked to Sean's crib. He watched his
sleeping son as seconds ticked by. Then he turned. He
picked up his plumed hat from where it sat on her bedside table, swept it low to her in a deep bow, and departed into the darkness of the predawn.

Dark days befell the Confederacy in February 1862.
They met with disastrous defeat at Forts Donelson and
Henry in Tennessee, and the Secretary of War ordered
General Robert E. Lee to withdraw all forces defending
the seaboard of Florida and report to Albert Sidney
Johnston in Tennessee. The east coast was to be aban-
doned, left entirely to its own defenses.

Julian prepared to pull out of St. Augustine along with
the rest of the military. Alaina was torn, certain that Ian
had known full well that the Confederacy was going to
virtually rape the east coast of Florida when he'd made
her promise to stay. Watching Julian pack up his medical
supplies, she wondered if she shouldn't accompany him
anyway; circumstances had changed.

Peter O'Neill came to see her before pulling out with
his company.

"It's deplorable, what has happened here! But don't
despair, Alaina—there will be Rebel soldiers nearby, just
across the river."

"I know, Peter."

"You haven't become a traitor, too, Alaina?" he
asked her.

"My heart is with the Confederacy, you know that."

He smiled at her. "You're a regular Rebel angel,
Alaina. I know we'll meet again. I'll be with the fighting
men still in the state, don't you worry. And . . ."

"And what?"

He hesitated, then swept off his hat. "I'm sorry, but
I'm going to kill your husband. I'm going to hunt him
down in his lair and kill him. The Panther will die before
this war is over."

She stepped back from him, appalled. He quickly tried
to rectify his words.

"Alaina, I'm sorry. This is war, and he is the enemy, and I want you to know, I will be there for you. I will be there."

"Don't say this to me, Peter."

"You'll see . . . I'm afraid that one day you'll need me," he told her.

He tightened his mouth grimly, mounted his horse, and rode away.

Alaina debated what to do until the last minute. But even as she did so, Dr. Percy came to see her in the guest house. He looked very old, sad, and tired. "A physician, a surgeon in this war must have tools with which to work! Morphine, quinine, and chloroform, astringents, stimulants, and escharotics like nitric acid to burn out bad tissue, form scars! We must keep our men alive; we must keep abreast of the movements of the Union army."

She stared at him determinedly. Percy knew full well that he could sway her by convincing her that she could save lives. "Percy, I'm not certain that I should abandon St. Augustine."

"Ah, my dear! You *can't* abandon St. Augustine. I will take over Julian's practice in this house. You must stay here and assist me. There will be a skeletal force of volunteers just across the St. Johns River. We are both well acquainted with a certain cipher. If we can just keep them informed, which we should manage easily enough to do under the guise of medical necessity, we can still continue to serve the Confederacy."

Alaina hesitated, memories of Ian still very strong within her heart.

And memories of Peter's words to her. The war needed to end, to be over. And if she could do anything that might hasten the South to victory . . .

Or defeat?

She was good at espionage, she knew. And she knew her state, and the rivers, and the terrain.

Just as Ian did.

But Ian refused to see the duality of his position. He believed in the Union cause, and he had to fight for it. She believed just as passionately in the Confederacy. He would avoid bullets; she would do the same.

And he would never know anything about her activities.

He was known as the Panther, but very few people knew the identity of the Moccasin.

Yes, she would stay in St. Augustine. Just as she had been told to do.

Chapter 26

The Union had actually not hurried to occupy Florida—even though it had been pointed out frequently enough that the state was scarcely defended—because it was of so little strategic importance. The priority on the South Atlantic coast was Charleston.

But in spring 1862, Union General George McClellan decided that St. Augustine might as well be taken.

The first scout ship arrived off the St. Augustine inlet on March 8, leaving buoys in the channel for the ships that would follow behind. Four days later, Union Commander Rogers left the *Wabash,* flagship of Flag Officer Samuel Du Pont, in a small boat that flew a white flag.

Abandoned, left completely undefended, St. Augustine surrendered to the Federal forces without a whimper. Perhaps the surrender was made easier by the fact that the city had been down to its knees in financial woes. Without Northern tourists to fill the hotels and keep the merchants in business, it had steadily become almost impossible for the citizens to pay their taxes. City government had come almost to a standstill, and food had become as scarce as medical supplies.

Alaina took the carriage with Lilly and Sean, keeping a distance as Mayor Cristobal Bravo met Commander Rogers at the seawall. Rogers appeared quite dignified and assured the mayor and his council and the Unionists who gathered there that he was anxious to restore St. Augustine to the happy state of affairs it had enjoyed before the South's rebellion.

Watching the event, Alaina felt her heart sink, because she could remember how Ian had told her all along that the South couldn't possibly win the war. In St. Augustine that morning, it seemed true—for all the reasons Ian had stated. The Union could tighten a noose around the South. Starve the people. The Union had pharmacies and could produce life-saving drugs, just as the Union had the arsenals and the capability of manufacturing weapons. St. Augustine had been seriously weakened long before it had fallen to Commander Rogers.

She was glad, however, to realize that although the men of the town had given in quietly, a number of the women had chopped down the secession flagpole so that the union flag couldn't fly from it. And one of the ladies, Hannah Jenckes, called the men who so willingly cooperated with the Union "a bunch of grannies."

It didn't matter. Within a few days, the Union had settled into St. Augustine.

And even when, a few days later, Federal troops pulled out of Jacksonville, they remained in St. Augustine.

The Union had apparently come to stay.

The Panther's men rowed silently through the night, heading toward a landfall against a smooth stretch of beach a good fifty miles south of St. Augustine.

Sam Jones, in the front of Ian's dinghy, shook his head. "Don't see you how you're gonna do it, Major. Can't see a blasted thing in this darkness!"

"You'll see. When the clouds lift, we've got a full moon," Ian told Sam. "They'll have been transporting heavy materials, and there should be a trail through the brush and foliage as clear as an ink line."

The moon shifted obediently to Ian's will.

"There!" he exclaimed triumphantly.

Sam stared at him, as if Ian might have had a bit of warlock in him.

Their dinghy beached, Ian lifted a hand, indicating that his men should come ashore quietly. The men moved quickly to hide their boats. He led the way, moving swiftly across the sand toward the patch of sea grapes and low brush that lined the beachfront. With such foliage, there would have been no way to move any number of men and materials without leaving a flattened trail.

Ian had seen it from the water.

"I'll be damned, I'll be damned," Sam said.

"Wish we had the horses, Major," Simon Teasdale complained with a sigh. "A cavalryman—walking the beaches. Sir, I ask you, what's this war coming to?"

The men laughed.

"Quiet, men," Ian warned. "There's a mighty slim possibility of us running into other Union troops here. They have been saying that folks east of the St. Johns River are sympathetic to the Union now, but there still is a damned good chance of us coming upon a company of Rebs, so keep it quiet."

"Yessir!" he heard in the night.

"Whichever side we come upon, I hope they've got some horses," Simon grumbled.

Once again, they moved in silence.

They were after the goods taken off of the *Stalward,* a Union ship trapped by the Reb raiders just three days ago. The *Stalward* had been sunk; her cargo of ammunition, on its way to Key West, had been taken. They'd heard about the ship's fate through her sailors who'd been set off in dinghies by the captain of the Rebel boat who had attacked them. Apparently the captain had admitted to knowing about the plans of *Stalward,* which had anchored off St. Augustine before starting her ill-fated journey south. Intelligence reports had named a Rebel spy who was somehow slipping information to the Confederate volunteers in the interior of the state—the east side of the St. Johns—and then to the blockade runners. Three ships had been lost since the Union had taken St. Augustine. The spy was called the Moccasin; Ian had seen broadsides posted in Union-held towns and bases. There was a reward out for the Moccasin—dead or alive.

Ian and his men had already been shipboard, heading north for a consultation with General Brighton, when word of the *Stalward*'s demise had reached them. A large cache of arms had been taken, and they'd been close enough to attempt to do something about it. There might be little opportunity to bring the weapons back, depending on the size of the Rebel forces they came up against, but if they couldn't reclaim the arms, they could at least see them destroyed.

They followed the trail through the night, not a man complaining about the insects, the sharp foliage along the trail, the bog they traveled at one point. Near dawn, he called a halt for two hours, allowing his crew to catch an hour's sleep, taking turns at guard duty.

Ian didn't sleep at all himself. They were so close to St. Augustine, he felt that he could almost smell Alaina's perfume, feel her flesh, taste her. . . .

He lay in the darkness, eyes open, staring upward at the heavens and feeling as if beasts gnawed at his heart. This was war, and he had his part in it. But God knew, there were times when he wanted nothing more than to forget the conflict, times he prayed that someday, somewhere, he'd have a peaceful home and family again. The one night he'd slipped into St. Augustine seemed little enough to survive by now. Yet he'd held her, and in that time, whether he'd been a fool or not, he'd believed in what lay between them, in what strange bond had been forged by time and passion. He'd believed that she loved him.

Even if he was equally certain that she'd damn well been guilty of some sort of espionage in Washington. And even if . . .

Even if he had the sinking feeling that she might well be involved in it still. The Moccasin. The name haunted him. He was afraid. Anxious to return to St. Augustine, and assure himself that all reports he had heard were true: His wife had remained in the city. She'd accepted no social calls from Union officers, but she had remained in the home his brother had rented, working with Dr. Percy, and neither had ever refused medical care to the occupying Union soldiers.

Still . . .

Ian knew Dr. Percy. He'd been a military physician in Washington in the days before the war, before his resignation, and he believed that every man owed his life to his country.

His country was now the Confederacy.

And Alaina was working with him, which could well mean that . . .

He didn't dare dwell on the edge of suspicion and fear that had so recently come to haunt him.

"Major!"

He jerked up, looking at Sam, who had come creeping

toward him. "Major, Billy just heard some noise . . . I think we've got our cache of weapons."

"Get the men," Ian ordered.

Within seconds, his company of eight was awake and in formation and moving silently through the brush. Billy led the way, pointing out the wagons in a copse just ahead. They fanned out into the brush, watching, waiting. But it seemed that there was a lone sentry on, guarding the wagons, pacing back and forth, as if anxious to know himself why he'd been left alone so long.

"We rush him?" Sam asked.

Ian shook his head. "We want him alive. Get me Reggie."

Reggie was his best sharpshooter, so precise with his aim that the men said he could knock the eye out of a mosquito at a hundred feet.

"Make him drop his weapon; I'm not trading his life for yours, but we've got to talk to him, find out why he's hidden here—and how many other Rebs are near."

Reggie nodded, dropped, took aim. He nicked the fellow cleanly in the upper arm. The man howled, dropping his rifle, gripping his arm, and looking around wildly. Ian moved in, Colt aimed at the man's heart.

Man—he was little more than a boy. Ian felt a sudden sickness that his beloved state had been so ravaged by the war that now children were fighting. Thank God he hadn't had to kill the youth.

The boy, tall and lanky but no more than twelve, stared at him with wide eyes.

"What's a boy doing with a cache of weapons?" Ian asked him.

"I'm not a boy. I'm Private Elisha Nemes, Florida Volunteers!" the youth announced proudly. He had brown eyes, freckles, and wore a ragged slouch hat and huge brown overcoat. He lifted his chin, but he looked scared.

"Private Nemes, you must be a fine soldier to be trusted so," Ian said, watching the boy shake, "but you've been captured now, by—"

"McKenzie," the boy spat out. "You're the Panther."

Ian nodded. "I need to know where the rest of your party is, Private."

The boy's eyes darted nervously along the trail toward

the north. "I ain't telling you. I ain't telling you nothing," he said firmly. "Am I going to lose my arm?" he asked, face twitching.

Ian looked at Reggie. Reggie shrugged, then walked to the boy. "Major, how could you doubt me?" Reggie queried, smiling. "I gave him a flesh wound, no more. You just take care of that wound and you'll be fine, young man."

"Yeah," Sam said softly. "He'll live to lift a rifle again, and maybe die next time he's fired on."

"Where's your party?" Ian insisted.

The boy stared at him, tremendous conflict raging through his eyes. Then he seemed to make a decision; not that he liked Ian, but that Ian might be better than some other evil that threatencd him now.

"They went northward, yonder," he said.

"How many?"

"Just three. They went . . ." he hesitated, then spat. "They went to decoy some Yanks away from the guns. Animal Yanks, beast Yanks! Fellows walked just down the next trail from us, saying as how all Rebs should be hanged, all of them. They think we were the ones shot up some Yanks out of St. Augustine last week; they think we're a whole party of spies."

"Are there spies in your party, Private?" Ian asked, his mouth suddenly very dry.

The boy hung his head. "Patriots, sir!" he said, lifting his head again. "Just patriots."

"Simon, Billy, Gerald, secure the arms," Ian said, "and take them and the boy back to the boats."

"Am I going to a prisoner-of-war camp?" the boy asked.

"You're going to St. Augustine," Ian told him.

"It's in Union hands."

"From there, someone is going to find your mother."

In all the time they'd been with Elisha Nemes, he hadn't looked quite so scared. Ian smiled. Once his mother got her hands on him, Elisha Nemes was probably safely out of the war for the next several years at the very least.

He turned to the rest of his men. "Let's find out what the hell else is going on here."

His men fell into step behind him and they started

north, as Elisha Nemes had directed. They moved
quickly, and within a half hour they started to hear the
men ahead.

"Bloody Reb! Cut him, Captain, cut him. Hell, we're
going to hang and bury the bastard anyway. Who the
hell's going to know the difference? This is God's will."

Ian looked back at Sam and the others. They pulled
out their guns, ready to slip silently into their fan formation around the copse ahead.

Ian ducked low against the brush and moved forward
to stand behind a thick pine. He leaned against the tree,
quickly counting the Union soldiers in the group. Ten
of them. They'd been on horseback, but now three of
their horses were lined up beneath the huge overhanging
branch of an old oak—and there three Rebel prisoners
were seated atop the horses, hands tied behind their
backs, nooses around their necks. The Federals were so
busy urging their leader to torment their prisoners that
they were oblivious to the men encircling them.

"God's will?" Ian murmured. Because the Union men
were behaving despicably.

He nodded to Sam, then stepped from the tree, his
Colt aimed at the sergeant, a middle-aged man with
graying hair and a cumbersome gut.

"Sergeant! What in God's name is going on here?"

The captain's company spun about, all reaching for
their weapons, then hesitating as they saw him and the
rest of his men stepping from the brush.

"It's Yanks!" someone called with relief.

Ian approached the sergeant.

"I'm in charge here, Major!" the sergeant called out,
sounding both aggravated and wounded.

One of his enlisted men stepped forward. "These
Rebs murdered a bunch of our fellows just last week.
Why, the boys had been asked to a dance at the Framington plantation, and they were shot down in cold
blood on the way back, and these are the bastard Rebs
who did it."

"How do you know that?" Ian demanded.

" 'Cause the fellow on the third horse admitted it."

Ian walked around. Two of the prisoners had their
heads down. The third, a man of about thirty with a
gaunt, dignified face, returned Ian's stare.

"Is that true?" Ian asked the man.

The man sighed. "Major, I'm not a murderer, and I've never shot anybody down in cold blood. We're Rebs, sir, and that's a fact, and we engaged fairly with those boys when they left the Framington place. They were killed."

Ian nodded, turning to the sergeant.

"Cut them down."

The sergeant stiffened. "You're not going to just let them go."

"No, sir, we'll bring them in as prisoners of war."

"Major, you don't understand what's going on here. We took them fair and square, just like they took our fellows."

"We're soldiers, not the law!" Ian spat back.

"Damn it, Major—"

"That's damned right—I'm *Major* McKenzie, and I'm giving you a direct order."

"Major," the sergeant protested, "the skinny one at the end there—the pretty-looking, girlish fellow—is a spy and we know it! Corporal Ader over there is the one survivor from the dance, and he saw the fellow slinking away from the party right before our folks were ambushed. We're *allowed* to hang spies, sir. In fact, I have direct orders to do so! I'll show you, sir!" He walked toward Ian, producing a frayed paper from his coat pocket. Ian took the orders and saw that they had been written by a Colonel Hirshhorn. There was a statement within the orders saying, "The capture of all spies engaged in direct action against any member of the United States military may be punishable as seen fit by the officer in command, not to exclude an instant death penalty for those whose actions directly involved the death of U.S. military men."

Ian shook his head, handing the paper back. "Sergeant, I'm now the officer in charge here, and there isn't going to be any hanging done by a damned lynch mob of rowdy soldiers. Now I'm telling you one last time to cut these men down!"

"Yessir!" the sergeant said, saluting stiffly.

But then a gun suddenly discharged.

Ian swung around to discover who had so recklessly

disobeyed his order, but he could see nothing because the frightened horses beneath the oak reared and bolted.

The Reb prisoners began to swing. . . .

"Cut them down!" Ian roared, with such a fury that even the sergeant's men scurried to obey, scampering up the oak to slice the ropes. Reggie, with Ian, took aim and shot through the farthest rope, and the skinny fellow fell limply to the earth. A second later, all of the men were down. Ian first approached the man he'd spoken with, but there was no saving him; his neck had been cleanly broken. The next fellow was equally dead.

The third, brought down so quickly by Reggie's well-aimed shot, might stand a chance.

Ian hunkered down by that Reb, whose face was now in the dirt. He frowned as he saw clipped, blue-black hair, uneasiness churning in his gut even before he turned the fellow over.

The Reb had been wearing a huge slouch hat and an encompassing coat. Now the hat was gone. And the Reb's face was fully visible.

With her crudely cropped hair, Jennifer could be taken for a very pretty boy.

Ian almost cried out loud. Dead or alive, he couldn't allow Jennifer to be taken by anyone other than himself. He thought briefly that he would rather die on the spot than have to let his uncle know that his daughter had been hanged by Union forces as a spy.

And that she was dead. . . .

With a furious strength he wrenched the rope free from around her neck and stood, hiking her over his shoulder. "Bury those two!" he commanded harshly. "And Sergeant! Don't think that this will go unreported, by God. I'll take it straight to Lincoln myself!"

"They killed good Union soldiers!" the sergeant protested in return. "They killed our boys! Damn, sir, but you are one of those Johnny Rebs yourself at heart. Why, everyone in hell knows your kin are killing us all over, Major."

Ian spun around, staring at the man. He fell silent. He turned blood red.

"Someone ought to shoot him and put him out of his misery!" Sam said audibly, staring at the sergeant.

"Yeah, someone should," Reggie said smoothly.

"Burial detail!" the sergeant ordered hoarsely.

Ian turned. Carrying Jennifer, he strode quickly down the trail.

Away from the others, he shifted her into his arms, seeking a pulse, some sign of life, as he moved.

Her eyes opened. Liquid and dazzling against the handsome contours of her face, beautiful despite her ragged hair and muddied complexion.

"Ian!" she mouthed. She had no voice.

She almost smiled. She tried to touch him.

But then . . .

Her eyes closed.

Chapter 27

A laina continually expected Ian to arrive.
He didn't.

As the weeks passed, she found herself growing more and more nervous. He had come when the city was Confederate; now it was Union, and he hadn't made an appearance, nor had he written to her.

The spring of 1862 had brought several bitter defeats to the Confederate troops, one of the worst being the loss of New Orleans. Alaina discovered through Captain Willoughby, a kindly old Union gentleman—liked by even the most bitter Rebels of St. Augustine—that her husband had most probably been involved. The Union had made use of a cover plan in which it appeared that the main attack would be against Pensacola or Mobile. Joint army and navy forces had taken the strategic Southern city, and Captain Willoughby told Alaina that she should be very proud; her husband's intelligence frequently kept the Union well abreast of Confederate troop movements.

Alaina returned from surgery one day to find that she had a guest. Walking exhaustedly toward her little guest house, she was startled to hear voices—Lilly's and another soft, feminine voice. And Sean, shrieking with laughter.

Frowning, she hurried to her door and threw it open.

"Risa!" she exclaimed.

Risa, who had been down on the ground wrestling with Sean, stood, smiling.

"Hello."

Alaina stared back at her blankly. Sean cried out a happy little "Mum" and came running forward on his short but sturdy legs, throwing himself at her. She picked him up and he kissed her cheek, then shimmied back down and flung himself against Risa's skirt again.

"Alaina—is everything all right?" Risa asked, since Alaina continued to stare at her blankly.

"I—I—"

A dozen thoughts sped through her head. She liked Risa, really liked her, respected her for her frankness, honesty, courage, and loyalty to her own beliefs. She was also grateful to Risa, and certain that Risa's intentions had really been the best when she had helped Alaina flee Washington.

But if Risa had come to St. Augustine . . .

She would have to be more careful than ever. It wasn't good. She was already a nervous wreck, worried that she would be gone from the city when Ian did decide to make an appearance. But now, every time she made a move, she would have to worry about Risa as well.

Yet Risa's smile as she faced Alaina was genuine, just as her affection for Sean was sincere. She stood with her beautiful aquamarine eyes alight, her dark hair wild after her play with Sean.

"I'm fine! Just so . . . so surprised!" Alaina said at last, and she smiled and hurried forward then, hugging Risa with warmth.

When she drew away, however, she thought a strange light touched Risa's eyes—if just briefly. And it nagged at her a moment as she wondered if Ian had sent her.

"When did you come? How did you get here? Er— why did you come?"

Risa shrugged, trying to smooth down her hair. "My father has been away with the Army of the Potomac so much that my being at home became ludicrous. I would walk around, wait, worry—and join sewing circles," she added, making a strange little face that caused Alaina to laugh.

"You don't like sewing?"

Risa shrugged. "I felt . . . impotent. A friend of my father's is a flag officer, and his ship was coming this way—and here I am."

"Ah!"

"I've taken a little house just a block down on the water."

"That's . . . wonderful," Alaina breathed. Thank God!

At first she had thought Risa had come to stay with her. Live with her, see and hear far more than she should. . . . "It will be so much fun to have company," she lied. She smiled, watching Risa. "But it is quite strange to see you here."

"Isn't it, though."

"Have you seen Ian?" Alaina asked.

"On his last trip to Washington. Have you seen him?"

"Once," Alaina admitted. "But he hasn't been here in quite a while."

"I believe he was involved in the operations around New Orleans."

"So I've heard."

"And you?" Risa asked her pointedly.

"I—I work with Dr. Percy," she said. "Let me just see to some supper and we'll talk. You can tell me all about Washington. I'm afraid that St. Augustine will be slow and mundane in comparison."

"Ah, but it is a change of scenery!" Risa assured her. "And I have done some nursing. Perhaps I'd be of some help to you and Dr. Percy."

"Well, it will be wonderful to have you with us," Alaina said smoothly.

Under different circumstances, it would have been wonderful.

The soldiers and the people were in love with Risa. She moved with quiet grace, the rustle of her skirts and the soft subtle scent of her perfume reaching the men when she arrived. She was an angel of mercy, more adept at administering chloroform than Dr. Percy was himself, and so charming and clever that she had the men laughing right up to the point that they passed out. Risa didn't blanch at blood, nor turn in horror when Dr. Percy needed assistance with an instrument. Alaina was surprised to realize that she gained strength from Risa— even if it was just a bit of an irritation that Risa should prove to be quite so perfect. Risa never turned away from any medical task, no matter how menial or displeasing it might be.

Risa had been there one week when Dr. Percy came to the guest house late one night. He had a ciphered letter for Alaina to bring to the company of men camped on the far side of the river, near the Englewood plantation. There would be no difficulty in her actually leaving the city; she and Dr. Percy were often visited by the Yankees in command, and the help they had given the Union soldiers was appreciated. They were granted passes to cross the Union lines whenever necessary.

Dr. Percy wouldn't be leaving with her, since she was ostensibly going to stay with Mrs. Englewood, who was expecting a child any day. Dr. Percy's services might still be required in the city, and Alaina had now assisted in childbirth many times. Women were best to deal with women's matters, especially when physicians couldn't be spared.

"This is simple courier duty, Alaina. But next week, the Moccasin must strike again."

"When? How? Union ships guard the harbor."

"I'll bring you south. We've men ready to bring you to a ship hidden in an inlet. It's another trip to the Bahamas and back. You'll be brought to Biscayne Bay and set ashore close to your own home; you'll be carrying some financial assistance from British friends, and supplies of chloroform and ether."

"Dr. Percy, what if my husband comes to St. Augustine and I am gone?"

"That's easy enough. I intend to say that you had an opportunity to go home to see your husband's family. This is the same story I will tell your friend Risa. Beautiful woman, isn't she? Proud, strong, competent, kind—beautiful!"

Alaina smiled. "Just lovely."

"Thank God for her! She just proves so darned useful when you're away!"

Alaina nodded wryly again, staring at Dr. Percy—and wondering if Ian didn't feel exactly the same way about Risa.

"Alaina, this is one of the most important things the Confederacy will ever ask you to do. The Brits who are donating their gold and medications are basically doing so because you were so passionate and convincing when you met them last. If I were to send anyone else, the supplies might not be forthcoming. And even with the Union here in St. Augustine, you see how short the city is, not just in medical supplies, but in food! We desperately need what foreign help we can get—and we desperately need donations of gold. You've seen amputations now! Can you imagine that horror for our men with no anesthesia?"

"No, Dr. Percy, I can't," she assured him.

She would be his courier this one last time, she determined. She'd sail to the Bahamas. Then she'd have to give the business of being the Moccasin some serious thought.

Alaina left very early the next morning so that she wouldn't have to explain her departure to Risa. She was afraid that Risa might determine to come with her. She still didn't know if Ian had perhaps been to Washington and asked Risa to come down and watch his wife's activities.

She rode out alone and was met by Mr. Englewood just across the river, who saluted to the Union guard on their side of the river. The Englewoods played their own brand of dangerous game, Alaina thought, pretending to be Unionists because of their proximity to St. Augustine, while offering their plantation as a meeting place for many of the Union officers and troops within the interior of the state.

Maggie Englewood and her new baby girl appeared to be in excellent health when Alaina arrived at their household. Englewood himself seemed completely unconcerned with the birth of his child—other than that it afforded a good opportunity to bring information across the river. Alaina remained at the house for about an hour before Englewood suddenly rose, went to the door, opened it, and allowed her contact to come in.

Alaina rose, uneasy to see that Peter O'Neill stood in the Englewoods' foyer.

He smiled with deep amusement and pleasure. It appeared he had been expecting her. Englewood left them alone together, and Peter approached her, taking her hands in his. "Alaina! How sad is war—except for this chance to see you!"

She tried to draw her hands away. "Peter—"

"You have something for me?" he asked gravely.

She undid her hair, finding the cipher she had meticulously folded into her coiffure, a trick learned from Rose and her courier Betty. She nearly jumped when Peter stepped forward. "Just helping!" he assured her, and he did use deft fingers to free the paper from the length of her hair.

"Thank you," he told her. "A job well done."

She nodded, feeling queasy. She was, in fact, feeling ill quite frequently lately. The war was taking its toll.

"Alaina, you don't realize. Your contribution to the Confederacy is inestimable."

"I have to get back."

"You don't really, do you?"

"Peter, please—"

"Alaina," he said passionately, "one day you will realize, you and I are on the same side in this war."

"Peter, one day you will understand that I'm married."

"I promise you," he said, the liquid blue of his eyes chilling, "when this war is over, you will be a widow."

"Peter, God knows, when this war is over, we could all be dead. But if you think that you will gain sympathy from me by threatening to kill my husband, you are sadly mistaken."

Peter stared at her, clenching and unclenching his fists at his sides. "If you don't see that the man is a vicious traitor, it is you who are horribly mistaken! I love you, Alaina, I always have—"

"Peter, you *chose* to marry elsewhere!" she reminded him.

"—and one day, you will see it. And if you must grieve for that damnable traitor McKenzie, then you must grieve, but our intelligence has it that the man keeps a camp in the swamp, and if I do nothing else this war, I will find that camp and I will kill him!" Peter finished violently. He stared at her for a moment as if he would like to strangle her himself, then he suddenly smiled. "You're meant for me, Alaina, and it will happen one day," he said simply. And, still smiling, he spun around and exited the house.

Englewood appeared the moment he was gone, and Alaina wondered just what the man had heard. "There's something for you to eat in the parlor," he told her. "Then we'd best be getting back."

There were biscuits, ham, and gravy awaiting her. She couldn't eat, but she pretended to—old habits died hard, and though a lady never consumed too much food too voraciously, it was equally bad manners not to enjoy a host's hospitality. Peter had upset her more than she wanted to admit. She picked at the food, then was grateful when Mr. Englewood said it was time to go.

As they rode, Alaina heard a woman's scream, then the crying of children. She looked at Englewood, who shrugged.

"What's going on?" she asked him.

He spat off the side of his horse. "Traitors!" he told her.

Alaina stared at him.

"Traitors!" he repeated. "Ain't no business of ours."

Ignoring him, she kneed her horse and cantered along the trail to the sound of the cries.

She came upon a handsome plantation house on a rolling lawn. A company of soldiers stood around the house, lighting fires at the four corners of it. A young woman had been dragged out on the lawn; soldiers teased and tormented her, throwing her between them, even though she held a small child, and three other children—perhaps ages seven, five, and three—looked on, huddled together and whimpering.

Furious and appalled—Rebel soldiers should never behave so despicably!—Alaina slammed her heels heedlessly against her mount and thundered upon the men. Hearing the horse come, they quickly parted; the young woman was left to herself as Alaina entered the circle, staring down at the men with her eyes flashing.

"What in God's name are you doing?"

"These folks are traitors," one of the soldiers declared, "and the place is to be burned, and that's that!"

"You've proof that they're traitors?"

"Captain O'Neill says they're traitors, and that makes them traitors!" the young man said.

"We're not traitors—we're Unionists, and we've stated it all along. And it doesn't even matter anymore—my husband was killed in action at New Orleans!" the woman cried.

Alaina dismounted, striding between the soldiers. "You are supposedly soldiers of the Rebellion, the last cavaliers—and this is how you behave?"

The group of them—four very young men—looked at her shamefaced.

But then she felt a pair of hands set down forcefully

upon her shoulders. She turned her head to meet Peter's eyes.

"This is the fate traitors meet, Alaina," he told her. "Turn, look!"

She had little choice, for he spun her around. As he did so, the beautiful house started to burn. The woman began to sob, sinking to her knees with her baby held to her breast, her other three children running around to her side.

Alaina slammed an elbow against Peter's ribs. When he grunted in pain, she escaped him, rushing forward, wrenching her riding cloak from her shoulders and beating out the flames that were beginning to eat at the house. She kicked the kindling into disarray. A minute later, Peter was at her back again.

"Her husband's dead!" Alaina informed him furiously. "She has four little children! How are they enemies to you? How are they dangerous?"

Staring at her, he let her go. He turned to his troops. "Douse the flames!" he ordered.

Relieved, Alaina felt her knees buckle. She knelt down in the grass. Peter hunkered down in front of her. "Happy, Alaina? Because I promise you, something else shall burn. Get up. I'll arrange another escort back to the river for you."

She stood, shrugging away from him. "There is no enemy I fear facing if you are my friend, Peter," she said angrily. She stormed away from him and mounted her horse. The woman came running to her, reaching for her arm, stopping her. "Thank you, thank you—"

"Please!" Alaina said, close to tears. "Don't thank me that they've had the sense to remember decency! Go, go in quickly, take care of those babies." She escaped the woman's hold and kneed her horse forward on the trail. She wanted to reach the river, and for once in her life, she wanted to be in Yankee territory.

She was in such torment that she rode recklessly and was in no way prepared when her horse suddenly reared with a vengeance. She plummeted to the earth, unhurt, swearing. "Why in the world did you do that, you idiot?" she cried to her mount, a skinny bay, The mare merely reared again and went tearing down the trail.

Alaina struggled up, testing herself for broken bones.

She heard a horse coming along the trail behind her, and she tensed, jumping quickly to her feet.

To her amazement, it was Risa riding a handsome roan. Risa reined in, and arched a brow.

"*You*—Miss Southern horsewoman—were thrown."

Alaina set her hands on her hips. "Yes, I was thrown. What are you doing here?"

"Following you," Risa said. Grinning, she dismounted.

"You just passed through Union lines into enemy territory—that easily?"

"I have a medical pass," Risa assured Alaina sweetly. "Want a ride?"

Alaina shook her head. "You're spying on me."

"I'm trying to help a friend," Risa said. She frowned suddenly, as if listening to something. "I wonder what—"

"Oh, Lord!" Alaina gasped, suddenly knowing why her horse had bolted. She had disturbed a batch of eastern diamondback rattlers.

"Move!" Alaina cried, springing forward, pushing Risa out of the way. Then, despite herself, she screamed.

Risa was in the clear, but even with the volume of her skirts, Alaina had been struck. The sudden pain was electrifying, and she staggered to her knees.

Risa flew into action, dragging Alaina quickly from the side of the trail and the offending snake. To Alaina's astonishment, she heard a sudden blast of gunfire. She realized that Risa had been carrying a gun—and that the snake was dead.

In the clear dirt center of the trail, Risa knelt down by Alaina. "You're a fool, getting bitten for me!" Risa told her, ripping up her skirt for a length of cotton with which to make a tourniquet.

Alaina, shaking, drew up her skirt and ripped her stockings, finding the ugly fang marks. "We need a knife." she began weakly, but Risa apparently knew what she was doing. She moved quickly to her saddlebags and came back with a huge Bowie knife. "Are you going to save me, or slit my throat?" Alaina asked.

Startled, Risa glanced briefly at the knife. "You never know who or what you might encounter," she said flatly.

Alaina smiled, fighting the pain, leaning back. Risa knew what she was doing. Alaina braced herself as Risa slashed the wound, then leaned over her calf to start sucking the poisoned blood out of Alaina's leg, spitting it to the side. Despite Risa's efficiency, Alaina felt first as if she were on fire, then she felt a numbness.

"You shouldn't have done this!" she heard Risa say between spits.

"I've been bitten before, twice," Alaina told her. "Remember, I come from the true savage swamp! I guess I'll be sick, but you . . ."

She was dimly aware of Risa leaning over her.

"I might have died, right?"

Alaina closed her eyes. And passed out.

The night was ominously dark as the small boat made its way, silently streaking through the water, beaching against the sand.

Ian immediately heard the sound of a rifle being cocked, followed by the demand, "Who is it?"

By the dim moonlight, he saw where his uncle stood. Behind James, also armed, were a number of Teddy's old grove workers. Ian hesitated briefly, his heart heavy. "It's Ian, Uncle James."

"You're not welcome here, Ian," James said flatly, but even in the darkness, Ian could see that his uncle lowered his weapon. James wasn't going to shoot him down in cold blood. James saw, however, that Ian wasn't alone in his boat. "You're not welcome, Ian, nor are your people."

"I've got Jennifer."

"What?" James demanded harshly.

Ian stepped from the boat, his cousin held tenderly in his arms as he approached her father.

Risa managed to get Alaina back to St. Augustine and under Dr. Percy's care. Percy assured her that she had done an exceptionally fine job, and that he was quite certain Alaina would come out of the ordeal all right. They'd just have a bit of a rocky road ahead of them.

Put to bed in her guest house, Alaina spent about twenty-four hours in which Risa, along with Lilly and Dr. Percy, diligently fought the fever that plagued her. Risa tended Alaina, watched the baby, and paid heed to all Dr. Percy's instructions.

That night, Alaina went through a spell of sweating, chills, and fever again.

She talked and talked, talked to Ian, to Percy.

"It's all right, it's all right, it's going to be all right," Risa assured her.

But Risa was heartsick. She was good at listening, and she'd listened very carefully to Alaina's ramblings.

And she wondered if any of it would ever be all right.

By nightfall of the second day, Alaina's fever broke completely. She was weak as a kitten the day after, then she seemed to make a miraculous recovery. Rising, bathing, and doing up her hair, she seemed especially well and in good spirits. Happy to be alive. "You brought me back, and you sat with me for days. Now you look exhausted, just like hell," Alaina told Risa with a smile. "Thank you."

Risa looked at her. "You threw me away from the bite—and wound up the victim yourself."

Alaina smiled. "But I knew I had an immunity."

"It was still incredibly brave—and quite a strange thing to do for *me!*"

Alaina shrugged. "It's war. We find strange enemies, and even stranger friends."

Risa nodded. "Still, I might have died. Thank you."

"Risa, are you watching me for Ian?" Alaina asked her bluntly.

Risa shrugged. "Actually, Alaina, I'm trying to watch you for yourself!"

Alaina walked to Risa and hugged her tightly. "Whatever the reasons, you're a good friend."

"Whatever the reasons, you are, too," Risa assured her.

"Go home. You're exhausted."

"I'm going."

Alaina hugged her one more time.

When Risa was gone, Percy arrived.

"Will you be all right?" he asked her worriedly.

"I'm fine."

"You gave us quite a scare . . . but you do seem to have an immunity. You're due to sail. Can you make it?"

"Yes."

"Perhaps we could postpone—"

"No. I'm going now. I'm going for medicine. . . . This time. I may not go again, Dr. Percy."

Percy nodded. "I understand. You have done your part."

He didn't understand. She loved her homeland, loved the ideal of freedom, and loved the gallantry that was supposedly a part of her South.

But she had also seen too much.

She would sail.

One more time.

It was time to go, and Ian stood with his uncle on the beach. He felt himself trembling along with James as his uncle embraced him. Three of his men waited in the small boat.

"Thank you," James told him. "Thank you."

"The ship's surgeon aboard the *Regard* assured me that she'll have few ill effects from the hanging," Ian said, "but she was suffering from malnutrition and a serious cold before it all happened, so it may take her a while to recuperate. She's not out of danger, and it will probably be quite some time before she can actually talk."

James nodded, his eyes filled with pain. "Teela and I won't leave her side."

Ian nodded. "I'll try not to come back and put you in an awkward position," Ian assured him quietly.

James drew away, staring at him with eyes as dark a blue as his own: his grandfather's eyes. McKenzie eyes.

"Ian, quite frankly, I have had it with war. I hated soldiers in blue, and I had a right to. But I'm not so sure about embracing those men who changed from blue to gray. I'm weary. I haven't seen my brother in well over a year, and whatever the sides in this, he has always been my brother, and if I have forgotten my own blood, by God, I am sorry. Ian . . ." He lifted his hands. "Well, we are still at war. But . . ." He hesitated a long while, staring at Ian, then he sighed softly. "I understand that Jen is still in danger, but you saved your cousin's life, and I will die grateful for that fact. So it seems that . . ." Once again, he seemed to have trouble finding the right words.

Then he stared firmly at Ian.

"There's been word that a ship is coming in south of here, next Wednesday night to be exact. The ship won't be able to come in too closely, of course, but it's supposed to carry . . . the Moccasin."

Ian felt cold fingers clamp around his heart.

Orders were clear regarding the Moccasin.

And if his uncle was actually giving him information regarding the spy . . .

"Thank you," Ian whispered.

James, studying him intently, nodded with a painful jerk of his head.

The two men embraced one more time.

Then Ian stepped into his boat.

The Panther and his men slid back out into the darkness of the night.

It was time to catch a snake.

Chapter 28

May 1862

The night was eerie.

A full moon rode the silken black sky, casting an iridescent ivory glow over the landscape. But there were clouds that night, puffy, billowing monsters that drifted along invisibly until they covered the moon and pitched land and sea into a darkness so deep it was like an ebony void.

And in the darkness, supported by his men, Ian waited.

And prayed that he was wrong. His uncle had warned him about the Moccasin in exchange for Jennifer's life, though he surely knew that Ian's love for his cousin demanded no payment in return.

But Ian was afraid.

Afraid that Alaina was guilty of espionage. Afraid that he wouldn't catch her.

That someone else would.

"A ship! Major, by God, you were right!" old Sam Jones whispered in the night.

Ian felt his heart quicken. His uncle had been right. His uncle had known.

He felt his men shifting in the darkness, amazed that he had known not just that a ship would risk the waters, but when it would do so. Sam, who had been the first man Ian had chosen for his company, probably suspected what Ian feared.

His men were anxious, he realized. He tried to speak calmly.

"Steady, boys, we can't take a ship right now, and we don't want anyone getting wind of us and carrying off the cargo. We want the landing party, gentlemen." He was silent. Then he reminded them, "We're here to seize the Moccasin."

Alaina stared at the fast-approaching coastline. *Almost home!* She was glad, so glad! The war was a wearying effort, more trying than ever recently. More worrying. She didn't know why she was so uneasy; she had slipped from St. Augustine with no difficulty, and everything had gone extremely smoothly in the Bahamas. Tonight, all she had to do was come home and turn her heavily laden coat over to her contact. Then she could go to Belamar, and sleep in her own bed. And perhaps . . .

She had believed, so passionately, in the Southern Cause. In States' Rights. In the battle cry that they were like the fledgling band of the colonies before the Revolutionary War, fighting for the right to independence, for the pursuit of life, liberty, and happiness—in their own way. If only others understood . . .

It was time to quit now. Quit. She had been a good spy, a good ambassador for the South. She had risked a great deal. Times were changing. Too many people knew her identity; too many people were beginning to guess at it.

And . . .

She wasn't sure about her convictions anymore. God forbid, she wasn't sure that the Confederacy was right! Perhaps it would be possible to slither into the water . . . and disappear into legend and history.

In the small inlet, just before they might have run aground, the ship was brought to a slow, smooth halt.

"Cast dinghy!" Captain Nasby ordered. He glanced at Alaina, and she knew he was worried. He had told her that he had seen the broadsides posted advising that the Moccasin was wanted—dead or alive.

Shot or hanged without mercy at the discretion of the captor.

Alaina didn't dare think about such threats—or the fact that they would be carried out. Fear made it impossible to function.

She touched the brim of her slouch hat, drawing it lower down her forehead. She drew her encompassing greatcoat with its numerous pockets more tightly around her. The coat was heavy, with gold, laudanum, letters, and Yankee dollars for the purchase of items that had become necessary to the South but that couldn't be bought with Confederate money. If she had to swim, the weight could drown her. She would have to slip out of it—and retrieve it later. She hoped she didn't have to swim. She felt that she had recovered entirely from her bout with the rattler, but she was still afraid that she wasn't as strong as she should be.

She stared at the shore, wondering again why she was so uneasy. She could see nothing amiss. The moon kept creeping behind clouds, but when the clouds parted, a strange yellow glow illuminated the earth. The water, with or without the moonlight, seemed black. Trees were encased in silent shadow. In a sudden burst of yellow moonlight, she scanned the shore. Nothing. Nothing . . . except . . .

"Wait!" she cried.

"You see something?" Captain Nasby demanded, frowning and trying hard to peer into the night.

Yes, something. Something had moved in the shadows. Alaina was filled with dread. Twin red lights suddenly seemed to peer from the trees. She felt a tightening grip of panic begin, but then breathed more easily again, nearly laughing aloud with relief.

"What?" the captain asked anxiously.

"A little deer," Alaina laughed.

"Ah . . . A deer. You're certain?"

"Yes."

"Jenkins, bring the Moccasin in," the captain ordered one of his young seamen.

"Yessir!" Jenkins said, saluting.

The captain turned to the Moccasin. "Be careful. Please."

"I will, sir," Alaina said, smiling.

"Remember," he told her firmly, "your life is far more valuable than your cargo, no matter how precious it may be. *You* cannot be replaced. You must remember that."

"I will!" she promised. Alaina realized then that she wanted it to be over. She wanted to get ashore, deliver her contraband, and be done. "And I must go now."

The captain nodded. He appeared unhappy, as if he struggled for the words to say more, but could not find them.

As if he, too, were suddenly filled with the same sense of dread.

For a moment, Alaina was made even more uneasy by his manner, and felt a strange chill, one as foreboding as the haunting night with its eerie yellow moon-glow.

"Be careful," the captain said again, gruffly.

"We should move now, sir," Jenkins said uneasily.

Alaina nimbly scrambled over the starboard side of the ship, following Jenkins down the small drop ladder to the dinghy waiting below. Jenkins quickly slipped the oars into the water, and the dinghy shot across the night-black sea. The coastline loomed ever closer.

"Stop!" she whispered, suddenly certain that all was not well. She felt as if the night was watching; she had the feeling of being . . .

Stalked.

Something awaited them. The heavy breathing of some great horrible creature seemed to echo in the darkness. The trees were too still. Nothing stirred; no insects chirped.

Jenkins ceased to row. The dinghy, caught by the impetus of his previous strength, continued to streak through the water despite Jenkins's efforts to position the oars to stop its progress.

Then the trees came to life. The moon was gone, darkness had settled, but the Moccasin heard the sounds as men slipped from the trees, rifles aimed at the dinghy.

And dreaded words in a more dreaded voice were suddenly issued.

"Surrender, come in peacefully, and your lives will be spared, you've my guarantee!"

The moon slipped free from the clouds. Eight men in hated Union blue had come from the trees. They were in formation at the water's edge: four on their knees, four standing, all aiming their rifles directly at the occupants of the dinghy. One more man stood slightly apart from the others.

Ian.

Her stomach lurched.

"Lord A'mighty!" Jenkins swore. He didn't even glance at Alaina, and she knew that he meant to surrender.

But she *couldn't* surrender.

"We surrender—" Jenkins began.

Alaina dove into the water. She dove very deep, slipped out of her coat, and swam hard, trying to pretend that she hadn't seen Ian, that he didn't suspect that she was the Moccasin. If he didn't know it was her, he might not catch her. He might swim straight for the boat and find nothing more than the coat she carried resting on the bottom.

She swam as hard as she could, trying to let the current help her, then surfaced. Keeping very low, she looked back to see that Ian's men still seemed far away. She scrambled up around the mangrove roots, certain that she could disappear into the foliage and away from the water, given half a chance.

But as she came ashore, she heard a sudden shout.

"Halt, or I'll shoot!"

She ran, expecting a bullet to plow into her back at any second.

But no weapon was fired.

Gasping for air, her lungs burning, she continued to run.

Then she heard racing footsteps. Close behind her, so close behind her . . .

She cried out even as his weight catapulted against her, bringing her down so hard she was winded and inhaled raggedly just for enough air to live, to remain conscious.

Oh, God, she knew it was Ian, knew it.

She wanted oblivion.

She was facedown in the roots and sand. He flung her over, straddling her with a staggering speed.

The moonlight suddenly seemed brilliant. She could see him clearly, so clearly.

He was as soaked as she, shirt and breeches plastered to the muscled hardness of his body. His dark hair was slicked back, his features like rock, cobalt eyes damning and cold and . . .

Strange. He had become a stranger. A hard, handsome stranger who stared at her now with such heated fury and hatred that she panicked, desperate to escape. She writhed, drawing back a fist to strike out with all the strength she could muster. She caught his jaw—but he barely seemed to notice. She struggled wildly to move him off balance, but succeeded only in winding herself further.

He caught her wrists and slammed her back to the sand with such brutal force that she cried out, panicked into silence. She went dead still and stared at him.

"So you are the Moccasin," he said. His voice was cold and harsh, and the fury within it increased as he added, "How dare you?"

She was so afraid. And even more heartsick. She wanted to explain, but she couldn't explain to him.

She could only keep fighting, because there was nothing left for them now except battle.

"And you're the Panther. The bloody, goddamned Panther. Stalker. Traitor! Dear God, this is Florida!" she cried. "You are the traitor here. How dare you?"

She was vaguely aware of footfalls on the sand. And then his men gathered around them.

"Major," one of them said quietly, "we lost the Reb from the ship. He panicked and drowned. We went in; there was nothing we could do."

Ian listened to his soldier speak, but his eyes never left her face, and not a flicker of emotion passed through them. She bit her inner lip, dismayed. Poor Jenkins! But he had given up so quickly. If only he had shown a little more courage . . .

Oh, God, he was dead. Another good man. These men hadn't even wanted to kill him, she realized, but he was dead.

"All right, Sam," Ian said calmly, still watching Alaina all the while with the deadly glitter of ice-fire in his cobalt eyes. "Brian, Reggie, see to the body. We'll head back to base camp." He spoke to Alaina then. "Don't try to escape me again."

She couldn't look away from him. "Will you shoot me?" she managed to ask him.

"My men get nervous in the swamp. God knows, sometimes we shoot at anything."

He stood suddenly, jerking her to her feet. He kept staring at her while his men moved about as bidden. Someone brought the horses.

Pye!

She suddenly felt like laughing. He even had his own horse here deep in the swamp.

He threw her up atop his mount, then leaped up be-hind her.

No more than thirty minutes of riding in a tense si-lence brought them to a small grouping of cabins, built up on stilts, deep within a hammock. The cabins were all but hidden by a massive wall of pines that broke just before the small clearing.

Alaina began to shiver. The night air was cool. With her coat gone, she was dressed in men's breeches, a cot-ton shirt, and high boots. Even her boots remained un-comfortably sodden with seawater.

The camp was amazing. She had heard rumors that the Panther was so good he had arrogantly settled in enemy territory. His cabins were so well hidden, and yet so close to her home. Close to where she should be handing over the items in the coat to her contact. Close to being saved. . . .

She was the Moccasin. She had been captured.

She would be hanged.

No!

Something in her heart cried out that it couldn't hap-pen. But, oh, God, what a naive fool she had been! It now seemed inevitable that this day should come.

She wished fervently that he had ordered his men to drag her through the swamp on foot. That would have been better than riding with him. *Feeling* his rage, his horror that she was the Moccasin. It seemed to burn from him, from the arms that held Pye's reins around her, from the hard-muscled wall of his chest. He was fire tonight, and she would be consumed in it. Cast into Rebel hell.

He seemed to be a mass of heat and muscled tension, and yet the very feel of him when he touched her was somehow colder than a northern ice floe. *As if he could not bear to touch her. . . .*

Perhaps that was well. Ian seemed to be a broad-shouldered, yet slender man. His appearance was decep-tive, for it was his height, over six feet, that made him seem more lithe and lean when he was actually quite powerfully built. If he were to touch her, he might readily snap her neck, break her right in two.

Yet when they reached the clearing, he jumped swiftly from Pye. Briefly, his cobalt eyes lit upon hers. Blue fire.

He turned to his men. "See to the prisoner!" he ordered brusquely, then quickly strode away. He couldn't bear to be near her, she thought. He was afraid that he'd strangle her, tear her limb from limb with his bare hands.

What would that matter, she wondered, feeling a sudden rise of hysteria, if she was to be hanged anyway? A quick death at Ian's hands might be preferable.

Ah, but he was the famed Major Ian McKenzie. He'd never lower himself to the cold-blooded murder of a prisoner. Justice—Union justice—would have its way.

When Ian was gone, she realized that his men had been left as surprised as she. But one of the men quickly sprang to action. "My name's Sam. Don't try to escape, now, Ma'am. Pye will just throw you, you know."

Pye would throw her. The horse was as irritatingly loyal to his master, as were Ian's men.

Sam reached up to help her down. She didn't know just how badly she had been shaken by the night's events until she realized she could just barely stand. Another soldier rushed to her side, supporting her. He looked at her with dazzled, dark brown eyes. Too bad this boy wasn't her jailer, she thought. She'd be free in no time.

"Thank you," she told him softly.

Ah, but that was why they called her the Moccasin. She'd eluded those sent to trap her time and time again.

Tonight, though, she would not escape.

Again she wished she could cry out; she wanted to explain. In a way she wanted to shriek with pain, for all she had seen in his eyes. And in a way, she wanted to rail and beat against him for being all that he was. The Panther.

"Come along, ma'am," Sam said. "I imagine the far cabin's yours for the night. Gilbey, see to fresh water for the lady. Brian, post a guard."

Sam escorted her to the cabin, keeping a hand loosely on her elbow as he helped her up a ladder to the platform flooring. Sam was polite, but firm. He lit a kerosene lantern, illuminating the cabin. "You should be comfortable enough . . . bed and blankets—clean sheets to wear while your clothing dries. Not much else here, I'm afraid. Ah, there's a sliver of soap and there's your pitcher and bowl. Gilbey will bring fresh water for washing and drinking. I'm afraid the bunk, the desk, and the chair are all the furnishings we have."

"Well, Sam, I am quite impressed as it is," she murmured, attempting to do so with spirit.

There was a light rapping on the door. The young soldier with the deep dark eyes, obviously fairly new in the command, appeared with a big pitcher of fresh water, pouring some directly into the bowl for her.

"Sam," he whispered, "it is a she, all right—is *she* really the Moccasin?"

"She's the Moccasin," Sam said wearily. "So it seems. Now get on down, Gilbey. Ma'am," he said to Alaina, "we'll leave you now."

They did so not a minute too soon, for the desire to wash the salt from her face became more than Alaina could bear. The fresh water felt delicious. She forgot her peril for a moment, drank deeply, then swore softly and impatiently and shimmied her way out of boots, breeches and shirt. She doused herself in the fresh water, even pouring it through her hair. Then she stood shivering again; there was no fire in the cabin, and though the late spring night was probably no less than seventy degrees, chills could set in. She found the clean sheet on the bed and wrapped herself in it. She sat cross-legged on the bed. They had left her water and a lamp. Probably far more than the Moccasin deserved. At least she would not die in sea-salted misery.

But that thought brought a sudden sob to her lips. Ian had been so terrifyingly furious and had dismissed her so cleanly! She might never see him again. She might die without ever having a chance to say . . .

To say what? They had chosen different paths, and nothing could change that. She had hated him often enough. She had to hate him now. She did hate him . . .

She didn't hate him.

She hugged the sheet around her. She seemed to be cold on the outside but ablaze on the inside, riddled with fear, with fury. She could demand mercy, surely . . .

Oh, God, not from him. Nor could she cajol, plea, bargain. She'd always told herself that she would die with dignity if she was caught. She'd never beg or plead . . .

But she'd do so tonight, just to touch him. Except that, oh, God . . .

She leaped to her feet in a whirl of frustration. She had to set her mind to finding a way to escape. She couldn't plead or cajol, because he wouldn't believe a word she said. She couldn't bargain, because there was no longer anything she had that he might want. Again, a soft sob of rising panic escaped her.

Then she heard footsteps on the ladder, and she swung around. The door to the cabin opened.

And he was there.

He had changed to dry clothing. His skin seemed very bronze in the lantern light; his eyes did not appear blue at all, but rather a deep and penetrating black. He stared at her so long that she thought she would scream and beg him to shoot her and get it over with. Just when she thought that she would simply save everyone trouble and die on the spot, he spoke at last.

"The Moccasin," he said softly. Then, "Goddamn you."

"No!" she heard herself cry in return. "Goddamn *you*, Major McKenzie. You betrayed your state, not I!"

"Indeed. My state betrayed my country, madam. But that doesn't matter now; politics don't matter now. And whether God Himself is on my side or yours doesn't matter, either. What matters, my dear Moccasin, is that you have been captured by the enemy, while I have not."

Involuntarily, she sucked in a quick, fearful breath.

"Yes, I've been caught. So . . . Major McKenzie, just what do you intend to do with me?" she demanded with a false bravado.

He raised an arched, ebony brow. "What do I intend, madam? How does one deal with a deadly snake? Perhaps I should use against you every atrocity blamed upon the Yankees by such delicate hothouse belles as yourself. Plunder, rapine, slaughter!"

"Ian, surely . . ." she breathed.

Cobalt fires of fury burned in his eyes, in the wired tension of his lithe, powerfully muscled body. He started toward her.

Despite herself, Alaina let out a terrified shriek. She had seen him angry before, seen him furious, but never like this. His fingers wound around her wrist, biting and cruel. She was jerked with such force that she lost her grasp upon the sheet and yet remained tangled in it when she was lifted and thrown, landing flat on her back against the bed, winded, so stunned that she saw blackness and stars floating before her face.

And then his hands were on her shoulders, and he was shaking her. "Damn you, damn you, damn you! How can you be so reckless, how can you risk your life when you're caring for our son—"

"How can you leave forever when you have a son?" she cried in return.

"Oh, my God, Alaina—"

"I've fought the same as you've fought!" she told him desperately.

"You've fought a losing battle."

"I had to do what I could."

"Damn it, Alaina, don't you know, haven't you heard—"

"What, *what*?" she demanded, trembling with such ferocity that she was barely aware of the force of his grip upon her.

"Jennifer was hanged!"

Jennifer! Alaina gasped, feeling as if he had slipped a knife cleanly into her. Her eyes must have echoed her agony, for he was quick to speak again, but so cold, so angry still! "I tried to stop what was happening. By a damned miracle, my sharpshooter hit Jen's rope. She's alive. Just barely."

Tears of relief stung her eyes. She blinked them back. His hands were suddenly on either side of her head. "Damn you, can't you get it into your skull just how dangerous these games are that you play?"

"Ian—" She sobbed, taking a ragged breath. Then his hold eased. And he cried out her name with a shattering anguish before his lips touched down on hers . . .

She thought bleakly that she was his prisoner. She had to fight him. She brought her hands pressing against the wall of his chest, but he didn't begin to notice. Her lips parted beneath his, and she felt the seductive power of his tongue sweeping into her mouth, bringing the force of his hunger, anger, and passion. She tried to twist, tried to writhe . . . yet even as she did so, she was threading her fingers into his hair, parting her mouth freely to taste more of his. Her tears dampened her cheeks, and she gasped and trembled, feeling him shudder as he moved against her with a wicked determination, lips, mouth, tongue, fierce, hot against her, her flesh, her breasts, nipples, navel . . .

She wanted him, oh, God, she wanted him. She was touching his hair, tearing at his shirt until it was peeled from his shoulders, and she pressed her lips against his flesh with equal hunger. She whispered no words of longing, said nothing of her emotions, for she didn't know what would be believed.

And if he thought that she made love in order to save her own life, it didn't matter. Having him mattered. Feeling him touch her mattered. The caress of his tongue against her belly and thighs, his weight atop her, his hands, fingers stroking, the feel of him beneath her touch, the shiver and convulsion of his muscles when she captured and stroked him. His violent shudder when she slipped low against him . . .

With barely tempered violence, he was within her, and she cried out, clinging to him. It was a tempest, a storm, sweeping with unbearable sensation and staggering, engulfing speed. She soared fiercely, violently to an apex, and felt the power and force of him as he reached a climax as well.

Then it seemed that the weight of his body fell flat against her own. His flesh was slick as hers, his breathing as labored. Yet she couldn't regain her breath beneath his weight, and he shifted from her, sitting at the foot of the bed, his back to her.

She watched him for several long moments, wishing she could still the silent, wet tears that came to her eyes and streamed down her face.

"Ian . . ." she tried, but speaking was so painful. "Ian, I know that this sounds absurd now, but . . . oh, God, Ian, I do love you!"

He didn't reply, and she closed her eyes, lying there in simple misery.

"It's amazing," he murmured after a long moment, naked back and broad, bronzed shoulders straightening. "There have been so many times when I wished that I'd never seen your face. And there are times when I remember Teddy telling me that he was only sorry about our marriage because 'she is the South'! And then there have been so damned many times when I've fought this war never sleeping, because I've been so damned afraid of what you might be doing. And after it all, the fear was for one reason. Damn you, I don't want to love you. But I do."

She wanted to touch him. She knew by the way he sat that she shouldn't dare.

"So where do we go from here? What do we do?" she asked him softly.

He turned to her at last. "Well, my love, according to my orders, we are to go to the center of the copse come the morning—and I am to hang you. Without mercy."

"You can't hang me, Ian."

"Why? Because you're my wife?"

She shook her head. "No. Because I'm carrying your child."

Ian didn't sleep with her in the cabin that night; he didn't dare.

He left his men on guard, well aware she could very easily escape, and returned to his own cabin.

He paced for an hour, then tried to sleep, then drank half a bottle of whiskey, and tried to sleep again. Nothing seemed to help as he battled for a solution as to what to do with her.

Sam came up at dawn.

Ian let him in, then sat at the foot of his bed, his head between his hands.

"The way I see it, Major," Sam told him, "we caught the Moccasin—and the man's already dead."

Ian stared at him, skeptical.

Sam lifted his hands with a grimace.

Ian allowed a rueful smile. "Well, Sam, obviously you can see that I can't hang or shoot the Moccasin. And neither can I turn her in." He hesitated just a moment. "We're going to have another child."

"Ah, the trip into St. Augustine!" Sam murmured. "You definitely can't hang her, Major."

"But how do I keep her from getting involved again—

and hanged in truth by some other Yankee commander? Not to mention the fact that she has admittedly been a thorn in our war effort? How can I make sure that she doesn't betray the Union—and me—again?"

Sam smiled. "I think I know a way," he said.

Chapter 29

Alaina didn't think she'd slept at all, but she must have, because someone had come in for her clothing, and when there was full light in the cabin, she realized that it had been washed and returned to her, sun-dried.

She washed and dressed quickly, extremely nervous as time passed and no one came near her.

Then finally there was a tapping at her door, and Sam came in bringing a cup of coffee, which he handed to her.

"The major's waiting to see you, ma'am. Whenever you're ready."

She looked surprised, but it seemed he intended to say no more. He led the way down the ladder to the center of the copse, where Ian waited. He was mounted on Pye, and held the reins of another horse at his side.

He nodded gravely to Alaina. "Let's take a ride."

Naturally, it occurred to her instantly that she could escape. Slam her heels against her horse's flanks and streak off into the trails . . .

No, she couldn't escape. She couldn't escape the fact that she loved her husband, no matter what battles raged between them.

She followed silently as he led his mount from the camp. They rode perhaps half a mile, coming to a pine bog very near the bay. Ian dismounted, pacing a few feet to a tree. He leaned against it, one booted foot raised up on a root, his eyes focusing like knives upon her own.

"Obviously, I'm not going to hang you."

She lowered her lashes and shook her head. "I wish I could make you understand how I felt."

"Felt. Is that past tense?" he inquired.

Alaina hesitated. She shook her head. "I don't know what I feel anymore. Tired."

"What should I do, Alaina?" he asked her very softly.

"I was going home," she told him, looking at him. "I swear to you, Ian, I was going to go to Belamar, and I'm not sure what from there, but I had decided . . . I had decided that the Moccasin had to slip away."

He lifted his hands to her. "Go."

"What?" she demanded.

"You've got the horse; you're a mile from Belamar. Go home. And decide what you really want. And when I come for you, you can let me know then."

She stood uncertainly. Of all the things she might have expected, this was the last.

"Ian—"

"Alaina, go now. I mean it. Go. Unless you're ready to swear an oath of allegiance to the Union this minute, go to Belamar."

She felt ill, faint. She realized suddenly that she didn't want to be sent away. She wanted to be held.

He strode to her. "Let me help you."

Before she knew it, he had set her upon her horse, and he looked up at her, eyes shaded by his plumed hat. "Of course, I'm taking quite a risk here. You know where our camp is now."

She started to answer him, but he slapped her horse's flanks, and her mount bolted forward, cantering down the trail.

Numbly, she rode.

She rode for at least fifteen minutes before she abruptly pulled back the reins.

She couldn't do it.

She couldn't part with him this way.

She turned her horse back, racing to Ian. She leaped down from her horse, hoping against hope that he might still be there. But she didn't see him; he was gone.

"Ian!" she cried out desperately.

Of course he was gone. He had let her free, and now he had other things to do.

"Ian!"

He came around a pine, hat still low over his eyes. She ran toward him, throwing her arms around him. She kissed his lips, and then she tried to talk, jumbling her words.

"I can't say that I've changed sides, Ian, because I haven't . . . actually. I mean, I think we're all wrong now to be at war, and I don't know the solution, but . . . at first I wanted revenge for my father. And I did believe very much in the simple right of states to be free. But then there were other things. . . ." She hesitated. It didn't seem the right time to mention Peter O'Neill's name. "There were troops ready to burn out a woman with four children because her husband had been killed fighting for the Union. And when the Yanks came to St. Augustine I began to realize what I hadn't wanted to see. It *is* about slavery, and slavery is wrong. Lilly is so many colors—black among them. I couldn't imagine someone owning her, whipping her, and it can't be right that white men can sell mothers and fathers and children just because they're black, and . . ."

She broke off, running out of words.

It didn't matter. His arms came very gently around her, and he was kissing her. And there was passion in his touch, and no anger now, and he was sensual and tender and forceful without being brutal in the least. . . .

And though they were in the middle of a pine copse, they'd had so little time together. In a matter of minutes, their clothing was in tremendous dishabille and they were entwined down on the pines, making love.

The sun broke through the branches of the pine above them. Alaina shielded her eyes. His mouth moved teasingly over her belly, planting small kisses. He commented on the baby, that he should have known . . . there was a slight swell about her. She grimaced ruefully and admitted that she hadn't really known herself until quite recently.

"You were too busy spying to pay attention," he told her.

"You could have come more often and made me so nervous I didn't dare spy," she told him.

He grinned at her. "Would it really have worked?"

"You can be very intimidating."

He soon found the fang marks in her calf, and she told him what had happened. Then she demanded to know, "Did you send Risa down to watch me?"

He shook his head after a moment. "I knew she was going South; she wrote to me. She really is a better friend than you can imagine."

"You're still a little bit in love with her."

"Only a little bit," he told her, then added sternly, "But Alaina, throwing yourself in front of a rattler even if you believed you might have an immunity—"

"I didn't intend to get bitten, and I'm really fine."

"And the baby?"

"I pray the baby survives me!" Alaina admitted.

On an elbow, staring at his wife, Ian wondered if they could possibly have reached a point where they could survive. She had been so impassioned when she had been speaking to him. No, she couldn't suddenly become a flag-waving Yank.

And yet . . .

She was so, so beautiful. So delicate, stretched at his side, dressed only in her long man's shirt, her bare legs sprawled across the ground beneath the pines. His own clothing lay in a tossed heap several feet away, his scabbard and sword under his breeches.

She smiled, her topaz eyes smoky against her porcelain complexion, her hair a tangle of sunlight and dappled shade. Then suddenly her eyes widened.

Too late, he heard the footsteps.

He, Ian McKenzie, the Panther, had failed to hear the approach of the men standing behind him now.

He stared into her eyes and was suddenly certain that she'd ridden straight to her Rebel contact. He knew by the silence of the men behind him that they had come to snatch a panther from a trap.

Bitterness assailed him, and he stared at her with an anger and hatred so intense it was nearly blinding. Then he rolled in a split second.

A pistol was already aimed at his head. A shotgun, held by none other than Peter O'Neill.

"Well, will you lookee here, boys, what do we have? A naked panther tangling in the grass with a snake! Guess who wins that fight? Get up, Alaina, good work!" Peter said.

She gasped, drawing her white shirt closed, leaping to her feet. Ian, tense upon his haunches, felt the knife of her betrayal work more deeply into his back. There were three men with Peter, all of them armed, aiming their guns at him. And he was naked on the ground, his sword and Colts a good ten feet away.

"This is like Goddamned Christmas!" Peter breathed, looking down at Ian. "I'm so excited, I just don't know where to start. I'm going to kill you, of course. You've needed killing for a long time. But how? Shoot you, hang you? Shoot your kneecaps out first, of course, but . . . I think I should tie you to a tree, let you watch me make love to your wife. What do you think, McKenzie?"

He thought he was in a damned wretched position. But he'd be dead a hundred years before he said such a thing to Peter O'Neill. The bastard had been warped to begin with. The war had given him a chance to become a monster.

And yet . . .

Alaina.

He was on Alaina's side.

"Peter, you are sick!" Alaina suddenly cried out. She stared at the men with him. "What's the matter with you all? You're Rebel soldiers. Peter doesn't have you fighting a war—he has you helping him with his personal revenge!"

Ian gazed at his wife.

She flashed him a furious look; she was well aware that he believed she had betrayed him.

"Get up, McKenzie," Peter said, "Alaina, shut up and get over here. My men and I are rescuing the Moccasin; we are heroes to the Cause, and that's a fact. Get over here!"

She stared at Peter, and Ian's heart nearly sank—because she moved. She moved to obey Peter.

But as she moved, she came upon the pile of his clothing and shoved his guns toward him, through the pine needles, still beneath his clothing. Then she pretended to trip against Peter, aiming his shotgun into the ground.

In those brief seconds, Ian rolled and caught up his guns. Peter's men both fired; Ian shot off defensive rounds without thinking, killing one of Peter's men, disarming and wounding the other two in a hail of gunfire. But when he rolled to Peter, he saw that O'Neill had taken Alaina, and that he was better shielded by Alaina's body than he might be by a steel fortress.

"Shoot him!" Alaina demanded.

She knew damned well that he couldn't.

Peter smiled, his colorless eyes hard on Ian. He started to lower and aim his gun again.

"No!" Alaina shrieked, slamming an elbow back against Peter.

She was good; she was tough. Ian knew that well enough. And Peter lost his gun. But before Ian could leap to his feet and tackle the man, Peter had whipped out a razor-honed army-issue knife and set it against Alaina's throat.

"She comes with me, and you stay there. Right there, where you are," Peter said. "Jarvis, Tatum?"

"Yessir!" One of the men replied, pain clear in his voice.

"Dammit, move on out ahead of me, get the horses. Is Pazinsky dead?"

"Yessir," the other man said.

"Stand still until we're out of here, McKenzie," Peter O'Neill warned him. "Dead still."

Ian stopped in his tracks, looking at Alaina. He stood watching, keeping his eyes on Alaina's, as Peter dragged his wife away.

Peter stepped over the body of his own dead man as he backed the entire way out of the copse.

"Not a word," Peter warned Alaina. She was mounted in front of him on a small gray mare. A good, sturdy, surefooted mount. Peter wasn't a fool. He did know how to navigate this terrain. His men followed behind them, silent—and in pain, she was certain. "One word, and I slit your throat."

She ignored him. "You can't kill me. You can't afford to kill me. Because he's going to get up, put on his clothing, and hunt you down."

"Do you think I'm a fool? Do you think I'm less than your arrogant husband? I know the hammocks and the swamps and the rivers just like he does, Alaina. I made it all the way down here with my company to root out the Panther. And by God, I will finish him!"

She turned slightly and saw that his mouth was in a

grim line. He was a dangerous man. Not the spoiled rich boy she used to know. He was honed and tight, and had been living a life, fighting. Always fighting.

She was suddenly afraid.

"Peter, ride to the rest of your men. I'll accompany you to them. I'll say that I am the Moccasin and that you did rescue me. You will be a tremendous hero in the South."

He smiled.

"I will take you to the rest of my men, Alaina. Tomorrow. Right now we have Privates Jarvis and Tatum. They'll stand guard, and tonight you spend with me. Before anything else can happen, my dear, I'm going to take what should have been mine."

Ian dressed in seconds flat. He whistled for Pye and leaped up on his mount.

He warned himself that he had to follow carefully. He had to let Peter O'Neill think he had a good lead on him.

Which, at the moment, he did.

The sun rose, yet Alaina was shaking.

They'd been riding for hours. Hours. She felt ill, nauseated.

The sun had begun to beat down cruelly; hot, sticky dampness was all around them. Her bare legs had been ripped by sawgrass and gnawed by mosquitoes.

Which didn't matter.

What mattered was that Ian hadn't come.

They had paused once by a freshwater stream. Tatum's wrist was shattered, and he was moaning and complaining that he had to get to a surgeon. Jarvis, as it turned out, had only sustained a flesh wound. He kept telling Tatum to be a man.

And still, Ian didn't appear.

It was a dangerous time, Alaina thought. Ian must know how volatile Peter was, how the thought of revenge had eaten away at his mind. Ian was surely being careful, very careful, tracking them until the time was right.

Unless . . .

Unless he believed that she had betrayed him one

time too many. She had seen his eyes when he had realized someone was there, watching them. . . .

"Keep an eye out, boys, keep an eye out!" Peter commanded his men.

"Hell, Captain, I think we've lost him!" Jarvis said happily.

Alaina began to worry.

If Ian didn't come before nightfall . . .

Peter O'Neill had picked a deserted Seminole outpost as his camp.

There were several chikees in the overgrown encampment, all built off the ground with thatched roofs and no walls. It was a decent choice, Ian admitted, watching the party from the cover of a stand of oaks. Peter and his men were elevated, able to see anyone or anything coming at them.

There was open space between the trees and the chikee they chose. It was going to be damned difficult to surprise the party.

Still, Ian waited. He couldn't take chances. He was afraid that Peter would gladly kill Alaina before allowing her to escape.

He leaned against the oak, trying to plan his strategy.

But then . . . Alaina screamed. Ian whirled to see her struggling with Peter, and before he knew it, he had let out his own Yankee brand of Rebel yell and gone charging for the chikee.

She had tried to be rational. She had reminded herself that she had once thought she was in love with Peter. She told herself that he wouldn't really hurt her, that she couldn't cry out. If she screamed, and Ian was following her, she could endanger his life, because he would certainly come after her. Throughout the day, she had known Peter's intent to rape her, and she had tried to tell herself she could endure such an event. She had to endure—she was carrying another child. And she had Sean.

Perhaps she even had Ian.

She had wanted to be rational. Brave—and so stoic she could perhaps dissuade Peter by her total disinterest.

But when he had dragged her to the rear of the chikee

and thrown her down while his men kept watch by the
fire they had built . . .

She screamed.

And all hell broke loose.

Ian came running out from the trees, yelling in a manner that rivaled a Seminole war cry. He started firing his
guns and hit Jarvis again.

Jarvis dropped. Dead.

But Tatum, despite his injury, was an adept shot with
his left hand, and he started firing back even as Peter
drew his rifle and fired shots off wildly into the night.

Then there was silence.

Peter, half atop Alaina, rose slightly.

"McKenzie!"

There was no sound at first.

"Fight me for her, O'Neill. Fight me for her!"

Peter started to laugh. "I don't have to fight you for
her, McKenzie. There's my man and me. And you, out
there alone."

But there was suddenly another blast of gunfire—from
a totally different direction.

Alaina felt Peter's sudden convulsion as he dragged
her around with him. She stared into the night, praying
for some kind of salvation.

Then she saw a man riding forward.

And her heart sank.

For he was in gray. A handsome gray uniform, with
a plumed hat.

Yet even as her heart sank, she saw that Ian had
slipped out from around the pole where he had taken
refuge from a hail of bullets.

And as she turned again, she recognized the rider
herself.

Jerome McKenzie.

Jerome rode straight into the camp, into the firelight.

"You!" Peter raged, looking at Jerome. "You'll hang!
You're a Confederate officer, by God! And you're supposed to be on a ship somewhere. You'll hang from the
highest tree, betraying your country for your kin."

"I wonder what your penalty would be for rape,
Peter," Jerome said coolly. "And you—you're a dis-
grace," he said contemptuously, looking at Tatum.

"She's the Moccasin—" Tatum began.

"I was afraid of that," Jerome said quietly. "Hello, Ian."

"Jerome," Ian responded.

"He's got to die," Peter said to Jerome. "And if the two of you think you're going to join McKenzie blood against me, remember we're in the middle of a war."

"This war is between you and me, Peter," Ian said flatly.

"Shoot him! Shoot him!" Peter commanded Tatum in a sudden frenzy.

But no one moved.

Ian walked forward then, determined. He walked right past Tatum, who seemed too stunned to waylay him. He leaped up to the platform of the chikee, striding toward Peter.

He threw his gun down and drew his sword.

"This particular war is ours, Peter. Let's finish it—without killing anyone else."

Peter hesitated. He still had Alaina.

He looked at Jerome. "If I kill him, you ride away."

"You kill him, and I ride away," Jerome agreed.

Peter smiled. He reached down, ostensibly for his sword.

He picked up his Colt six-shooter instead, but before he could shoot Ian point-blank, Alaina screamed.

She threw herself at Peter.

The gun went off.

"No!" Ian bellowed, bringing his sword down with a crushing blow against the butt of the gun.

Alaina fell; the gun went flying. Peter grasped for his sword then.

And Ian felt fear for his wife tear into his limbs, but he couldn't reach her. Peter was coming at him with his sword like a madman.

Ian fought the fear and saw red.

The war had improved Peter's abilities. He fought back with vigor and strength. But Ian was incensed, desperate to get to Alaina.

God!

He'd fought so hard.

He'd won so many times.

He was the Panther.

Yet this battle would mean nothing if she wasn't all right.

From the corner of his eye, he could see that Jerome had come to the platform of the chikee and was gently lifting Alaina into his arms. She wasn't moving.

Peter's sword tip flicked Ian's forehead. He felt a drop of blood fall into his eye, and he blinked furiously against the stinging sensation.

And fought back with a vengeance.

Peter made a wild lunge.

Ian was ready.

He didn't have to slay his enemy; Peter impaled himself on Ian's sword.

For once, he couldn't regret the blood spilled, the life lost. Heedless of Tatum, he rushed to where Jerome knelt beside Alaina.

"He nicked her temple. She's out cold. Let's get her to Belamar," Jerome said.

He rose, handing Ian his wife. "We're thirty minutes away. She needs help. Teela, my father, and Jen are at Belamar."

Ian nodded. But then he stopped, facing Tatum, who was staring at Ian and Jerome nervously, looking from man to man, licking his lips as he aimed his gun at them.

"This ain't right!" Tatum said. "You're both my prisoners."

Ian looked at Jerome, then handed Alaina back to him. He drew his bloodied sword.

"Fool, I'll shoot you," Tatum said. And he pulled the trigger.

But his gun was empty. He drew his sword.

Ian was tired, bone weary. He didn't want to kill. But Tatum wouldn't let it end. With one thrust, Tatum fell.

When the battle was over, Ian stared at his cousin. "God, am I sorry. God, am I sick of the killing."

"Some folk don't give you a choice," Jerome said. "At least the Moccasin can truly slip into legend now," he added.

Ian nodded.

"I'll hold Alaina until you're mounted," Jerome said.

"Thanks."

A few minutes later, they were riding together through the swamp and hammocks.

Jerome in gray.

Ian in his Union blue.

Ian looked at his cousin curiously. "How did you happen to find us?"

Jerome turned to him, opened his mouth, closed it, and looked ahead again, a strange light in his dark blue eyes. "A friend of yours arrived."

"A friend?"

"Miss Magee."

"Oh?"

"It was interesting."

"Oh. Are you going to tell me about it?"

Jerome looked at him again. "No," he said after a moment.

Ian arched a brow, but didn't push the point. He was becoming far too worried about his wife.

Jerome . . . thanks."

Jerome smiled and nodded. "You know," he said softly after a moment, "we are still at war."

But they both knew as well that a truce had been called for the night.

She was dizzy. So dizzy.

When she opened her eyes at first, the room was spinning. Slowly, it came to a halt.

She narrowed her eyes, then blinked furiously.

She was home! Really home. In her own room.

She tried to sit up. The room spun a little, then came to a stop. Someone was there. She blinked, and the visitor came into focus.

Jen.

She cried out, reaching forward, hugging Jen, being hugged in turn.

"How do you feel?" she asked Jennifer.

"Fine."

"But you were . . . hanged."

"And you were shot."

"I was?" Alaina said. Then she remembered. Remembered everything. "Oh, my God, Ian—"

"Is fine. He stayed awake all night, afraid that my mother was wrong, that you would stop breathing. He kept making sure that you were breathing, that your heart was beating. Then he said he had to let his men know what had happened. He promised he'd be back."

"Oh!" Alaina said with relief. She lay back, then sat up worriedly again.

"Your father won't shoot him, will he?"

"Ian brought me back here. My father wouldn't harm a hair on his head."

Alaina smiled. "Good. Oh! Jerome—"

"Is fine as well. But he's back at sea. With a passenger."

"A passenger?"

"Risa Magee. She came here and found my brother somehow. That's how he went after you and Ian. It was rather strange, but now . . . they're gone."

"Gone? Risa left here in a Rebel ship?" Alaina queried disbelievingly.

"So I was told; apparently they left at dawn."

"Why would Risa leave now?" Alaina wondered aloud.

"Maybe she thought you and Ian needed some time alone."

"After . . . helping us? And Ian isn't even here now."

Jennifer shrugged. "Ian will be back—and Jerome can be very persuasive—who knows?"

Alaina, frowned, still puzzled. It was her head, surely. She touched her temple, felt the bandage there. "I was shot?"

"Nicked. A flesh wound. You were lucky." Jennifer was silent a moment. She touched the scarf she was wearing around her neck and smiled at Alaina. "We were both lucky. We've served, Alaina. We've done our part. You know . . . wounded men are sent home."

"Meaning . . ."

"The war is over for me. I think you need to let it end as well."

Alaina shook her head. "Jennifer, we can't end the war."

"We can end the wars we wage inside," Jennifer said. She stood suddenly. "Go back to sleep; rest."

Jennifer left her. Alaina didn't think she'd rest; she was too anxious to see Ian.

But she did sleep.

And when she awoke again, she felt better.

More than better.

Alive.

And life was out there.

There to be taken.

He was standing on the little strip of beach that faced the mainland, looking toward shore. Out there where Alaina had nearly been drowned by the deserter the day Teddy had died. When the war hadn't really begun.

They had chosen separate sides.

But she had been willing to die for him. Even after he suspected her of the worst kind of betrayal.

He closed his eyes, and listened to the sound of the surf. From somewhere, he heard gulls cry. This was his home. Florida, with the water, the sun, the beautiful exotic birds. He loved his homeland.

Eventually it would return to the Union.

And so would he.

But now . . .

He smiled. He heard her coming, no matter how soft her footsteps.

He inhaled deeply, and breathed in her scent. She paused behind him, and he turned very slowly.

She was in white. A soft, simple, eyelet gown, no petticoats or corset beneath it. Her hair was free, streaming down her shoulders. She'd rid herself of her bandage and allowed a lock of her hair to fall over the healing wound on her forehead.

"Hello," she said gravely.

"Hello." He leaned against the small coconut palm at his side, crossing his arms over his chest.

"This is enemy territory."

"Is it?" he queried.

She shrugged slightly, walking toward him, smiling a sensual little smile that almost made him insane. He refused to touch her, though, waiting.

She punched him. Luckily, he was prepared, and tightened his muscles.

"Woah! So it *is* enemy territory!" he exclaimed, capturing her arms and drawing her against him.

"You thought that I would have betrayed you with that despicable man—" She broke off, lowering her head. "He's dead, isn't he?"

Ian nodded. "I'm sorry, Alaina."

"I'm sorry, too. Once, it was just my father. God, Ian, the cost of war is so very high!"

He pulled her closer. "I'm afraid it will be higher before it's over." He drew back slightly. "But I pray it will end soon. And I pray we'll be together then. All of us. As a family."

She stroked his face. "You're going back to war, aren't you?" she asked him.

He caught her fingers and kissed them. "Alaina, they send men to the firing squad for deserting."

She lowered her head, nodding. "But you'll believe in me now, won't you?"

"With my whole heart. Except that I'll wring your neck if you ever try to take a bullet for me again. A snake for Risa, a bullet for me. I need to have more faith in your need for self-preservation, especially since we're going to have another child."

"Did you see Risa? Is she all right?"

"Yes, I saw her. And she was fine. A bit strange, perhaps, but . . ."

"She left with Jerome willingly?"

"I imagine. I was with you. Why are you so worried about her?"

"Well, she does keep trying to save me."

"My cousin is a good man. You know that. And a Rebel, to boot."

Alaina nodded. "I guess." She looked up at him. "Have you fallen out of love with Risa yet?" She shook her head. "You never will, will you?"

Ian laughed softly. "She's a very good friend. I could have loved her, and I do—as a very good friend. Is that all right?"

Alaina nodded. "She's the very best friend!" she said softly, then added, "Oh, Ian, what are we going to do?"

"I don't know yet, except for one thing, of course."

"Oh?"

"We're going to love one another," he said very gravely. "And trust in that love, above all else."

Alaina nodded.

She smiled.

And the sun shone in a dazzling display upon the water.

And suddenly she was spinning away from him. "Remember how we first met as grown-ups?" she asked him.

He frowned. "Of course—" He broke off, for she was pulling the white gown over her head.

And he had been right. She wasn't wearing anything beneath it. Anything at all.

She let it fall to her feet in a cloud.

And smiled again. A wicked smile.

"Well . . . let's go swimming."

She turned and ran into the surf.

He stripped in a flash.

And followed.

He would be returning to the Union, he thought. But that would be later.

He would always love a Rebel.

Florida Chronology

1492	Christopher Columbus discovers the New World.
1513	Florida discovered by Ponce de Leon. Juan Ponce de Leon sights Florida from his ship on March 27, steps on shore near present-day St. Augustine in early April
1539	Hernando de Soto lands on west coast of the peninsula, near present-day Tampa.
1564	The French arrive and establish Fort Caroline on the St. Johns River. Immediately following the establishment of the French fort, Spain dispatches Pedro de Menendez to get rid of the French invaders, "pirates and perturbers of the public peace." Menendez dutifully captures the French stronghold and slays or enslaves the inhabitants.
1565	Pedro de Menendez founds St. Augustine, the first permanent European settlement in what is now the United States.
1586	Sir Francis Drake attacks St. Augustine, burning and plundering the settlement.
1698	Pensacola is founded.
1740	British General James Oglethorpe invades Florida from Georgia.
1763	At the end of the Seven Years' War, or the French and Indian War, both the East and West Florida territories are ceded to Britain.
1763–1783	British rule in East and West Florida.
1774	The "shot heard 'round the world" is fired in Concord.

1776	The War of Independence begins; many British Loyalists flee to Florida.
1783	By the Treaty of Paris, Florida is returned to the Spanish.
1812–1815	The War of 1812.
1813–1814	The Creek Wars. "Red-Stick" land is decimated. Numerous Indians seek new lands south with the "Seminoles."
1814	General Andrew Jackson captures Pensacola.
1815	The Battle of New Orleans.
1817–1818	The First Seminole War. Americans accuse the Spanish of aiding the Indians in their raids across the border. Hungry for more territory, settlers seek to force Spain into ceding the Floridas to the United States by their claims against the Spanish government for its inability to properly handle the situation within the territories.
1819	Don Luis de Onis, Spanish minister to the United States, and Secretary of State John Quincy Adams sign a treaty by which the Floridas will become part of the United States.
1821	The Onis-Adams Treaty is ratified. An act of Congress makes the two Floridas one territory. Jackson becomes the military governor, but relinquishes the post after a few months.
1822	The first legislative council meets at Pensacola. Members from St. Augustine travel fifty-nine days by water to attend.
1823	The second legislative council meets at St. Augustine: the western delegates are shipwrecked and barely escape death. The Treaty of Moultrie Creek is ratified by major Seminole chiefs and the federal government. The ink is barely dry before Indians are complaining that the lands are too small and white settlers are petitioning the government for a policy of Indian removal.
1824	The third session meets at Tallahassee, a

halfway point selected as a main order of business and approved at the second session. Tallahassee becomes the first territorial capital.

1832   Payne's Landing. Numerous chiefs sign a treaty agreeing to move west to Arkansas as long as seven of their number are able to see and approve the lands. The treaty is ratified at Fort Gibson, Arkansas. Numerous chiefs also protest the agreement.

1835   Summer. Wiley Thompson claims that Osceola has repeatedly reviled him in his own office with foul language and orders his arrest. Osceola is handcuffed and incarcerated.

November. Charlie Emathla, after agreeing to removal to the west, is murdered. Most scholars agree Osceola led the party which carried out the execution. Some consider the murder personal vengeance, others believe it was prescribed by numerous chiefs, since an Indian who would leave his people to aid the whites should forfeit his own life. December 28. Major Francis Dade and his troops are massacred as they travel from Fort Brooke to Fort King. Wiley Thompson and a companion are killed outside the walls of Fort King. The sutler Erastus Rogers and his two clerks are also murdered by members of the same raiding party, led by Osceola.

December 21. The First Battle of the Withlacoochee—Osceola leads the Seminoles.

1836   January. Major General Winfield Scott is ordered by the Secretary of War to take command in Florida.

February 4. Dade County established in south Florida in memory of Francis Langhorne Dade.

March 16. The Senate confirms Richard Keith Call governor of the Florida Territory.

June 21. Call, a civilian governor, is given

command of the Florida forces after the
failure of Scott's strategies and the military disputes between Scott and General
Gaines. Call attempts a "summer campaign," and is as frustrated in his efforts
as his predecessor.

1837   June 2. Osceola and Sam Jones release or
"abduct" nearly 700 Indians awaiting de-
portation to the west from Tampa.

October 27. Osceola is taken under a
white flag of truce; Major Sidney Jesup is
denounced by whites and Indians alike for
the action.

November 29. Coacoochee, Cowaya, six-
teen warriors, and two women escape Ft.
Marion.

Christmas Day. Jesup has the largest
fighting force assembled in Florida during
the conflict, nearly 9,000 men. Under his
command, Colonel Zachary Taylor leads
the Battle of Okeechobee. The Seminoles
choose to stand their ground and fight, in-
flicting greater losses to whites despite the
fact they are severely outnumbered.

1838   January 31. Osceola dies at Ft. Marion,
South Carolina. (A strange side note to
a sad tale: Dr. Wheedon, presiding white
physician for Osceola, cut off and preserved Osceola's head. Wheedon's heirs
reported that the good doctor would hang
the head on the bedstead of one of his
three children should they misbehave. The
head passed on to his son-in-law, Dr. Dan-
iel Whitehurst, who gave it to Dr. Valen-
tine Mott. Dr. Mott had a medical and
pathological museum, and it is believed
that the head was lost when the museum
burned in 1866.)

May. Zachary Taylor takes command
when Jesup's plea to be relieved is answered at last on April 29. The Florida
legislature debates statehood.

1839   December. Because of his arguments with

federal authorities regarding the Seminole War, Richard Keith Call is removed as governor. Robert Raymond Reid is appointed in his stead.

1840   April 24. Zachary Taylor is given permission to leave command of what is considered to be the harshest military position in the country. Walker Keith Armistead takes command.

September. William Henry Harrison is elected president of the United States; the Florida War is considered to have cost Martin Van Buren reelection.

December 1840–January 1841. John T. MacLaughlin leads a flotilla of men in dugouts across the Everglades from east to west; his party becomes the first white men to do so.

John Bell replaces Joel Poinsett as secretary of war. Robert Reid is ousted as territorial governor, and Richard Keith Call is reinstated.

1841   April 4. President William Henry Harrison dies in office: John Tyler becomes president of the U.S.

May 1. Coacoochee determines to turn himself in. He is escorted by a man who will later become extremely well known—Lieutenant William Tecumseh Sherman. (Sherman writes to his future wife that the Florida war is a good one for a soldier; he will get to know the Indian who may become the "chief enemy" in time.)

May 31. Walker Keith Armistead is relieved. Colonel William Jenkins Worth takes command.

1842   May 10. Winfield Scott is informed that the administration has decided there must be an end to hostilities as soon as possible. August 14. Aware that he cannot end hostilities and send all Indians west, Colonel Worth makes offers to the remaining Indians to leave or accept boundaries. The war, he declares, is over.

It has cost a fledgling nation thirty to forty million dollars, and the lives of seventy-four commissioned officers. The Seminoles have been reduced from tens of thousands to hundreds scattered about in pockets. The Seminoles (inclusive here, as they were seen during the war, as all Florida Indians) have, however, kept their place in the peninsula; those remaining are the undefeated. The army, too, has learned new tactics, mostly regarding partisan and guerilla warfare. Men who will soon take part in the greatest conflict to tear apart the nation have practiced the art of battle here: William T. Sherman, Braxton Bragg, George Gordon Meade, Joseph E. Johnston, and more, as well as soon-to-be president Zachary Taylor.

1845 March 3. President John Tyler signs the bill that makes Florida the 27th state of the United States of America.

1855–58 The conflict known as the Third Seminole War takes place with a similiar outcome to the earlier confrontations—money spent, lives lost, and the Indians entrenched more deeply in the Everglades.

1859 Robert E. Lee is sent in to arrest John Brown after his attempt to initiate a slave rebellion with an assault on Harpers Ferry, Virginia (later West Virginia). The incident escalates ill-will between the North and the South. Brown is executed Dec 2nd.

1860 The first Florida cross-state railroad goes into service.

November 6th: Abraham Lincoln is elected to the presidency and many of Southern states begin to call for special legislative sessions. Although there are many passionate Unionists in the state, most Florida politicians are ardent in lobbying for secession. Town, cities, and counties rush to form or enlarge militia companies. Even before the state is able to meet for its special session, civil and military leaders plan to demand the turnover of Federal military installations.

1861   January 10th: Florida votes to secede from the Union, the third Southern state to do so.

February: Florida joins the Confederate States of America. Through late winter and early spring, the Confederacy struggles to form a government and organize the armed forces while the states recruit fighting men. Jefferson Davis is president of the newly formed country. Stephen Mallory of Florida, becomes C.S.A. Secretary of the Navy.

April 12th–14th: Confederate forces fire on Ft. Sumter, S.C., and the first blood is shed when an accidental explosion kills Private Hough, who then has the distinction of being the first Federal soldier killed. Federal forces fear a similiar action at Pensacola Bay, Florida. Three forts guarded the bay, McRee and Barrancas on the land side, and Pickens on the tip of forty-mile long Santa Rosa Island. Federal Lieutenant Adam J. Slemmer spiked the guns at Barrancas, blew up the ammunition at McRee, and moved his meager troops to Pickens, where he was eventually reinforced by 500 men. Though Florida troops took the navy yard, retention of the fort by the Federals nullified the usefulness to the Rebs of what was considered the most important navy yard south of Norfolk.

July 18th: First Manassas, or the First Battle of Bull Run, Virginia—both sides get their first real taste of battle. Southern troops are drawn from throughout the states, including Florida. Already, the state which had been so eager to secede sees her sons being shipped northward to fight, and her coast being left to is own defenses by a government with different priorities.

November: Robert E. Lee inspects coastal defenses as far south as Fernandina and decides the major ports of Charleston, Savannah, and Brunswick are to be defended, adding later that the small force posted at St. Augustine was an invitation to attack.

1862   February: Florida's Governor Milton publicly states his despair for Florida citizens as more of the state's troops are ordered north after Grant captures two major Confederate strongholds in Tennessee.

February 28th: A fleet of 26 Federal ships sets sail to occupy Fernandina, Jacksonville, and St. Augustine.

March 8th: St. Augustine surrenders, and though Jacksonville and other points north and south along the coast will change hands several times during the war, St. Augustine will remain in Union hands. The St. Johns River becomes a ribbon of guerilla troop movement for both sides. Many Floridians begin to despair of "East Florida," fearing that the fickle populace has all turned Unionist.

April 6th–8th: Union and Confederate forces engage in the battle of Shiloh. Both claim victories. Both suffer horrible losses with over twenty thousand killed, wounded or missing.

April 25th: New Orleans falls, and the Federal grip on the South becomes more of a vise.

Spring: The Federal blockade begins to tighten and much of the state becomes a no-man's land. Because of the rugged terrain, the length of the peninsula, and the difficulty of logistics, blockade runners dare Florida waterways because the Union